Can't Get Over You

ERIKA KELLY

CAN'T GET OVER YOU

Erika Kelly

Formatter: Erica Alexander at Serendipity Formats
Developmental editor: Olivia Kalb at Olivia Kalb Editing Services
Editor: Sharon Pochron
Editor: Jenny Sims at Editing4Indies
Proofreader: Jaime Ryter at The Ryter's Proof Editing Services
Cover design: Sarah Kil at Sarah Kil Creative Studio

This book is dedicated to my husband.

*I never dreamed about fame or fortune. I only ever had one
fervent wish: to have one great love in my lifetime.
I never take for granted—not for a single second—the
fulfillment of that wish.*

Acknowledgments

🤍 To Superman: My books wouldn't be nearly as good without your help.

🤍 To Sharon Pochron: You've been there from the start, and no book gets published without your eyes on it.

🤍 To Erica Alexander: I love working with you. Always have.

🤍 To Melissa Martin: I am so grateful for you and all you do for me.

🤍 To Melissa Panio-Peterson: My partner on this journey…thank you!

🤍 To Olivia Kalb: Oh, man. What you did for this book… I am wildly grateful to you. Thank you!

🤍 To Jenny: Thank you for untangling my sentences and being the second-to-last set of eyes on this story!

🤍 To Jaime: Thank you for making this book shine!

🤍 And thank you to the readers, bloggers, reviewers, and all my author friends who make this job so richly rewarding and worthwhile.

The Renegades (Hockey)
THE DEEPER I FALL
LOVE ME LIKE YOU DO
TRULY, MADLY, DEEPLY
NEVER IN MY WILDEST DREAMS

The McKenna Brothers
(The bad boys of Calamity Falls)
CAN'T GET OVER YOU
UNTIL I FOUND YOU

Mistletoe and Silver Foxes
ALL I WANT FOR CHRISTMAS IS YOU
WHEN YOU WERE MINE

The Wild Wolff Village Serials
KISS ME SLOWLY
ANYWHERE WITH YOU
BABY I'M YOURS

Have you read the Rock Star Romance series? Come meet the sexy rockers of Blue Fire:

YOU REALLY GOT ME
I WANT YOU TO WANT ME
TAKE ME HOME TONIGHT
MORE THAN A FEELING

Get ready for Until I Found You, the next book in the McKenna Brothers series, coming June 2026! You're going to love watching this pie-making quarterback fall in love with a strong, feisty woman…and the little girl he didn't know he had. #footballromance #singledad #surprisebaby #steamy #foundfamily

Come hang out with me on Facebook, TikTok, Instagram, Goodreads, and Pinterest or in my private reader group!

SWEET WATER
RESORT AND SPA
LA
WILD
WOLF VILLAGE
HOMESTEAD
INN
River
BISON
PRESERVE
Snake

TY
Bowie Brothers Ranch
Highway 191
EXHIBITION OF
BROKEN HEARTS
WILD BILLY'S
COCO'S
CHOCOLATE
BLISS
ICE CREAM
PARLOR
HARLEY LU
EMPORIUM
AMITY
OE'S
WILD ROSE INN
LCOME TO
mity Falls
E HEARTS ARE WILD

Prologue

WHEN FINLAY O'NEILL LIFTED THE PILE OF LAUNDRY off the floor, something hairy brushed against her wrist.

It was bristly. It was big. And it was alive.

With a shriek, she dropped the clothing, and out scurried a baby raccoon.

Fear ripped through her, making her hair stand on end.

She bolted out of the apartment, only realizing she didn't have her phone when she ran down the flight of stairs. And since she could never go back inside as long as she lived, she couldn't call anyone for help.

Her heart thundered, and the ice-cold air burned the back of her throat. The moment she hit the sidewalk, she collided with a large, hard body. "Oh my God. I'm so sorry." Flustered and sweating, she locked eyes with the guy.

No.

Not him.

Of all the people in the entire town, why did it have to be Jude McKenna?

"Fee?" Concern tightened the skin around his eyes.

Any other time, she'd be thrilled to see him. But not when she was wearing fuzzy brown moose slippers, gym shorts, and her dad's Golf Pro sweatshirt.

And no bra.

Her arms crossed over her chest, and she wanted a sinkhole to open under her feet and swallow her up.

"What's wrong?" The two words shot out of his mouth, clipped and urgent.

She couldn't think, let alone speak. Not when her feet were tucked into the belly of a stuffed moose, the antlers sticking out and bobbing when she moved.

But as much as she didn't want to see him looking like this, she needed help. "Jude, I—"

Her jaw snapped shut when she noticed his companion.

Leia Collins.

Her former best friend.

The sting of betrayal traveled through her body as fast as a bullet.

No.

She bolted. As she hurried off, snowmelt dampened the bottom of her slippers. She wished she had her phone. Then again, who could she call? Her parents were working. Neither could take time off to rescue her from a freaking *raccoon.*

Her best friend would drop everything and come running. She knew that, for sure. But Willa was at the salon, getting ready for prom. No way would Finlay bother her for something so silly.

Boots hitting pavement caught up with her. "Hey," Jude called. "What the hell's going on?"

Unable to even look at him, she waved him away. "Nothing. I'm fine."

But he reached for her arm and turned her to face him.

God.

It happened every time she saw him.

Every single time.

He was just so big, so handsome, so…dark and brooding and *sexy*. With his shoulder-length, dark, glossy hair and bold tribal ink, he was the biggest, baddest, biker boy in town. Girls chased him, and boys secretly wanted to be him.

He was her obsession. Her crush.

And her deepest source of heartache.

Because even though they talked outside of school, he ignored her when they were in it.

He might flip through girls like a deck of cards, but he'd made it clear he had zero interest in her.

At that moment, Leia caught up with them. No matter how much Finlay needed Jude's help, she'd rather keep walking in her slippers till she hit the California coast than ever acknowledge her former friend again. She wrenched her arm out of his grip and spun around.

"Dammit, Fee." Jude kept up with her. "Tell me what happened." The concern in his voice brought her to a stop. He studied her eyes.

"Come on," Leia said. "It's cold. I want to go home."

"Go without me." Jude never once pulled his gaze away from Finlay.

"I thought we were hanging out?" Leia asked in a nasty tone, but when he ignored her, she stomped off. "Screw you, Jude. You're such a jerk."

"Now, talk to me," Jude said in a softer tone. "What's going on?" His dark hair brushed the tops of his broad shoulders and framed a strong jaw and high cheekbones. Those startling green eyes burned with concern.

How could she not be obsessed with a guy who looked at her like she was the most important thing in the world? "It's stupid."

"Tell me anyway."

She had nowhere to go, and she needed help. What choice did she have but to make a fool of herself? "There's a raccoon in my bedroom. And I can't…I can't go back there. And I forgot my phone. Not that my mom could come get me. But I'm just freaking out—"

"Is the apartment unlocked?"

Warmth spread through her, and she nodded. Because he was going to help her.

"Come on. Show me where you live."

"Oh no." She shook her head. "Absolutely not. I'm sorry, but I can't go in there."

"You'll wait outside."

Even as she said, "You don't have to do that," she was on the move, heading back to the employee housing complex. Every step ramped up her anxiety, and she climbed the stairs as if heading into a burning fire. At the landing, she stopped and pointed at her mom's unit. It was the only one with an open door. "That one."

With a curt nod, he strode off and disappeared inside.

It's kind of crazy, right?

That Jude's going on a search-and-rescue raccoon mission for me?

Usually, she didn't waste time thinking about Leia or wishing bad things would happen to her, but watching Jude shut her down so coldly had somehow managed to heal the nick in her heart.

When he finally trampled down the stairs, he held a shoebox. He moved right past her, crossed the street, and disappeared into the woods.

Relief loosened her anxiety, and she broke into a huge smile. She hadn't expected to run into anyone from her class today, since it was prom, but for Jude to sweep in and save her? It just made her so happy.

When he emerged from the thick grove of trees, he dumped the box into a garbage bin and headed back to her.

"Thank you—"

But he brushed past her and loped up the stairs.

Surprised, she followed him into her apartment. "Do you think there are more?" Her skin prickled, and she couldn't help scanning the room. "Is the mother living in my apartment? Raising her entire litter in my room?"

"I didn't see any others, so I don't think so." He swiped a bath towel off the floor and headed straight for the kitchen.

"Where'd you find it?"

"Under the dresser." He dropped it into the washing machine and fiddled with the dials. A moment later, water rushed through the pipes.

"You didn't have to do that. You've done more than enough."

"I used it to catch the raccoon. I didn't think you'd want to touch it."

This guy. She wanted to throw herself against that big, broad chest and feel the shield of his powerful body. She wanted his big, strong arms to squeeze out all the loneliness.

Instead, she said, "You're right. I would've burned it." She smiled. "Thank you. I really appreciate it. I know it seems ridiculous, but it was a *raccoon.*'"

"That motherfucker went Cujo on me." He washed his hands at the sink.

Other than Willa, she wasn't used to having people over, so with his size, Jude took up all the space in her small kitchen.

It was thrilling, and she loved it.

Loved him.

Wanted him with her whole being

"So what's your beef with Leia?" he asked.

The question hit like a hard slap across her cheek. Why had she assumed he'd chosen her over the most popular girl in school? He might still be planning to catch up with her. "Uh, I was on the run from a wild animal in my slippers. I wasn't exactly in the mood to socialize."

"Nah. You're the nicest girl in town. You've never been rude to anyone."

Was that affection in his eyes? *For me?* "Yeah, well." She didn't want to share her ugly past. She especially didn't want Leia to come out looking powerful. But at the same time, she wasn't going to shy away from the truth. "We were best friends until sixth grade."

"And then?"

"And then, she dumped me." And before he could think she was a loser, she added, "Because I'm not rich like her."

"What does money have to do with friendship?"

Coming from a guy who used to live in a bike club, the question surprised her. As if he hadn't experienced it, too. "You think she wants to have playdates in employee housing?" But she could tell he still didn't get it. "While her family was in Paris for spring break, I was teaching kids on the bunny slope at the ski club."

"Maybe she was jealous of you."

"Of me? Ha." Well, honestly, she loved that his mind went there. But no, he didn't get it. "Trust me, it's the money. Her parents live in a fancy house, and her mom stays home. Mine are divorced and work full-time. That meant all the playdates could only be at her house. And when her mom took us back-to-school shopping, it wasn't like I could afford anything. It was all very one-sided. Whatever." She shrugged it off. It was a long time ago. "She dropped me."

"How'd she do it?"

"She was mean, okay? Why're you pushing this?"

"If she treated you like shit, I want to know."

A burst of pleasure had her fingers and toes tingling. She loved that he cared. "There were four of us in the group, and one of the girls was having a birthday party. It seemed like every year, the events got bigger and more outrageous, as if they were all trying to outdo one another.

And for this one, her parents rented out the Owl Hoot amphitheater and hired a semi-famous band. They had food trucks and fireworks. It sounded like so much fun, and I couldn't wait to go. But when I showed up at Leia's house, there was no one home. She'd left a letter for me taped on the door."

"What did it say?" The skin around his eyes crinkled with concern.

"Basically, that she didn't want to be friends with me."

"Fee. What did it say? I know you still remember every word."

"Why do you care?" She was a little too heated, too emotional, and she didn't want him to see her as some pathetic loser.

"Because I do. Now, spit it out."

"Fine. It said, *'Finlay, you can't be our friend anymore. And don't give us your stupid puppy-dog eyes. It won't work.'*"

She could've sworn his features hardened, but she was probably reading into it, looking for the support she wanted. Because, in reality, he didn't say a word. He just stood there, giving her no emotion whatsoever. Her heart seized up.

But she had to shake it off. He didn't have to join her in hating Leia Collins. "Well, thank you for catching the raccoon. I still won't sleep tonight, but it's better than running away from home when I'm so close to graduating." She smiled, hoping he'd get the humor.

He didn't. "No problem."

As he headed for the door, her pulse rioted. Because he was leaving. And it struck her that, in a matter of weeks, school would end. All the moments she lived for—waiting for him to saunter into Algebra or pass her in the hallway on his way to gym—would be gone. Over.

Forever.

This obsession had filled her every waking hour, kept her company, and let her escape into a world of fantasy. And not once in all these years had she let him know how she felt. She'd never asked him to go for a hike or get a smoothie. Nothing.

Did she really want to wonder if something could've happened between them if she'd only had the courage to ask him out?

The moment his hand closed over the doorknob, she blurted out, "Do you want to go to prom with me?"

He shot a look over his shoulder. "*Prom?*"

Shame burned a path from deep in her gut all the way up to her earlobes.

He'd spat the word out as if she'd asked him to play Barbies. He might've been a senior at Calamity Falls High School, but he was nothing like the other kids. He didn't go to football games or dances. He cruised on the outer edges.

"What happened?" he asked. "Your date bail on you?"

It was a fair question. The dance was in a few hours, after all. But she shook her head. "I don't have one."

"Why not?" He seemed truly confused, which, she supposed, was flattering.

"No one asked me." It drove it home, though, how different their experiences were. She wasn't a nerd or an outcast or anything like that. She was friendly with a bunch of different people, but she didn't have a group of her own.

And she'd never had a boyfriend.

Because she'd only ever wanted *him*.

He grew thoughtful. "I saw your vision board."

Oh God.

She wanted the floor to give way so she could go crashing to the bottom of the earth.

She'd been so worked up over the raccoon, she hadn't considered that Jude McKenna had been *in her bedroom*.

What else had he seen? Her bras. Her underwear?

Oh, please. Not the journal. She'd for sure left it out. She knew that because she'd been writing in it.

Had he noticed his name scrawled all over it?

Drowning in mortification, her chest squeezed tightly. She could barely take a full breath.

"I'm not that guy," he said.

"What guy?" Her voice came out as a hoarse whisper.

"The guy who wants to live on Bloom Lane and do block parties and shit. Can you imagine me coming home from work, roaring up the street on my Harley? The moms, in their designer jeans, would snatch up their kids and get them inside their houses, pulling the curtains shut. Me, mowing a fuckin' lawn? Yeah, that's not gonna happen."

She didn't like that he'd seen right down to her most tender core, but at the same time, his assumption pissed her off. "I'm not asking you to marry me, Jude. It's a dance."

"You got your whole life planned out," he said with a hint of accusation.

"What's wrong with that? People with goals wind up more successful in life."

"Nothing wrong. I just don't know why you're asking me now, when school's almost over, and we're going in very different directions." He shrugged. "You want to be a teacher, have kids, live on Bloom Lane."

He made it sound like it was the most boring life in the world, but she wouldn't apologize for the future she longed for. "And you want to go ride free—or whatever the club motto is. Cool. But I love it here. Calamity's the most beautiful place in the world, and it has literally everything."

Including you.

For now, anyway, it has you.

"And yet, no one asked you to prom. And other than Willa, you don't have many friends."

He'd plunged a blade into her heart. "God, Jude."

"No, I don't mean it like that."

"Well, how did you mean it? Because I just told you what happened in sixth grade. It was literally the worst thing I've gone through in my entire life, and I'm sorry, but it's not easy to trust people after something like that." She let out a huff of exasperation. "It's not like I don't want to have friends."

"No, I get it. I'm just saying… Forget it." He opened the door.

"No, you don't get to leave me hanging like that. What do you mean?"

But he'd already walked out.

What just happened?

How had it all gone so wrong?

She stood there, reeling, wishing she'd kept her mouth shut about Leia.

Worse, why had she asked him to prom?

He'd seen her vision board and knew what she wanted out of life. Leia probably wanted to become an ambassador. Travel the world. No doubt, she'd become someone important, live an international life filled with State dinners and yacht parties hosted by celebrities.

And as interesting as that might sound, it left Finlay flat. She didn't want any of it.

A lot of things embarrassed her—*and trust me, asking Jude to the prom just shot to the top of my list*—but not her vision board. Not her dreams. She wanted them fiercely.

So Jude could hook up with Leia. Hang out with his biker friends. He could think she was a prissy, naïve little girl with small dreams of being a teacher, getting married, and living in a pretty house on Bloom Lane.

But it wouldn't change who she was and what she wanted.

She went to close the door but found Jude on the landing.

Lowering his chin, he flicked a thumb over his bottom lip. And then, he looked up at her. "Yeah. I'll take you to prom."

What the hell were you thinking?

Unfortunately, Jude knew exactly what he'd been thinking.

As he stood in the living room, strangled by a monkey suit, he knew he could never say no to Finlay. She was just so pretty and sweet. She didn't know it, but the way they "randomly" ran into each other after school was neither an accident nor a coincidence.

He went looking for her.

"Here." His dad lifted the collar of Jude's white dress shirt and wrapped the black bow tie around it.

To say they ran in different circles was an understatement. She was a good student, and the teachers loved her. If she were associated with Jude McKenna, it would ruin her reputation. He wouldn't do that to her.

Worse, if she hung out with him, she'd be around his friends. That would be bad.

But most days, he couldn't stop himself from visiting Wild Wolff Village just to catch a glimpse. Didn't she wonder what he was doing there? He didn't live anywhere near the ski resort.

Today, though, seeing that vision board in her pink bedroom with the frilly bedspread—with all her hopes and dreams on display like that—had weakened his resolve to keep his distance.

In his world, people were jaded—no, guarded. It seemed like, after enough brutal disappointments, they'd stopped allowing themselves to hope. It hurt too much when expectations were dashed.

But not Finlay. She was strong. Courageous. The fact that she wasn't afraid to dream, to put herself out there… He admired the hell out of her.

He wouldn't expose her to his ugly world, but now, with school ending in a few weeks, what would it matter if they were seen together at prom?

His phone vibrated on the coffee table, but he ignored it. As usual, his friends were up to something he didn't want any part of. He'd take this one night to be the kind of man Finlay would be proud to date.

A yearning took hold of him, a longing. He could almost see himself on her vision board—

But he shut it down. He could never give her the kind of life she wanted. He wasn't built like that.

The stiff shirt was buttoned to his neck, cutting off his air supply, and he jammed a finger under the collar to loosen it.

"Stand still." His dad fiddled with the tie.

Ava came into the house and dropped her purse on a side table. "Oh, don't you look handsome?"

"I got the wrong size." Of course, he had. Everyone else had rented their tuxes months ago. He'd had to take what was left.

"Should've gotten the clip-on." His dad wasn't having an easy time with it.

"Here." Ava hip-checked his dad and took over, her familiar perfumed scent calming him. She'd been their nanny and babysitter from the day they'd arrived in Calamity when he was six, and the closest thing to a mom since his had passed away. After getting the job done in thirty seconds, she stepped back and patted his chest. "There you go." She turned to his dad. "You got a limo?"

"No," his dad said. "They're going with other couples. There's a party bus."

"Perfect. Okay." Ava ran her hands through Jude's hair. "You want to comb it?" She tugged on his scruff. "Maybe trim your beard?"

"I'm good." He didn't see the point. No matter how he dressed or shaved, people still saw him as a scary biker.

Except for Finlay.

Huh. So for her, yeah, maybe he'd do it.

He headed up the stairs.

"Where're you going?" his dad called. And then to Ava, he said, "He just said he wasn't going to trim his beard."

"Well, don't make a big deal out of it," she whispered. "Just let him do it."

Jude flicked on the bathroom light and shut the door. In the mirror, he saw the man people crossed the street to avoid and the bad boy girls handed dirty notes.

Meet me under the bleachers.

Gazebo tonight at midnight.

My parents are out of town this weekend…

And the thug teachers and cops eyed with disgust because he'd been such a pain in the ass as a kid. Somewhere around middle school, though, pranks started veering into criminal activity, and that was when Jude's path began to separate from his friends.

He might've stopped being reckless a while ago, but people in small towns had long memories.

It was different with Finlay. She got all bright and shiny when she looked at him. Made him feel like…well, like the man he wanted to be.

As he picked up the comb, he noticed a slight tremble in his hand.

It only took a second to figure out why.

Hope.

No matter how hard he tried to smash it, hope pulsed in his gut. It had him leaving his friends after school to go find a pretty girl in the village.

And, you know, why can't I be the man she sees?

She'd gotten into UCLA, so he'd figured they'd never see each other again. But if he went to Los Angeles with her, he could build a brand-new reputation.

After trimming his beard, he shaved. Then he dragged a wet comb through his hair.

In his tuxedo, clean-shaven, hair tamed, he looked… all right.

Like a man who could be with a woman like Finlay O'Neill.

Feeling lighter than he had in years, he came downstairs to find two of his brothers in the living room with Ava and his dad. Wyatt wasn't around, but then, that wasn't a big surprise. That dude was always holed up in his room.

But Jude didn't want them to make a big deal about his date, so he breezed right past the lineup. "I'm out of here."

Boone, the youngest—and his polar opposite, with blond hair and blue eyes—stepped in front of him, shoving something into his pocket. "Wrap it up." He burst out laughing.

Jude pulled it out. "What do you know about condoms?" He gave him a shove. "You're twelve."

Boone just laughed. "I took 'em from your drawer."

"Stay out of my room," Jude said.

"Know what else I found?" Boone's eyes glittered.

God only knew what his friends had left there. Probably a joint. Jude rushed him. "Shut your mouth."

"Boys." Ava clapped her hands. "Game on."

The two of them froze. Decker tensed.

"You've got three minutes to grab anything that starts with the letter C," Ava said. "The one who collects the most gets a tank full of gas. Go."

The three brothers scattered. Jude didn't have time for this shit, so he headed into the kitchen and got an entire bag of carrots. He'd argue that each one was a separate C, but just in case, he grabbed cauliflower, half a cake, and as many packets of his dad's hot cocoa as he could carry.

"Time," Ava called.

Jude stopped, just as he knew his brothers had done. The McKennas might be competitive, but they were honorable.

"Bring everything to the table." She stood there with her hands on her hips.

Boone came downstairs at the same time Decker came up from the basement. When Ava saw Jude's pile, she just shook her head.

"Grand slam," Jude said. "Am I right?"

Ava laughed and lifted his arm. "Winner. Now, go on." She waved him away. "Get out of here. I owe you a tank of gas."

As he crossed the living room, the front door opened, and the fourth brother walked in.

The moody, quiet, second-born son had a box in his hand. He didn't break his stride as he handed it to Jude and headed up the stairs.

"What is it?" Boone asked.

"It's a corsage." Ava sighed. "That's so sweet." She nudged Jude. "Your brother went out of his way to get this for you. Thank him."

"Thanks, man."

But by then, of course, Wyatt was gone.

"All right, I'm out of here." Jude headed for the door.

"Well, wait," his dad said. "You taking your bike?"

"Yeah." He hadn't thought it through. Finlay would be wearing a fancy dress and high heels. "Actually, no. I need to borrow your truck." Jude wasn't used to formal dates. The girls he hung around with wore as little as possible.

His dad pulled the keys to his truck out of his jeans. "Here."

"You might want to go to Bliss after," Ava said. "Get some ice cream."

Unexpectedly, Jude's heart pinched hard. That was the kind of wholesome thing Finlay would love. He'd definitely do that for her.

He headed outside into the crisp early evening air. The sharp scent of pine cleared his head. He'd had a lot of fantasies about Finlay, but it was like lusting after a model or movie star. Now, though, a world of possibilities cracked open.

When he got in his dad's truck and started the engine, he realized his fingers were tingling.

What's wrong with me?

Sweat broke out on his hairline.

After a three-point turn, he made his way down the long driveway. His fingers flexed on the steering wheel.

And then, he did something bizarre. Something totally out of character.

And he only knew he did it because he checked in the rearview mirror and saw it with his own eyes.

He smiled.

Because he was fucking happy.

He couldn't wait to see her. To spend a whole evening with her.

No one in the world was as pretty and smart and strong. He didn't know for sure, but it looked like she had the softest skin in the world. And he'd only gotten whiffs, but her scent drove him wild.

All this time, he'd thought she was off-limits. But tonight, he'd get to touch her, dance with her. He imagined them swaying together, her cheek resting on his shoulder, his arm belted around her waist, those big, plump breasts pressed against his chest. Damn, just the thought of it got him half hard.

As he turned onto Highway 191, his cell phone rang again. He glanced at the screen.

Marco.

Nope. Not tonight.

Tonight, he was ignoring his friends.

But it rang again. And then, a third time.

Something's wrong. He picked up his phone. "Yeah?" The background noise was staticky. He heard panting. Feet pounding. Alarm sounded through his body. "What's going on?"

"You gotta come get us," Marco said. "Now."

"Where are you?" Jude demanded.

"On Crested Bluff. Heading into the woods off Robin's Lane. You know the house there?"

"The abandoned one?" Jude asked.

"Yeah." Marco was out of breath. "Cops are on our fuckin' asses. Hurry."

He pulled the truck over and closed his eyes. Finlay

was his north, and his body's compass strained in that direction, demanding he stay on the right course.

But fragments of memories flickered somewhere in the depths of his mind.

Boys laughing. Kicking him.

Holding him down.

That terrifying helplessness, weakness. The rage, fear.

And then, a curly-haired boy rushing in with a guttural shout, punching and head-butting with reckless abandon. *All to save me.*

For his first few months in Calamity, until he'd found his place in the club, Marco had protected him. Saved him.

"Get in the bushes," that same boy shouted to his friends right then. "Jude's on his way."

"Shit." Jude slammed his fist on the steering wheel. "Fuck." No, he didn't participate in their criminal activity, but they were still his friends. And Marco had been there for him when he needed it most. What kind of man would he be if he turned his back on him when he no longer needed the protection?

"Hurry, man," Marco shouted. "You know what they said last time. We're eighteen now. We'll go to jail."

Crossing lanes, he turned the truck around and headed in the opposite direction.

He's coming.

He wouldn't blow me off.

Alone, Finlay stood on the front lawn. Everyone had

boarded the party bus, but she was still watching for a motorcycle to come roaring down this quiet, suburban street.

Where was he? What was he doing?

"Fee?" Her best friend stepped off the bus. "Forget prom. Let's make nachos and watch dirty movies."

"No, you're going." Finlay had only been included in this group because of Willa, but man, it sure had seemed like the dream prom night. Jude as her date, and a group of friends to pre-party with. What could be better?

Instead, it was turning into a nightmare. Because Jude still hadn't shown up.

But Finlay wouldn't ruin this night for her friend, so she plastered on a smile. "Don't worry about me. Let's not forget that three hours ago, I was planning on doing laundry and adding pictures to my mood board." She tried to sound like she couldn't care less.

But Willa knew her too well. "He's forty-five minutes late. I don't think he's coming."

The sickly sweet scent of her friend's corsage made Finlay a little queasy. Because the truth was, she knew her friend was right.

"I'll tell Josh I'm not going." Her friend turned and started off.

But Finlay grabbed her arm. "Stop it. You're going to prom."

"And what're you going to do?"

"I'm going to wait a little longer." When her friend started to protest, she said, "If you're right, and he doesn't come, my mom'll come get me." That was a lie. Her mom was working. So was her dad. No one was coming. "Either way, I'll be fine. It's not like I've been planning for months to go with him."

But Willa wasn't buying her false cheer. "I can't have fun if you're sad."

"Okay, fine. If he blows me off, you can come over tomorrow and feed me tubs of cookies and cream ice cream, okay? But tonight…" The smile died. There was no point in faking it with someone who knew her as well as Willa. "I just want to be alone." It was how she handled things. She needed time to process. By herself.

That's how I'm built.

Willa's date stepped off the bus and joined them. "He's not coming." He held out his phone. "Look."

Finlay's stomach twisted into a knot as she processed the image on the screen.

It was a Splashagram photo of five boys huddled together in a dark space. They were laughing hysterically.

It took a moment to find Jude because he was in the back. But she'd know those eyes and that mouth anywhere.

He shaved.

Why would he do that if he never planned on coming?

It didn't make sense.

"What is it?" Willa asked.

Finlay heard their voices like she had cotton stuffed in her ears. Because it finally broke through, how delusional she'd been to cling so tightly to the idea that Jude would go to something as lame as a prom.

She'd actually thought he'd rent a *tuxedo.* She'd pictured him in a flower shop, deciding which *corsage* to get.

Even as her heart ripped in half, she burned with shame.

"Hey, I'm not going, okay?" Willa said to her date. "I'm really sorry—"

"No." Finlay stepped away from her friend. "I'm fine."

"Fee, if you're not going, I'm not going." Her date looked confused and unsure, so Willa said, "Give me a second." He hesitated but, with a nod, returned to the bus.

"You're not blowing off your date." She loved her friend too much to ruin one of the most important high school events. Besides, Finlay really didn't want company.

"Come on." Willa nudged her. "Chicks before dicks."

Finlay stood her ground. "You spent two hundred dollars on that dress and a hundred getting your hair done. You're going."

"Ovaries before brovaries."

"What does that even mean?" It was all Finlay could do to keep it together, but she'd save her breakdown for when she got home. For now, she gave a playful push. "Just go."

"Sluts before nuts. You're coming with me, and we're going to dance and have fun. Please, Fee?"

She honestly couldn't think of anything worse than being the third wheel with a group of people who weren't even her friends.

Oh wait.

Yes, she could.

It was being played by the boy she loved with all her heart.

Chapter One

TWELVE YEARS LATER

THE MERMAID'S SHANTY WAS HOPPIN' TONIGHT. They'd had to call in all their servers to keep up with orders.

Merry fuckin' Christmas.

Jude twisted the caps off six ice-cold beers and set them on a tray.

Before grabbing it, the server slapped a cocktail napkin on the counter. "This is from the blonde at table nine. She wants to know if you're single."

He gave a curt nod of acknowledgment. Ignoring the napkin, he dropped lime wedges onto the rim of two mojitos and handed them off.

He'd been working at this bar in the Florida Keys for a few weeks and had a running list of pros and cons. The owners of the bar wanted to retire, so they'd neglected some upkeep. But the shitty speakers and broken faucet were easy fixes. The pros were the great location and demographics. If he flipped this place, he'd bring in live bands and host events. Make it the social focal point of the area.

He'd wait for the financials, but it seemed like a winner.

The worried expression of the woman at table six caught his attention. A while ago, some guys had joined the group of nurses. It had taken a matter of minutes for them to couple up. Lots of laughter, lots of flirting.

Except for that one woman. She didn't seem to be enjoying herself. He lined up glasses for espresso martinis. He poured vodka into the shaker but kept his eye on her as she got up, grabbed money from her wallet, and threw it on the table.

The guy who'd been hitting on her watched her walk away. Jude didn't like the hard look in his eyes as he tracked her progress toward the exit.

But his skin went tight when the asshole got up to follow her out.

Jude set the coffee liqueur down. "Take over for me," he said to another bartender before lifting the bridge. He came out from behind the bar and strode across the room. By the time he caught sight of her, she was outside and heading for her car. The guy lagged just a little behind.

"Hey," Jude called.

Both of them whipped around at his harsh tone.

The woman noticed the creep not five feet from her, and her eyes went wide in fear.

"What's up?" Jude asked the guy.

"Just came out for a smoke." His gaze slanted sideways, as if looking for a way out of the conversation.

"Yeah? Where are the cigarettes?" The guy clearly

didn't have any, so Jude got right up in his face. "Get the fuck out of here and don't come back."

After giving Jude a quick once-over—taking in his height, ink, and muscles—the guy pulled his keys out of his pocket and headed off to his truck.

"You okay?" Jude asked the woman.

Relief softened her features. "Yes." She hitched her purse onto her shoulder. "I had no idea he was following me. God, if you hadn't noticed…" She hit the button on her remote, and the lights flashed on her car. She tossed her purse onto the passenger seat before turning to face him. "Thank you. I really appreciate that."

"No problem. Have a good night." As he hustled to get back inside, he took a moment to check his phone. The family chat was on fire tonight.

Boone: Nice catch, butterfingers.

Jude smiled at his youngest brother's comment, but it also reminded him that he'd missed Decker's game against Cincinnati.

Decker: Fuck off. We won. That's all that matters.

Times like this, he regretted the distance. With Decker in the NFL and Jude in Florida, their schedules rarely aligned for family get-togethers.

Ava: Congratulations, Decker. It was a nail-biter.

Dad: Who the fuck took my work gloves?

Decker: Oh, hey, thanks, Dad! Appreciate the support!

Dad: After you pulled your head out of your ass, it was a good game. That was a nice forty-five-yard strike on a third-and-fifteen play. Now, who took my fucking work gloves?

Boone: 😂😂😂

Wyatt: Me. Remember, we had to sedate that wolf with the abscessed thigh? You helped me crate it.

Dad: Oh yeah. Well, bring them back. Half my fence came down with that last snowstorm.

Boone: Should he wash the pus off first? Or just leave them on the kitchen counter for you?

Dad: Fair point. Keep them. I'll get a new pair.

Ava: Decker and Jude, will you boys be home for Christmas?

Boone: One of you guys better be. We lost Snowfest for the first time last year 'cause you both fucked off.

Decker: No, got a game in Detroit.

Ava: Oh shoot. I'm sorry to hear that. We'll miss you.

Ava: Give me an address where I can mail you something. I hate to think of you alone in a hotel room.

Boone: I don't know what lies he's telling you, but that's not what life on the road is like for a football player. 😂😂

Decker: Says the guy who plays circle jerk with his hotshot buddies out in the forest.

Decker: But yeah, I won't be alone. We'll have a team dinner. And then, family members can come over for the team snack after we do a walkthrough on Friday night.

Ava: What about you, Jude?

He'd just started to type his reply when his phone rang. He didn't get many calls. Every now and then, one of his Marine buddies needed to talk. He'd drop everything for them. Same with his family. But that was about it. He didn't stay anywhere long enough to make friends.

He might've ignored it, but the area code was Calamity. Just in case it was important, he answered. "Yeah?"

"Are you Jude?" It was a kid's voice.

What the hell? "Who's this?"

"It's Cody. Will you get me a bike? Please?"

"What?" Jude wanted to hang up, but it was a kid. He could at least figure out what was going on.

"I got to go to school, or I'm gonna get in trouble, and Amy's my friend, and she doesn't got any other friends 'cept me, and if I'm not there, she's sad."

Wait a minute. Am I being pranked? "Did Boone set you up for this?" Jude pulled the phone away to check the number again. He had no idea what was going on.

"Who's Boone?" the kid asked.

"My brother."

"Oh. I don't got a brother. So will you get me one?"

"Kid, you've got the wrong number."

"Are you Jude?" the boy asked. "My dad's friend?"

"Who's your dad?"

As he crossed the patio, the roar of conversation drowned out the kid's voice, but a familiar name snagged his attention. "Say that again."

"My dad said to call you. You're his friend."

"You said Marco? *He* was your dad?"

"Yeah. My dad's dead."

Holy shit. "Hang on." Instead of entering the bar, he hurried around to the side of the building, where it was quieter. His boots sank into the sand, and he leaned against the rough wood siding. "Say that again. Marco Rossi's your dad?"

"Yeah. He died. And now, I live with my grampa."

"Okay, but how'd you get my number?" He hadn't talked to his old friend in years.

"My dad gave me a picture of you and him together. On the back, it says, 'If I'm not around, call Jude. He's me just in another place.'"

The words echoed inside his brainpan.

Me in another place.

Sorrow sliced through him.

Regret.

That was the thing about Marco. He could be a total

fuckup—he had the worst judgment of anyone Jude knew —but then, he'd say something like that. Something insightful. Sensitive. And it exposed a whole other side of him.

A side worth knowing.

The side that saved his ass when he was the soft new kid dropped into a strange and scary biker world.

His eyes squeezed shut, and he dropped to a crouch, lowering his head into his hands and letting the pain engulf him.

After the Marines, Jude made the decision not to go home. As much as he loved his family, he knew there was no way to reinvent himself in a small town. So he'd hit the road. He'd seen a lot of this country. It was easy to get bartending jobs. Hell, his dad owned Wild Billy's. He'd grown up in one.

It was only last year, when he'd heard Marco had died, that Jude wished he hadn't cut him out so completely.

And yeah, he'd known about a son. He just hadn't given it much thought. Having a kid was outside his realm of understanding.

"Mister?" the kid asked. "Are you still there?"

"Yeah, I'm here. So you need a bike, huh?"

"Yeah. Can you get me one?"

The waves crashed and dragged on the shore, and a salty breeze cut through the humidity. Things just weren't adding up. "Where's your mom?"

"I don't know."

A couple staggered past him, heading for the shore. "Where are you right now?"

"In the club."

Marco's son was living in the bike club? "And you're with your grandpa?"

"Yeah, but he's sick and can't take me to school, and I really need to go."

Jude watched moonlight hit the surface of the ocean and splinter. A group gathered around a bonfire. A couple humped each other in the shadowy space underneath a house on stilts.

Marco's *son*. It was taking him a minute to wrap his head around it. "How old are you?"

"Five."

In Calamity, all grade levels were housed in one complex. The club was a good fifteen miles from the school. Yeah, not a chance a kid could ride a bike there.

"Please, Mister? Will you get me a bike?"

The urgency in his tone had Jude standing. "Yeah, I'll get you one."

"Thanks."

Before he could ask to speak to the grandfather, the kid disconnected.

He'd give the guy a call in the morning, get a better understanding of the situation.

But he guessed he had an answer for Ava.

Jude: Yeah, I'll be there.

Chapter Two

I'm getting married.

Finlay barely recognized herself in the mirror. The stylist had tamed her curly hair into glossy beach waves, her makeup was a little heavy (but that was for photographs, so she understood), and she wore an absolute explosion of a wedding gown.

Her best friend stood beside her. "You're stunning. You know that, right?"

"Thank you." Finlay reached for Willa's hand. "I'm really doing this."

Somehow, she'd made every dream on her vision board come true.

Well, not the kids. Not yet. But she and Matt wouldn't wait even a day. She hoped to get pregnant on their honeymoon.

"All right." Stella, the wedding planner, waved her hands. "It's showtime."

Willa smiled. "Let's do this."

Lifting the skirt of her dress, Finlay headed out of the

dressing room with her bridal party, but just as she reached the door, she remembered the gift. "Oh, wait. Hang on a sec. I forgot one thing."

"Are you serious?" Stella asked.

"What is it?" Willa asked. "I'll take care of it."

"No, it's okay. It's something I have to do."

"Sweetie, you walk down the aisle in five minutes," the wedding planner said.

"I know. I promise it won't take me longer than that." She just had to run to the car. Once they left, she dug her groom's present out of her tote bag. Her heart did a little jig.

He's going to love this.

Matt's dad had passed away when he was a teenager, and he didn't have much to remember him by. The one thing he'd always wanted was his dad's watch. It had gone missing after the accident that took his life, and no one had been able to find it.

With permission from his mom to go through old boxes in the attic, Finlay found the purchase order and serial number, so she'd been able to track it down at an estate jewelry store in Spokane. She couldn't wait to give it to him.

Tucking it under her arm, she hurried out. As she made her way along the empty hallway, she caught the hum of conversation in the church and the smell of pine and cinnamon from the candles for her winter wedding.

A frisson of happiness sped down her spine.

This is really happening.

She and Matt were two peas in a pod. They wanted the same things out of life: a home full of soccer shoes and holiday decorations and big family dinners. She wanted laughter around the table, toys in the bathtub, and the entire family smushed together in bed, reading stories.

All the things she'd never had growing up.

Hitting the lever of the side door, she stepped out into the frigid air of the Teton Range. Good thing Matt had parked his BMW right there. She opened the trunk to find it stuffed with their luggage. They'd spend their wedding night at the Homestead Inn, then leave for their honeymoon the next day.

She couldn't wait to start her life with him. *He's going to be a great dad.*

Out of nowhere, she got an unwanted flash of her childhood.

A boy with bottle-green eyes. Long, dark hair and scuffed motorcycle boots. In school, he'd revealed nothing. No emotion. No interest.

But the moments they'd had together were intense, fun, exciting. Her best childhood memories were with Jude. She'd thought there was a spark, a connection.

But she'd been so wrong.

Lesson learned.

He's not mysterious… He's just not into you.

And she needed a man who adored her. Who communicated with her.

No more crushes on wounded men.

Besides, it was a waste of time and energy to think about what might have been.

"Finlay?" The wedding planner leaned out of the doorway. "You coming?"

She gave Stella a thumbs-up and wedged the gift into the back of the trunk.

Something crinkled. *That's weird.* She dug around and unearthed a wrapped present tucked away in the corner.

See how cute we are?

We both bought something for each other.

Peas in a pod.

Except…the wrapping paper had colorful balloons. It looked like something for a child. She shouldn't do it, but curiosity got the better of her, and she tugged the white envelope out from under the red bow. Fortunately, it wasn't sealed, so she pulled out the card.

DEAR CHLOE,

I'M SORRY I COULDN'T BE THERE FOR YOUR BIRTHDAY, BUT I PROMISE TO MAKE IT UP TO YOU.

LOVE,

DADDY

Daddy?

Her stomach plummeted, and she went lightheaded.

No, no. Don't freak out. There's an explanation.

There has to be.

But fear fractured her mind, and she couldn't think straight.

She forced a few deep breaths.

Okay, wait.

Maybe it wasn't Matt's. He could be holding it for his sister. His brother.

A friend.

Sure, one of his friends.

But none of them were dads.

Look at the handwriting.

It was definitely Matt's.

But he's not a father.

Is he cheating on me?

He went on a lot of hunting and fishing trips with his friends, but he always sent pictures and texts. He always came home with stories and stinky clothes.

What about an ex? His only other serious relationship was with his college girlfriend, but they broke up six years ago and she lived in another state.

Just talk to him.

Now? Two minutes before walking down the aisle?

No, I'll wait till we're in the car, heading to the inn.

I'm not bailing on him because I found a present in his car.

That'd be ridiculous.

Closing the trunk, she hurried back inside, determined to put the gift out of her mind.

As she approached the bridal party, the wedding planner spoke quietly into her microphone, and the chamber trio launched into the processional.

Her best friend handed her the bouquet. "Everything okay?"

In the vestibule, with butterflies in her stomach and toes pinched by the fancy shoes her soon-to-be mother-in-law had gifted her, Finlay nodded and tried for a smile.

But as the maid of honor and best man made their way down the aisle, she grew more agitated. More anxious.

Her dad stood beside her. "You don't look good."

Finlay laughed. "Thanks, Dad."

"You know what I mean. You're beautiful, angel. But you don't look happy." He jingled the keys in his pants pocket. "Car's outside."

She wished so badly she hadn't seen that present. But now wasn't the time to talk about it. "I'm good."

"You sure?" Her competitive, athletic dad took no crap. If she told him her concerns, he'd march right up to the altar and confront the groom.

She set her hand on his arm. "Positive."

The wedding planner gave a nod, and they stepped into the church. Amid a shush of fabric, the congregants rose to their feet.

But she didn't look at them. She was focused on her fiancé, who stood at the end of the aisle, watching her.

Are you lying to me?

Are you cheating?

Now that she'd had some time to think about it, she could say that, yes, Matt had been acting differently. The other day, she'd looked out the window of their new home and found him on the walkway. He'd been upset. She'd figured it was about work—there was always a crisis in the finance world—but instead of coming inside to tell her about it, he'd gotten into his car and driven off.

When he'd finally come home, he'd told her it was just some work thing.

But see, he never said, "work thing." He told her every detail of his job as a wealth manager. She knew the lingo.

Still, she kept marching forward. She'd hear him out. He'd have a logical explanation—even if she couldn't think of one herself.

Except… That was his handwriting.

No doubt about it.

But it was confusing because, as Matt watched her approach, he radiated pure happiness. He lowered his face into a hand and used two fingers to wipe away the tears.

He loves me.

He wants a life with me.

Her gut knew it.

So what's going on?

A rustling sound caught her attention. She glanced over to see a mother struggling to keep her antsy child seated. As she slowly moved by, Finlay registered that the girl was trying to peel off her tights while the mom fought to keep them on.

As a kindergarten teacher, she was used to kids acting out. They often resisted wearing coats, shoes…anything that felt restrictive. She didn't fuss over it.

Finally, she reached the altar. Her dad kissed her cheek and took his seat. Finlay handed her bouquet to Willa.

This is it.

No turning back.

The butterflies in her tummy turned to swooping bats. She pressed a hand to her stomach. But nothing felt right.

Everything was off.

The dress she'd loved and tried on a dozen times felt itchy. Her skin was damp. Hot. One of the bobby pins dug into her scalp just behind her ear.

"Good evening, everyone," the pastor began.

But as he continued, Finlay could only hear a muffled murmur, as if the ceremony took place underwater. She was sweating now, and she thought she might pass out.

The pastor kept talking, the congregants laughed every now and then, and her groom couldn't keep the grin off his face.

Finally, Matt said his vows. He slid a ring onto her finger.

The gold was shockingly cold.

Only when he said, "I thee wed," did the fog clear. Because it was her turn.

Unfortunately, her mind was preoccupied with balloons.

Love, Daddy.

Again, it was unquestionably Matt's handwriting. He hadn't written the card as a favor for a friend. He wasn't helping a sibling.

No.

"And now, Finlay, you may say your vows," the pastor said.

Instead, she turned to the congregation. "Is there a Chloe here?"

Strangely, her gaze landed unerringly on the little girl who'd won the battle over her tights. The one who stood on the padded pew and shouted, "I Cwowie."

Finlay's gaze shifted to the mother. She sucked in a harsh breath. "Your ex is here?" she asked Matt.

He jerked around. When he spotted the woman and her child, he let out a deep exhalation. His shoulders slumped.

"You invited her to our wedding?" she asked.

Instead of answering, he squeezed his eyelids shut. His head tipped back. "Fuck," he whispered.

"Is Chloe your daughter?" she demanded.

His eyelids flew open. "Yes, but I can explain. It's not what you think."

"Yes?" Her dad shot out of his seat. "You have a *daughter*? What the *hell* are you talking about?" He made a beeline for the groom.

Matt's mom popped out of her seat as if she could intercept Finlay's burly dad. "We can talk about it later."

"No, we can't." With her child in her arms, the ex hurried down the aisle. "I'm sorry, Finlay, but you deserve to know the truth before you exchange vows."

Finlay turned to her groom for answers. "How long have you known?"

"I just found out. I swear."

Love, Daddy.

No, he did not just find out.

"When?" she insisted.

"I told him three months ago." The ex reached the altar and pushed through the throng of family and bridal party. "He said he wanted to be part of her life, so I moved here. We're not together. It's not like that. But he *is* her father. He took a DNA test."

Finlay's dad went ballistic, Matt's mom tried to deflect, and Willa looked ready to punch the groom in the face. The guests were whispering, talking, and shifting in their seats.

Her vision went foggy at the edges, and a low current of energy buzzed in her ears.

Finlay slowly backed away. Unseeing, she walked to the back of the sanctuary and down a short flight of stairs. She pushed through a door and found herself in the frigid cold air once again.

Good thing she was numb. But as she looked around the parking lot, she realized she had nowhere to go. They'd just moved into the house together, so she couldn't go there. Not yet.

So then, what? *Where do I go?*

Her mom's apartment? Her dad's? Just the thought sent a flood of unpleasant memories through her. No, neither of those places.

A roar of motorcycles invaded her thoughts.

Even though she hadn't seen Jude in over a decade, she still thought of him every time she heard that sound. She looked for those intense green eyes inside every helmet.

But none of that mattered right now. She needed to go. She wasn't about to steal Matt's BMW or go back inside and pull Willa away from the melee.

Besides, she found herself drawn to the bikes. Gathering the tulle and silk of her gown, she started in their direction. A walk turned into a run when she realized the light would change, and the motorcycles would leave.

At that moment, they seemed her only solution.

The light turned green, and the engines sputtered and growled. And then, they were gone, their exhaust leaving plumes of white exhaust.

Except for one rider. He remained in the middle of the street, his eyes on her.

She knew him. Of course she did.

She would recognize the breadth of his shoulders, his muscular frame—that *swagger*—anywhere, anytime.

She walked right into the street and stood beside him, gazing at the face that still haunted her dreams.

"Need a ride?" he asked in that deliciously deep voice.

She nodded. But they both looked down at the billowing material of her seven-thousand-dollar gown—a gift from Matt's mom. He pulled a knife from his boot and jerked his chin at it.

Finlay loved this dress. She'd been building a mood board of gowns for two years, but she'd never once imagined she could buy one from a couture designer like Knox Holliday.

It was truly the gown of her dreams.

But here's the thing. Matt might have a very good reason for not telling me.

"I wanted to wait until after the wedding."

Sure, she could see the logic in that.

Maybe. Kind of.

Actually, no. Not really.

"I didn't want to ruin this special time for you."

"I was waiting for the results of the DNA test."

But he already had those. His ex had made that clear.

Nothing could excuse waiting *three months* to tell her life-altering news.

Finlay was sure some women could forgive what he'd done. Eventually, she probably could, too.

But she'd never trust him the way a woman needed to trust her spouse.

And so, she nodded, taking in those intense eyes and the thick beard that framed a full, kissable mouth.

He gathered the layers of material and plunged the blade in, hacking away until the bottom half dropped to the ground. Then he pulled off his leather jacket and held it open for her.

Turning, she slid her arms inside. It was warm from

his body, and it smelled like woodsmoke and pine, like the crisp night mountain sky.

Finally, he peeled off his helmet and offered it. She didn't know her hands were shaking until she pulled it over her head. Once she got it on and smashed all those pretty beach waves, she climbed onto the back of his motorcycle and wrapped her arms around his waist.

He twisted the throttle and shot forward.

She never once looked back.

Chapter Three

WITH HER ARMS BANDED AROUND HIS CHEST, FINLAY clung to him like her life depended on it. Her cheek was smashed to his back, and her bare thighs clamped around his hips. She had to be freezing her ass off.

This is wild.

Jude had only landed in Calamity an hour ago. His dad, Ava, and two of his brothers met him at the airport. Even brought him a bike to ride.

And the moment I cross the town line, I find her?

That was bizarre enough, but to catch her right as she was running from her own wedding?

Typically, they didn't ride in December. It was too damn cold. But it was sunny, and the roads were clear. Hadn't snowed for a week. And of course, no one had anticipated a companion in a wedding dress.

He had a lot of questions.

Like, who was she marrying, and what had the asshole done to make her pull a runner?

And had she ever gotten her house on Bloom Lane?

But he didn't have time for that. He had to get to the club. Had to see about Marco's son.

When he reached a safe distance from the church, he pulled onto the shoulder of the road.

"Oh, okay," she said. "Sure. I'll just…um…" She released her hold on him. "Can I borrow your phone? I have to…" She glanced from the bison preserve to the motel and gas station across the street. "Call…someone. A cab." She set one pink satin heel on the asphalt and clutched his shirt as she tried to slide off the back of his bike.

She was a mess, and he didn't like seeing her so rattled. It stirred something in him. Something that made his hands clench into fists. Because she wouldn't be running if the groom hadn't done something.

It's none of my business.

When she pulled off his jacket and handed it to him, he shook his head. "Put it on and get back on the bike. I'm not abandoning you on the side of the road."

"Are you sure?" When she saw his stern expression, she scrambled to slide her arms into the sleeves. She was shaking, and he didn't know if her ghostly pallor was because of the temperature or shock. "Thanks."

"I only stopped to find out where I'm dropping you."

"Oh." She looked overwhelmed and overwrought. "I don't know."

That fancy makeup, the shiny wedding hair, the expensive gown…none of it fit with the anxiety pinching her features. "I can't go home. We live there together. And I don't want to hear his excuses. I need…I need to *think*."

"What about Willa?"

"I mean, she's at the church. She was my maid of honor." Tears glistened, and her voice was thick. "But she has to go back to the city in the morning. She's working on a case. I can't mess it up for her."

No one on this earth tugged at his heart the way this woman did. But as much as he wanted to help her, he had a kid who might try to walk fifteen miles along a highway to get to school. "Look, I have to get to the club. I can drop you at a hotel—"

"I don't have a wallet." She looked down at her ruined dress. "I don't have clothes."

"Then I'll take you to your mom or dad's."

"No." She had a frantic look in her eyes. "I can't. They're going to want to talk about it, dissect it. Analyze every single detail. They're going to try to fix it."

"But it can't be fixed?"

"No. It's over."

"Then you'll have to come to the club with me." It might not be the ideal place, but they'd take care of her. "They'll get you some clothes, and I can give you cash. You can figure it out from there, yeah?"

"Yes." She nodded, clearly still in shock. "Thank you. I won't get in your way."

That was it. He'd reached his limit. Gripping both forearms, he jerked her to him. "You are *not* in my way."

She didn't believe it. He could tell from the way she wouldn't look him in the eyes.

She'd spent a lot of time alone as a kid, which made her self-reliant and independent. It also made her feel like she couldn't impose on anyone. Like she was a burden.

No, she'd never told him shit like that. But he'd paid attention. He knew.

Well, he'd make it clear. "If I could help you right now, I would. But I'm in town to handle some business, and I have to get going." He let her go. "Now, get on." He knew he said it too gruffly by the way she flinched, but at least she did as he asked.

Whatever shit her groom had dished out, Finlay didn't deserve it. She was sunshine and kindness and everything good in the world.

As she got settled on the back of his bike, he glanced at the gas station, half-afraid old man Keller would stalk out with a baseball bat and tell him to get the hell off his property or to empty his pockets so he could see how much candy he'd stolen.

It was only when his dad sat him down and explained the repercussions of stealing—not just for Jude but for store owners—that he'd begun to separate from his friends and make better choices.

Jude remembered so clearly being seventeen and idling in this very spot, waiting for his friends to come running out with their arms loaded with chips and beers, wondering what life would be like somewhere else.

Well, now he knew.

Which made it surreal to be back in town and with Finlay clinging to him like he was her only hope against the hordes of zombies chasing her. He liked it.

That was not good, so he pinned it and took off.

When he got to the club, he didn't recognize a lot of the bikes and trucks. He had no idea what happened to most of the guys he'd once known.

He only knew one thing: Marco was gone.

A sharp twist of regret had him lowering his gaze to the snow-covered ground. He and his friend had gone in different directions. There was nothing he could've done about that, but it didn't take away the disappointment that life hadn't gone better for his oldest friend.

While waiting for her to get off his bike, he checked the family chat.

> Dad: What the hell was that?

> Ava: Need us to come back?

> Boone: Jude, the legend. Bagging a date his first five minutes in town.

He wrote them back.

> Jude: She's an old friend from high school. She needed a ride.

> Boone: 😭😭😭

> Dad: You need us for anything?

> Jude: No. I'll be home after I figure things out with the kid.

Once off the bike, Finlay handed over the helmet and jacket. "Thank you."

Her shaking hands and voice messed with him. "What'd that fucker do?"

"He kept a secret."

He studied her for a moment. That wasn't always a dealbreaker. Not when you loved someone.

What the fuck do I know about love?

Not a damn thing.

"Don't look so murderous." She cracked a half-hearted grin. "He didn't cheat on me. At least, I don't think."

Her hair was a mess, so he bit the tip of his glove and tugged it off, freeing his hand to brush strands off her forehead. "You okay?"

"I don't know. I feel like a rubber ducky floating in a bathtub. I don't have legs, so I can't kick toward the side, and I'm just…bobbing."

"All right, ducky. When you figure it out, let me know. For now, let's get you warmed up."

As she held his gaze, she broke into a soft grin. It lit her eyes and put color back into her pale complexion. "You know what I just remembered?"

"What?"

"That day you rescued me from the raccoon."

He'd never forgotten. For a lot of reasons. First, she'd been wearing the cutest fucking slippers he'd ever seen. Second, because of the fear in her eyes. It had been real. And third, because that was the day all the pieces had come together, and he'd understood her. Her essential loneliness.

He'd never talked to Leia again.

She nodded. "Today's the second time you happened to be there right when I needed you."

"You didn't need *me*. You just needed a ride."

"But it was you who showed up." Her eyes went soft. "Both times."

"Yeah, because everyone you know was in that church."

"It could've been anyone. But it was you. Thank you, Jude."

Whatever held him upright—his bones, his resolve, his instinct for survival—softened, nearly taking out his knees.

How the hell could anyone hurt this sweet, sincere woman?

But he had a purpose, so he turned away from her. "Let's go." His boots crunched on snow and gravel, and he wouldn't let himself check to see if she followed.

The moment he opened the club door, the roar of conversation and the smell of pot hit him. The juke-box blasted out a Slipknot song, while people laughed, shouted, and hung out. It was a late Saturday afternoon, and the party was in full swing.

When he was a kid, his dad would take them camping most weekends. Of course, at the time, they had no idea he was keeping them away from the decadence of the club. For a few years, they'd loved it, but then, they'd reached a point when they'd started making friends and had sports commitments, and disappearing every weekend hadn't been viable anymore.

It wasn't the reason his dad moved away—no, that was because of what happened to Wyatt—but it was certainly a major factor.

Finlay entered ahead of him but came to an abrupt stop, forcing him to grab her hips so he didn't slam into her.

The feel of her body sent him back to all those restless nights when he'd dreamed about her. He wouldn't say he had a type. Generally, he was attracted to a smile, confidence, and a lack of inhibitions.

But something about Finlay's curves had always driven him wild. An image hit of pulling her up hard against him, cupping her full breasts, and grinding his cock on her ass.

He let her go as if she were on fire.

He didn't know where that thought had come from, but it was an unacceptable reaction to someone he hadn't seen in twelve years. Someone who'd just run from her own wedding.

She cast a glance over her shoulder as if wondering what she'd done wrong.

Trust me, Ducky, it's not you. It's me. He pushed in front of her and said, "Stick close," as he moved into the room.

The massive warehouse space featured an active bar, four pool tables, and several couches that faced a giant TV with a video game playing on the screen.

An old friend spotted him. With a lift of his beer and a smile, Jordan sauntered over. "Dude. What're you doin' here?"

"Came to see Carlo."

"Ah." The smile faded. "Is this about Marco's kid?"

"Yeah, he called. Guess he needs some help?"

Jordan gave a curt nod. "Carlo's having a hard time keeping up with him. We try to pitch in, but everyone's got their own shit to deal with. Come on. Let me take you to him."

"Thanks."

Jordan clapped him on the shoulder. "Afterward, we'll grab some beers, catch up."

"Another time. I need to get my friend something to wear and then take care of the kid."

Finlay stepped forward and reached out a hand. "Hello, I'm Finlay. It's nice to meet you."

Even with her wind-blown hair and savagely cut wedding gown, she was still gracious.

"Hey. Jordan." He shook her hand. "And I got you. Hang on." He waved to a woman at the bar who came right over. "Marta, you got something for her to change into?"

The woman touched the shredded dress. "I don't have anything so fancy, but I can set you up with jeans and a T-shirt."

"Oh, I don't normally dress like this." Finlay tried for a smile. "Today was a special occasion."

The woman laughed. "I can see that."

"Jeans would be perfect." Finlay's grin was like sunshine, warming his heart. "Thank you so much."

As the woman set off through the crowded room, Finlay hesitated to follow. "Where will you be?" she asked Jude.

"We're going in the same direction," Jordan said. "We'll be right behind you."

The four of them headed off, he and his old friend lagging behind on their way to the living quarters.

"So what's up?" Jordan asked. "You steal a bride?"

"Friend from high school." He gave chin nods to familiar faces but noticed a lot of people he didn't recognize. "Club's grown a lot."

"What's it been since we graduated, twelve years? Long time to be away."

True.

"You probably weren't paying much attention at Marco's funeral, but most of these guys were there." Jordan's features tightened. "That was a rough day."

As they turned down the hallway, Jude couldn't help watching the sway of Finlay's hips and the fall of her long, dark hair. He wasn't so sure about sending her off with a woman he didn't know. "Is she gonna be all right?"

"Oh, yeah. Marta's the best. Ugly divorce. Her ex made sure she didn't get a thing. She was a mess when she showed up here, but now, she's like the club mom."

Jude never understood men like Marta's ex. *No matter what happens between a couple, assets should be divided equally. Just split everything and move on.* Before the women dipped into a room, Jude called, "I'll be in here, okay?"

Finlay gave him a relieved smile and nodded.

"Not sure where the kid is, but his pops is here." Jordan stopped outside a closed door and knocked.

"Yeah?" An older man cleared his throat. "Come on in."

"You good?" his friend asked.

"Yeah. Appreciate it."

"You got it," Jordan said before taking off.

Inside the small room, Jude took in a black dresser, an unmade bed, and a window that looked out to the backyard.

In a small recliner, an older man sat, watching kids play outside. The man planted his hands on the armrests and tried to get up, but pain twisted his features, and he hissed.

"Sit." In three strides, Jude stood before him and held out a hand. "Jude McKenna."

The man was unshaven with a shock of gray hair and watery eyes. "Carlo Rossi." He smiled. "You came."

"Of course." They'd only had a brief conversation on Jude's way to the airport, so he hoped to get a clearer picture of the kid's situation. "I wasn't expecting to get a call from Marco's kid."

"No, I'm sure you weren't. And I'm sorry about that. The little runt took my phone." His words might've sounded harsh, but the affection in his eyes made it clear how much he cared about his grandson. "I'm sorry he made you come all the way out here."

"He said you're sick, and he needs to get to school. What can I do to help?"

He chuckled. "It's preschool. He doesn't have to go. I only put him in it because I've been having trouble with my hips. Gonna need both replaced." Again, he tried to get up, but pain dug deep lines around his eyes and tightened his jaw. He took a moment to pull himself together before speaking again. "But you know what it's like here. I got plenty of people who can pitch in."

"Where's his mother?"

Damion shook his head. "Right from the start, she couldn't handle it. My grandson raised him solo. He did a good job, too."

"Sounds like you've got it under control. He asked for a bike, so I'll get him one for Christmas. Is there anything else you need?"

"There is." The old man's eyes sharpened. "And I'll get

right to the point. There's a risk with any surgery, but I'm eighty-six years old."

There was a plea in his eyes that Jude found unsettling. "Okay."

"Other than me, the boy's got no relatives. If something happens on that operating table, I need to know someone will take care of him."

A cold fluid shot through Jude's veins. Where was he going with this? "Nothing's going to happen." Though that seemed a stupid thing to say. Any surgery had complications, but at an advanced age… Sure, he got it. "But even if it did, like you said, you've got a club full of people here. Some of them already have kids."

The old man held his gaze. "Your dad got you boys out of here for a reason, yeah?"

This man was painting a picture Jude didn't like. "Hang on. What exactly are you asking me to do?"

"I need to assign temporary guardianship, and I'm asking you to do it."

Jude took a step back. "Me? You can't just ask a stranger to take care of your grandson. And even if I wanted to, what judge in his right mind's going to let a guy like me raise a kid?"

"What do you mean, 'a guy like you?' You come from a good family. You served this country. You don't have a record that I could find. And you're reliable. Responsible."

"You don't know anything about me."

"You're here, aren't you? A kid called, asking for help, and you flew out the next day. What more do I need to know? Besides, Marco talked about you all the time. And he's not the only one. Been living here about a year now, and I've heard stories about you and your family." Carlo pointed a crooked finger at him. "Your dad's the reason these folks have work. He gave this club a living and the members a purpose."

"That's got nothing to do with me taking care of a *child*. Trust me, I'm not parent material."

"Why not? You're the oldest of four kids. You've got the instincts. Thing is, I've got to have the surgery in Idaho Falls so my sister can help me rehab after. And I can't go unless I know Cody's in good hands."

The energy in the room changed, lightened, and a sweet, feminine scent filled the air. He turned to see Finlay in a Metallica T-shirt and tight jeans. She brightened when she saw the old man. "Oh, hey, Mr. Rossi." But the smile faded into concern. "Are you okay? How're you feeling?"

"Eh, I'm all right. This guy flew all the way out here just to get Cody a bike."

"Aw, he'll love that." Finlay flashed him a luminous smile that made his heart skip a few beats.

"How do you know the Rossis?" Jude asked.

"I'm a kindergarten teacher."

Of course, she was. And he bet every kid in that class had a crush on her.

"I know most of the preschool kids," she said, "because we have conferences to see if they're ready to move up."

He didn't ask the question that came to mind. Was this kid going to make it? Because education wasn't a priority for Marco or anyone in the club. They liked to say they graduated from the school of hard knocks. How could they "live life full throttle" if they had to "work for the man" to pay their bills? For them, that wasn't what life was about. It was about living free.

Jude jerked a thumb over his shoulder. "I'm going to head out. Stop at my dad's to borrow a car and then get to the bike store. Can I get you anything?"

There was no denying the panic in the man's eyes. "No, I'm good."

"All right. Be back in an hour or so." With a chin nod, he ushered Finlay out of the room.

In the quiet of the hallway, she asked the obvious, "Are you taking Cody with you?"

What would he do with a kid? "No. I have a motorcycle."

"You could come back for him. You need to know his size. Plus, it'll be more fun for him to pick one out. It's Christmas."

"Can you imagine me showing up in town with a kid? Everyone will think I kidnapped him."

"Oh, I don't know about that." But she didn't push the issue. "Mr. Rossi doesn't look so good. What's going on?"

"He's having hip replacement surgery. He'll be gone for six weeks." *Or longer.*

Fuck.

"What does that mean for Cody?" she asked.

They entered the main room, where a few people were dancing. Several groups gathered around three of the pool tables, and one couple was getting hot and heavy on the fourth one. A pair of blue jeans pooled around ankles, a white ass thrusting, and a pair of sky-high heels were right there on display for the whole club to watch.

Finlay's features froze in a mask of horror. "Cody lives here?" Her gaze took a quick tour around the warehouse, noting the curls of smoke from cigarettes and weed, the fight that was about to break out at the bar, and the woman straddling the guy on the couch. "Where is he? I need to see him."

Through the kitchen window, they could see children of all ages racing around in the snow. "Maybe outside." When he grew up here, his dad tried to protect him from this lifestyle. And, of course, they'd had Ava.

But who did Cody have? He went tight thinking about an innocent kid running wild in this place. "Carlo wants to make me a temporary guardian while he's recovering."

Hope sprang to life in her eyes. "And what did you say?"

"I didn't say anything. No court's going to give me legal rights to a kid I don't know."

"Well, that's not true. Carlo's the grandfather, so they'll listen to his request."

"Carlo doesn't know me."

"Well, I do. Your brothers do. I'm sure we could find a hundred people who'd speak well of you."

"I'm not looking for people to testify on my behalf." She didn't get it. "I don't *want* to do this." She watched him with concern. "And after the shit I put you through back in high school, why do you have such a high opinion of me?"

"You mean prom?"

He nodded.

"Yeah, well, I have my theory about what happened that night."

"And what's that?"

"I kept torturing myself by looking at the picture your friend posted on social media."

"Oh, the one the cops used to find us?" Now, he could laugh at it. "They weren't exactly known for their genius IQs."

"It took me a few days to see the bow tie you were wearing."

How the hell had she seen that? "You could hardly see me in that photo. Besides, I'd shaved. No way could you tell it was me."

"The other guys were laughing, but you were behind them, looking pissed off. Your white shirt stood out in the darkness." She tipped her head, her warm amber eyes studying him. "You were coming to get me, weren't you? When the guys called, you were on your way?"

All he could do was nod. It was such a relief for her to know the truth.

"I wish you'd told me. I get that you had to leave town, but why did you let me believe you'd been playing me? That was mean, Jude."

It was. "Because I needed to cut ties with this town."

"There's nothing wrong with the town. The only ties you needed to cut were with your friends."

His breath hitched. "Yeah, well, the biggest tie's been cut."

She touched his arm. "I'm sorry about Marco."

"Yeah." Instead of offering comfort, the warmth of her hand stirred something deep inside. Something he didn't want to analyze too closely. "At least he died exactly how he wanted."

"How's that?"

"Riding with his boys."

"Well, I guess the tie wasn't cut after all, because now, you have Cody."

"I don't *have* him. And I'm out of the business of saving Marco's ass." Even back then, he'd understood it wasn't his friend's fault. The guy's dad bailed, and his mom had been more focused on partying than parenting.

The only reason Jude hadn't wound up like him was because he had a great family.

"If you don't take guardianship of him, what happens?" she asked.

"His life stays the same. He'll hang out at the club until Carlo gets back." But if Marco could've made something of his life if he'd had a decent parent, what did that mean for Cody?

"Okay, well, let's check on him. He shouldn't be around this"—she gestured to the party—"kind of thing."

They crossed the kitchen to the back door, but before she could open it, he pulled a parka off the hook and shoved it at her. "Here."

"Oh. Thank you." She quickly shrugged it on and headed outside, where kids of all ages chased each other, shouting and throwing snowballs.

"You know which one he is?" Jude asked.

She looked around. "I don't see him."

"Hey," Jude called out to a girl running by. "Where's Cody Rossi?"

She shrugged and dashed off.

He had his hand at his mouth, ready to shout the kid's name, when Finlay pointed. "Oh my God. That's him. That's Cody."

Chapter Four

JUDE DIDN'T KNOW WHAT HE WAS EXPECTING WHEN he'd spoken with a five-year-old on the phone, but it definitely wasn't the thin little boy wearing jeans and a long-sleeved T-shirt, squatting at the base of a tree and sticking pine needles and rocks into a mound of dirty snow.

"He's not wearing a coat." Finlay was already on the move. When she reached him, she crouched, using her fingers to get the boy's unruly curls out of his eyes. "Hey, Cody." He neither answered nor looked at her, but she persisted. "What're you making?" Her breath came out in white puffs.

"A fort."

"Are these windows?" She touched some of the rocks.

"No. They're guards."

A visceral memory hit of being outside in the cold, just like this kid. That feeling of being exposed and vulnerable rocked him to his core. Because at least he'd had Marco. This boy didn't seem to have anyone.

"Oh, that's really cool," Finlay said. "I bet the people inside feel really safe. Hey, guess who's here to see you?"

The boy's gaze flicked up.

Several emotions ran wild inside him. First, the boy's uncanny resemblance to Marco threw him back to his own childhood when his friend was a scrappy, skinny kid who wouldn't back down from a threat. But also, with the same wild black curls and dimples on either side of his mouth as his dad, the boy reminded him of the quieter moments with his friend when they'd hike or build forts away from the chaos of the club.

But man, it was like looking right into Marco's hazel eyes.

Until this moment, Jude had understood intellectually what Carlo was asking of him. But right then, he got it on a much deeper level.

Because this is Marco's son.

And he's out here alone in twenty-degree weather with no supervision. Did he even have food in his belly?

If something happened to Carlo, this boy would grow up in the club. He wouldn't have a traditional education, celebrate holidays, or know the kind of love only a parent could give a child.

Cody would live by his desires and not his obligations. Like Marco, he might never realize his potential or become the man he was born to be.

"Cody," Finlay said. "This is Jude."

"You came." The boy's eyes widened with awe.

"Of course. I said I would."

"Are you really going to get me a bike?" Cody asked.

"Yes."

"Can we go right now?" The boy scrambled to his feet. His hands were red from the cold. His clothes were filthy and damp. "Please?"

Jude knew what he had to do. "Yeah. You're coming with me." He had no other choice. "Come on."

Finlay picked up the boy. "We need to get him washed up and into dry clothes. Which do you want to do?"

"I'll find something for him to wear."

After they entered the kitchen, Finlay went straight to the sink while Jude headed into the mudroom to pick out a kid-sized coat, hat, and gloves. Next, he had to get jeans and a shirt from Carlo.

Turning back to tell Finlay where he was going, he saw she'd propped Cody on the counter to wipe his hands and face with a dish towel. The intimacy between them was like mother and son. There was so much trust in the boy's eyes as he turned his palms up and tilted his chin to let her clean him.

An image of her in a home, a kitchen, the smell of chicken roasting, two kids on the floor, playing with toy cars, blew through him. It was so vivid, so…*good*…that he immediately shut it down.

What the fuck was that?

Jude had zero interest in a family. A mortgage. A dog shitting in the yard.

Imagine me selling insurance and mowing the lawn.
Yeah, right.

He strode over to her. "Come on." He lifted Cody off the counter. "We need to talk to your grandpa."

The boy went stiff, and he clung to Finlay's T-shirt. "Can Miss O'Neill come, too?"

"Absolutely." Before Finlay could even reach for the boy, he flung himself into her arms. "*Oh*. Okay. I got you." She ran a soothing hand down the back of his head. "It's all right."

"Will you come with me to get a bike?" Cody asked her.

"You don't have to do that," Jude said quietly. He couldn't involve Finlay in this situation. She had enough of her own shit to deal with. "He'll get used to me. We'll be fine." He reached for the boy.

But that only made him more anxious. "Please, Miss O'Neill?"

Finlay's gaze dropped to the floor for just a moment as she grew contemplative. She drew in a breath. "Sure. That sounds like fun." She shot Jude a rueful smile. "Better than dealing with my own life, right?"

He didn't think it would work without her. "Maybe if you come with us to get the bike, it'll give him time to get used to me. After that, I'll take you wherever you need to go."

"Deal."

They headed back to Carlo's room. As he knocked on the door, he turned to her. "Can you give me a minute to talk to him alone?"

"Of course."

"Then bring Cody in so he can say goodbye."

She eyed him curiously, but as soon as Jude heard, "Come in," he entered the room, leaving her and the boy in the hallway.

He stood before the older man. "What exactly do you need from me?"

Relief softened the man's features. "Take care of him while I'm away."

"I just take him home with me? That's it?"

"I think that's best. I can't look after him right now. Will you stay here, though?"

"I can stay in town, but you don't expect me to move into the club, do you?"

"Trust me, if I could live independently, I sure wouldn't be raising Cody in a bike club," Carlo said. "But what can I do? I can barely walk to the bathroom."

"You don't mind if I take him to my dad's? We can give him a nice Christmas." The idea of his dad, brothers, and Ava helping made the prospect of looking after a kid much more doable. He could hire a sitter or a nanny. Cody might get a kick out of doing Snowfest with them.

"That's good." Carlo smiled. "That's real good. I've already written up a schedule, though I didn't think anyone here would keep it. It's just preschool, but it means a lot to him." His gaze cut away. "The guys here don't always take him."

"Is this legal? I feel like people would call the cops if they saw me with a kid."

"I've been looking into this," Carlo said. "Got a lawyer who's gonna file a petition for emergency temporary guardianship. It'll last ninety days, but like I said, I should be back in six weeks. The judge'll likely set the hearing for Monday morning. Now, I can't be there in person, but I'll write up my reasons for wanting you. It shouldn't be a problem."

"All right, then. You've got my number, so let me know if you need anything. And feel free to call him any time you want. I'm sure he'll want to know you're okay."

"I'll do that." He clutched the arms of his chair, his fingers turning white from the effort. Jude wanted to tell him to stay seated, but he could see the concentration, the determination, so he kept his mouth shut. By the time Carlo rose, perspiration gleamed on his skin. He reached out a hand. "Thank you, Jude. This gives me real peace of mind."

The gravity of the situation sank like a stone in his stomach. This commitment, along with its longer-term implications, made him want to cut and run. Wash his hands of the whole thing.

Not because he didn't care about Marco, Carlo, or the boy, but because it was a big fucking deal to be responsible for a little boy. How could he be slinging drinks one day, and the next, agreeing to take on the role of guardian for a kid he'd never met before?

Yet, at the same time, he knew he was making the right—no, the only—choice he could live with. "You're welcome."

The door creaked open, and Finlay came in, the boy still clinging to her.

Sensing the man didn't want his grandson to see him in pain, Jude helped Carlo back to his chair.

The grandfather patted his leg. "Come here."

The boy wriggled free, and Finlay set him down. He approached his grandpa. "Mister's gonna get me a bike so I can go to school."

"That's right." The tenderness in Carlo's eyes, the way

that gnarled hand cupped the back of the little boy's head, made Jude's chest ache. "Now, you know I've been sick, right?"

The boy nodded, so sincere, so trusting.

"And, thanks to Jude, I get to see a doctor who'll make me better. You're going to stay with him for a few weeks, and Jude's going to take you to school every day. Sound good?"

The boy swiveled around and looked at Jude, hesitant and a little fearful.

While Jude stood there like a tree trunk, unsure what to do, Finlay said, "Did you know that Jude was your dad's best friend? They knew each other from the time they were little boys. There's no one else your dad would've chosen to take care of you but him."

Jude felt pretty stupid. He should've been the one to say that. Should've gotten down on a knee and talked to the boy at eye level.

But he'd learn. He'd have to.

"Do I still get the bike?" Cody asked.

Carlo laughed. "Yeah. You still get it."

"You'll be with Jude for Christmas," Finlay said. "He's got a big family, so that'll be a lot of fun."

"There's a backpack over there." Carlo pointed at the corner. "And his things are in the top drawer of that dresser."

"All right. Let's get you packed for a fun adventure." She reached for Cody's hand. "Come help me so I don't forget the important stuff."

"Will you be there too?" Cody asked. "With me and Mister?"

"I can hang out with you sometimes, sure," Finlay said. "I'd like that."

As the two set off, Jude pulled out his phone. "Let me text my dad. He can pick us up."

"No need. Take my car." Carlo tipped his chin at the top of the dresser. "I won't be driving for a while."

Jude picked up the car keys and jingled them. "Anything else of yours you want me to take?"

"Eh. You can't bring anything with you when you go. Besides, the car's got his booster seat in it."

"You're not going anywhere, old man. At least, no farther than Idaho Falls. Just focus on getting better, and I'll see you in six weeks." He headed out.

"Jude." The urgency in Carlo's voice stopped him, but it was the pleading look in his eyes that wrenched his heart. "Take care of my boy."

Jude gave the man a solemn nod. "I will." He meant it with every fiber of his being.

He stepped into the hallway to text his family.

> Jude: Looks like I'll be staying in town for a few weeks.

Dad: Sounds good.

Boone: Yes! Snowfest trophy is ours!

> Jude: I'll be bringing a friend.

Boone: Is she hot?

> Jude: It's a he. And he's five. The kid I came here for. Seems like he needs more than a bike.

Decker: What's this now?

Wyatt: You need anything?

That last question pricked his heart.

He'd been on his own for twelve years, out in the world, making his way. He'd served this country, started a business, and hadn't needed a damn thing from anybody.

Until now. Because he couldn't pretend he could handle this situation. He needed to lean on his family.

Jude: Yeah. I'm going to need help.

To avoid exposing Finlay and Cody to the club's party, Jude led them out the back. The snow-covered ground had him glancing down at Finlay's delicate pink shoes. "You need to swing by your house?"

"No." She must've been surprised by her own vehemence because she closed her mouth and looked away. "Sorry. I'm just not ready to see him yet." When they reached Carlo's black Mustang, she busied herself with helping the boy into his booster seat.

After they got on the road, Jude asked quietly, "Are you afraid of him?" Only when she glanced at his hands did he realize how tightly he gripped the leather-wrapped steering wheel. But he couldn't relax until he got an answer.

"Not at all. It's nothing like that. Honestly, I just need time to process." She spoke in a whisper so Cody wouldn't hear the conversation, but with the loud, rumbly engine, he didn't think the boy could hear anything.

"You said there's no hope of getting back with him?"

"None."

As much as he wanted to know what the fucker had done, it was none of his business. "Well, remember, say the word, and I'll take you where you need to go."

"Thank you. Believe me, I know it's bizarre that I ran out on my wedding an hour ago, and now I'm on my way to buy a bike for Cody, but seeing him in that situation, knowing how scared he is… All I know is he's become the priority for right now, you know?"

He nodded, a little overwhelmed. Because a whole human was being buckled into the back seat, and he didn't have a clue how to make this turn of events easier for the boy. Well, for either of them, frankly.

"You know how they say kids are adaptable?" she asked. "Well, Cody's had way more than his share of upheaval. But this is good. He'll get to be around your family. He'll have his first real Christmas." She raised her voice. "You two are going to have so much fun together."

When she turned to smile at the boy, Jude noticed her arm was stretched behind her.

They were holding hands. Her natural instinct was to comfort the boy, while he was thinking about himself. Not that Cody was an inconvenience, but more that he wouldn't know what he was doing.

He had to stop that. *If you do this, you have to think of what's best for him. All the damn time.*

"But what about your job?" she asked. "Can you take this much time off?"

He shrugged. "I mean, it sucks. They're not going to be happy with me for bailing during a busy season, but they'll function without me. Like you said, he's the priority." He glanced in the rearview mirror to see Cody watching out the window and talking to himself.

"What if you get fired?"

"I'm a bartender. I can get a job anywhere."

"Like Wild Billy's?" She smiled. "Your dad'll love that."

"Yeah. His bar's crazy any time of year, but during ski season, it's out of control. He can always use the help." He lowered his voice even more. "You mentioned kids being ready for kindergarten. How's he doing?"

"Why?" She arched a brow. "Are you going to be with him more than six weeks?"

The idea sent a jolt through him because the possibility seemed both inevitable and impossible at the same time. "Just curious. Seems like the more I know, the better I can help."

"See? A guy who's not cut out for this role wouldn't have asked that question." She leaned a little closer. "To be honest, he's behind with literacy and numeracy, but that's not a problem at this age. It's easy for them to catch up. Really, he just needs someone to talk to him. Like, you know, count jellybeans, point out colors, read books…talk about animals. Just expose him to things and use it all as a learning experience."

"I can do that. And what about his behavior?"

"I'm not his teacher, but from what I understand, he mostly keeps to himself. He's quiet. I don't think he's suited for the, uh, unstructured environment of a bike club."

"I was like that." He kept his focus on the road. Probably shouldn't have brought it up.

"What do you mean?" She leaned in again, and this

time, he glanced over and couldn't miss the swell of her breasts in that tight T-shirt. "I thought you loved it there."

"Not even a little. Why would you think that?"

"Because you only hung out with your biker friends. You pretty much ignored everyone else."

"No one else wanted to be my friend." He'd never talked to anyone about his childhood, so hearing it out loud made him anxious. Why change her view of him?

"Huh. That's not how it looked from my perspective. I mean, the guys tried to copy you, and the girls wanted to date you. It seemed like you were living your best life and couldn't be bothered with kids your own age."

"Not the case at all. I was constantly getting into trouble, letting my dad down. I couldn't pull my head out of my ass."

"That's so funny to hear because you had so much attitude. You'd laugh when you got in trouble in class."

"I'm sure I did. But honestly, it was embarrassing to be tagged as the pothead or the loser. It didn't feel good."

"I had no idea. Couldn't you have changed all that if you'd played football or run for class president or something? You know what I mean? If you'd joined a club or a sport, maybe you'd have made friends that way."

His fingers clenched the wheel. "Those weren't possibilities for me."

"You're blowing my mind right now. I thought you hated the jocks and student council geeks."

"I hated them for the way they treated me when I was a kid. Like in third grade, when Joey Gillespie invited the whole class to his party—except me."

"Jude." Her voice got all soft.

"It is what it is." He made it sound like it didn't matter, that it hadn't hurt him. But it had. "Ava used to say I was a 'rough-and-tumble' kid. I was too loud, too aggressive." How else could he have survived life in the club? "Parents thought I was a bad influence, and I get that. I remember showing up at Mason Watter's house for his birthday, and his mom blocked the door. She got right up in my face and said, 'I only invited you because Mason made me, but I don't want you here. You'd better not start anything.'" He couldn't believe he was telling her this. He'd never told anyone.

"God, Jude."

"I don't need pity."

"Yeah, well, it's called compassion, and little boy Jude is going to get it, because that was an awful thing for her to do. I'm sorry it happened."

"It was a long time ago, and it all worked out in the end."

"True. Maybe you didn't get to play football, but you had an entire roster of girls to hook up with."

"Sure, girls who wanted to fuck a bad boy out of their systems." He glanced at Cody again to find him drawing in the fog that steamed up his window. No way could he hear over the throaty growl of Carlo's engine. "But it's one of the reasons I agreed to take him. In a small town, when you get tagged as a bad kid from day one, it defines you for the rest of your life. I don't want that to happen to him."

"I'm so surprised to hear this. Is that why you didn't talk to me during school? You thought I didn't want to be your friend?"

"No." He knew she did. He saw the lingering looks, the longing. Of course he did.

"I don't understand. Then why did you ignore me?"

"Didn't want you associated with me."

"Where's my grandpa?" Cody's little voice held fear and uncertainty.

Finlay twisted around. "Remember, he has to go to the doctor to get better? That's why we packed a bag for you, so you could stay with Jude for a few weeks."

"How long is six weeks?" the boy asked.

How the hell do you answer that?

But Finlay didn't miss a beat. "You know how you go to school Monday, Tuesday, Wednesday, Thursday, and Friday? And then you're home for the weekend?"

"Yeah."

"That's one week. So it's six of those." Finlay raised her hand and lowered a finger at a time. "One, two, three, four, five, and six."

The boy nodded like he understood. "Grandpa takes me fishing on the weekends. We get lots of fishies. They're slimy."

"I'll bet they are. So yeah, that's how long it'll take for your grandpa to get better. Six weeks of school goes by fast, right?"

Cody nodded.

"And in the meantime, you'll get to spend Christmas with Jude. Your dad's best friend."

With a troubled look, Cody looked back out the window. "I don't know."

"What don't you know, sweetheart?" Finlay asked.

"He's the man in the picture?" Cody caught Jude's eye in the mirror.

The direct eye contact forced Jude to find his voice. "I am. I met your dad when I was six years old, and we stayed friends till I moved away."

"He was your best friend?" Cody asked.

"Yes, he was."

"Amy's my best friend."

"There you go," Finlay said. "Same thing."

The boy still seemed uneasy, but he looked away.

"It's hard to be with someone new," Finlay said. "Would it help if I spent some time with you, too? The three of us?"

Shyly, Cody's gaze flicked over to her. "Yes."

"Oh, good. Then I'll come over sometimes, and we can all play."

Jude kept his mouth shut until the boy settled back in his seat and resumed doodling on the steamed window. "You don't have to do this, okay?" This wasn't her burden. It was his. "You've got enough on your plate. Don't feel obligated to hang out with us."

"I'm sure once he gets used to you, he won't need me. In the meantime, I'll do what I can to make it easier for him."

As they approached town, the traffic grew thicker. "Last chance for me to drop you somewhere."

"Uh…" She glanced at Cody. "Not yet. I don't think either of us is ready."

"You know everyone's worried about you, right? You want to at least let them know you're all right?"

"Yeah, I guess." As he sailed through the Main Street intersection, she leaned across the console. "Wait. Shouldn't you be turning? That's the way to Bazoo's Mercantile."

"Not going there."

"But that's the only place in town that sells bikes," she said.

"We've got a garage full of them at my dad's house. He can have his pick."

"Oh. I thought you were going to get him a new one."

"You're a runaway bride. Do you really want people to see you with me forty minutes after leaving your groom at the altar?"

"No, sir." She settled back in her seat. "I do not." Her eyes widened. "Good call."

"Miss O'Neill?" Cody called.

"Yes, sweetie?"

"Did you bring my blanket?"

"I did. We put it in the duffel bag, remember?"

"Can I have it?"

"Of course." She unbuckled, sat up in her seat, and reached around back.

He heard the zipper and the soft rustle of clothing as she handed over a red-checkered fleece blanket with frayed edges. "Here you go, sweetie."

"Thank you." Clutching it to his chest, Cody rested his cheek on it and turned back to the window.

"You're welcome." Finlay quickly dropped back down and latched herself in. "I asked him what he wanted to pack, and you know what he said? Well, besides the blanket."

"No idea."

"He asked for three things. The first was a picture of you and his dad."

His chest tightened. "You've got it?" He wanted to see that.

"I do, yeah." She went quiet for a moment. "He showed me what his dad wrote on the back."

He didn't want to talk about this. Not when a knot formed in this throat.

"Do you want to know what it says?" she asked.

"I know. Cody read it to me." His voice came out rough and raw. It meant a lot that Cody kept it with him.

But what Marco wrote on the back gutted him.

"What do you mean?" she asked. "He's five. He doesn't read."

"I don't know what to tell you. On the phone, he said, 'If I'm not around, call Jude. He's me just in another place.'"

"Are you serious? I can't believe he memorized it."

"That's how scared he is at the club. He's holding on to that picture, making sure he'll have someone to take care of him."

"I think you're right." She gave him a helpless look. "He needs stability. Safety. Every kid deserves that."

Is that me?

Am I the only one who can provide that for him?

It didn't seem possible, but Carlo wouldn't have chosen Jude if there were an alternative. He couldn't think that far ahead, though, so he got the conversation back on track. "What else did he bring?"

"A box full of his 'special' things."

"What's in it?"

"Rocks, feathers, buttons. Stuff like that."

Ah, hell. "Did you see a metal gear about this big?" He showed her his palm.

"Yes. How'd you know that?"

"That's Marco's. We started that collection when we were kids. We'd wander around the woods, picking up cool things. I can't believe he kept it." Man, he wished things had turned out differently.

"That's sweet that he did," she said softly. "It says a lot about your friendship."

"Yeah." *Dammit.* He had a lot of regrets in life, but at that moment, with Marco's son in the back seat, his old friend was the biggest. He shouldn't have cut him off completely. They could've stayed in touch.

"You seem surprised, though."

"Well, yeah. Things changed as we got older. I didn't hang out with him as much. And then, of course, I left town." He'd never forget the time he'd gone to Bazoo's to buy a pair of jeans. The moment he and his friends left the store, a clerk ran out after them, demanding to see what was under Marco's sweatshirt. His friend had bolted, dropping the item on the ground, and Jude had wound up paying for it. He'd felt intense shame that day.

He supposed he needed that reminder. They'd grown apart for a reason. As Marco headed into illegal activity, the friendship hadn't been sustainable.

"What're you thinking?" she asked.

"Mostly, how different Marco's life would've turned out if he'd been born into another family. He might've gone to college, majored in geology or engineering or something."

"It's kind of sweet, though, isn't it?" she asked. "You couldn't save Marco, but you have a real chance to help his son."

Her words rang true. "You're jumping the gun here. I have him for six weeks. That's it. Don't start making a vision board about some happy family, okay? It's not going to happen."

"We'll see." She pushed her bottom back in the seat and tugged on the waistband of her jeans.

"You okay? Jeans not comfortable?"

"When you have a butt and hips, it's hard to find pants that fit. And don't tell me to work out. I promise you, no matter what I eat or how much I exercise, this is my shape. It's just my body type."

"Why would I tell you to work out? You have a great body."

She rolled her eyes. "Please. I know what I am."

"What does that mean?" Didn't she get that curves were a big fucking turn-on? Watching an ass jiggle or tits bounce was hot. What man didn't get hard with a handful of plump flesh?

He'd spent years imagining sweet, innocent Finlay in bed. But now, after a decade of relationships, she'd know exactly what she liked, and that was even hotter.

"It means I have a booty and boobs, and I can only wear certain brands that fit my shape."

Your shape's always been my favorite. But he wouldn't tell her that. Not an hour after she'd run from her wedding. "Other than the jeans, how're you feeling?"

She tipped her head back. "Nothing's really sunk in.

Well, except the fact I left everyone to deal with the fallout."

"Go ahead and use my phone."

She eyed it in the cupholder like it was a rabid animal. "Yeah, okay. Thanks. I'll text my parents and Willa." She picked it up. "What's the passcode?"

"66673."

As she punched in the numbers, she said, "That's random."

"Not really. It spells out moose. I've had it since high school." Hopefully, she wouldn't figure it out. He didn't see how she would.

"Thanks." She swiped and started tapping. "I'll tell them I'm okay, I'm with a friend, and I'll get in touch in a little bit." She put it back and slunk lower in her seat. "They're going to blow up your phone. You know that, right?"

"It's fine. At least they'll know you're alive and well."

"I know I should be crying my eyes out or…something. But right now, I'm numb." She lifted her hands. "I mean, literally, I have no feeling in my body at all." She pulled the waistband of her jeans. "Except here." She laughed. "This, I feel."

"We'll get you something to wear at my dad's house." He flicked on his turn signal, braking for the unmarked street that led to his dad's place deep in the woods. "Do you want to talk about what he did?"

"He didn't cheat."

"Yeah, you said that."

"I did, right? I guess I'm trying to minimize it." She pressed her hands over her stomach. "I found out he's got a daughter. Like, literally five minutes before I walked down the aisle."

"So he hid the fact that he had a kid?"

"Yes. He did. He said he only found out three months ago. That his ex called out of the blue and told him they had a child."

"But he didn't tell you?" *What an asshole.* "Isn't that something you share with the person you're going to spend your life with?"

"Exactly. And I know a lot of people will say it's not a reason to end a relationship. They'll think I have a problem raising some other woman's child."

"That's not the point."

"No, it's not. But I should've handled it better. Like you said, it's a small town, and everyone's going to talk about what I did. They're going to think I'm a fool for walking away from a good man just because he was still processing the fact that he had a child."

"Well, who was he processing with? It sure as hell wasn't the woman he planned on marrying. For three months, he's talked to you, brushed teeth next to you, and made plans with you, and the entire time, he was grappling with a huge secret. How can you ever trust him again?"

"And just like that"—she snapped her fingers—"feeling came back into my body."

"I think you'll be surprised how many people will agree with you. Who wants a lifetime of trust issues?"

"You're exactly right. I can't marry a man who hides things from me. We need to be a team, to handle things together."

"What was his reason for keeping it from you?" Sounded manipulative to him.

"I don't know. We didn't get that far. I hate that he was going to put a ring on my finger before telling me, but at the same time, I can't help but wonder why he felt he had to deal with it alone."

"He didn't. He's been handling it with her."

Finlay winced, slapping a hand to her heart. "Oof. You're right. Oh man, that hurts." She stared ahead, unseeing. "All this time, he's been talking to his ex. They got a paternity test and discussed the results together." She went quiet, staring at her laced fingers. "No, I can never trust him again." As he drove down his dad's long driveway, she sat up. "Is this where you grew up?"

"Pretty much. We moved here when I was twelve."

She shifted in her seat to take in the view from all directions. "Teenage me is dying right now."

"What do you mean?"

She let out a laugh. "I used to dream about coming home with you, hanging out with your brothers and your dad."

He'd always admired her courage, and this confession was exactly why. Because she owned her truth. She'd had a crush on him. She'd fantasized about him, and she wasn't afraid to let him know.

Unlike me. Maybe, if he got to spend more time with her, he'd tell her exactly what he'd once thought of her.

Yeah, maybe he would.

She leaned forward. "It's beautiful. You must've loved growing up out here with your brothers."

"I did." As kids, they'd used every square inch of the property to go fly-fishing, build forts, and run wild.

"Hey, Mister?" Cody called.

"Yeah?"

"When are we getting my bike? I don't see a store."

"You're right. There's no store here. This is my dad's house, where I grew up. We've got a whole garage filled with bikes."

"Why?"

"Why do we have so many bicycles?" In the rearview mirror, he watched the kid nod. "Because I have three brothers."

"And I can have one of their bikes?"

He caught the brightness in the boy's eyes. "Yes. Any one you want."

You just can't ride it because it's winter, and there's three feet of snow on the ground.

"Thank you." His feet kicked out in a show of excitement.

"You're welcome." As he rounded the bend, his dad's home appeared. The view never ceased to impress him, and he knew Finlay felt it, too, when her lips parted, and awe flared in her eyes.

The stone-and-timber house was set in a grassy valley with a backdrop of the towering Teton Range. He'd added on a lot over the years, so the original rustic cabin had become a sprawling lodge-like home. Given the remote location and weather, it was pretty self-contained, with a big game room and an indoor pool.

"This place is amazing."

"Wait till you see it without snow on the ground. The

meadow's filled with wildflowers." He had no idea why he'd just said that, considering she'd never get to see it.

She had a life to get back to.

Very soon, she'd be gone, and he'd be alone with this kid.

And he didn't know which scared him more, stepping up to take care of Marco's son…

Or losing her.

Chapter Five

FINLAY WAS ON OVERLOAD.

Which explained why, after Jude put the car in Park and got out, she just sat there, listening to the engine tick.

She was inert. Exhausted.

And yet, at the same time, strangely wired.

It didn't make sense.

Well, of course, nothing made sense right then.

Her fiancé, the man she'd chosen to build a life with, turned out to be a total stranger.

At the same time, she happened to run into her childhood crush, who'd grown into a man so freaking hot she could barely make eye contact with him.

Like, literally, the only thing I should be feeling is anger, guilt, regret…something…about Matt and my wedding, but instead, my heart's beating out of control for the boy I never thought I'd see again.

She'd never felt this kind of excitement for her ex. And she'd almost *married* him.

No, only Jude. What was it about this man that made

her want to climb onto his lap and grind on him? He was just so big and muscular. She wanted to run her fingers through that long, silky hair and skim her hands down his powerful chest.

After all these years, she still lost her mind for him.

She breathed in the scent of cologne and leather in Carlo's car. The black interior made it feel cave-like, and she thought, if they gave her a blanket, she'd curl up and lie there for a couple of hours until her mind stopped spinning and her heart stopped hurting.

But Cody unbuckled his seat belt and crawled onto the console. He knelt on it, patting her hand. "You sad, Miss O'Neill?"

Affection warmed her, bringing sensation back into her fingers and toes. "Thank you for asking, Cody. Yes, I'm a little sad, but I'll be okay."

Jude opened her door and stood there, arms crossed, like a Viking. "You good?"

In his black Henley, black jeans, and black boots, he was tall, intimidating, and utterly delectable. But best of all was the way he looked at her with concern, like he needed to know she was okay. She knew without a doubt that, if she asked him to take her to Alaska, he'd get in the car and peel out.

Jude was a ride-or-die kind of man, and she loved that he had her back. "Yep. Just peachy."

He dropped to a crouch. "What're you thinking about?"

Where to even begin? Certainly not the part about grinding on him. *No, don't say that.* But then, it all just sort of welled up, and the words spilled out of her mouth.

"For three months, I thought we were excited about the house. I thought we were deciding between the sunset dinner cruise or the Michelin-starred tasting menu on our honeymoon. I thought the biggest decision we had to make was whether to splurge on a new couch or wait and see how things went after paying the mortgage for a few months. But that entire time, he was consumed with finding out he had a daughter."

"Can we go now?" Cody asked.

She started to swing her legs out. "Yeah, of course—"

But Jude clamped a big hand on her knee. "You were living two different realities."

"Yes. Exactly. And now, I feel stupid for comparing the rattan and leather barstools when he was dealing with something so massive."

"Nope. You were operating in separate worlds. That's not on you. You did nothing wrong."

Cody watched the two of them intently. And then, he put his hand on top of Jude's, so all three of them were connected. As he leaned across her, she could smell the soap she'd used to clean his hands and face and see the constellation of freckles on his wrist. His fingers were so thin and fragile, and she just ached for this lost little boy.

"I'm okay, sweetheart," she said. "And I'm lucky to be with two friends who really care about me." As she got out of the car, she automatically reached for a purse that wasn't there. It drove home that she had nothing. No money, no phone. Nothing.

And you know what? She didn't mind one bit.

It was freeing. Just for this tiny slice of time, she wanted to linger in someone else's world.

Once on her feet, she reached for Cody's hand and helped him climb out of the car. "Let's go inside."

But the boy pulled away, staring at the big, imposing house. "Do I have to go in there?"

"Only if you want to," a deep voice called.

Standing on the porch, a strikingly handsome silver fox leaned against the doorway with a steaming mug of coffee. He stood idly, like he didn't have a care in the world. At the same time, Finlay, who'd grown adept at reading people, thanks to parents who viewed her as a burden and a group of friends who'd dropped her, noticed his watchful gaze.

"Dad." Jude's pace quickened, and he loped up the porch stairs.

"Jude." The muscular man pushed off the frame, set his mug down on a table, and drew his son in for a bear hug. "Long time."

"Too long," Jude said.

Watching these two big men cling to each other so forcefully made her wonder why Jude had stayed away so long. She knew why he'd left, of course. But why—when he had a dad and three brothers—hadn't he ever come back?

"Glad you'll stay for Christmas." His dad's voice was gruff.

Jude stepped back to include her and the boy. "Dad, this is Finlay O'Neill."

"The runaway bride. I know." He reached for her hand. "Gunnar McKenna."

He might as well have lobbed a potato at her head. "It happened an *hour* ago. How did you find out?"

"My son Boone knows the wedding photographer." Gunnar ushered everyone inside. "Come on. Let's get you all set up. Wasn't sure how many rooms you'd need."

"Oh, I'm not staying." In the entryway of this home, standing beside Jude and his father, she finally snapped out of it. This man did not need to take on her problems. "If I can borrow your phone again, I'll call my mom or dad." An inner voice shouted down that idea. Neither was her go-to person. "Or Willa." *Yes, her.* "She'll come get me." Her mind was spinning. Her chest went tight, making it hard to breathe.

Why was she so resistant to talking to anyone?

"How 'bout you come sit by the fire and warm up?" Gunnar asked. "You hungry? I have cookies in the oven, and I'm just about to put a roast in. Just waiting on Wyatt to get here with a bottle of red wine."

"Sounds good," Jude said. "I'm starving."

Reality crashed over her. "I didn't even think…I'm so sorry for intruding."

"What're you talking about?" Jude asked. He truly didn't get it.

"It's your welcome home dinner," she said.

"Yeah, well, now we're welcoming a kid and a runaway bride." Jude set his hand on her lower back and led her deeper into the room.

The house was warm and inviting with the scents of melted butter, cinnamon, and pine. Cody stayed glued to her side as they headed for the hearth. The moment she sat down, he crawled onto her lap.

Placing a hand on each of her knees to balance himself, Jude squatted. "You can stay here as long as you want. If you want to stay overnight, we can get you some clothes, a toothbrush, and whatever else you need. You call the shots."

"Got plenty of bedrooms," Gunnar said. "And no one's going to get in your business." He glanced down at the boy. "Now, you must be Cody."

Cody squirmed. "I'm here to get a bike."

"Is that right?" Gunnar stood. "Well, you're in luck. I've got a whole garage full of 'em."

"Can I see?" the little boy asked.

"You sure can. Which do you want first? A cookie or the bike?"

"The bike, please." But the little boy didn't budge.

"You got it. Come on." Gunnar waved him over. "They're in the garage."

Cody looked up at her, uncertainty in his eyes.

"If you need me, I'll be right here. I'm so close that I'll hear you if you call my name."

Cody deliberated for a moment before scrambling off her lap and joining Gunnar. The big man reached for the boy's hand, and they headed toward the kitchen. When he turned back to look at her, she gave him a reassuring smile.

"He'll be okay," Jude said. "My dad raised four boys."

"It's not your dad I'm worried about. It's the situation. He's been handed off to so many people. Who can he trust?"

With his stony expression, Jude looked like he couldn't care less. But it was the roiling emotion in his eyes that left no doubt he was worried. He reached into his pocket and pulled out his phone. "Here." He swiped the screen, tapped in his password, and thrust it at her. "Phone's been blowing up, so you can check your messages and make your calls."

"You're awfully trusting for a single bartender." She tried to inject levity, but it didn't work. Not when her hand trembled, and her voice came out shaky. She looked at the device as if she'd never used one before, not wanting to tell him she'd blanked on Willa's number.

"You're welcome to scroll through all the naked selfies women send me. It might take your mind off things."

She couldn't believe he'd just said that. Only when she saw the glint in his eyes did she know he was joking, and she let out a breath. "Okay, lover boy. Hard pass on that one." She set the phone on her lap and closed her eyes.

"Hey. It's all right." Jude's deep voice soothed her. "Take the time you need to figure things out."

"That's the thing. Everyone's going to come at me with their opinions and advice, and it's only going to make things worse. I need to think. I need to process. I just need…time."

"You got it." He sat down beside her and reached for her hand. "For now, just breathe, okay? You're good here. You don't have to do a single thing."

The warmth and strength of his touch did wonders for her nerves. "Thank you." They sat in silence for a moment while she took some calming breaths. The fire crackled and popped, and she breathed in scents of smoke and leather. "I can't believe you grew up here."

The dark paneled walls and built-in bookcases gave the

impression of a high-end lodge. The cathedral ceiling was reinforced with massive wooden beams, and a wall of windows let the forest in. Green couches built for a family of boisterous, large men fit beautifully against the dark gray river stone walls. "It's gorgeous." She smiled at him. "Your dad has amazing taste."

"It's all Ava. My dad would happily live in a yurt."

"Are they together?" No, that made no sense. She'd worked with Ava at the school for years. She'd know if her friend had a boyfriend. As far as she knew, Ava hadn't dated anyone seriously since her divorce.

"It's not like that. She's family." Abruptly, he got up. "I'll check on Cody."

Twelve years, one master's degree, and a whole fiancé later, Jude still had the power to mess with her emotions. In high school, every time they got close, got that surge of intimacy and connection, he'd just shut down and walk away. Like he was bored with her.

Leaving her to wonder: Was her crush too obvious?

Was she immature? Too inexperienced?

And just then, he'd done it again. His abrupt dismissal made her shrink.

A hot mess of emotion, she looked at the phone in her hand. Anyone she called would come out here and pick her up in a heartbeat. Her parents, the teachers at her school, and her wonderful friends… They'd come.

But they'd all want to fix her problem.

Her dad would bring her to his apartment in Wild Wolff Village. He ate like a child, so he'd give her a bowl of sugary cereal with marshmallow stars and moons. He called his one-bedroom apartment a crash pad because he let childhood friends, college pals, and any acquaintance he'd ever met stay there so they could ski or visit Calamity. But guests stayed on the pull-out couch, which was where her dad watched TV until he fell asleep.

She'd have noise and food and no chance to think.

So no, she wouldn't call him.

Her mom would heat two of her microwavable meals, and they'd share a pint of her favorite peanut butter brittle ice cream. The whole time, she'd be ranting about Matt's betrayal and telling her how to handle the situation. Finlay wouldn't have a second to process anything because her mom held such strong opinions. Plus, her childhood bedroom remained intact, and she couldn't bear to see that stupid vision board she'd based all her life decisions on.

It wasn't appropriate to bother her teacher friends. That just wasn't the nature of their relationship. They went for drinks, shared funny stories, showed pictures of their kids or new cars, and bitched about the parents of their students.

No, there was only one person to call.

Chapter Six

It took half a ring for Willa to connect. "Quiet," she snapped, her voice nowhere near the receiver. "It's her."

"Willa?" Finlay called.

Air whooshed, and then her friend's voice was right in her ear. "Are you okay? Where'd you go?"

"I'm fine. I promise."

"Well, thank God for that. Where are you? I'll come get you."

"No. I'm fine right where I am. I just wanted to check in, let you know I'm okay. What's going on over there?"

"Your ex—and I sincerely *hope* he's your ex—took off with his mommy. The coward got his feelings hurt when your dad and I ripped him a new asshole while his ex kept trying to claim her moral high ground—"

"Excuse me? That little girl has to be four years old. Why did she only tell Matt about her three months ago?"

"Oh, you left before that one, huh? She said she didn't tell him because she wanted to live in North Carolina. She wanted the help of her family, and she knew Matt would never leave Calamity. Can you believe it? Exactly what moral high ground are we talking about?"

"I can't even imagine what this has been like for him."

"Wait a minute. Fee, are you still going to marry him after all this?"

"No, I can't. If he can keep a secret that big, then I'll never trust him again." She could never look into his eyes and see anything but shadows.

"Oh, honey. I'm so sorry. I know this sucks, but we're going to turn this whole situation around."

Her friend had no idea what hearing *we* meant to her. "I'd love to hear how because, right now, my brain is closed for business."

"Don't worry about a thing. I'm going to borrow my dad's car and come get you. We'll go on the honeymoon together. I only packed for winter in Calamity, but I can buy everything I need on the island."

For the first time that day—or really, who knew how long?— tears brimmed, and she blinked them away. "You're the best friend in the world."

"Yeah, yeah. You can tell me all about it while we're sipping pretty cocktails by the ocean. For now, send me your flight details, and I'll try to get on the same one."

"No." As tempting as it sounded to spend a week with her best friend, she couldn't do it.

"What do you mean, 'no?' You can't stay here. You just ran away from the town's golden boy. It's all everyone's going to talk about. Come on. We'll get out of here, let the scandal die down, and give you some time to figure things out."

"I love you, Willa. In every way other than DNA, you're my sister. And because of that, I'm not letting you take more time off work. If you bail on this case, you'll lose your shot at making partner. You've worked too hard for it."

There was a tiny pause. "I don't give a damn about that right now."

But it was enough to confirm what Finlay already knew. "You know what? I believe you. I believe you'd blow up your career for me, but I'm not going to let you do that. I promise, I'm going to be just fine."

"I don't know how. You were one minute away from marrying the love of your life."

She shot to her feet as if a spark hit her back.

Those four words rang through her. *Love of your life.*

Boy, oh, boy, oh, boy.

There was so much tied into marrying Matt. They shared the same vision of a house on Bloom Lane, a bunch of kids, a dog.

The annual traditions of pumpkin patches and chopping down Christmas trees.

Waiting for the bus every morning, along with all the other families on the block.

Matt was her partner in making her dreams come true. "I can't believe I'm going to say this." Tears came back in a rush, and she got all hot and sweaty. "But he's not."

"You're killing me here," Willa whispered. "Not what, sweetie?"

"He's not the love of my life." She paced to the bay window, barely seeing the forest, because at that moment, the fog in her mind cleared, bringing sorrow—

fear—into high relief. She crossed an arm over her stomach when she realized losing Matt wasn't what she was sad about.

She was thirty years old, and giving him up meant she might never live her dream. It'd be years before she'd find someone to love again. Even more time before she'd have a child.

So much for a house full of kids.

Despair slid into her bloodstream. But she wouldn't tell Willa any of it, because if she did, her friend would stay in Calamity to support her. All her hard work to get on the partner track would go out the window.

"To be honest," Willa said, "I think most people get married because they're ready. And that means they only have the pool of people around them at that moment in time to choose from. I don't think it's about finding the love of your life."

"You're probably right about that." She needed to burn her vision board, forget some stupid, self-imposed timeline, and focus on how damn lucky she was to be a teacher and have good friends and decent parents.

"Putting aside my job for the time being, what do you want to do?" Willa asked. "Just tell me, and I'll make it happen."

Cody raced over to her, eyes bright and grinning. "I got a bike. Come look, Miss O'Neill. It's so cool."

Finlay held the phone away from her mouth. "Yay! I can't wait to see it."

"Mister's gonna take those big trucks out of the garage so I have room to ride. You have to come watch."

"Who's that?" Willa asked. "Where *are* you?"

"That's Cody." She spoke with the intention of letting her friend know she couldn't give any details.

"Come on, Miss O'Neill. Watch me ride."

Jude's tall, dark, and imposing form blocked the doorway to the kitchen. With his legs braced apart like that, his biceps bulging, and his hair tousled and shiny, she wanted to climb him like a tree.

"Let's go," he said to Cody in a commanding tone no one would ignore. "Miss O'Neill will join us when she's off the phone." When Cody did little more than inch closer to her, Jude frowned. A little crease formed between his eyes, and she knew he was trying to figure out what to do. "Remember, I told you my brothers are coming over? We'll all ride together."

The boy's eyes widened in alarm. "Are you gonna ride, too, Miss O'Neill? You're not gonna leave me, are you?"

Her decision was made. "No, Cody. I'm not leaving you. Not tonight." She glanced at Jude to see if that was all right, but his expression, of course, revealed nothing.

But this wasn't about him. It was about Cody feeling safe.

Nothing else mattered. "Hey, Wills? I have to go."

"You're seriously getting off the phone?" her friend asked.

"I am." She had a little boy depending on her for his well-being.

"I don't understand any of this."

"I know, and I promise to explain tomorrow. But for tonight, I'm going to stay at a friend's house."

"Blink twice if you've been kidnapped."

Finlay smiled. "I promise you, I'm fine."

Willa sighed. "Let the record show, I'm opposed to this action. But just so we're clear, I'm coming to pick you up tomorrow, and we're either going to get drunk or make a whole new vision board."

"Your flight leaves in the morning, remember?"

"Yeah, well," Willa said. "I'm changing it to Monday." And with that pronouncement, she ended the call.

Finlay stared up at the ceiling, hands overlapped on her chest like a body in a casket.

Which was fitting because part of her died when she'd run from the church. A whole life she'd once wished for with her every breath.

Once, in eleventh grade, Willa asked how she could have such a huge crush on Jude when he so clearly didn't fit her type. It was a good question then, and an even more important one now. She'd just run from the town's golden boy and jumped onto the back of the bad boy's bike.

Maybe it was as simple as knowing she couldn't have him. That he didn't want a relationship or have any interest in settling down with a woman and a lawn mower.

The confusion had ended when he'd left town, and she could get back to manifesting her dream man.

Matt was everything she'd ever wanted. He was handsome, clean-cut, and polite. He had a big group of friends, so they were always socializing and vacationing in big groups. It was fun.

But boy, had she gotten it all wrong.

It was a different kind of dark out there in the forest,

so she'd left the curtains open. Milky moonlight cut through the trees and painted stripes on the walls.

The quiet was haunting.

She strained to hear voices, a faucet running… anything that let her know she wasn't alone in this big, unfamiliar house.

Imagine what it's like for Cody.

He was in the room right next door to hers, and she'd lain in bed with him till he'd fallen asleep. She'd been checking on him every hour, but now, he was out cold.

She wished she could stay with him, but she couldn't.

She had to pick up the pieces of her life.

A light knock had her jolting up. "Yes?"

"It's me."

Jude. Hearing that deep, rugged voice in the darkness awakened something wicked in her. *Cut that out.*

It's not like that.

It'll never be like that.

"Can I come in?" he asked.

She sat up, tugging the fabric of the huge T-shirt Gunnar had loaned her so it didn't cling to her breasts. "Of course."

When he opened the door, a sliver of yellow light from the hallway cut into the room. Folding his arms across his chest, he leaned against the threshold. "You want to keep it down in here?"

"What?" She sat all the way up and flicked on the lamp. "What're you talking about?"

"I could hear you thinking from down the hall."

"Oh." She smiled. "Sorry to keep you up."

"You want to yap to someone who won't give you advice?"

Yes. That's exactly what I want. "I don't even know where to begin."

He pushed off and entered her room. "Anywhere you want. I won't even be listening." He pulled his phone out of his back pocket and waved it at her. "*Call of Duty.*"

She laughed. "Fine. Twist my arm."

He sat on the mattress and placed his elbows on his knees, pretending to stare at his phone. But while the game played on his screen, he never tapped the keys.

His easy silence gave the threads in her mind a chance to pull together into coherent thought, and words started tumbling out of her mouth. "I'm going to lose the house, and you know what it's like on Bloom Lane. There's a waiting list a mile long, so they never go on sale. We only got it because Matt's mom used to play mahjong with the owners. And yes, I hear myself. My marriage blew up, but I'm babbling about a stupid house."

"Didn't even hear a word you said." He held up his phone. "I'm crushing this game. Besides, this is a no-judgment zone."

"Okay, but I'm judging myself. Because, really, how shallow am I?"

"You grew up in apartments with parents who worked a lot. Why wouldn't you want the stability of a home?" He gave her a chin nod. *Go on.*

"Says the man who saw my journal and gel pen collection." She covered her face with both hands. "How mortifying was that?"

"Oh come on. That wasn't nearly as lame as the frilly bedspread."

"And it was *pink*." It not only felt good to laugh, but it also opened space inside her. "I want to be angry with him. I keep trying to drum it up, but how can I when I'm just as much to blame?"

He tensed. "Blame for what? You had no part in his deception."

"No, not that. I keep thinking… How can you live with someone for three months and not have a single clue he's going through something so big? I mean, did I even know him at all? And worse than that, how well did I *want* to know him?"

"You only knew the part of him he wanted you to see."

That was a good point. "But shouldn't I have sensed he was hiding parts of himself? When we were kids, I wanted to know every single thing about you. I dreamed about going into your room and opening your drawers. I wanted to know what you thought about, what you wanted in life, what books you read, and what you snacked on during road trips. I wanted to know whether you shower in the morning or before bed, and if you wear boxers or briefs or go commando. And maybe that's just because you were so closed off, and I couldn't read you. Man of mystery and all that. I don't know. I just know I was never that interested in Matt."

He set the phone down on the blanket. "I wanted to build things. I wasn't sure if that meant houses or motorcycles, but after working with a contractor for a few months, I realized I preferred houses. I liked imagining how the family would use each room. I read apocalypse books and was never much of a snacker. Don't like chips or pretzels. Not a fan of packaged desserts."

It was the first time he'd ever shared himself with her, and she loved it. "That's because Ava spoiled you."

"Fair. I always shower in the morning, but sometimes I do it at night too. Depends on the day. And boxers bunch up when you wear jeans, so I prefer briefs."

"Well, there you go." She smacked the mattress with her hand. "You've proven my point. Now that the mystery's gone, I've lost all interest in you."

He barked out a laugh, and it was so rare and so beautiful that her pulse beat out of control. That rush of connection between them came flooding in. It kicked up the long-buried yearning that defined her childhood.

No. Nope.

Absolutely not going back there.

She'd come too far to go back to obsessing over a man who, she knew from experience, would get up abruptly and leave her feeling like she'd done something wrong. And she really couldn't bear to pile on any more emotion today, so she cut the intimacy and returned to the conversation. "Bottom line, I didn't like Matt in the way a woman should like the man she's going to spend her life with."

Shifting a knee onto the mattress, Jude faced her.

"And now, I'm left with a million unanswered questions."

"Like?" he asked.

"Where am I going to live? I'm too old to sleep on my dad's couch, and my mom's so set in her ways, she'd hate having to share her space with me again."

"There's an apartment over Wild Billy's. You're welcome to stay there."

She smiled. "You have an answer for everything."

"I'm not the one in the middle of a hurricane."

"Are you sure about that?" she asked. "The single bartender who roams from one city to the next has just been saddled with a five-year-old. You must have big thoughts, too."

"Nah, I can do anything for six weeks." He scowled. "My only big thoughts involve ripping your ex a new asshole for putting you through this."

This man. He roped her in with his big heart but then left her cold and alone when he shut down. "You know what I just figured out? I think maybe you care about so many people—your dad, your brothers, Ava, your friends —that you don't need romantic love."

He reared back. "Where the hell did that come from?"

"Have you ever had a girlfriend?" She added another pillow to the stack behind her, plucking the T-shirt away from her chest.

"No."

"And you don't get lonely?"

He shrugged. "Not really. Hard to do that when my phone's always blowing up with texts from my idiot brothers. Plus, I work in a bar, so I'm surrounded by people all the time. I like coming home to quiet."

"Yeah, but there's an intimacy with a lover you can't get from friends and family."

He let out a huff of breath. "I get plenty of *intimacy.*"

Of course he did. "But is that satisfying for you?"

"Well, I can't think of a time when I wasn't *satisfied.*"

"Okay, but the women are mostly strangers, right?" she asked.

"Yeah."

"So you don't really know them."

"I know as much as I need to."

"That's what I'm saying. We're total opposites. You have so many people in your life that you don't need an emotional attachment, and I have so few that I crave it. Like I can't have sex without it."

"And now you know why I kept my hands off you in high school."

"Oh, please. Let's be real. You didn't like me like that."

Something about his expression was off as he studied the blanket. It was hard to read him, but she only had this one night to get the truth. And she needed it. She needed to know.

The quiet, the darkness of this room… now was her only shot. "I don't know if I wasn't cool enough or hot enough, but I mean, you slept with everyone except me. I figured I was too… plain Jane or something."

His gaze swung up and looked her right in the eyes. "What the hell did you think I was doing in Wild Wolff Village all the time?"

"I don't know. You worked there?" She hadn't really questioned it.

"No, I didn't." He shook his head. "Drop it. Anyway, go on with what you were saying about the douchebag."

"No, Jude. This matters to me. Why were you in the village all the time?"

"I was trying to run into you." His tone sounded

assertive, almost like an accusation. "That day with the raccoon? That was no coincidence."

"Did you know where I lived?"

His gaze dropped to his phone. "I knew your parents lived in employee housing."

"Wait. Are you saying you came by to see me…with your *girlfriend*?"

"No—" He must've remembered who he was with that day because his eyes lit up. "Leia was never my girlfriend. And I never slept with her. I was already in the village to get my Fee fix when I ran into her, and she asked to hang out."

"Your *Fee* fix?" *Is that what he called it?* That meant he'd had a thing for her.

Me.

Emotion erupted hot and fiery, like a solar flare.

He *liked* me.

"Yeah." He broke into a soft smile, like he was happy the truth was finally out. "I spent a lot of time thinking about you, and sometimes, when I couldn't take it anymore, I'd prowl the village, hoping to run into you."

"Are you serious right now?"

"It would be less embarrassing if I wasn't."

Wow. Wow, wow, wow. He'd just changed the entire landscape of her heart. "I wish I'd known."

"It wouldn't have changed anything."

"Believe me, it would've changed the world for me." All the confusion, the longing, the pain… Yeah, it would've healed her.

"I still wouldn't have asked you out."

"Why?" It made no sense. "We liked each other."

"I told you. You were the good girl, and I was a troublemaker. In a high school as small as ours, reputations don't change. No matter what you do, they'll never see you differently." He seemed resolute. "The only way to reinvent yourself is to leave."

"And you did that?" She took in his black jeans, biker boots, and long-sleeved T-shirt. Her fingers brushed the tips of his silky, shoulder-length hair. "You reinvented yourself?"

"Okay, Ducky. Calm down. Outside of Calamity, no one remembers me putting dish washing soap in the Wild Wolff Village fountain, so they can't throw it in my face. I call that a win."

"Yeah, I can see that." She really could. *But…he liked me.* The beauty of it swirled inside her. She wanted to live in that dreamy space for the rest of her life.

"My little obsession with you got me through a lot of hard times," he said. "I needed it."

"Is that all it was for you? A distraction?"

"No, of course not."

"How do you know?" She'd often wondered that about herself. Was her obsession a way to fill the loneliness?

His chest expanded as he drew in a deep breath. "Because even after I left town, I never stopped thinking about you."

She might need to record this conversation and replay it a hundred million times until it sank in. "What did you think about? My moose slippers?"

"You know."

"No, I don't think I do." She gave him a sly smile.

He grew impatient. "Us."

"What about us?"

"This crazy fuckin' attraction." He stiffened. "That we're not going to act on."

Even if she accepted it was true, she still needed to hear it from him. "Because you don't want to ruin my reputation?"

"Sure. But also, you just said sex means something to you."

"And sex with me wouldn't mean anything?" She was pushing too hard, making him uncomfortable. But today, her entire life had gotten dismantled. She had nothing left to lose.

"I think you know it would, but it's not going to lead anywhere. I'll be gone in six weeks, and you haven't even talked to the man you were supposed to marry."

"Ouch. But yeah, that's fair." She'd talk to Matt. Of course, she would. She just didn't like to have big confrontations until she could think clearly.

When she plucked the fabric of her T-shirt again, his hand shot out, wrapping around her wrist. "Is the shirt uncomfortable? Do you want one of mine?"

"No, it's fine."

"Then why do you keep pulling it away like that?"

"Because I have big boobs, okay?" Nothing a man with a perfect body could ever understand. "And I'm not wearing a bra."

"I had a lot of fantasies about those tits." He seemed surprised he'd said it out loud, and he glanced up with a worried expression.

She'd love to reassure him that he hadn't overstepped, but sensation burst in her chest, and it was sending a shower of sparks through her body, so she had no control over her facial features. It was like being caught mid-orgasm. "Well, believe me, I had fantasies about you touching them."

Fire burned in his eyes. "Yeah?"

"Yeah." The word came out shaky, thin as gauze. "I didn't know much about sex back then. I only knew I had this weird feeling, you know…between my legs."

"But you didn't know how to relieve it?" Even though he didn't move, he felt closer, like he was taking up all the space around her.

And she loved it. "Not back then, no." She wanted more. She wanted his weight on her body, his silky hair on her skin.

"You're killing me. You know that, right? It's been twelve years, and you still make me so hard I could pound you into next week."

"Aw, Jude," she whispered. "That's so romantic."

Shifting closer, he cracked a smile. His gaze drifted to her mouth, and when he ran a thumb over her bottom lip, his forearm brushed her nipples.

Goose bumps exploded on her skin.

"We don't make sense." His voice came out rough and raw, heavy with need.

It was so hot. "I know."

"You're so beautiful, Fee. I don't know what you ever saw in me."

"I saw a loyal friend. A smart student. I felt safe around you. Seen. I thought you were the sexiest man in the entire world." She let out a shaky breath. "I still do."

His expression hardened with need. "Fuck it." His

mouth closed over hers, and the boy she'd once loved with all her heart kissed her. Only it was nothing like she'd imagined. It wasn't sweet, and he didn't take his time. There was nothing romantic about it at all.

It was fierce. Pure, unleashed hunger. As he took possession of her mouth, his hand clamped the back of her neck, holding her in place.

He kissed her like the world was on fire, and he needed to get as much of her as he could.

This man was starving for her.

No one had ever wanted her like this. The backs of his fingers skimmed down her neck and swept across her collarbone. He cupped her breast, closing his warm hand around it, and he groaned.

Pleasure flooded her. The way he devoured her mouth stirred up a frenzy of desire. And just when she reached for him, her hands clasping behind his neck, he tore his mouth off hers and pushed her away.

Her arms fell gracelessly to her sides.

His eyes narrowed, his lips still shiny from their kiss. "You're my kryptonite, Fee. I can't help myself around you." He stood. "But you ran from your wedding seven hours ago, and I've got Marco's kid to deal with." In five long strides, he was at the door. "This isn't going to happen." Without looking at her, he disappeared down the hallway.

Chapter Seven

Jude woke up with a monster erection.

Which was crazy because he'd already jerked off twice during the night.

But he couldn't stop thinking about that kiss, the sexy sounds she'd made, and the way she'd pressed herself against him. When she'd clasped her hands around his neck, trying to topple him over, he'd nearly lost it.

He'd wanted to yank up the T-shirt and press her tits together, lick the nipples, and suck them into his mouth. Wanted to feel them hardening into beads on his tongue. Wanted her squirming beneath him, grinding on his cock.

All night, he'd imagined flipping her over and hiking up her hips. He fucking loved Finlay's ass. He wanted to get his hands on it, spread her cheeks, and slide his cock right into her juicy, hot core.

And yeah, he was a dirty son of a bitch for thinking about her like that. Her life had just blown up, and the last thing she needed was some creep fantasizing about her.

But he had no control over his dreams.

And it wasn't like it'd come out of nowhere. No, it had been building from the moment she'd clung to him on the bike. The press of her tits against his back, the scent he caught every time she shifted, the way she'd bent over to pick up wet towels after Cody's bath… Jesus, the denim had clung to her ass so tightly he'd itched to peel them off and replace them with his hands.

The way her breasts bounced when she'd chased Cody to his room… It was hot.

Everything about her was fuck-hot.

He gripped his cock and squeezed. Without a doubt, he'd never been this attracted to anyone. Ever. At the church, he might not have recognized her. She'd tamed her curls, and the makeup was something a movie star might wear. Had he not known the way she carried herself, he'd have driven off with his family.

But he'd known. And he'd waited for her to come to him as he'd known she would.

In some inexplicable way, they were tied to each other.

His hard-on wasn't going anywhere, so he'd have to rub one out in the shower. But just as he started to throw back the blanket, the door burst open, and Cody came careening into the room.

"Hey, Mister. Are you gonna teach me how to ride a bike now?"

His legs jerked and got tangled in the sheet. "Yeah. Sure. Where's Miss O'Neill?"

"She's outside. Talking to some guy."

Some guy? Had to be the fuckwad. "Do me a favor?" He slept naked, so he wasn't getting up. "Go get your socks and boots on while I take a quick shower and grab some coffee."

But the kid didn't budge. He stood there, watching him.

"What?" Jude asked.

"Are you really gonna get up?"

Ah. Okay. He wasn't used to reliable people. Hanging onto the sheet, Jude jackknifed up and looked Cody square in the eyes. "Yes. I'm going to shower, brush my teeth, and then I'll come get you."

The answer seemed to satisfy him. "Okay."

As soon as the kid left, Jude headed into the bathroom.

Tension tightened his muscles as he imagined the conversation Fee was having right then. She said she wouldn't forgive the guy, but she'd had time to get over the initial shock. Maybe she'd change her mind.

He turned on the faucet. *Good for her. Let her have the life she's always wanted.*

Restless and impatient, he didn't wait for the water to warm up before stepping under the spray. Because it was bullshit. That wasn't the right life for her. She'd never be happy with a man who kept things from her. She needed honesty and full disclosure. And she shouldn't marry a manipulating son of a bitch.

When he closed his eyes and let the water saturate his scalp, all he saw was Finlay's haunted expression when she'd run into the street in her wedding gown. The plea in her eyes.

Get me out of here.

Her life had flipped upside down. Everything she'd

ever wanted was slipping through her fingers—including the house on Bloom Lane. And she didn't deserve that.

That woman deserved everything.

Fuck it. Fighting the pull to her was exhausting and impossible. He needed to know she was okay. He needed to see if there was anything he could do to help her. In record time, he took his shower, brushed his teeth, and got dressed. He trampled down the stairs, ready to bust through the front door, but when he looked out the window, he found her making a snowman with Cody.

Just the two of them.

Which meant "that guy" was probably Jude's dad.

Shake it off, man. Grab a coffee. He was home for one reason. *Cody.* And for the next six weeks, he had to make that boy his entire focus. Not Finlay.

As he headed to the kitchen, he heard laughter and deep voices.

Boone.

Wyatt.

And his dad.

The knot in his chest eased. He didn't have to do any of this alone. He had his family.

Damn, he'd missed them.

As soon as he entered the kitchen, his dad said, "Meeting called. Let's go."

As they trooped toward the pantry, Jude said, "Cody said she was talking to a guy. Did her ex stop by?"

His dad shook his head. "That was Wyatt."

But as they filed into the pantry, he got that weird tug again to see her. "Give me a second. I want to check on them."

"They're fine," Boone said.

"I have to let her know what I'm doing." *Cody's my responsibility*. He couldn't just foist him on Finlay. Hurrying across the living room, he opened the door to a blast of cold air and stepped out onto the porch.

They'd built a big snowman, complete with a carrot nose and beets for eyes.

"Let's give him hair," Finlay said.

"But how?" Cody asked. "Where do we get hair?"

"See those pine needles over there?" She pointed to the woods on the other side of the driveway.

"Yeah."

"Wouldn't it be funny if we stuck them straight up out of his head?"

Cody's eyes lit up. "I'll get 'em." He took off, but his boots sank, and he tripped, landing face-first.

Jude leaped off the porch, landed on the snow, and took off.

But Finlay didn't budge. "Okay?" she called to the boy in a calm voice.

Before Jude could reach him, the boy stood. "I'm okay." He wiped crystals off his face, blinking back a sheen of tears.

Clarity hit. Up until this moment, he'd viewed the boy as a responsibility. A task he had to manage.

But for the first time, he saw a person with complex emotions and thoughts. A little boy with big feelings. Cody wasn't crying because he got hurt. He was crying because he was overwhelmed. He was in a new place with strange, scary people. He couldn't begin to understand that his mom didn't want him, his dad had died, and his grandpa couldn't look after him anymore.

There was no getting around it. Jude could make himself feel better thinking in terms of "six weeks" or "until Carlo recovers," but the truth was, this boy needed a guardian for the rest of his life, and if Jude didn't step up, he'd go into the system.

Softening, he let out a frosty breath and reached for the boy's hand. "Come on. Let's get those pine needles."

Cody's gloves were way too big for his little hand. Jude would have to buy him clothes. Some toys and books. He'd have to do more than feed and water him.

They gathered pine needles. "Did you have breakfast?" Jude asked.

"Yeah." The boy moved around the tree to grab a few more.

Of course. Because Finlay had seen to it. "When you're ready to come in, we'll warm up with some cocoa. Sound good?"

The boy looked at him warily. "What's cocoa?"

"You've never had hot chocolate before?"

"No, but I like chocolate."

"Well, good, because my dad's weird. He doesn't drink coffee or tea. Only cocoa."

The boy cocked his head. "I only like chocolate."

Right. He was confusing Cody. "Yeah, sorry. Hot chocolate and hot cocoa are the same thing. And let me tell you, my dad stockpiles it. He's probably tried every brand out there."

"Why?"

Okay, this is good. Conversation. "He's on a quest to find the best."

"I can help your dad do that."

Cute. Jude smiled. "He'd appreciate it."

They brought the needles back and dumped them in front of the snowman. Finlay grabbed a handful, lifted the boy, and showed him how to stick them around the head.

"I'm sorry for sleeping in," he said quietly. "I'm a bartender, so my hours are off." But that was just an excuse. "I shouldn't have assumed someone else would take care of him."

As he looked into her eyes, he couldn't help remembering her sultry expression as he'd leaned in for the kiss, the way her lips had parted, and the soft heat that greeted him inside her mouth. She'd been so responsive, so fucking sexy.

"I'm a teacher." She smiled. "I'm used to getting up early, so it all worked out. Now, you'd better get in there. Your brothers came to see you, and I said I'd keep him occupied while you guys talk. Go on. We're fine."

Flame doused, he focused on business. "When I'm done, I'll take you wherever you need to go."

"Oh, that's all right. I have a ride."

He fought the urge to say, "*I'm* your ride." But he had to cut that out. His time with her was almost up.

That shouldn't make his chest tighten.

But there you go.

In the kitchen, he poured himself a cup of coffee, then headed for the pantry. Before entering, he checked to be sure Finlay and Cody hadn't come inside. They hadn't.

His dad's shelves were crammed with food. Even

though none of the brothers lived there anymore, he still hosted the holiday parties, summer barbecues, and birthdays. He was also somewhat of a survivalist, as evidenced by the hefty bags of rice and canned tuna and sardines.

Jude reached behind the canisters of flour and sugar and pulled the lever.

The door gave easily and silently, and he pushed it along its runners. Checking behind him one more time and finding no one around, he slipped into the pitch-black darkness of the cellar staircase. Once the door closed behind him, he flipped the switch. Light flooded the concrete walls and wood steps.

The secret basement was divided into two sections. One housed storage boxes, and the other held his dad and Wyatt's abandoned furniture projects. There was no evidence of the safe room—not even a seam in the wall—and it was fully soundproofed, so Jude couldn't hear his brothers or smell the inevitable cigars they'd be lighting.

Kneeling, he lifted the wood panel from the floor and pressed the button. The bolts slid open, and he got up and headed inside to find his brothers laughing their asses off and his dad pouring a drink at the bar.

"It's not even nine in the morning." Jude pressed the button that sealed the door shut behind him.

"Thanks for the update, Father Time," Boone said.

As Wyatt nipped the butt of his cigar, Boone flicked the switch to the ventilation system.

His dad handed him a whiskey.

"I'm good with coffee."

Wyatt pulled the drink out of his dad's hands and tipped it into the mug. "You're gonna need it."

Probably. Jude dropped into a leather club chair.

"Give us the backstory." Wyatt sat on the ottoman. "Marco died a year ago. Where's the boy been living since then?"

"South Dakota," Jude said. "With his grandfather. But Carlo was already dealing with hip issues, so he couldn't handle raising the boy on his own. That's why he moved into the club."

"He's eighty-six, though, right?" Boone asked. "What happens after he comes back?"

Leave it to his family to get right to the point. "First of all, a judge has to grant me temporary guardianship, and who knows if that'll happen. But even if it does, it only lasts ninety days. I have no idea what happens after that."

An image struck of Cody gazing up at him, eyes glazed with tears. Lost. Scared. Confused.

"Unless you start the process, he'll either go into the system or back to the club, right?" Boone asked.

"Process?" But even as he said it, he knew exactly what his brother meant. Adoption.

He'd never seen himself as dad material. He wasn't the type to put down roots. Buy a minivan. Get a real job. The idea of making sure the kid had three meals a day and washed behind his ears seemed foreign to him.

Yet… It was a very real possibility. "We'll have to see what Carlo wants."

"And if he does?" his dad asked.

"I don't think I could say no. Which is wild because two days ago…" He didn't bother finishing the sentence. It didn't matter who he was two days ago. That life was over. He leaned forward, elbows on his knees, and stared into his steaming mug of coffee.

"What're you thinking?" Wyatt asked.

When he looked up, he found all three of them watching him, as if his emotions were playing across a big screen. "Even if I'm open to it, there's not a chance in hell a Calamity judge is going to let me adopt a kid. I think we all know I'm the worst guy in the world to do that."

"Not really," Wyatt said. "A serial killer would be worse."

"No, a cult leader," Boone said. "For sure."

"You got me there." Wyatt nodded.

"Would you shut up?" Jude couldn't believe they'd fuck around at a time like this.

For about three seconds, they both looked contrite. Until Wyatt snapped his fingers and said, "Pennywise. You know that crazy-ass clown from the Stephen King movie? Now, that dude would hands-down be the worst."

"Oh fuck, man." Boone shuddered. "That's probably my only memory of the club. Waking up one night to find a bunch of guys watching it. I about pissed my pants." He shot a look at both brothers. "I didn't, so don't start with me. I did not piss my pants."

"You know who'd really be the worst, though?" Wyatt asked. "Farrah from *Teen Mom*."

"Teen what?" Boone asked.

"It's a reality TV show about pregnant teens," Wyatt said.

"Since when do you watch shit like that?" his dad asked.

"Not me." Wyatt held up both hands. "It's what they've got playing in the break room at the clinic."

"If you dumbasses are done, do you think we could get back to my situation?" Jude asked. "Or do you want to compare your favorite hair products first?"

"Actually, I used someone else's shampoo at the station last week," Boone said. "It smelled like fruit salad. Made my hair nice and soft." He flicked Jude's hair. "You should try it, Straw man."

"I don't have—" Jude began.

"Boys," his dad snapped before turning his attention to Jude. "Let's be clear on something. You don't *have* to do anything. You can go back to Florida and get on with your life. It's been twelve years since you were friends with Marco, so nothing says you have to raise his kid."

"I couldn't live with myself if I didn't." Jude paced across the spacious room, which had six Murphy beds hidden in the walls, closets stacked with enough food to keep them fed for ten years, and shelves filled with books, satellite equipment, board games, flashlights, and lanterns. "I owe it to him."

"Did you know Marco nearly got arrested for stealing motorcycles?" Boone asked. "Griffin James was hauling a bunch of custom bikes to a show, and he and his guys went inside the shop to grab the last one. When they came back out, they found him and his friends trying to pull one off the truck."

"The only reason they didn't call the police is because they were caught before a crime was committed," Wyatt said.

"I didn't know about that, but the Marco I knew was a

good friend. He was there for me. And now that he's gone, I owe it to him to take care of his son."

"There for you how?" Wyatt asked quietly.

He supposed if they were decent enough to take off work to meet with him, he owed them honesty. "I didn't really talk about it, but I didn't do well when we first moved here. There was a lot of bad shit in the club—"

"We know," Wyatt said. "Because you were the one who protected us from it."

Jude nodded. "But I got roughed up one day." While he wouldn't go into detail, he could tell from his dad's pinched expression that he remembered when his six-year-old son had a split lip and black eye. "And I took off. Got lost in the woods, and Marco found me." As he tugged on his beard, he looked into the sober expressions of three of the McKenna men. "In the middle of the damn Tetons, that kid found me. I was alone. It was dark, and I was scared shitless. And when I saw that flashlight in the woods, I broke out crying. I know it didn't seem like it, but he was a good friend. And for a lot of years, he was my only friend."

"I didn't know about that." Boone looked concerned.

"I didn't say anything." He figured he ought to get to the point. "But I'm pretty sure if I don't step up, Cody's going to turn out the same way I did."

"What're you talking about?" his dad asked.

Well, hell. He didn't want his dad to feel bad. None of it was his fault. He'd done his best to provide for his kids in an impossible situation. "When we got here, I had to wear whatever the club gave me, so at school, they tagged me as a biker kid. When anything went wrong—if a kid got hurt on the playground or someone's Tamagotchi got stolen—the finger was pointed at me." He remembered when Gwynn Morrison came in after recess with bloody hands and her ponytail askew. The teacher looked right at Jude and accused him of pushing her down.

"I got a lot of calls from the school," his dad said. "You saying you didn't do all that?"

"No, I did some of it. I was a jerk, I'm not saying otherwise. But I'm not sure I had a chance to be anything else since I got blamed for things anyway. And Cody's walking the same path. Last night before bed, I told him we needed to get him new clothes for school, and he got this panicked look. He started to argue with me about it, and I figured the do-rag, boots, and vest were all he had left from his dad. So I have to let him wear them, but at the same time, it's going to get him in trouble in school. Parents aren't going to want their kids to play with him."

He didn't like the concerned look in his brothers' eyes, so he drank his coffee, forgetting that Wyatt had spiked it. Warmth sped through his bloodstream.

"Well, whatever happens, just know we're here for you," Wyatt said. "You're not in this alone."

"I appreciate it." He'd always been closest to Wyatt. Certainly because of the two-year age gap, but also because he'd had to protect him in the club. "And I'm going to need the help. The last anybody heard of me was when Judge Adams kicked me out of town. He called me a loser."

"He didn't call you a loser," his dad said.

"He looked right at me when he said it. Trust me, I heard." Maybe it was the booze, but he felt compelled to let the deeper truth out. "I just don't want my reputation to impact him." Because associating with the guy who'd raised hell in this town for half his life might be a lot worse for Cody than wearing a vest.

"I don't know why you say that," Boone said. "You didn't steal cars. You didn't hurt people. The worst thing you did was put a snake in someone's mailbox."

"When dad was out hustling for work, you're the one who took care of us," Wyatt said. "When shit happened to me, you're the one who stepped in. You're a good man."

"And we'll stand with you in a courtroom," his dad said.

"That's good." Jude doubted a judge would care what his family had to say. "Because Carlo thinks we'll get a hearing Monday morning for temporary guardianship."

"We'll be there." Wyatt stepped closer and pulled him into his arms. His big, burly lumberjack of a brother gave him a bear hug. "The right man for the job isn't someone who checks off a list of qualities on a piece of paper." He pulled away. "It's a man who steps up for a kid who needs a father."

"Dude, you're wasting your time with animals," Boone said to Wyatt. "You should make inspirational posters. That kitten hanging off a rope? '*Hang in there.*'"

"'*Don't follow your dreams,*'" his dad said. "'*Chase them.*'"

"Fuck off." But Jude was laughing, too. "I have to go check on Finlay. She's done enough childcare."

As he climbed the stairs, he felt lighter. He didn't know how things would turn out, but it helped to know his family was there with him.

At the landing, he checked the cameras. No one was in the kitchen, so he pulled open the door and—just to be sure—grabbed a box of crackers on his way out of the pantry.

After setting his mug and the box on the counter, he crossed the living room. Sunlight glinted off metal, and he saw a white BMW parked out front.

Finlay's ride.

Shit.

She's leaving.

Chapter Eight

He'd known this time was coming, yet he wanted her to stay. Not for the boy.

For me.

Because he finally knew what it felt like to touch her, kiss her.

Aw, hell.

But he had to let her go. Both of their lives were too complicated.

When he stepped onto the porch, he found her in a heated conversation with a man he assumed was her fiancé, while Cody made snowballs nearby and hurled them at a tree trunk.

"I messed up, and I'm sorry," her fiancé said. "But I'm not like you. You need to talk everything out. I had to wrap my head around it before I told you."

What? That wasn't how she worked at all. She got quiet and introspective. She had to figure things out on her own first.

"But you did talk, Matt." Finlay's tone was calm and rational. "You talked to your ex."

"Yeah, of course, I did. What other choice did I have? I needed answers. I needed to know why she kept Chloe from me for five years."

Jude had no business listening in on the conversation, so he headed over to the boy. Jesus, it was cold out there. But the kid didn't seem to mind. "You ready for that cocoa?"

Cody's gaze darted to Finlay. "Can Miss O'Neill come?"

"Well, she's talking to someone right now. But when she's done, she can."

"I want to wait."

Boone peered out from the garage, holding up a box. "Anyone down for a popsicle before we ride bikes?"

"I want one." After a lingering look at Finlay, the boy trudged over.

"Nice," Jude said quietly to his brother. "Maybe *you* should adopt him."

"Oh, hell no. I'm the funcle."

"The what?"

"The fun uncle."

After they each grabbed a Fudgsicle—his dad's favorite—they watched Cody gape at all the big toys.

The large space housed a snowplow, a Ford F-150, his dad's convertible for nice weather, and a boat for the section of Lake Calamity that sat on his property. Even with all that, it still had plenty of space for Cody to ride.

His dad and Wyatt joined them, grabbing popsicles. The

way that little boy stood among the four of them solidified something in Jude. He couldn't explain it, but he just knew he had to protect this boy. If the judge gave him any shit, he'd get right back in his face and let him know the McKennas would bring him into the fold. Keep him safe. Loved.

I'm not just the only man for the job. I'm the right one.

When Finlay's voice came closer, he grew distracted. He'd never heard her teach, but he imagined she'd sound just like this—steady, strong, and brooking no argument. He'd have liked to have been in her class.

Though he'd probably have stared at her tits too much. And instead of listening, he'd have imagined skimming his hand up her thigh, under her skirt, his fingertips brushing her bare pussy.

Would she be wet for him if he pulled her into the pantry and touched her?

Desire surged through him hard and fast.

You've got to stop this shit.

Her voice grew louder as she walked her ex to his car. "I'm sorry this happened to you, Matt. I really am. I can't imagine finding out I had a child. But you decided to tell me about it after we got married, and there's just no coming back from that."

"Look, I don't know what else you want me to do, but you don't bail on me the first time we have a problem. That's not how marriages work. Maybe it's because your parents are divorced, and you don't have a good example of how to handle problems, but mine were together till my dad died. They never once considered breaking up. That's the kind of marriage I want."

"Well, then, you'd better learn how to communicate,

because no one's going to put up with a man who withholds life-changing information until after she's legally bound to you."

"It's not like that, and you know it."

"That's exactly how it played out, so don't pretend otherwise. But I'll tell you what I *do* know. For three months, you talked about barstools for the kitchen island when the entire time you were struggling with something huge. I'm not going to spend the rest of my life wondering if you're hiding something or what piece of information you're choosing to withhold. I'm sorry, Matt, but you've lost all credibility."

"You're seriously talking to me about credibility right now? You left the wedding on the back of some dude's motorcycle. You spent the night with some other guy."

"He's a friend. And believe me, after the news I got yesterday, I needed one."

"Come on, Finlay." The man tipped his head back, a burst of white fog shooting out of his mouth. "I've been nothing but a good partner to you. I'm sorry if I got thrown sideways and didn't handle it the way you wanted, but you're really not going to forgive me?"

"At some point, I'll forgive you. But that's not the issue. I'll never completely trust you. So no, I'm not marrying you."

The man let out a deep sigh. "You know what? I'm *glad* we didn't work out. You want some kind of Prince Charming, and no one can live up to your expectations. Forget it." He reached to open the door. "I'll tell the realtor we're selling the house."

"Wait." For the first time, Finlay sounded frantic. "Don't do that. Not yet."

"Why?" Matt asked. "Why would you even want to live there by yourself? It's a family neighborhood. That's no place for a single woman. Besides, I paid half the down payment. You'd have to buy me out, and you don't have that kind of money."

"I'm well aware of my financial situation, but I'm asking for a little time to figure things out. Can you just do this one thing for me? You owe me that."

"You'd seriously live there alone? Without me?" The man's voice cracked.

For the first time, Jude felt bad for the guy. He was an asshole, no doubt about it. But he was losing Finlay.

Big loss.

Huge.

He'd never find anyone like her again.

"You just blew up my life. I don't know what I'm going to do five seconds from now, let alone five years. I can't think straight, which is why I want you to leave things alone. Give me a minute to calm down and think clearly. Can you do that for me?"

"Sure." Emotion died in the man's eyes. "I'll give you till after Christmas, but then, I'm calling the realtor."

He got in his car and drove off, leaving Finlay alone on the driveway, staring after him.

Jude had to stop himself from pulling her into his arms. He wanted to comfort her, but he didn't think she'd welcome his touch right then—even one meant to be platonic.

Well, let's be honest. It's never been platonic between us.

He didn't know how to help her, only that he had to do something. "You want a Fudgsicle?"

She looked at him like he was speaking a foreign language. And then, when she saw all of them licking away, she burst out laughing. "You know what? That's exactly what I want."

"Is he right, though?" Finlay lay on the bed, gazing up at the ceiling. "*Was* he my Prince Charming?" The room smelled a bit like feet, and the mattress had a dip in it. Which was confusing because the Wild Rose Inn and Saloon had always been the best hotel in Calamity.

"Maybe." Willa stretched out beside her, digging into a bag of Moose Munch. She only liked the chocolate-covered nuts and left all the kettle corn behind. "He sure looks like one."

With his dark hair and medium build, Matt had classic good looks. He ran six days a week, detailed his car once a month, and had weekly get-togethers with his frat brothers from the University of Western Wyoming.

"Well, it fits because Cinderella didn't even know the prince," Finlay continued. "She had one dance with him and *bam*! He's the one. Same with Snow White. She's basically dead, and the dude revives her with a kiss. When she opens her eyes, *boom*, there's her soulmate. I mean, seriously, isn't that what Matt was for me? He walked right off my vision board. He checked all the boxes."

Not like Jude. Who was dark and menacing.

Except not when he's with me.

With me, he's sweet and protective.

Generous, loyal, and kind.

And a really good kisser.

The memory of his hungry mouth sent a hot current through her body, making her restless.

I kissed Jude McKenna.

And it was so, so good. He wasn't tentative and careful. He wasn't being gentlemanly like Matt always was.

No, he'd grabbed the back of her neck. He'd plundered her mouth. He'd taken what was his.

No, I'm not his. I know that.

I do.

But God. The way he'd cupped her breast so possessively, like he'd longed to do it for ages and had finally gotten a handful. Well, more than a handful. *Let's be honest.* His palm pressed over her nipple… She'd felt his restraint, and it had made her desperate to be naked with him when he lost control. She wanted it rough, hard, wild.

She just knew it would be like that with him.

He'd given her a taste, and she wanted more. She wanted Jude McKenna unleashed.

"That's extremely insightful for someone who's had two and a half peach wine coolers. And I'm sure it's true for all of us." Willa had grabbed snacks from the convenience store on her way to pick her up from Jude's house. But she had a flight in the morning and needed to go right to the office to catch up on work, so she wasn't drinking much.

But this conversation was helping. Because fantasizing about Jude: Bad. Figuring out what went wrong with Matt: Good. "He thinks I'm being unreasonable. Like, you know, everyone makes mistakes. No one's perfect. I should forgive him and move on."

"Honestly?" Willa said. "I don't care what he thinks."

Ha. Fair. Still, she had to probe a little deeper. Root out every shred of doubt. "I'm sure he has a million things he can't stand about me, but he's willing to get past them. Why can't I do the same for him?"

"Oh, for sure. I'm surprised he's put up with you this long." Willa held up her free hand. "You have no athletic ability at all." Her pointer finger folded after revealing the first flaw.

"Excuse me?" Finlay swiveled her head to stare at her friend.

"Remember when we tried out for softball, and you ran your little heart out to first base all while peeing your pants?"

Finlay burst out laughing. "That's because you were making fun of the way I ran, and I was laughing so hard a little bit of pee came out. *Also,* I'd just had a Gatorade. And anyway, how is that a flaw?"

"Bladder control issues. And your cooking? That's another thing." Willa set another finger down.

"Well." While she couldn't argue with that one, she felt compelled to try. "I make grilled cheese sandwiches. And quesadillas." Unsuccessfully, but she got an A for effort, right?

"You literally only bake things. When have you ever made an actual meal?"

"I don't like meat." And she hated preparing it. It was the raw *muscle* of an animal. "And what even are vegetables?"

"Uh, the bounty of nature, that's what."

"Okay, but do you strip bark off a tree and steam it? Do you stuff a handful of grass in your mouth and call it salad? What's grown in the earth—"

"Gets peed on by bugs and four-legged creatures," Willa said. "I know. You've said it a million times. You like baked goods. But Matt's a beer-and-steak kind of guy. What kind of life is that for him? 'Honey, I'm home.'" She lowered her voice to sound like a dude. "'What's for dinner?'" She raised her pitch to say, "'I made yummy brownies and cinnamon rolls.'"

Finlay laughed. "That's fair."

"And don't get me started with your craft shit." Willa lowered another finger. "Girl, you leave glitter everywhere. I don't think I've ever come home from visiting you without finding it in my suitcase or under my fingernails."

"That *is* a problem."

"Oh. Oh." Willa got excited and hiked up on an elbow to roll over and face her. "And what about your laugh? Birds scatter. Dogs hide under the bed, and little children clutch their mommy's legs."

"Hey. I can't help how I laugh." When her friend broke out in shrieking laughter, her mouth stretched impossibly wide, Finlay whacked her. "Okay, now, you're being mean."

"Oh, come on." Willa leaned in and smacked a kiss on her cheek. "Everyone loves your laugh, and you know it. It's one of the best things about you. You let it rip. Free and unfettered. It's awesome. My *point* is your 'flaws' aren't even in the same ballpark as Matt's."

"He said my expectations aren't realistic."

"Yeah, well, he can go screw himself." Willa reared up, snatched the plastic bag off the floor, and began tossing empty cans and wrappers into it. "You know how I feel about this. We run from anyone who tells us to lower our standards. We hold out for what we want. Now, we've got Malibu Barbie cocktails with our names on them waiting for us at Wild Billy's. You want to fix yourself up, or are we going like feral women who just raw-dogged six days in the wilderness?"

That was *not* going to happen. She hadn't told Willa—or anyone—about the kiss. She was holding on to it like a gift. Or a dirty secret. *It's mine.* But her friend knew all about her childhood crush, so she'd understand. "Jude's working the bar tonight, so I want to look as fine as wine." She cringed. "That's bad, right? Two days ago, I was getting married, and now, I'm glamming up for some guy I knew in high school?" *Who touched my boob last night.*

"You know the old saying." Willa swung her legs off the bed. "The only way to get over Prince Charming is to get under a bad boy."

<h1 style="text-align:center">Chapter Nine</h1>

WILD BILLY'S WAS THE MOST POPULAR BAR IN TOWN, so it was no surprise that every table and barstool was filled. The dance floor was crowded with people two-stepping to a live country band.

While their friends were dancing, Finlay sat with Willa, but she couldn't take her eyes off Jude. She loved the way his biceps flexed as he held a vodka bottle with one hand and deftly caught the lime another bartender tossed him with the other. He had his hair tied back, which only accentuated his high cheekbones and strong jawline. The man was gorgeous.

Yeah, but you know what? It was his confidence that made him so appealing. That made him stand out.

"I could just take a picture of him," Willa said. "That way, you could just stare at your phone all night. Might be easier."

Finlay laughed. "Oh, let me have some fun. My entire life went up in smoke. I've lost the father of my future children."

"Yeah, you for sure look torn up about it. Probably, Jude McKenna's the only one who can relieve your broken heart."

"Keep your sarcasm in New York, where it belongs. It's not welcome in my lovely mountain town." Her phone buzzed with a photo Willa sent. In it, she was gazing longingly. And since she recognized the taxidermy moose head protruding out of the brick wall behind her, she knew she was staring at Jude.

The yearning, the raw desire, need—*whatever you wanted to call it*—made her sick to her stomach. "What's wrong with me? Why am I still so obsessed with him?" She flipped her phone over. She couldn't look at that lonely, pathetic high school girl who dreamed about him all while cutting out photos of clean-cut, handsome actors and models. "Do you think he saw?"

"Who cares if he did?" Willa asked. "You're allowed to be attracted to a man. You get to be whoever the hell you are. And personally, I think you're fantastic. You're a great friend. A great teacher. You're smart, creative, and you're fucking hot."

Impulsively, she wrapped her arms around her friend's neck and hugged her. "I didn't know how much I needed to hear that. Thank you for being here."

Willa clung to her. "I'll be here as long as you need." She pulled back. "Speaking of which… Are we going on the honeymoon?"

Settling back in her chair, Finlay shook her head. "No." She wiped the moisture under her eyes. "I've already canceled the hotel and my flight. In fact, I'm going back to school for the next three days until Christmas break."

"Sweetie, I know how much you want to keep the house, but I'm not sure you'll be able to come up with that kind of money in a week."

"I know. But I'm not giving up yet. I'm holding on to every ounce of hope until the clock runs out."

"What if I give you a loan?" Willa asked. "We could come up with a payment plan."

"I love you. And I appreciate that you'd do that for me, but I'm not taking your money. Realistically, I know I can't come up with that kind of money. I know I can't keep the house. And it's okay. I'll be fine. I just need to peel off one piece of the dream at a time."

"The easiest part was the groom."

"I *know*. How awful am I? I mean, did I even love him?"

"That's a good question," Willa asked. "Did you?"

But she already knew the answer. She'd spent half the night contemplating it. "I loved what we were building." It was hard to think with rum sloshing around her brain, but she was sure of one thing. "That's how we connected from the very beginning. We both had our lives mapped out, and they were perfectly aligned. It was exciting, and it made me feel close to him. But…" She glanced back at the bar—well, at Jude. "But now it's over, and the only thing I can think about is the timeline. I'm thirty, Wills. This is when I need to buy a house and have a baby. Don't get me wrong. I love my job and my friends and my family. I love my life, but I've had this dream for so long, and now it's just been…erased."

"I get what you're saying. For the first time in your life, you're driving without a map, and that's scary."

She could only nod because it was terrifying not to see the road ahead.

"I think the vision board made you feel safe." Willa ran her fingertip around the rim of her glass. "I mean, one day, you're living with two parents, you have a close group of friends you've known your whole life, you're happy as a bug in a rug, and the next… it all blows up. Your parents divorced, your friends cut you out… Both of those things happened in the same year. I can't imagine how helpless you felt. And maybe taping pretty images to that board gave you some control, you know? It made you feel like you had the power to make the life you wanted."

"You're pretty smart for a girl who once stripped naked in Tommy Pederson's bathroom."

Willa balled up her napkin and threw it at her. "It was my first date, and I got spaghetti sauce all over my white dress. I was panicking. And how was I supposed to know his brother would walk right in?"

"I'm just saying, you're a lot smarter now."

She slunk down in her chair. "Oh, my God. I can't believe you brought that up when I'm sitting here feeling all sophisticated and shit. Listen, lady, the person whose life isn't a dumpster fire gets to act like she has her life together and dole out the wisdom like a Pez dispenser. That's how it works."

Finlay patted her friend's hand. "Don't worry. You've come a long way since you told Tommy Pederson's brother your dress was wet because the family dog pushed you into the pool."

"I hate you."

"Which is a real shame since you're my favorite person

in the world." She picked up her glass only to find it empty. Eyes flicking over to Jude, she pushed back her chair. "I'll get us another round."

Willa reached for her. "I think that's why God invented servers."

She paused, hesitant, knowing she should listen to her friend but driven by the absolute compulsion to be near him.

"I'm going to ask you this as a friend who loves you. Before you go over there, what do you want? Because you're not in a place to start a relationship, and you already know the only thing he's interested in."

"You mean a quickie in the bathroom?" Fire raced along her nerves. She could picture it. Jude's strong arms holding her up as he thrust into her, the tile cold against her back. Desire coursed through her, dampening her panties.

"Unless he's changed…?"

"No, he hasn't." Finlay scooted her chair closer to the table. "And I really, really don't want to be that girl anymore." The one who filled her loneliness with a crush on a boy she could never have. "I have a good, full life, and a quick bang from the boy I'm still susceptible to would throw me right back into that obsession." She could already feel it. The way she constantly snuck looks at him. Already, she was slipping back there. "And I don't want that."

"No, I didn't think you did."

"It's just…" Finlay tapped her fingers on the wooden table. "You know what I realized somewhere around two in the morning?" She didn't even wait for her friend to respond. "With Matt, I'd have the husband, the house on Bloom Lane, the children, the dogs, the dream job…and then, once the excitement leveled off, when we got into the routine of life, I'd be hit in the face with the reality that I wasn't in love with my husband. Like, Wills, that was *going* to happen. It was inevitable. Because when Matt and I talked this morning? Neither one of us said, 'I love you.' The word never came up. Not for either of us."

And that scares the crap out of me.

Because what the hell was I willing to settle for?

Willa's features scrunched in discomfort. "Okay, but at least you got out. It won't happen now."

"And on top of all that, how bizarre is it that I run out of the church, and it's Jude McKenna I see? He hasn't lived here in twelve years, and he's the first person I ran into? I can't believe it."

"Can't you?"

"What does that mean?"

"I don't know. I mean, what better way to drive home that Matt isn't the man for you than to be with Jude?"

Maybe she'd thrown up a wall between the two sides of her—the vision board Finlay and the wild woman who ran free—but at that moment, she became painfully aware of the contrast between her feelings for the two men. The life she wanted versus what her soul craved.

But wait, why would there be a difference between the two?

She knew the answer. Of course, she did. Willa had just spelled it out for her. When her parents divorced, she'd been gutted. Countless nights curled up in bed, crying her eyes out, the loneliness of being a latchkey kid.

And then, being blindsided by her friends when they'd cast her aside. She'd gone from safety and security to being alone and vulnerable.

After two hits like that, why would she open her heart to another devastating loss? So she'd chosen a tepid relationship and denied herself true, passionate love.

It was such a terrible truth that she pushed her chair back. She wasn't ready for a night out yet. *This is a mistake.* "I'm going to the bathroom." She needed a break from thinking.

"Do you want to get out of here? We can leave."

"I just… I need a minute, okay?"

Willa watched her with concern. "Of course."

She took off, passing tables filled with laughter and flirty, loud conversation. While everyone around her had a great time, she was carving herself wide open and looking into the deepest, darkest parts of herself. *I should've stayed home.*

Yeah, but where's home? Matt said he'd move in with his mom till he found a new place. Did she really want to be alone in that big, empty house? Maybe she *should* let it go.

The dance floor was packed, so she made her way around the perimeter, which put the bar directly in her sight. *Don't look at him.* Because if she did, she'd have to face the fact that Jude was the man she craved. Jude was the only man she'd ever truly wanted.

But, of course, she looked. She had no control when it came to him. His form-fitting black T-shirt accentuated his musculature, drawing her in like a powerful magnet. She wanted to get her hands on his chest, trace the V that led to the bulge beneath the waistband of his jeans.

No one excited her the way he did.

In high school, the boys had tried to outdo each other with their trucks. They'd show up with new lift kits or knobby tires, custom grilles, and LED light bars. Finlay had been oblivious to all of it.

It was only when Jude rode in on his Harley, his long hair fluttering beneath his helmet and the silver studs on his leather jacket catching the sunlight, that her heart had thundered and her skin had bristled with awareness.

Her reaction had never made sense because she'd wanted a good, clean, beautiful life. She hadn't wanted to be caught having sex in a public place like the other girls he'd hooked up with. And yet, there'd been that one time she'd seen his bare butt thrusting in the back seat of Laura Edelson's mom's Jeep, and a rush of desire had swept through her with such force, she'd nearly lost her footing.

She'd tucked away that memory, playing it repeatedly all these years. It still had the power to get her worked up.

It was the way he hadn't held back. The way his hips had reared up, and he'd thrust so hard and deeply.

No one had ever wanted her so badly they'd bruise her skin or make her sore. It was such a familiar ache, a yearning for that kind of physical contact. Needing it. She was desperate for the kind of love Jude gave.

Do you even hear yourself?

He doesn't love you. He's not built like that. He said so himself.

The most she could hope for was a night of great sex.

And that would never be enough for her. In fact, a night with Jude would ruin her.

Finlay only realized she'd made it to the bar when a

bartender with giant, sparkly earrings asked, "What can I get you?"

She didn't even know how she'd gotten there. "Can I get another round of Malibu Barbies for my table?" Fortunately, Jude had his back to her as he poured draft beers. That man could read her like no one else, and he'd see how badly she wanted another kiss, how the only thing she could think about was his big, warm hand sliding under her shirt and skimming her belly till he reached her breasts.

A sudden jolt of pleasure ignited a pulse between her legs.

You have to stop this.

"You all right?" the bartender asked.

"Sure." Her gaze flicked over to Jude. "I'm just…"

"For what it's worth, I'd have walked, too." She leaned over conspiratorially. "After a stunt like that, I'd never trust that man again."

Yanked from her preoccupation with Jude, she was momentarily confused. "You know who I am?"

"Oh yeah. One of your guests recorded the whole thing and posted it online. It's all anyone can talk about." She must've noticed the alarm on Finlay's face because she hurried to add, "Everyone's on your side. No one can believe he didn't tell you before the wedding. Anyhow, I'll get your drink order started."

"Thank you."

Jude coasted over, setting a big, warm hand down over hers and looking deeply into her eyes. "You okay?"

For just a moment, the whole world quieted. Sound

blanked out. And it was just Finlay and Jude locked into each other's orbit. "I really don't know what I am."

"She just found out she's gone viral," the bartender said before ducking under Jude's arms to grab glasses.

"Don't look at the comments," he said. "Social media trolls get off on stirring shit up."

Someone called his name from the other end of the bar. A scuffle had broken out, and Jude was called into the action. He gave a chin nod to her table. "Who's the designated driver?"

"Well, it was supposed to be Eloise." Her friend and wedding photographer had a baby at home, so she'd volunteered, but she'd had a few drinks and definitely wasn't safe to get behind the wheel.

"Let me know when you're ready to leave." He gave her that intense eye contact that made her bones vibrate. "I'll see you, though. I always do." He hurried off, placed both hands on the pass-through, and leaped over it.

The agility in his hard body and his absolute confidence made her swoon. Everything about him—

"Don't go there," the bartender said, a hint of warning in her tone. "Anyone but him."

"Oh, I'm not…" Finlay's thoughts scrambled. "I knew him in high school. I…"

"Yeah, I get it. He's hot. But trust me, you can't tie that one down." The woman held up a ticket. "Go back to your table. I'll get these to you in a minute."

"Thanks." Well, that was mortifying. On her walk of shame, she moved awkwardly, like she hadn't yet figured out how to use her legs. Her stupid feelings were so obvious that a stranger could read them. *You can't tie that one down.*

Yeah, believe me. I know.

But when she got to her table, she saw Eloise and Ava had returned, so she pasted on a smile and sat down. "Drinks are on the way." She reached for her glass and tipped it over to swallow the dregs. "What did I miss?"

"Willa's dating a finance bro," Eloise said.

Ugh. She'd been so preoccupied with her own problems that she hadn't caught up with her friend. "Willa *only* dates finance bros." Finlay shot her a look. "She's got issues."

"Okay, but are they faithful?" Ava asked. "That's what I want to know. They have a reputation."

"Everyone deserves a fresh chance." Willa laughed. "Or so I keep telling myself. New York City is like a smorgasbord of single, gorgeous people. No one's looking to settle down. And who has time for a relationship? I'll be choosier once I make partner."

"Here you go, ladies." The server held a tray of drinks. They all leaned back as she set a sugar-rimmed pink martini glass in front of each woman.

"Oh, yum. Thank you." Lifting it, Finlay said, "To new beginnings."

"To new beginnings," her friends said, and they all clinked glasses.

"You guys." Eloise looked tortured. "I have a confession to make."

Chapter Ten

"WE'RE LISTENING," FINLAY SAID.

Willa made a circling motion with her finger. "You're in the vault."

Eloise nodded. "I went on a date. Is that bad? Am I awful?" She'd lost her husband in a fire a year ago. She was now raising their baby as a single mom.

Just like that, all of Finlay's troubles blew away. They were trivial in comparison. "No, honey. Not at all."

"I loved my husband, you know?"

Willa set her hand over Eloise's. "Of course, you did."

"But I'm so angry." Tears glittered in Eloise's eyes. "I begged him not to join the hotshot team, but he wouldn't listen."

"People can be so stubborn," Ava said.

"Why did he always have to do what Boone did?" Eloise's husband was the youngest McKenna's best friend. "I just don't get it. What's so special about the McKennas?"

"Don't ask me." Willa couldn't have cared less about

bad boys. If Jude hadn't been Finlay's obsession, the brothers wouldn't have been on her radar at all. "I couldn't pick any of them out of a lineup."

"Well, I wouldn't touch a McKenna if they were the last men on earth." Eloise gulped down half her drink.

Finlay and Willa shared a concerned glance.

"Sweetie, who's watching the baby for you?" Finlay asked.

"I swap with someone in my neighborhood."

"You're not picking her up tonight?" Willa asked.

"Nope. I'll get her in the morning."

"Tell us about the date," Ava said.

"Oh." Eloise clicked her tongue on the roof of her mouth in a sound of disgust. "You're not going to believe this. So I'm shooting the opening of this new boutique in Wild Wolff Village. This place is ridiculous. It's got maybe twenty things to buy in the entire store, and nothing is even slightly affordable. We're talking five hundred dollars for a pair of jeans."

"Guess I won't be shopping there," Finlay said.

Eloise smiled. "Trust me, there's nothing you'd want to buy."

"I'm assuming the jeans come with the keys to a Ferrari?" Willa asked.

"Ha. Right?" Eloise took another swig. "Anyhow, the owner's designed it like a penthouse apartment. There's an actual *Picasso* hanging on the wall."

"What's the name of this place?" Ava asked. "I have to see it."

"It's called Fredericka's. The moment you walk in, she hands you a glass of champagne. Anyhow, I'm shooting away, and this guy starts chatting with me. Really nice, really hot, extremely well-dressed."

"You've got my attention," Willa said.

"Oh, he had mine. That's for sure. And he's not hitting on me at all. He's real. Genuine. Asking me questions about my life. He hears I'm a widow, a single mom, and he doesn't bat an eye. Which, trust me, is rare. Men disappear like vapor when they hear my sad story. So I'm talking to him, and I start to feel like, I don't know, maybe this could be something. Especially when he says he's the CEO of a business and keeps hours that prioritize his big, extended family. I'm thinking, wait a minute, a man who's actually home? Who spends time with the people he loves? In my mind, I'm packing for the next flight to Vegas." Eloise flashed her bare ring finger. "But, of course, I'm there to shoot the event, so I keep doing my job."

"I really wish you were telling this story in a less hostile tone because I want to be excited for you," Willa said.

"Yeah, wait for it. It's coming. Anyhow, the event ends. I'm packing up, and this guy walks me to my car. He goes, 'I could ask for your number and play the waiting game, but can we just skip the bullshit and go on a date Friday night?'" Eloise shook her head. "Hold on. He didn't say go on a *date*. He said, 'go out Friday night.'"

"I'm not unhappy about any of this," Finlay said.

"At this point, I wasn't either. I was all in. So I get a sitter, and I dress up like I've never had my heart broken. Like I'm not a single mother who lives in lint-covered leggings. And we have the best time. It was fantastic. Sparks flying, conversation flowing. He's telling me how much he loves kids and what a great *uncle* he is. I…" She drained her glass and licked her lips. "I can't believe I'm saying this out loud. I kissed him good night. That might seem like nothing to you guys, but I haven't…touched anybody since my husband. It *meant* something to me." Tears glistened, and she blinked furiously. "Oh, dammit."

Finlay's heart hurt for her friend. Bailing on a wedding was nothing compared to losing the father of your newborn baby.

"What happened?" Ava asked quietly.

"I mean, it was a good kiss, but it wasn't easy for me to do, you know? I wrestled with it, trying to convince myself it was okay to love again, that it's what my husband would've wanted. I reminded myself that my baby needs a dad…" She reached for a napkin and dabbed her eyes. "I knew I wasn't going to fall asleep, so I went to the boutique's Splashagram page to see the comments about the opening, and guess who's all over it?"

Dread snaked through her. "Your date?"

Eloise nodded. "Who just happens to be Fredericka's *husband*."

"*That's* the family business?" Willa asked.

"Yep. Apparently, she comes from serious money, and he's just along for the ride. They gave him the title of CEO."

"But he's really the president of pussy?" Willa asked.

"The CEO of sneaky links?" Ava said, laughing.

"The boss of booty calls?" Finlay added, though really, her heart ached for her friend's grief. "I'm sorry, honey."

"Yeah, well. Let's just say lesson learned. I'm not ready to date, and the only thing that matters is my baby. The worst thing I can do is crash out over some guy. I'm going to focus on what matters—growing my business and being a good mom. That's more than enough."

"It's absolutely enough," Ava said.

"Ugh, look at me," Eloise said. "I'm supposed to be the designated driver, and I'm drunk."

"Don't you worry about it. We've got this." Finlay knew Wild Billy's had a Safe Ride Home program. She'd ask the server about it when they got the next round.

Turned out, she didn't need to do that because, minutes later, Wyatt and Boone strode over, parting the crowd like movie stars with their intensely masculine swagger. There was something so deliciously naughty about these men. Sure, they were gorgeous and fit, but it was their don't-give-a-damn attitude that captured everyone's attention.

They were so self-contained, like they didn't need anybody but each other, and people couldn't help wanting to break into the inner circle. Of course, few ever made it, but what a validation it was to be included if you were deemed cool enough.

"Looks like you ladies need rides home." Boone flashed his signature smile to Eloise that let her know all the dirty ways he'd used women.

It had the intended effect because she gave him a disgusted look. He was, after all, the reason her husband had become a hotshot.

"Oh no, I'm fine. I can call a cab." The moment Ava stood, she swayed, grabbing for the table.

Wyatt got a grip on her arm and pulled her chair out

farther. "I got you." Before he led her off, he said, "Stay put. Someone's coming for you two."

"That's okay," Willa said. "We're right across the street."

Jude appeared, his tall form looming over the table. "I've got them."

Her sharp intake of breath at the sight of him sounded like an explosion in her ears. She was certain the entire bar heard her reaction to this hot, sexy man. "No need." Finlay's tone came out a little haughtier than intended. "We're staying at the inn."

"Good," he said. "Then it'll be quick, and I can get back to work."

"We can walk ourselves across the town square." *Oof. Do you have to sound like a prim schoolmarm?*

"It's ski season," he said. "The town's full of assholes looking for trouble. I'm walking with you."

They heard a shriek and turned to see Eloise flying into the air and flopping over Boone's shoulder. As he carried her off, she said, "I hate you."

"Yeah, keep it that way." Without a glance back, the youngest McKenna hauled their friend out of the bar.

She gazed up at Jude. *What was that about?*

Instead of answering, he had a grip on both their arms. That turned out to be a good idea, since she found it harder to walk in a straight line than she'd expected. In fact, her brain was floating in a sea of alcohol. "How much did I drink?" she asked, mostly to herself.

"You had three cocktails," Jude said.

How did he know that? "Yeah, but they're mostly fruit."

"And coconut rum."

He didn't know about the wine coolers. "I like rum." She tried to make an "mmm" sound—like something was tasty. Instead, it came out sounding suggestive. As if she'd said, *"I like it doggy style."*

"You just like the fruit juice."

"I do." She grinned, mostly happy that he couldn't hear her thoughts about him taking her from behind as he led her across the crowded bar.

Jude pushed the door open, and they stepped outside.

Ice-cold air stung her cheeks and made her eyes water, and she moved behind Jude's big, solid body. She pressed her face to his back and couldn't resist squeezing his biceps. "You're such a manly man."

Thankfully, he ignored her, stepping off the curb and heading across the street. Instead of going through the park, he guided them on the sidewalk that framed it.

You really need to shut your mouth.

No, but literally, don't say another word.

Except her brain was bobbing like a scoop of sherbet in a punch bowl, and she kept losing her train of thought. "Do you still bang all the girls? You know, like you did in high school?"

"Shh, Fee," Willa said. "No talking."

"I saw your butt once." She giggled.

"Finlay," Willa warned, but she stumbled, and she'd have gone down like a rag doll if Jude hadn't caught her. "Dammit. I have a flight in the morning. I wasn't supposed to drink tonight."

"No, but I did," Finlay continued. "He was banging Laura Edelson in her mom's Jeep, and his butt was going like—" She thrust her hips back and forth so hard she got dizzy and spun in a circle.

A group of tourists had to break apart to avoid getting hit by her whirling dervish dance.

"Whoa." In apology, she held her hands out in front of her. "Sorry." After they passed, the trio continued in lock-step. "Anyhow. It was *hot*."

"Okay, Fee," Willa said. "Use your inside voice."

"But I'm outside."

"I know, but he's right there." Willa pointed at Jude.

"I know. I'm talking to him." She looked at Jude. "I'm talking to you." Still, he ignored her. "Do you hear me? You're not saying anything."

"When you say something worth responding to, I'll talk," Jude said gruffly.

"But I did," Finlay said, confused. "I asked you a question."

"You asked me if I still bang all the girls."

"That's right. Do you?" she asked.

"Sure, Fee." He released a long-suffering sigh. "I bang."

"Just not me. That gave me a complex. For the longest time, I thought I wasn't bangable."

"Oh, honey, you are," Willa said. "You're so bangable. If I were a guy, I would totally bang you."

"Bang me," a guy shouted as he passed by with a few friends.

"Okay, ladies." At the Wild Rose Inn and Saloon, Jude opened the door.

Unlike the riotous bar they'd just left, the red, gold, and dark wood-paneled saloon was quiet, with only a few patrons talking at tables.

Where was everyone? Finlay was used to costumed servers who'd break out in song and dance. "Where's the piano lady?" she asked.

"My dad said she moved to Las Vegas." Willa sounded genuinely baffled. "And you know what else?" She gestured around the spacious room. "He didn't put up the Christmas decorations this year. And worst of all, there's no yummy food. I have to talk to my dad about it before I leave."

"You need help up to your rooms, or are you good?" Jude asked.

"We're good," Willa said.

"Thanks for walking with us." Finlay followed her friend across the saloon. But at the bottom of the grand staircase, they crashed into each other, laughing hysterically as they went down.

Two strong arms jerked her back up, and suddenly, the saloon was a blur. Even drunk off her ass, she recognized Jude's scent. "Mmm. You smell good." Her feet bumped into his hard, round butt, and her face was nestled into his neck. "Like snow. And sunshine. And pine trees. And manly man."

"Which room?" he asked.

"This one." Willa tried to stab her big brass key into the lock, but it didn't slide in.

Jude snatched it out of her hand and turned it neatly. Kneeing the door open, he carried Finlay to the bed as Willa went into the bathroom and closed the door. Right away, water started running through the pipes.

The room was dark, so he must not have seen the suitcase on the floor. He tripped but somehow managed to keep hold of Finlay, flipping around so he landed on the mattress with her safely cradled in his arms and lying on top of him.

His arms felt so good, his chest so warm and strong, that she couldn't help but cling to him. "Jude?" She sighed. He felt so good.

"Yeah?"

"Would you hold me? Please? I need a hug."

He answered by wrapping his arms around her more tightly.

"Yeah." She exhaled. "Just like that." He smelled like a piney forest and clean sheets, and she never wanted to be any place other than in his arms. "You make me feel safe."

"I'm not safe, Fee." His voice was a dangerous growl. "You understand? You are not safe with me."

His warning tripped a switch, heating her up and making her burn for him. Her hands wandered underneath his shirt and explored the hard planes and ridges and valleys of Mount Jude. "Mmm."

"You've got to stop making that sound," he said into her ear.

"But you feel so good."

"You've had too much to drink."

"Or maybe I've had just enough to relax me. I'm too uptight, don't you think? I take things too seriously." She loved the feel of his warm chest and silky hair. She loved the power of his big body. "I want to be just like this, only naked with you."

"Cut it out, Fee. Willa will be out of the bathroom any minute."

But his erection was hot and hard in his jeans, and she

could feel it on her stomach. Her nipples hardened, her fingers curled into his biceps, and her hips—God help her —rocked downward, sandwiching his cock between her thighs. Her body sizzled with pleasure.

To her surprise, he dug a hand under her ass and moved her up and down his shaft. "Not safe." He thrust a few times, roughly, to make a point. "You get me?"

Sensation streaked through her, an electric, neon burst of pleasure so intense every cell in her body lit up.

But it only lasted a moment before he peeled her off him.

"I'm not sorry." The world might be spinning, but she was sure that if she didn't have sex with him, she would die.

Jude got out of bed and rapped lightly on the bathroom door. Light pierced her vision, and she heard the two of them talking. The faucet ran. Pills shook in a bottle.

And then, Jude was back, setting a glass of water on her nightstand. He hauled her up the bed until her head rested on the pillow. He lowered his face—so close she thought he might kiss her. Instead, he whispered, "See you around, Ducky."

Chapter Eleven

When Jude opened his eyes, the sunlight blinded him.

Wait, what time is it?

Oh shit. Cody. Throwing off the covers, he jumped out of bed. He skipped the shower and hurried downstairs.

Still groggy, he found his dad in the kitchen. "Where is he?"

His dad had a hand braced on the stone counter and a leg crossed over the other. "Dropped him at school."

His dad's calm and steady demeanor eased his anxiety. "Good. Thanks for that. I know how much he wanted to go today." The last thing he wanted was to disappoint the boy.

"No problem."

Jude poured himself some coffee. "I haven't figured out how to make my work schedule fit with babysitting." But he'd better. He had him for another five weeks.

After the bar closed at two, he had to count the cash drawer and lock it in the safe, run a quick check of the booze, clean up…and a hundred other things. He didn't get home till four.

His father eyed him carefully. "I didn't ask you to work."

"Well, I'm not going to just live off you."

His dad's eyes darkened, his features pulling tight. "This is your home. You do whatever you need, and I'm here to support you. You get that?"

He looked away. "Sure." He hadn't lived here in twelve years. He didn't know what home felt like anymore.

His dad came right up to him. "You know I didn't send you away because you were a bad kid, right?"

"Yeah." What was his point?

"Judge Adams left us no choice. Either we got you out of town, or you boys would've wound up in juvie."

"Dad, I was there. I heard."

"Yeah? Then how come the other guys came back, but you never did?"

"Because I needed to cut ties." *To have an identity outside them.* "I didn't want to get drawn back into their shit."

"And how'd that work out for you?" Humor glinted in his dad's eyes.

"Not so good." He lifted his mug. "Here I am." Drawn right back into Marco's drama. But he wanted to make sure his dad understood. "I hope you know I never blamed you for what happened when I was a kid. You had four boys"—one of them a *baby*—"and no income. You did the best you could."

"Well, that's a nice way to say it, but nothing changes the fact that you were the oldest and got the worst of the situation. You've never been much of a talker, so I didn't know what was going on. I only knew you were taking care of your brothers. Now I know there was no one looking out for you."

"But that's the point. There was." *Marco.*

"Yeah, I get it." He stepped back to wipe the counter. "In any event, while you're here, I don't expect you to work. As far as I'm concerned, you've got one job, and that's to take care of the boy."

"Thanks, Dad. I appreciate it." He took a slug of Ava's dark roast. His dad might not drink coffee, but he kept it in the house for her and his sons.

"Now, if you decide to go through with the adoption, I assume you'll stay in town so we can help."

"I haven't given it a lot of thought, but yeah. That makes sense."

His dad gave a curt nod. "If that's the case, the bar's yours."

Jude straightened so quickly that the coffee sloshed in his mug. "What do you mean, it's mine? You're not retiring, are you?"

"Got other shit I want to do. And if it's something you'd like, I think now's a good time to start transitioning it over to you. If you want it."

"I don't think that's a good idea."

"Why not?"

"Dad, come on. I don't exactly get along with the people in this town."

"First of all, I don't give a shit what the ten thousand locals think about a kid who ran wild for a few years. You took my truck out for a joyride and knocked out someone's mailbox. So what? I care about the three million tourists who come to Wild Billy's each year to ride the mechanical bull. They're the ones who pay my bills."

A strange warmth flooded him, loosening the tightness in his chest that he lived with. "Fair point."

Right then, the front door opened, and boots treaded on the wood floors. Wyatt came into the kitchen holding a bag and a big box. "This is for you." He handed the package to his dad.

"What is it?" His dad grabbed a knife from the block and cut it open.

"Don't know." Wyatt tossed the bag onto the counter. "It was sitting on a snowbank on the driveway."

"Damn delivery drivers." Beneath the packing ice, his dad unearthed a fancy wooden board. "What is this?"

Jude pulled out the accompanying container and peeled off the plastic wrap to reveal a variety of meats, nuts, cheeses, and crackers. "It's a charcuterie board."

"The fuck?" His dad read the card. "It's from Finlay." He barked out a laugh. "She's thanking me with a meat board for letting her stay the night."

A clutch of protectiveness had him yanking the board out of his dad's hands. "That was nice of her."

"Not sayin' it wasn't." His dad pulled out almonds, figs, prosciutto, and olives. "Just didn't expect it."

Jude had to grin. It was a nice gesture but probably sent to the wrong crowd. Not because they didn't like the food. They did. They just weren't delicate eaters. One of them could polish it off single-handedly and then sit down to a full meal of steak, potatoes, garlic bread, chips, and guacamole.

Grabbing a butter knife, Wyatt cut off some soft herbed cheese and smeared it on a thin cracker.

"This is the kind of thing Ava would do," his dad said.

"Yeah, that's because she's civilized," Jude said.

Wyatt gave a chin nod to a bag he'd also brought in. "Got gloves for Snowfest. Don't know Cody's size, but they're pretty much one-size-fits-all."

Jude rooted through the bag, pulling out a tiny pair. "Appreciate it, man." He didn't know why his voice came out so rough. But his chest tightened, and he found himself caught between sorrow and a ferocious anger.

"You okay?" Wyatt asked.

Of course, his brother would notice. Jude held up the gloves. "He's just a kid."

"Yeah."

Wyatt had been the same way. A little, lost boy. Neglected. Teased relentlessly. No one looked out for him. "He needs protection. He needs…" He looked at his brother and dad. "Family."

"Yeah, he does." His dad clamped a hand on his shoulder. "But he's got it now. He's going to be all right."

Was he, though? Jude didn't even have temporary custody yet. He had no idea what life would be like for this boy.

"We'll make sure of it," Wyatt said.

Jude could almost believe them. His phone buzzed, and he glanced at the screen. He wouldn't usually answer if he didn't recognize the number, but now, he had Cody to worry about. "Yeah?"

"Is this Jude McKenna?" a woman asked.

"Who's this?" he asked in his *don't fuck with me* voice.

"This is Jenna Halston, a lawyer from Winter, Browne, and Sampson. We're handling the guardianship case?"

"Oh, right. Yeah, this is Jude. What can I do for you?"

"Well, we've got a hearing." She sounded pleased. "Can you be at the courthouse in twenty minutes?"

"I can. What do I need to bring with me?"

"Wear a coat and tie. If you can get your father to show up with you, that should help."

"Sounds like there's a possibility the judge will say no." He'd hoped the legal guardian's choice would be honored.

"There's always a possibility when a child's well-being's at stake."

Jude came to a stop the moment he entered the courtroom.

"Is there a problem?" the attorney asked.

"No, it's just… That's Judge Adams. I have history with him."

"Anything I should know about?" she asked.

"In high school, Jude was the getaway driver when his friends stole a car," his dad said.

"That's right. High school." That was twelve years ago. The judge would be a dick to hold that against him.

They all headed down the center aisle, parting when his dad, Ava, and brothers sat in the first row, and he took his seat beside his attorney. He barely registered the formalities of the bailiff announcing that court was in session and everyone rising as the judge entered, because he was preoccupied with his attorney's advice to keep his cool and be respectful, not defensive.

And the hope that, maybe, the judge had forgotten about him.

It's been twelve years. He's seen hundreds of cases since then.

Once finished, Judge Adams peered over his glasses. "Mr. McKenna, let's catch up. In the twelve years since you last stood before me, I became the Wyoming chess champion two years in a row, a grandfather of seven, and, if I may brag, quite a good pickleball player. What have you accomplished?"

"Your honor, I've served eight years in the Marines."

"I thank you for your service. And how have you filled the remaining four years?"

"I'm a bartender, currently residing in Key Largo." He wished he had a more impressive résumé, but he'd still done well for himself. "I also flip bars. So I'm comfortable financially."

Judge Adam held Jude's gaze, his expression unreadable. "I've read Mr. Rossi's affidavit. I'm curious why he chose you."

"I grew up with his grandson, Marco, Cody's father." It was true Jude didn't share much, but if he wanted to win over this judge, now was the time. "I don't have a lot of memories from before I moved to Calamity. I remember a big pile of presents under a Christmas tree, and my mom reading books to me before bed."

She'd had soft hair and a soothing voice, but he'd long forgotten what she looked like. His only recollection was how she'd made him feel. "I remember the shock of moving into the bike club when I was six. The specific age sticks with me because I'd just started kindergarten and had a crush on a blue-eyed, blonde girl named Melissa and didn't want to move away from her."

Laughter in the courtroom had Jude pausing, but the judge didn't crack a smile.

So he drew in a breath and continued. "Anyhow, I'd just moved into the club, and I remember being outside with a bunch of kids. We heard gunfire—something I'd obviously never heard before." In his peripheral vision, he saw his dad stiffen. Yeah, he'd never shared that one. "Scared the life out of me. Turns out, some of the members were drunk and shooting bottles lined up on a wall. But it was Marco who grabbed me and brought me to his hideout, a place he went when things got too crazy. And it was Marco who protected me at school when kids made fun of the way I dressed."

"Are you making excuses for your dangerous and reckless behavior as a teenager?" Judge Adams asked.

"No, sir. I'm trying to explain my loyalty to Marco."

The judge made a gesture with his hand. *Go on.*

"I know I did a lot of stupid things, but that ended by the time I hit high school because I had a dad who cared. Who disciplined me and had expectations of my behavior."

For a moment, the judge's hard mask softened.

It gave Jude hope. "Marco didn't have any of that. I'm the man I am today because of my father, and Marco turned out the way he did because he was raised without parents in the club. I want to give Cody the life Marco should've—no, *deserved*—to have."

Judge Adam's head tilted as he gave him an assessing look. Something that looked like approval registered in his eyes. "Besides your family, who will you spend time with while you're in town? Your former friends from the club? If they need a getaway driver, for example, will they call you?"

This is bullshit. I'm not that kid anymore. "No, sir. I've cut ties with everyone. Look, I understand that I'm set in your memory as a troublemaker, but I'm not the same man at thirty that I was at eighteen. And there's no one better to be this boy's guardian than me because I won't let him take the path I took."

The judge nodded. "You're right. You *are* set in my mind as a troublemaker, and after three decades on this bench, I've come to the conclusion that most people don't change. Because it's not your circumstance that matters. It's how you handle it. You've shown me your character, and it doesn't give me confidence in your ability to raise a five-year-old boy. Frankly, I'm not convinced the best choice is a single bartender whose motto is 'live full throttle.'"

Before he could articulate his defense, he heard a rustling sound, and a familiar voice filled the courtroom.

"Your honor, if Jude's single, then he's got some explaining to do." Everyone swung around in their seats to find Finlay holding up her left ring finger. "Because we're engaged."

Chapter Twelve

THE TENSION IN THE ROOM SNAPPED LIKE A LIVE wire.

"Is that so?" Judge Adams asked. "Miss O'Neill, two days ago, you ran away from your wedding to Matt Jones, and now, you want me to believe you're suddenly engaged to *this* man?"

"This man" is a United States Marine who has a clean record and a successful business.

It didn't matter that he'd shaved off his beard and borrowed his dad's khakis, coat, tie, and dress shoes because Jude was frozen in the judge's mind as a scruffy teenager. But the question wasn't directed at him, and Finlay had just dropped a bomb in the courthouse.

How the hell's she going to explain this one?

"Well, you don't know the whole story." She sounded almost defiant. "Jude McKenna's the love of my life. We were torn apart the night of our prom when you sent him away. Yes, he was the getaway driver, but did you know he was on his way to pick me up when Marco called and asked for a ride? He didn't commit the crime."

"Aiding and abetting a criminal is still a crime, Ms. O'Neill."

Jude watched her carefully to see if she'd lose steam after being called out. But she didn't even flinch.

"He knows he shouldn't have responded to their call, but there was history there and a deep sense of loyalty. Since then, he's served in the Marines and built a life outside of Calamity with the express purpose of reinventing himself."

"I always wondered why he was wearing a bow tie in that mug shot," the judge said. "Still, Miss O'Neill—"

But Finlay held up a hand. "Please, let me finish. When he came to town to see Cody, he heard I was getting married, and he told me he still loved me and that if I held on to any of the feelings I once had for him, then he wanted us to be together. And I'm sorry for what I did to Matt—I truly am—but the only thing we shared was the same goals. We're not, nor have we ever been, the loves of each other's lives, and I will not apologize for saving him from a doomed marriage and giving myself the happy ever after I've dreamed about for half my life."

Anyone could see the judge's demeanor change. Jude's attorney looked like she was reading a romance novel and had just gotten to the swoony part. Hell, even he was moved by her speech.

"I see." The judge turned back to Jude. "So if I place him with you, where will Cody live? Are you taking him to Florida?"

"No, your honor," Finlay said. "We're going to live in

my house on Bloom Lane." She smiled proudly. "We're going to be a family."

His dad stood. "And they'll spend Christmas with us."

Boone rose, too. "My dad makes the best chocolate chip pancakes you've ever tasted."

Wyatt stayed seated but chimed in. "And I have a litter of puppies that need a good home if anybody wants one."

Laughter filled the courtroom, and the judge looked at Ava. "And I assume you're going to take the boy caroling and buy the family matching onesies?"

Ava grinned. "And if I wasn't going to, I sure will now."

The judge lifted his gavel. "All right, take the McKenna show on the road and get out of my courtroom. The petition is signed."

"I'm going to get arrested." Anxiety had her pacing the room she'd shared with Willa. "Why didn't I give Matt back this stupid engagement ring? The fake engagement idea would never have occurred to me if I hadn't been wearing it. I mean, it's so traceable. You just have to check my social media to see it's the ring Matt gave me."

"Are you done?" Her best friend had landed in New York less than an hour ago and was currently in a cab heading to her apartment.

But Finlay's mind was racing. "And what about the position I just put Jude in?" A tremor of fear ran through her. "If he gets arrested, too, then what happens to Cody?"

"Fee, listen to me. You weren't sworn in, so no one's

arresting you for lying to a judge. That's number one. If he does find out the truth, there might be consequences, but you're not going to jail. Number two, you were thinking about that little boy. If Jude didn't get custody, they would've put him in foster care. The judge expected his dad and brothers to stand up for him, but you're outside the McKenna clan. In Calamity, you're as trustworthy as they come. Fee, you saved the situation."

That made sense. Finlay pressed a hand to the cold window. It was a front-facing room that overlooked the town green. Blinking multicolored lights festooned the gazebo, and town trucks unloaded folding tables and erected white tents in preparation for Snowfest. "I hate that the judge holds his childhood against him. Shouldn't he be impressed by how well he's turned his life around? He's a good man. He's got such a big heart. I know he looks all grumpy and dark and broody—"

"*We* know that, but keep in mind who his friends were. From the judge's perspective, he hung around hoodlums."

"Hoodlums." Finlay smiled. "Okay, Grandma."

"Do you remember the big freeze during freshman year of high school?"

"Of course."

"There were parts of town that didn't get their power back for ten days. My dad let people stay in the B&B for free. And guess what Marco did?"

"I don't even want to know."

"He raided housekeeping's utility cart. Yes, that's right. He stuffed complimentary soap and shampoo into his pants. I mean, he would've stolen the false teeth out of an old man's water glass if he'd found them just sitting there."

A knock on the door wiped the smile right off her face. Terror sliced through her. "They're here."

"Who's there?" Willa asked.

"The police. I don't know. Maybe Family Services."

"So Family Services is showing up at the inn to cuff you and do a cavity search? Is that how it works now?"

"Okay, but who else would it be?"

"In an inn? How about housekeeping?"

Reality broke through. "You're right. But just in case it *is* the police, I'll come clean. I'll tell them I acted impulsively because it looked like the judge wasn't going to grant Jude custody, and they have to know Jude's a good man, and there's no one better to take care of Cody than him."

"I'll make you a deal. If it's the police, I'll walk naked through Times Square with a sign around my neck that says, *Spank me.*"

"This conversation is being recorded for quality assurance purposes and to hold you to your promises," Finlay said on her way to the door. "Stay on the line with me."

"Switch the call to FaceTime so I can watch them drop you to the ground and handcuff you."

"That's not funny." Of course she trusted her friend, but she was a hot mess. It was enough that she'd blown up her life and was going to lose her house, but now, she might've compromised Cody's safety.

She peered through the peephole to find a broad chest covered in a white dress shirt, and when she opened the door, she found it wasn't the police at all. It was a tall, broad-shouldered man with green eyes and a mouth that unleashed her deepest, darkest desires. "Jude?" Without his beard, boots, and worn jeans, she almost didn't recognize him. "What're you doing here?"

"Figured you'd be spiraling."

"What? No." She sputtered. "That's not…" She let out a huff and brought the phone back to her ear. "It's not the police."

"No shit." And then, Willa shouted, "She's spiraling," making Jude chuckle.

"You two suck," Finlay said.

"But you love me anyway," her friend said. "Let me know what happens."

"I will. Thank you." After they disconnected, Finlay stood aside to let him in but couldn't help checking the hallway.

"Coast clear?" Jude asked.

She closed the door and bolted it. "Yes. And I don't know what led you to believe I wasn't handling the situation well. I was perfectly composed in the courtroom."

"Until you ran out of the building like your ass was on fire."

She clasped her hands together. "Well, Jude. I might've ruined everything for you. What was I thinking, announcing an engagement…" She held up her finger. "While wearing Matt's ring? But how *dare* he reduce you to a single bartender—"

"That's what I am."

"No, you're not. You're so much more."

"Well." Pink tinged his cheeks. "It all worked out."

"We don't really know that yet." There was one part that could blow the whole deception wide open. "Not only aren't we engaged, but I might not even have a house."

"Yeah, that's what I came to talk to you about."

"The house?"

"I don't know how it works—whether Family Services will check on me and Cody—but since I have a history with this judge—"

"And I've just told them you'll be living on Bloom Lane." Her eyelids squeezed shut. "I can't believe I did this to you. You were probably hoping to live with your dad." How did she fix it? "Look, I have to put it on the market, but I don't have to move out right away. It'll take time to get financing, and, you know, there's escrow. So we should be okay. And if someone wants to move in sooner, then we can live at your dad's house. I don't think the judge will care about our address as long as we're a couple and giving Cody a good home."

"That won't be necessary."

What have you done? "Look, right now, we're the only ones who know. Well, except for Willa. If we live together for the next six weeks, we can pull this off. For Cody's sake. I promise you won't be responsible for me. You can do your own thing. Work…" *Hook up with tourists at Wild Billy's.* "I won't cramp your style. We'll hardly even see each other."

His expression changed. "My style, huh?" Was he amused by all this?

"Yes. You just go on about your business like I don't exist."

"But you do exist."

She grew even more agitated. She couldn't tell if he

was playing with her, and that made her want to clarify. "Just because I forced this situation on you doesn't mean I expect us to be something we're not. You don't have to entertain me."

The longer she babbled, the higher his brows arched, and the wider his smirk grew.

"I'm just *saying* we're not a couple. There won't be any expectations. No…touching or whatever."

"Well, there might be a little touching, right?"

Her heart flipped over. What did he mean?

He came closer. "Like when we're both reaching for the same mug, our hands might brush. Or if there's a storm, and the power goes out, we might bump into each other in the hallway. I'm a pretty big guy. I might knock you over, and I'll have to catch you"—he put his hands on her hips—"like this, so you don't fall."

"I didn't mean that kind of touching."

"No? What kind did you mean?" His fingertips landed on her cheek, soft as a butterfly, and he tucked a strand of hair behind her ear. "Something a little dirtier?"

He was messing with her, and she didn't appreciate it. "I only meant you don't owe me anything. I have no expectations."

"Fee." He tipped her chin with a finger. "I'm not mad at what you did. You stood up for me, and I appreciate it. But yes, I do think we have to live together for the next six weeks."

His scent filled her senses, making her acutely aware of him. Her pulse fluttered in her throat, and she had a hard time breathing. "In my house?"

"Yes." He grew serious. "Listen, I heard what your ex

said yesterday, that he'd give you a week to come up with his half of the down payment."

Where had she been when they'd had that conversation? She was pretty sure she'd walked Matt to his car. That meant Jude and his family were in the garage, listening.

Awesome.

"I can give you the money."

"No." She stepped back from him so fast she bumped into the bed frame. "Thank you, but no. And before you say anything, Willa's already offered. I'm not borrowing money from anyone."

"Good. Because it's not a loan."

"I'm not taking your money."

"Hear me out. Right now, you're supposed to be on your honeymoon. Then you're off for winter break, right?"

"Right."

"That's three weeks. The next three weeks, he can go to and from school with you, so that covers the whole timeframe."

"And you want to hire me?"

"I do. And I can pay you exactly what you need to buy him out."

"Are you serious?" She was afraid to get her hopes up. Could this be real?

"I've done the math, and for six weeks of work, it comes out to the same amount."

"Well, imagine that." She didn't believe him for one second. "How convenient."

"Let's remember this is happening over the holidays," he said. "So it's more than reasonable. And my dad's buddies with the bank president, so if you can afford the mortgage on your own, we can refinance the house and put it in your name."

"Seriously?" *So, wait.* Did she really get to keep her house? Excitement bubbled up. "How much will you really need me, though? He'll be with you and your family a lot, and you work at night, so maybe you just need a babysitter?"

"Are you talking yourself out of the job?"

She laughed. "I guess I am."

"Look, it's the holidays. I want to spend time with my family. Go skiing. Shit like that. And my work hours are off from the rest of the world, so yeah, Cody needs someone who'll be there just for him."

She didn't like the sound of this. "What do you mean?"

"As a bartender, I'm not home till four in the morning. Which means I sleep late, run some errands, and then, it's back to the bar."

"I'm not following. You're busy all day, and you work all night. When are you going to see Cody? What about this family Christmas you promised the judge?"

"I'll be around. Just like any parent who works full-time, goes to the grocery store, has appointments... You know."

Yes, she did. She knew all too well how severely lonely that life was. "When exactly will you be around Cody?"

He shrugged, clearly uncomfortable. "When I can."

"Deal's off." She couldn't believe his attitude. She'd stood up for this man in a court of law. "I'm willing to help you, but that doesn't mean you get to run off. You're his guardian, and it sounds like you're hiring me so you don't have to do anything."

He hardened. "I'm a bartender. Those are my hours."

"Not for the next six weeks, they're not. Not if you want me to be his nanny. This child's mother abandoned him. His father died. His grandfather left him in the care of a total stranger. It's not your fault, but Carlo did nothing to help Cody transition. He didn't give him a few days to get to know you. He literally handed over his grandson to a man he'd never met."

Awareness sharpened his gaze. "You make a good point."

"This child comes to school with dirty clothes and no lunch, and his attendance is irregular. He deserves a guardian who cares about him, and if you want me to help you out, I'll only do it if you take a real role in this."

"I hear what you're saying." He reached for a beard that wasn't there and wound up rubbing his clean-shaven jaw. "The thing is, he's going to get attached, and then, in six weeks, we'll probably be gone, too."

So it wasn't because he wanted to party or hook up. It was fear. "I don't have any control over the outcome of Cody's situation, but I can be damn sure that, while he's in my care, he gets all the love and stability he deserves."

"Yeah, okay. I hear you."

"Are you sure? You'll be there for Cody? Not just hand him off to me?"

He rubbed the back of his neck. "Yeah. I guess so."

"I don't believe you." She headed for the door, ready to show him out. "We don't have a deal."

"Fee. All you have to do is babysit, and you get to keep your dream house."

"If you think a house has a higher value to me than a little boy, then you don't know me at all. I don't care how much money you're going to throw at me, I won't let anyone else treat that boy carelessly."

He caught her upper arm and pulled her to him. "This is dangerous. You get that, right? Playing happy family on Bloom Lane? It's going to end badly."

She held her ground. "I won't do it any other way."

"Fine." He let her go. "I know you're right. I'll be there for Cody, and I'll give him the best Christmas he's ever had."

"I doubt that'll be hard, but okay. We have a deal." She held out her hand, and they shook.

"This is a small town. How're you going to handle it when people find out you dipped on Matt only to wind up engaged to a guy like me? Living in the same house you and your fiancé bought together? The town sweetheart isn't going to come out looking too good."

"You know, not everybody's as obsessed with their reputations as you are. Some of us just want to build a beautiful life and be happy."

"And pretending to be married to me and a mother to a kid that's not yours is going to get you there?"

Well, no. She didn't want to play happy family.

She wanted to be part of one.

Chapter Thirteen

SINCE FINLAY AND HER EX HAD ONLY MOVED INTO the house a week prior to the wedding, they hadn't even finished unpacking boxes. He'd already taken his things—and that included the couch his mom had given them, the TV, and the fancy grill he'd bought with this year's bonus—so she didn't have much to do to prepare for her new roommates.

Mostly, she had to finish putting her stuff away. She unloaded quickly and methodically, leaving the empty boxes in the hallway. She'd break them down and get rid of them right before Cody got home from school.

It should be sad, she knew that. She should be crying for all she'd lost.

For the *husband* she'd lost. The babies she'd planned on having.

Instead, her head was spinning with the absolute thrill of being with Jude McKenna. Even if it was fake, she got to live with the man she'd once wanted body and soul.

And pretending to be married to me and a mother to a kid that's not yours is going to get you there?

Well, that was the thing. It would be the worst kind of torture. But if she went in knowing it was temporary, maybe she'd be okay.

And you know what? Maybe living with Jude would make her see him in a whole new light. Maybe he'd be all dark and moody and keep to himself. Or he'd chew loudly. See, those were all the details she didn't know about him. He might not brush his teeth every day. That would be gross. Or what if he left clipped toenails all over the bathroom counter?

No, you know what would really do it? Turn her off completely? If he ignored Cody. If he scrolled through his phone instead of actually getting on the floor and doing puzzles with him. If he didn't tuck him in at night—well, she wouldn't stand for that.

As a child, she'd put herself to bed most nights, and the loneliness… Yeah, it wasn't something she could bear to watch with Cody.

After cleaning the bathrooms, she checked the time. Jude would be there any minute. She collected the packing paper and hauled it into the garage. Both the recycling bin and garbage can were full, so she rolled them down the driveway to the curb.

The cloud cover made it extra cold, and light snow flurries had crystals dancing and swirling around her. What would Jude think of her neighborhood? It didn't fit him at all.

Across the street, as a mom unloaded groceries from her SUV, her toddlers made snow angels on the lawn. *I want that. I want that so much.* Next door, a neighbor chatted with a friend through the window of an idling car. Plumes of exhaust rose into the frigid air.

She loved how everyone went all-out with Christmas decorations. Strings of lights dangled off eaves and wrapped around bushes. Front doors held wreaths with bright red bows, and giant ornaments hung heavily from branches. Some of the lawns had blow-up Santas, snowmen, and reindeer. It was magical.

When she started to turn back, she noticed a woman crossing the street.

Oh. Excitement sped through her. *Is this it? Is it happening?* She wasn't sure if this was the woman who hosted the annual Christmas open house, but if it were… she'd waited a lifetime for this moment.

She checked her mailbox every single day in the hopes of getting that coveted invitation. Silly to have worried. Of course, she'd be invited. She lived there now.

With a welcoming smile, the older woman approached, clutching a dark green envelope in her gloved hand. "Well, hello there, neighbor. I'm Janice Atherton."

"Finlay O'Neill. So nice to meet you."

"Are you all settled in?" The woman tipped her head to the house.

"Getting there." Finlay had wondered what kind of reception she'd get after running out on Matt, but it looked like everything would be all right. That was awesome because she didn't have grandparents, so the idea of this kind woman taking her under her wing just made her feel all kinds of good things.

"Well, that's just great." The woman smiled. "Let me

know if there's anything I can do. I was an interior designer back in the day, so if you need help with décor, I'd be glad to take a look."

"I would love that." On a teacher's salary, that wouldn't happen anytime soon, but it'd still be fun to make a batch of shortbread and a pot of tea and at least talk to her.

The woman's arm lifted.

Here it comes. The invitation I've dreamed of getting since I was a teenager. She had pictures on her vision board of candlelit homes, a grand Christmas tree laden with glittering ornaments, guests dressed up in holiday outfits—the women in sparkling jewels, the men in sweaters and slacks—and a buffet table crowded with festive platters.

Just when Mrs. Atherton started to extend her arm, a motorcycle roared up the street, and the woman froze.

The envelope hung between them. Not close enough for Finlay to take it.

The woman glanced around, as if making sure there were no kids for the rider to mow down. But it was Jude, and he'd never be that careless. After parking in the driveway, he got off the bike and set the helmet on the seat.

She had to make a split-second decision to either address the fiancé switcheroo or ignore it. But with Cody's safety at stake, she had to keep up the fake engagement. "Hey, honey. Come over and say hello."

He sauntered over, cutting across the snow-covered lawn, and just stared the woman down.

Not the time to scare the neighbors, honey. "Mrs. Atherton, this is—"

"I know Mr. McKenna." The woman's mask of politeness turned brittle.

Clearly, this woman had a history with Jude. Well, Finlay wouldn't allow him to feel unwelcome over something he'd done as a child. She slid an arm through his and drew him up close. "He's my fiancé."

For the first time, Finlay understood the expression *the color drained from her face.*

"I see." The woman lowered her arm. "Well, I'll get out of your hair and let you settle in." With that, she turned and walked away, taking the envelope with her.

"What was that about?" Jude asked.

"She was just welcoming us to the neighborhood." She hurried back to the garage, her eyes stinging.

Jude followed her, hitting the remote to close the door and plunging them into darkness. She was about to head into the kitchen when his deep voice issued a command. "Hold up."

She kept her back to him. He didn't need to see how upset she was.

"Let me explain. A bunch of us went to the bonfire out at the Anderson's farm back when they hosted them for the Fourth of July. We had no business being there, and her son let us know that. He and Marco got into a fight. I wasn't part of it. I'm not the reason her son went to the hospital."

"No, Jude." He'd gotten it all wrong, but he didn't need to know he'd cost her that invitation. She turned to face him, his features harsh in the dim light. "I'm not angry with you. Not at all."

"Then what's the problem?"

"It's nothing."

"Look, if this is going to work, if we're going to *live*

together, then we have to be honest. Besides, I can read you like a book."

"It's too dark in here to see anything." That wasn't entirely true. Light came from the bottom of the garage door.

"I see you. I always see you. Now, tell me what's wrong."

Oh, that was really sweet. And had he moved closer? She didn't think so, but it felt like he was crowding her against the door. "I've done a really stupid thing, and now I'm dealing with the consequences."

"Meaning?"

"Well, I mean, two days ago, I was living here with Matt, and now, I'm here with a different guy and a little boy. How do I explain it?"

He gave a curt nod, as if to say, *I can fix that.* "We don't have to live together to be engaged. Cody and I can stay with my dad."

No, she wanted them there with her. She wanted her house to smell of pine from a freshly cut tree and warm, baking cookies. She wanted to hear laughter coming from another room while she wrapped presents. But also, his idea wouldn't work. "Your dad lives too far away, especially in winter. I'd hate for Cody to miss more school when it's so important to him."

"I'll do whatever's best for you. I don't want to embarrass you in your new neighborhood."

"I think we have to remember why we're doing this." Especially since, after the way that woman had treated Jude, Finlay's interest in making friends had dropped several notches. "The only thing that matters is Cody, and as long as we give him the best Christmas, I don't care what they think of me."

"You might not feel that way after we move out. They're going to be your neighbors for the rest of your life, and we'll be long gone."

It stung to hear that. *We'll be long gone.* But it was a good reminder not to get too attached. *This is just temporary.*

And it wasn't even the point. "I don't think there's much I can do about it. I've just become the woman who ran from one fiancé into the arms of another. It is what it is. You and Cody are moving in, and if they don't want to invite me to their block parties, then they can go—" Her jaw snapped shut before she said a cuss word.

"Fuck themselves. Come on." He tipped her chin. "You can say it. They're just words."

She tried not to swear at all. If it became a habit, it'd slip out in front of her kids, and she didn't want to do that. But this situation merited it. "They can go fuck themselves." Ooh, that felt good.

His thumb and finger tightened on her chin, and his gaze lingered on her mouth. "Say it again. Only take out all the other words."

She laughed. "You're an idiot. And you've just proven my other point. This situation I forced on you is going to cramp your style."

"That's the second time you've said that. Why don't you just tell me what 'style' is code for?"

Did he really need her to spell it out? "You're a man with needs. If we're pretending to be engaged, you can't hook up with other women. It's a small town, and people will talk."

"Then how will I get my needs met?"

"Well, I don't know. Maybe you can go to Victor or Driggs. Or Idaho Falls or something."

"You want me to drive an hour and a half one way to get my needs met? Well, which is it, Fee? Yesterday, you said you wanted me to spend time with the boy. Now, it's okay if I spend three hours on the road to get my daily needs met? And that's just commuting time. How long can I stay with my 'friend'? Do I have time for a second round?" He grabbed his genitals and gave them a shake. "I'm pretty quick to reload. And it might make sense to get as much out of my system as I can with each session."

"Oh, cut it out. You can make fun of me all you want, but you know you're going to need…"

"To fuck some bitches?"

"Okay, forget it." She laughed. "I'm sorry for bringing it up. I feel awful for forcing you into this situation, and I'm nervous about how it's going to work out." She tried to open the door, but he held it firmly. "Can we just drop it?"

"Fee, I don't plan on embarrassing you, and I can go six weeks without getting laid."

"Okay, but I don't think a day went by in high school that you didn't have a girl grinding on you."

"Well, I'm thirty now. Maybe I don't need a daily grind."

"Please. You reek of testosterone. Your pheromones are practically radioactive. I can't imagine much has changed."

"You know, you're the one who keeps talking about it.

Maybe the problem isn't me. Maybe you're the one who needs a daily grind."

"No, trust me. I'm fine."

"I see. I'm getting the picture now. You just got out of a relationship where you got it on the regular, and now, you're gonna be wanting to get some. Tell you what, since we're living under the same roof, how about I give you permission to grab me every now and then."

"Grab you?"

"Sure, when we pass each other in the hallway, and you're jonesin' for some action. You turn around…" His finger made a circling motion, and he popped his butt out and did a slow twerk. "And grind on my dick."

She burst out laughing at how ridiculous he looked. "You win. Conversation dropped. You can just drag a woman into the bathroom at Wild Billy's and bang her brains out."

"Huh. That's a very specific scenario. So specific it makes me think it might be *your* fantasy." He backed her against the door. Lifting a lock of hair off her shoulder, he twirled it around a finger. When she sucked in a breath, his eyes went hot. "Oh, yeah. You're definitely the one with needs to be met."

Her heart pounded, and her panties got wet. "Trust me, I have no interest in having sex in a bar."

"In case the police come in and arrest you?"

"It's public indecency. You could get arrested for something like that."

"Actually, it's called indecent exposure." His eyes were full of humor. "Public lewdness. And depending on how hot it gets, it could even be disorderly conduct."

"Sounds like you know your way around bar hookups."

He chuckled. "I'm a bartender. I've seen it all."

"Yeah, but have you done it all?"

"There you go again. So interested in my sex life."

"Well, sure. You were like this mythic character. You walked the halls like a king, and all the girls were your concubines…" She wasn't ashamed to admit it. "Sure, I was."

"Was or are?"

"Both." Something about her honesty shifted the balance of power. He went from teasing her to looking out of his element. And that emboldened her. "I've always wondered what it would be like with you. I had a lot of fantasies as a girl when I didn't know what French kissing meant. When the only sex I'd ever seen came from PG-13 movies."

"And now that you've fucked?"

She suspected his crudeness was a way of regaining his footing in the conversation. But in the darkness and having spent some time with him, she wasn't afraid to tell the truth. "Now, I want different things."

He licked his bottom lip, and his features hardened. He caged her in, and even though their bodies didn't touch, she could feel desire radiating off him like heat. "Different how?"

"Someone who's not so careful with me." She shook her head because that wasn't it. "You can feel it in the way a man touches you, kisses you."

"Feel what?"

"How much he wants you. And with Matt, I never felt swept away. I never felt he had to have me."

He gripped her arm and yanked her closer. "Say that name again, and I'm going to have to kiss it out of your mouth, you hear me?"

"You mean..." That rough voice, the clutch of his hold... It sent a punch of adrenaline through her. Her body went hot and electric, and she literally could not help herself from unleashing the beast. "Matt?"

"Dammit, Fee." He gripped her wrists and held them over her head, his hips slamming her ass against the door. With his gaze locked on her mouth, he leaned in and plundered her with a voracious kiss.

This man took what he wanted. He didn't wait. He didn't try to seduce. He groaned deep in his throat while his tongue took possession and swept out every last remnant of the man who'd come before him.

The passion of his kiss swept her under, and her mind shut down. She became pure hot lust. Wrenching her wrists free, she wrapped her arms around his neck and grabbed a fistful of his silky hair at the base of his neck.

The hard tug unleashed something in him because he reached for her ass and lifted her. Stepping between her legs, he rocked his thick cock against her. The rhythmic pressure on her clit had sensation exploding in a shower of fiery sparks.

She wanted his hunger, his clutch, and his ferocious desire for her to never end.

Because it spilled into the lonely corners of her heart, it heated the places that had long gone cold and made her feel vitally alive. It yanked her from the soft space of her dream world and dropped her into a sizzling, raw reality she knew she'd never want to leave.

And just when the pulse between her legs grew unbearable, he set her on her feet, spun her around, and braced her hands on the wall. He unzipped her jeans and reached beneath the elastic of her panties. The moment his finger grazed over her clit, a flash fire tore across her skin.

"You're so fucking wet." As he started to yank down her pants, a rumble of engines ripped through the haze of intimacy. He froze.

She needed his touch, his urgency…his friction. Glancing over her shoulder, she eyed him with desperation. *Come on.*

"We've got company." He lowered his chest to her back. "Dammit."

Chapter Fourteen

As the trucks turned into her driveway, she jerked up her jeans and quickly zipped and buttoned them.

But before she could hit the remote, he cupped her chin. "You okay?" He held her gaze.

"If you regret what you just did to me, I'm kicking you out on your ass."

He cracked a grin, his thumb stroking her jaw. "Not a chance."

Engines cut off. Car doors slammed shut. "I don't know who it could be. I'm not expecting anyone." She punched the button, and the garage door rattled and creaked as it opened. Light flooded the space. Outside, two giant black pickups were parked in the driveway, and a moving van was pulling up to the curb. "What's going on?"

But Jude already was on the move, greeting his two brothers. "What're you guys doing here? Does anybody have a *job*?"

"Not a lot of forest fires in the dead of winter," Boone said.

"We're not set up for company," Jude said.

"That's why we're here, big brother." Boone clapped him on the shoulder.

Wyatt approached her. "Heard fuckface took most of the furniture, so we got some stuff."

"Well, I mean, he took what he owned," Finlay said, painfully self-conscious. Was her hair a tangled mess? Did her lips look red? Could they tell what she'd been doing?

And why did she find it more thrilling than embarrassing?

Because I've never had that just-fucked look.

And I think I like it.

"How'd you hear about that?" Jude asked.

Wyatt pointed down the street. "Bernese Mountain dog got into it with a snowmobile. Owner saw your ex take his couch."

"So you brought me a new one?" She couldn't believe it.

"Yeah," Boone said. "But also, Miss Marlee's son's a probie, and she told him she saw a bunch of frat guys clearing out the house. She said you could land a plane on that big screen TV." He tipped his chin to the back of his truck. "So we got you an even bigger one."

"You guys." She was unbelievably touched. "Thank you. This is so nice." Across the street, curtains parted, and her neighbor peered out. Finlay didn't know what they'd think of the big, scary men with tattoos and black trucks, but Jude's family was so wonderful, she'd be damned if anyone made them feel unwelcome.

The passenger door on the box truck opened, and yet another brother came out. He was big, muscular, and rough-looking.

Jude headed toward him. "What the hell're you doing here? You've got a game tomorrow."

"Oh shit. You're right. Thanks for the reminder." Even though he wasn't as tall, the quarterback pulled his older brother into a hug, lifting his feet off the ground.

Jude got free and shoved his younger brother. "You get kicked off the team?"

"No. But you've got a lot going on, and I wanted to see how you're doing, meet the kid."

"I'm fine." Jude gestured to his family. "These clowns shouldn't have involved you."

"Hey, who're you calling a clown?" Boone grinned.

"You're going to pay a big-ass fine for leaving your team," Jude grumbled.

"Since when is money more important than family?" the football player asked.

Jude stood back to let her into the circle. "Finlay, this is my baby brother, Decker."

Never in her life had she felt petite—until she stood beside these giant, rugged men.

"Hi, it's nice to meet you."

"Nice to meet you, too. Now, I know you stepped in to be his fake fiancée, but I don't know how you two know each other." Decker wagged a finger between Jude and her.

"We were friends in high school," she said. "And now, I'm helping with Cody. I'm the nanny."

"But we're not talking about the fake part, okay?" Jude

asked. "I already have enough shit stacked against me with the judge. That can't get out."

"Got it," Decker said with a nod.

"Now, come on." Jude stalked down the driveway. "Dad's unloading by himself."

As they all headed to the street, Gunnar set aside the dolly to hug his sons.

"You buy out a whole furniture store?" Jude asked.

"Pretty much," Decker said.

"You've got the boy for six weeks." His dad went back to stacking boxes. "And it's Christmas. You want it to feel like home for him, don't you?"

Jude looked from one man to the next. She didn't think she'd ever seen him display his feelings so clearly. He seemed unable to speak.

Finlay stepped in. "That's so nice, Gunnar. Thank you." She hugged him, breathing in the scent of leather and pine. And even though the gifts weren't meant for her, she said, "This means so much to us."

"All right." Gunnar patted her back awkwardly. "Now, don't go sending me another meat board. Let's get this done."

But as they all started for the trucks, Jude stood there, unseeing, his eyes clouded with emotion. She didn't even ask if he was okay because he clearly wasn't. So she reached for his hand.

He could've brushed it aside or given a polite squeeze and release. But to her surprise, he clasped it, holding it tightly for a moment as though it were a lifeline. He lowered his chin and blinked.

"Good to be home?" she whispered.

"Yeah."

The four men did all the heavy lifting, relying on Finlay to show them where to put things. It would've taken her a decade or more to acquire the furniture and toys they'd bought, so she was overwhelmed by their generosity.

When they finished unloading the truck, they brought in their tool kits to assemble bookcases and bed frames and peel the plastic wrap off the mattresses. Finlay didn't have siblings, so she wasn't used to the way they constantly joked with each other, recounting childhood stories and making fun of each other's jobs.

She loved every second of it and got to see Jude in a whole new light. He might act like a broody loner, but he was surrounded by love and support. For some reason, he didn't feel he deserved it, and she wondered why when it was clear his siblings looked up to him.

With an armful of moving blankets, Gunnar crossed her living room that now had a couch, loveseat, ottoman, television, and media center. Her four bedrooms were fully furnished, and one of them doubled as a guest room and a play area for Cody. It was filled with books, a kitchen with fake food, several Duplo Lego sets, and art supplies—including a finger-painting kit.

"I can't thank you enough for everything you've done," she called out to him. "You've given Cody a real home."

He gave a curt nod and headed for the door, but she couldn't miss the pink staining his cheeks.

Was filling up her entire house over the top for a six-week visit? Yep. But Jude's family expressed themselves through action. And she heard them loud and clear. They loved Jude and wanted him to come home.

The man himself came trampling down the stairs. "We're about finished up there, and we're running out of time. What's next?"

They were trying to get everything done before Ava brought the boy home from school. "The last thing we have to do is decorate."

He eyed the stacks of boxes. "Do we really need all this crap?"

"Maybe not, but did I need a ping-pong table in the basement?"

Jude cracked a grin. "That's my dad's way of making sure everyone spends time here so Cody has a big family around over the holidays."

"I love that." For Cody, but also for herself. She'd always wanted a full house.

"Yeah, he's a good guy. Well, let's get started." He pulled out his folding knife and slit each box right down the middle of the packing tape.

She stepped in to pull out the contents. "You have the best family."

"Yeah. They're cool."

She set all the ornaments and tree lights on the floor by the hearth. It seemed a shame to stay away just because of encounters like he'd had with her neighbor. "How come you didn't tell Mrs. Atherton the truth? You had a chance to say you had nothing to do with what happened to her son."

He'd finished opening the boxes, so she handed him an evergreen and berry-laden garland. Just for a moment, his hands stilled as he seemed to consider whether he wanted to answer. And then, he lowered his arms. "When I was about ten years old, I was walking down Sundance Road. A couple of kids from school ambushed me with a pile of snowballs they'd stockpiled."

"Was it intended for you, specifically? Did they know you'd be walking by?"

"No. They couldn't have known I'd be there. Anyway, I retaliated. Nailed 'em with their own weapons until they ran crying into their house. Their mom came at me with a broom, telling me to get the hell off her property and leave her poor little boys alone. I told her I didn't start it. I even showed her the arsenal of snowballs sitting right there behind the bush, but do you think she believed me?"

"No, I don't." Her heart ached for the boy who'd been so completely misunderstood and all alone. "I get it. That really sucks."

"Whatever."

As he hammered the second nail to the other end of the mantel, she watched the play of muscles across his back, her gaze tracing broad shoulders that narrowed to a defined waist and flared to a hard, round ass. "It isn't everyone, you know that, right? If you totaled it, you'd probably find there are maybe ten stupid people who have a bad opinion of you. The rest of the town doesn't know you. They don't care. You can't let ten people keep you away from your family." *From me.*

"Why do you care so much?" He sauntered closer, his gaze turning lazy when it landed on her mouth.

"Maybe I want more kisses." She couldn't hide the hint of defiance in her tone because she didn't see why she had to keep hiding her feelings for this man. If they were going to live together, it was bound to come out.

"You really think that's a good idea?" He smelled of pine and cinnamon. "You think I stay away from this town because I'm butt hurt about how people treat me, but I don't give a fuck what they think." He studied her features. "Mrs. Atherton was about to hand you an envelope. What was it?"

Of course, he'd seen it. She had no choice but to tell the truth. "It might've been an invitation to the Christmas open house."

"And she pulled it when she saw me?"

"Yes."

His features shuttered, and he went back to the mantel.

"I don't care about a stupid party."

"Yeah, Fee. You do. It's the whole reason you moved here."

"Well, it's not more important than you and Cody."

"Okay. But now you get why I'm not so excited about moving back here."

She'd just experienced it, so of course, she got what he was saying. "I'm not sure that should keep you away from your family, though. You're not friends with anyone in the club anymore, and I think people will come to see you for the man you are."

"Maybe." He didn't sound convinced.

He was being his usual stubborn self. "What happens when your brothers start settling down?"

He glanced over his shoulder, eyebrows raised.

"What? At some point, they're going to get married and have kids. You'll want to be here for that, right?"

"We're not built like that."

"Like what?"

"The whole domesticity thing. That's just not who we are."

She'd heard this nonsense before. If he was still spewing it after twelve years, then there was no point in discussing it. She focused on the trio of brass stocking holders, pulling them out of a shopping bag and placing them on the mantel. "Where should we put the tree?" In the corner of the room, sunlight flooded in from adjacent windows. "Maybe there?"

"Sure. Let's take Cody to the Merry Bright farm this weekend. He can help us chop one down."

"He'll love it." Happiness rushed through her. "I've always wanted to do that."

"Didn't you have a tree growing up?" he asked.

"My mom kept one in a box under the bed. And my dad always grabbed one from the lot on his way home Christmas Eve."

"Why'd he wait so long to get one? They were cheaper?"

"They were *free*. For most of the residents of Wild Wolff Village, those are just vacation homes. They pay an annual fee that covers a full-time concierge who takes care of everything for them—"

"That's your mom, right?"

She nodded. "Before they show up, they fill out a form to stock their wine cellars, refrigerators, whatever, and around the holidays, they can order a Christmas tree and all the decorations. The team will even go in and set it all up."

"Where's the fun in that?" he asked.

"Right? Anyhow, they always get extra trees in case guests come into town at the last minute, and my dad just charms the guy who runs the lot on his way home. Everyone loves my dad, you know? He gets all kinds of gifts."

"Did you ever ask if you could cut one down instead?"

"Sure, but it's expensive, and neither of my parents could spend that kind of money for something we'd toss out in a week. I don't blame them. It wasn't that big a deal."

"They didn't listen to you. That's the point. It's not about shelling out cash for a tree. It's about giving your kid an experience. I'll bet they spend that much to go out to dinner, right? Or on drinks at the bar. Why not give their daughter the gift of a magical Christmas?"

He didn't know it, but he'd plugged in the connection between her heart and her mind. Because she'd had those sentiments as a child, but she'd never really allowed them to take form. If she had, she'd have wished for more—demanded it—and that would only have driven her parents further away. So she'd taken whatever she could get and stuffed down her feelings. "I think I know why I liked you so much."

His gaze jerked over to her.

"Every time my parents couldn't be bothered to look at the picture I'd drawn or take off work for the science fair to see my project, it made me feel like I was a burden. And now that we're talking about it, I remember showing my mom the Merry Farms website." It was covered with photos of happy families on a hayride and kids drinking cocoa, wearing colorful knit hats and gloves. "When she saw the prices, she rolled her eyes and said it was a 'racket,' and I remember shriveling up inside."

"She's no fun, but what's that got to do with me?"

"You listened. You blew off Leia Collins to save me from a raccoon." She grinned at their shared joke, but it was so true. "And with you, I can feel myself unfurling."

"*Unfurling?*"

She laughed, and it felt so good. "There's no better word to describe it, so I'm standing by it. I don't shrivel when I'm with you. I unfurl."

"And with Matt?"

"Oh." Well, that one was obvious. "With him, I stayed neatly in the box."

"He didn't want to see your science projects, either?"

Her gaze dropped to her hands, and she examined the ring she was now stuck with since lying to the judge. "Our project was building a life together, you know? We looked at houses and couches and vacation packages." *Wait a minute.* A sharp memory hit her. She could smell the lavender as if she held it in her hands. "Actually, I used to make soap." She watched him carefully to see if he'd look at her the same way Matt did, when he'd wait for her to finish talking before redirecting her to a topic that mattered to him. "It was a fun little hobby."

"And you stopped?" Jude asked.

"I did, yeah. But, I mean, he was right. We had a busy life, and it didn't fit."

"For him or for you?"

"Good question." She smiled. "He thought it was a waste of time since you can find handmade, small-batch soaps everywhere you go. There's nothing different about mine."

"Is that true?"

"Not really. I created my own scents."

His eyebrows shot up. "Explain."

The way she'd caught his attention only confirmed that she did have a unique product. "Okay, so it all started with my cookie-cutter collection."

He folded his arms across his chest, the hammer dangling. "A collection?"

"That's right." She laughed, not even slightly embarrassed. "A couple of times a year, I make homemade playdough for my kids. It started out as a holiday thing, you know, making ornaments or hearts. But then, on vacation at the beach, I found really cute seahorse and shell shapes. After that, I started noticing them everywhere, and it became a whole obsession. Anyhow, one day, it occurred to me that I could do the same thing with soap. Can you imagine a powder room in Calamity with soap in the shape of a moose? How cute would that be?"

"Very."

"I started playing with essential oils and making scented soap."

"What does the moose smell like?"

"It's pine and cinnamon. I have a flirty line, too, with lips and hearts and high heels. I use sexy perfume for those."

"That sounds like a good idea."

"I thought so, but was it the best use of my time?

Because we wanted to buy a house and save money for our honeymoon, and all that stuff, so working at a daycare in the summer and tutoring after school made a lot more sense."

"That's bullshit." He stepped around the boxes. "Where're the molds and essential oils?"

"Matt put them in the attic."

He set the hammer down and started off.

"Jude, wait." She laughed. "I'm not making soap right now. I'm your nanny, remember?"

"You're making holiday soaps. That's what I want for Christmas. A bar of moose soap."

A flash of sunlight glinting off metal drew their attention as a car pulled into the driveway. "They're here. Let's put the bags away so Cody doesn't see the mess." She couldn't give him magic with store-bought boxes and receipts lying around.

Jude headed to the bottom of the stairs and called, "Ava's here." When he came back to the fireplace, instead of cleaning, he cupped her elbows. "Just so we're clear, you're not a burden, and there's nothing sexier than you unfurling."

"Really?"

"Fuck, yeah. You know, the night you ran from your wedding, you said you weren't ready to talk to anyone, that you needed to process everything on your own." A car door slammed, and he collected the boxes and stomped on them with his boot. "But it's probably more that you don't want to drive people away. As long as you're fun and sweet and easy to be around, they'll stay."

His words hit the bull's-eye, sending a jolt that

straightened her spine. "I think you're right about that." He'd nailed that one.

He carried the boxes into the kitchen and tossed them in the garage. On his way back, he said, "I get that you don't have the most supportive parents, but you have a lot of people who love you. If someone pulls away because you ask for what you need, then they're not for you." He set the hammer in the toolbox and locked it up. "The right people will be honored to be there for you."

"Hello. We're here." Ava came into the house, handing Jude a stack of pizza boxes.

But Finlay was still stuck on what he'd said. *Honored to be there for you.*

She knew it was true because that was how she felt when Eloise lost her husband, and Finlay put together a meal chart for their friends and family. And when Willa broke her ankle, Finlay didn't think twice about taking a few days off to fly to New York and help her. She'd wanted to do it. Jude was right.

I felt honored to be the friend who got to do that for her.

"Wow, look at this place," Ava said.

"I know, right?" It looked like a family had lived there for years, and Finlay loved it. "It's all Gunnar."

Ava cocked her head, confused.

"The couch, the TV…" Finlay gestured to the staircase. "The beds and dressers. Pretty much everything you see, the guys brought over."

"They did that?" Ava's smile was filled with affection. "That's so sweet." She stepped back to reveal Cody, who stood behind her. "And look who I brought with me."

"Yay. Come on in, sweetie." Finlay headed for him as Ava unzipped his coat and tugged it off his shoulders.

The boy's gaze roamed the room. "Is this your house?"

"It is. And while your grandpa's with the doctor, you and Jude are going to live here with me. Does that sound good?"

"I get to stay here?" His eyes widened in marvel. "With you?"

Chapter Fifteen

Finlay's heart melted like chocolate in a warm pan. "You sure do. We're going to spend Christmas together. With Jude."

Cody slid a furtive look over to the big man with the dark expression before reaching for Finlay's hand. With a tug, he led her to the fireplace. "What're those things?"

"They're nutcrackers." She lifted one and brought it down for him to hold.

"You're telling me Gunnar bought *those*?" Ava asked.

"He did," Jude said.

"What is it?" Cody examined it, playing with the jaw.

"It's a Christmas decoration," Finlay said. "But also, if you put a nut in its mouth and press the lever, the shell will crack."

"Can I try?" the boy asked.

"Absolutely." Finlay added it to her mental shopping list. "Next time I'm at the store, I'll get us a bag of nuts, and we'll do it together."

"Why're they dressed like that?" He kept watching the

row of toy soldiers as if trying to make sense of them. "Are they fighters? Do they keep bad guys away?"

My God. Finlay sat on the edge of the coffee table, wishing so badly she could make this boy feel secure. What had he seen in his short life? Had he ever felt protected? "That's exactly right. They stand watch over the fireplace where they can see the doors and windows and keep us safe."

Jude stood behind them like a warrior. He had his hands on his hips as he seemed to assess the situation. "You want one in your room?"

Cody looked at Finlay for approval, but Jude needed to have the authority, so she waited for him to answer. "Um…" The boy glanced at the front door. "I want to leave them down here." He clutched the one he was holding to his chest. "Except this one."

"Okay, so just one for your room?" Jude asked.

Cody nodded, his expression earnest and so trusting.

"You got it." Jude's demeanor softened. "This is my first time at Miss O'Neill's house, too, and I think you're brave for staying here. It makes me want to be brave, too. I think the three of us are going to have a lot of fun together."

Cody gazed up at him, unsure.

"Have you ever made Christmas cookies before?" Jude asked.

Still wary, the boy shook his head.

"What about ornaments?" Jude pulled a sparkly gold one out of a box.

"In school, we made them out of popsicle sticks."

"Cool. So we've already got two fun things to do. Bake cookies and get ourselves a Christmas tree to decorate."

The boy didn't show much emotion, which had to be hard for Jude. How could he gauge what the boy needed or wanted if Cody didn't make it clear? She wanted to help but knew the two had to find their way together.

"Have you ever had a Christmas tree before?" Jude asked.

"We have one at my school."

"Well, now, you can have one right here." Jude pointed toward the corner of the living room. "And that means you can decorate it, and Santa can put the presents underneath. Sound good?"

The boy nodded, still not quite trusting. And it was hard to watch because, even though Jude was way out of his comfort zone, at least he was trying.

"There's lots to do in town over the holidays," Jude said. "We can go ice-skating and get hot cocoa."

The boy perked up. "I want hot cocoa."

"Then we'll get some."

Finally, the boy smiled. "Can we have it now?"

"Yeah." Jude's features relaxed. "We can make some right now."

"That pizza sure smells good," Finlay said. "How about you guys handle the drinks, and we'll set up for dinner?"

"Good plan." Jude reached out a hand, and to everyone's surprise, Cody took it. "Let's get busy."

Ava got to work setting the table while Jude rounded up a pan, whisk, and measuring cups. Once he had the ingredients, he brought a kitchen chair over for Cody and started on the cocoa.

"I'll get mugs." Just as Finlay opened the cabinet, Jude came up behind her and reached over her head.

"Here." He grabbed a few and set them on the counter.

"Thank you." She turned to face him, placing a hand on his chest. "That was beautiful, how you handled the nutcrackers."

He read her expression, as if he wanted to know if she meant it.

She did. "See what happens when you're less scary?"

"It's not like I try to be."

As she reached for water glasses, it all clicked into place. "Well, you know, I think you do. You were an open-hearted kid who expected to make friends, and instead, you were rejected. You didn't know why, so you adopted this"—she made a circular motion around her face—"*don't mess with me* mask. And it's worked. It's kept people from hurting you. But maybe now, as an adult, you don't need it anymore."

"Fee." He sighed.

"Yeah, yeah, I know. You don't need to be psychoanalyzed." She stood before him, brushing the hair off his forehead. "But I want everyone to know you the way I do. You think Mrs. Atherton hates you for what happened to her son, but I saw your expression when you came over. You looked dark and scary and mean. The message you gave her was, 'I haven't changed one bit, and if you mess with me, I'll knock you on your ass.'"

"I don't care what she thinks of me."

"I think you do." She reached for his big, calloused hand. "So maybe, instead of telling the world you're a badass biker, you can let them see you're sweet and generous and smart." She laughed when she saw his appalled expression. "Okay, fine. But at least stop scowling. I promise, people will see you differently."

Trampling on the stairs alerted them that the brothers and Gunnar were coming down for dinner, so she filled the water glasses while Jude helped Cody adjust the sweetness of the cocoa.

The men immediately descended on the food, pulling apart slices, taking huge bites before the pizza hit their plates, and arguing over topping choices. Wyatt thought mushrooms and peppers were slimy, Boone only wanted meat and cheese, and Decker didn't "eat shit like this during the season."

And then, Gunnar made everyone laugh when he said in his gruff voice, "It's just food. Who the hell cares?"

Growing up, Finlay either ate dinner alone in front of the TV or with one of her parents. With her mom, it was quiet. The scrape of a fork on a plate, the rustle of paper from a catalog as her mom sorted through the mail. Sometimes, she'd ask a few polite questions about her day.

Her dad almost always brought someone home with him. They'd tell drinking stories, swap worst skiing accidents or chunked golf shots, and hang out. She never had much to contribute, so she'd often take food to her room.

In contrast, the McKennas were boisterous, loud, and constantly messing with each other. There was so much laughter that her stomach muscles ached. She couldn't keep up with all the swearing and inside jokes, but she loved every second of it.

She loved how their tight bond made them confident.

These men did what they wanted and didn't wait for anyone to join them.

Because they had each other.

And that was enough.

That's why they don't need wives and children. Because they're complete in their own McKenna universe.

She had to let that sink in. There was no bridge across the chasm separating her and Jude. He had no need for the life she craved.

Well, that's depressing.

But it was a good reminder to tread carefully during the next few weeks. She absolutely could not fall in love with him.

"What's up, little man?" Decker tapped Cody's uneaten pizza. "Not hungry?"

"I'm saving room for my hot chocolate." The boy eyed Gunnar.

"I thought you and Jude made some," Ava asked.

"We did." The boy blushed all the way to his ears.

"It wasn't good?" Ava asked.

Cody gave Jude side-eye, and everyone burst out laughing.

"Hey, *I'm* not the aficionado," Jude said.

"No, you're not." Gunnar reached into his back pocket and pulled out two shiny red packets. Waving them, he said, "Salted caramel." He shoved his chair back. "Let's go."

The boy dropped out of his chair, running to keep up with the McKenna patriarch.

As they headed into the kitchen, Boone smiled. "Bonding with Grampa. Nice."

"It really is." Ava's gaze lingered on them as Gunnar filled a kettle.

"When's your flight?" Jude asked Decker.

"I have a car coming in an hour to take me to the airstrip." The quarterback pushed his salad aside and wiped his fingers on a napkin.

"Actually, Decker's here for a reason," Wyatt said. The table went silent. "We want you to know we're all in this together."

"If you do this, we're doing it with you," Boone said.

"I know I have a tough schedule," Decker said. "But I came home when you *didn't* need me to show you how fast I'll be here when you do."

Finlay sucked in a sharp breath. *What a lovely thing to say.*

When the three brothers put their hands in the center of the table, Jude stared at them, as expressive as a slab of granite.

Ava put her hand on top of the pile. "If you adopt him, I'll treat your son the way I treated all of you."

Finlay wasn't part of the family, so she wasn't sure if she should join them, but she had to let Jude know he could count on her, too. She added her hand. "I know you only hired me for six weeks, but I'll do anything I can to help. As long as you need me, I'll be here."

Jude examined his slice of pizza. He cleared his throat. "I guess I'm doing this, huh?"

Everyone remained quiet, but the way he was already changing for this boy, making space for him, was a pretty clear indication.

"It's a lot, you know?" Jude said. "Hard to wrap my head around."

"Which is why we're here." Wyatt clapped a hand on his brother's shoulder. "To help you get there."

"I appreciate it," Jude said slowly and deliberately, and she could see the effort it took for him to look each of them in the eyes. "I mean, Judge Adams isn't wrong. I am a single bartender, and I don't know that I'm the best man for the job." He took a breath, looking contemplative. "But with all of you beside me, I can't think of a better life for him."

"Aw, sweetheart." Ava got up and came behind him, throwing her arms around his neck and hugging him.

He reached for her hands, clinging tightly. "Thanks, guys."

Finlay knew at that moment she'd made a terrible mistake. She couldn't be his nanny, live under his roof, and be around his family without getting her heart thoroughly and mercilessly destroyed.

How the hell was she supposed to walk away after the holidays? She'd promised to stay in Cody's life, but what would happen when Jude settled down? And he would. No matter what he said about not being cut out for it, he'd eventually fall in love. He'd want a mother for Cody.

Interrupting her pity party, Boone pointed at Wyatt's last slice of pizza. "You gonna eat that?" Even as his brother said, "Yes," the hotshot yanked his plate away.

Unfortunately, he'd thrust it near Jude, who easily snatched it up.

"Hey." Wyatt stood. "That's the only kind I like. Give

it back." He motioned to the remaining boxes. "You guys like that slimy shit on top."

"You want it back?" Before his brother could answer, Jude tipped his head back and slowly lowered it into his mouth.

"You're an asshole," Wyatt said.

Jude shoved the entire slice inside and grinned.

As Decker burst out laughing, Wyatt reached behind his head and swatted the bill of his backward ball cap, sending it flying across the table.

"Jerk." Decker didn't react quickly enough because Boone snatched it out of the air. "Hey. I've had that since I was thirteen." The quarterback's chair nearly toppled over as he lunged for his hat. "Give it back. That was Tom Brady's. He signed it for me at football camp."

But Boone was up and tossing it to Jude.

And then, it was pure chaos. The men chased each other around the table, their big bodies slamming into it so hard they shoved it an inch to the left. Somehow, Boone got Decker to the floor, and the guys were full-on wrestling, shouting, and laughing.

But when Ava noticed Cody standing in the doorway of the kitchen watching, she clapped her hands. "Game on."

As if she'd Tasered them, the men leaped to their feet, staring at her like runners at the starting gate.

"Ten minutes to collect the boxes and packing paper. Biggest pile wins a care package from the aunties."

"Teams or solo?" Boone asked.

"Solo. You're on your own for this one." Ava checked her watch. "Three…two…one… Go."

The men scattered. It was the strangest thing Finlay had ever seen. Jude took the stairs like the house was on fire and he had to save the family dog. Boone grabbed a knife out of the block and followed him. Decker raced to the basement, which Gunnar had filled with a couch, a basketball arcade game, a ping-pong table, and a huge television that occupied half the wall. And Wyatt found a giant black trash bag under the sink and tore across the living room.

"What on earth?" Finlay asked as she picked up Cody.

"You know how in class we use distraction when we want to stop kids from fighting or throwing a tantrum?" Ava asked.

Finlay nodded, hitching the boy more comfortably on her hip.

"So with four brothers, you can imagine how wild they'd get. That's when I came up with this game. Basically, I give them a task. Whoever finds the most pinecones in ten minutes wins a prize. Whoever can make the tallest stack of rocks gets to put the star on top of the tree. That kind of thing."

"They still do it now? Jude's *thirty*."

Ava laughed. "Oh, they're as competitive as ever."

"And who're the aunties?"

"That's my family. My dad was basically raised by six very strong women."

"Got it." Finlay glanced to the top of the stairs to find Jude standing in the shadows, watching Cody intently.

He seemed torn. But then, he raced down and hurried over to them. "You on my team?" he asked the boy.

Cody nodded, holding his arms out. Jude gently took

him and carried him across the living room. "Team Grizz. Let's go." He raced back up the stairs.

"Hey, man, not fair," Boone shouted. "You got two extra hands."

"Suck on it," Jude called, and just before he disappeared down the hallway, she caught Cody's smile.

Watching him, Ava said, "He's a good man."

"I know."

I'm in so much trouble.

Chapter Sixteen

Living under the same roof with the only woman he'd ever really wanted was the worst kind of torture. Her sweet scent lingered in the hallway, and her laughter filled the house whenever she played with Cody or talked to a friend on the phone.

It gave him a pang of jealousy because he wanted to be the reason she smiled.

Though he didn't give her much opportunity to do that, did he? He'd have to work on that. Be less...gruff. He needed to be gentler for both her and the boy.

Or maybe just in general. He remembered a bar owner once telling him to be careful because the lethal look in his eyes could "incinerate" their customers. He'd argued that it was only particular patrons, but okay. He saw her point.

The problem with Finlay was that sparks flew whenever they were close. He wanted to get his hands all over her, but he shouldn't do that, right? Not when their focus had to be on the boy.

It was too complicated.

No, don't go there.

He set his toothbrush on the counter and flicked the light switch. The darkness made him think about Cody. Was he scared all alone in that big bed? He'd check on him one more time. As he headed down the hallway, he wondered if he should sleep in the boy's room.

He was way out of his element. Not only did he know nothing about being a dad, but the boy's past brought an extra layer of complexity. How did Cody understand the difference between his father dying and his grandpa having surgery? Bottom line: Both were gone.

Do I ask him how he feels about these things? Or wait till he brings shit up?

Maybe best to consult a therapist. *Yeah, I'll do that.*

As he passed Finlay's room, he found her door ajar, her nightstand lamp on, and the covers thrown back. It made him wonder what she did before bed. Read? Watch TV? Scroll through social media? He wanted to know her habits, her routines.

He'd thought he wasn't cut out to live with someone, yet all he wanted was to be with her. He wanted to share coffee in the morning before work and go grocery shopping together. He liked the idea of shoveling the driveway while she was under a blanket on the couch, reading.

If they shared a bed, he'd reach for her all night long, slide into her first thing in the morning, and come home for a quickie a couple of times during the day. He'd never stop wanting her. He couldn't think of another person he'd ever been so comfortable with. So *happy* with.

As he approached Cody's room, he found her coming out of it. "Everything okay?" he asked.

She held a finger to her lips and waved him down the hallway. "When I checked on him, his eyes were wide open, so I stayed till he fell asleep."

He liked everything about this woman, but her purity, her essential goodness, really set his gears churning. When he looked into her eyes, he had a clear shot straight through to her soul. He knew where he stood with her. He trusted her.

"Why're you looking at me like that?" she asked.

The yellow glow from the hallway night-light gilded her. It turned her dark hair bronze. "Because you're beautiful." *Oh, shit.* He probably shouldn't have said that. "And I admire you."

"Oh." A flush swept across her cheeks. "I just left my groom at the altar. I'm not sure there's much to admire."

"You starting to have regrets?"

"Not at all. I'm just lost. I've been walking this path for a long time, and suddenly, the road"—she pinched her fingers together and released them quickly, her hand opening wide— "blew up. It's scary."

"But maybe a little exciting, too?"

"Oh, well." She let out a shaky laugh. "I'm pretty sure the exciting part is living with you for the next five weeks. It definitely distracts me from the bad stuff."

"You know, your honesty's a big fucking turn-on, right?"

The vulnerability shining in her eyes, the raw openness of her heart, undid him. Desire slammed into him, and he wanted to haul her up against his chest and carry her to that unmade bed. He was desperate to learn every curve of her lush body.

"Yeah, well, I'm never going to survive if we keep having midnight talks like this." She slipped into her room. "Good night, Jude."

"Wait." He couldn't say what came over him, but he couldn't let her go. His hand shot out, blocking the door from closing.

Her eyes went hot, and he got a flash of her naked on the bed, ass pitched high, his red handprint on her cheek. His mouth watered as he imagined licking into her from behind, holding her squirming hips in place with his hands. He could imagine her cry as he flipped her onto her back, hiked up her knees, and spread her wide for his mouth and tongue. He knew her neck would arch, her eyelids would flutter shut, and her moans would send him out of his mind.

"Fee." His voice came out strangled. Heat flashed up his neck.

She waited for him to say more, but when her pink lips parted, and her chest rose and fell with shallow breaths, he lost his train of thought.

The truth lit him up like a firecracker. "I've already ruined your reputation."

She's mine. Always has been.

I have a chance to be with her.

All I have to do is get out of my own way.

"Totally destroyed it." She gave a helpless shrug. "There's nothing left to salvage." She gazed up at him, sultry-eyed, and licked her bottom lip.

"So there's nothing standing between us anymore." *Fuck the excuses. The made-up complications.*

"Not a thing." She tugged his black T-shirt. "Well, except this."

Without a moment's hesitation, he yanked it over his head and tossed it into her room.

"And this old thing." She began undoing the buttons on her pajama top, exposing her big, bouncy cleavage.

He went painfully hard. His hands flexed, then squeezed into fists so he wouldn't grab her.

And that was when she abandoned her task, lowered her arms, and the light died in her eyes. "Looks like you're trying to find a new excuse to keep your hands off me, so I'm going to leave you to it."

He yanked her back to him. "I'm trying to keep from fucking you into next week."

"That's not really the problem, is it, Jude? It's obvious we both want that. But what happens in the morning? Are you going to be all weird and awkward? Are you going to say you're sorry, you don't know what came over you, and you think it's best if we remain friends, for Cody's sake?"

"No. Once I finally get my hands on you, I'm not going to be able to stop. I've wanted you since I was fourteen years old, and spending this past week with you only proved that grown-up Finlay is even better than my teenage fantasy."

"Yes, I get that. I know that from the way you kissed me, but it doesn't answer my question. I'm not asking for forever, but you can't just have sex with me once and then think we can go back to being roommates. So I'm asking you. After you get what you want, are you going to shut down on me and walk away? Because that's all you've ever done. You—"

"I know what I've done." He cupped her ass and lifted her, backing her against the wall. "I'm an asshole, but I'm trying to be better."

She scraped her hands through his hair. "If you're still in the trying phase, then I'm not interested. You have to know what you want because you don't get to play with my heart."

"Jesus, Fee. I want to *own* your heart."

With their bodies pressed together, he could feel the tremor run through her. "Do you deserve it?"

He had to give that some thought. He'd never lie to her. Honestly, he didn't think anyone deserved a woman like Finlay. "No, but I'll die trying."

"Good answer." She grinned, but her gaze was fixed to his mouth. "But here's the thing. If you fuck me into next week, then we lose six whole days. Why don't you just rail me into tomorrow morning so we can take advantage of every delicious moment we have left together?"

He was so relieved, he was shaking. "Since when're you so filthy?"

"Since I climbed onto the back of your bike in my seven-thousand-dollar wedding gown."

He kicked the door wide open and stepped into the room, bumping it shut with his hip. Dropping her onto the mattress, he kneed her legs open and stepped between them. Grabbing both sides of her top, he yanked them apart. Buttons went flying, pinging on the nightstand.

He didn't know what would happen with them—

couldn't see past the next five weeks since he had no idea what Family Services would think about him adopting Cody—but he would worship this woman every chance he got while he had her.

"It doesn't feel dirty to me," she said. "It just feels good."

He cupped the tits he'd fantasized about for years. "It'll feel real dirty after I come all over these." Her eyes went wild with excitement, and it ignited the beast in him. It made him want to slam inside her and thrust decades of lust for this woman out of his system.

But there was a whole other side, one filled with so much tenderness he could barely stand it. He just…liked her so much. She was so damn special.

He had to get out of his head. Because the only thing he'd told her was that he wanted to come all over her tits.

She deserved so much more.

And so, he kissed her. With handfuls of her plump breasts, his thumb flicking over the hard peaks, he let his heart speak through the dance of his tongue inside her impossibly soft, warm mouth.

Pleasure streamed through him, exciting a spray of goose bumps across his skin. She smelled good, she felt good, she tasted good—*My God, I want this woman*. In a rush of affection, he deepened the kiss. He needed her to know how much she meant to him, how much he cared, so he poured it into her, hoping she heard she was perfect just as she was.

Her arms wrapped around him, holding him tightly against her, and her ankles locked around his waist. The way she was grinding on him—the urgency, the little sounds of desperation—turned him feral.

Straightening, he shucked off his sweatpants. "Do you have protection?"

"No. We were planning on…" She looked away. "Never mind."

He fell forward, planting a hand at either side of her head. "Don't hold back with me. There's nothing you can't say."

"No, forget it. I don't want to ruin the moment."

See, that was his point. She'd heard the lust part but not the devotion. "Finlay. There's nothing you could do to ruin anything. I've wanted you since I was a teenager, and I want you even more now."

She gripped his aching cock. "You sure know how to turn a girl on." She let out a dreamy sigh. "I was going to say we were planning on getting pregnant, so we didn't need protection."

"You think I don't know you want kids? I know, Fee. I know what you want."

Her eyes flared. "Why did you get harder when you said that?"

"Because the idea of putting a baby inside you turns me on." He was probably more shocked than she that he'd said it, but it was true. "Our lives are too messed-up for that, but…" He put a hand on her belly, could imagine it swollen with his child, and he lost his shit.

Kissing her, he dragged her up the bed. He had sweet, good Finlay O'Neill naked beneath him, and he reverted to a shaky, fumbling boy. His heart raced, and his hands wanted to cover more territory than they could, making his touch rough and awkward. His cock hurt with the need to release.

He just wanted her so much. All of her.

He needed to slow down. Get a hold of himself.

"What's wrong?" she asked breathlessly.

"I'm too excited. I need to make it good for you."

"What do you mean?"

"If we keep going like this, I'm going to come on your belly like it's my first time touching a woman." In some ways, that was exactly what it was.

She grinned, her hands clasping the back of his neck. "I like this side of you."

"Yeah, well, I don't. It's embarrassing." He buried his face in her neck and breathed her in. But it only fueled his hunger. "I need to calm down."

"That's the last thing I want. I want you to come unhinged around me. Give me everything, Jude. Give it to me hard and wild, sweet and gentle, whatever you're feeling…God, just give it to me. Show me how much you want me."

It was just what he needed to get out of his head and back into the body shaking with excitement. "I'd burn the world down to get inside you." He squeezed his eyes shut. "But I can't if we don't have condoms."

She reared up. "Well, I can have *you*." Planting both hands on his chest, she knocked him sideways. In one swift move, she had him on his back and was straddling his thighs. With a sexy grin, she held his cock with both hands and licked from tip to stem.

The electric sensation had him arching his back and crying out.

She ran her tongue all around the head and up and down his length, getting him wet and so worked up he was going to explode—there was no way to stop the freight train of an orgasm roaring through him. But wasn't that what she wanted? For him to lose control?

She sucked him into her mouth—*oh, fuck*—and the sensation was so intense, he couldn't hold back. Clamping the back of her head, he punched his hips off the mattress and thrust with abandon. Stars exploded behind his eyes. "Jesus. *Fuck*. Holy shit." That was it. Wracked with shudders, he held her tightly as the spasms rolled through him, one after another.

Her fingers dug into his ass, and her wet pussy rubbed over his thigh. It was so fucking hot he couldn't stand it.

The moment his ass hit the bed, he loosened his hold and flung his arms wide. It took a moment to catch his breath. "That's the single most embarrassing thing that's ever happened to me."

Eyes blazing, she wiped her mouth and sat up. Her chest rose and fell with harsh breaths, making her tits jiggle.

Unbelievably, desire flowed back into him. "Got to get a mouthful of those." He tugged on her arm, settling her beside him.

Nuzzling her neck, he held the weight of her breast in his palm. He kissed the tip, pushing them both together and learning her pleasure points from her breathy sighs and shuddery gasps. As he sucked the other nipple into his mouth, his fingertips grazed her stomach, dipping into her slick, hot core. He lazily stroked her—everywhere but where she needed it most. And when he slid inside to caress the sensitive patch, he was rewarded with a rush of desire coating his fingers.

When her hips rocked impatiently and her gasps turned into desperate cries, he skimmed his mouth down her torso. Shifting between her legs, he held her thighs open and licked inside. Her knees lifted, and her fingers tangled in his hair.

The moment his tongue licked her clit, her hips shot off the bed, and she pressed herself to his mouth. Another rush of pleasure coated his tongue, and she yanked his hair so hard it stung at the roots.

He loved it. He loved arousing her, tasting her, and feeling her everywhere on his body.

Her sounds were so erotic, so exciting, he went mindless, sucking and licking, gripping her ass with one hand while rubbing that inner patch with the other.

She came with a cry, her neck arching, her heels digging into his lower back, and her hips slamming hard against his mouth. "Yes, yes, yes. Oh, *God.*"

After the tension left her body, she collapsed like a rag doll. One more tremor went through her, and she let out a breath. "Mmm. So good. *So* good."

There was a moment when the familiar sense of *time to go* hit him. It was just what he did, a habit. He never slept in the same bed with a woman. But this time, the impulse sputtered out and died. Because the idea of tearing himself away from the warm body curled up beside him made his heart thunder and perspiration break out behind his neck.

No, he didn't think he could leave her.

"So much better than my fantasies." She sounded sleepy.

He reached over to turn out the light.

"If you wake up and want some boom-shakalaka," she said, "look in the nightstand. He took the big stuff, but I doubt he bothered to clean out all his drawers."

"Now you tell me," he muttered.

"Got to give you something to look forward to."

Chapter Seventeen

In the middle of the night, Jude awoke with a start.

Curled up to him, Fee slept deeply, peacefully. Her hair spilled across his chest, and he breathed in the scent of her perfumed shampoo and body lotion.

Gratitude flooded him. He couldn't believe it. Couldn't believe he got to be with her.

But not knowing how much time they had together made him greedy for more. He wanted to slide into her from behind, take his time fucking her. Slow, deep thrusts, filling her, working them both up into a frenzy.

But he had the strangest sensation. An urgency to go check on Cody.

Carefully, he slid out from under her arm and leg. He drew the covers over her shoulders and brushed a strand of hair off her cheek, tucking it behind the prettiest little shell of an ear.

His heart was so full, he couldn't help pressing a light kiss on her cheek. Then he threw on his sweats and a T-shirt and headed into the hallway. He didn't want to leave her, wanted nothing more than to crawl back under the covers with her, but he couldn't ignore the alarm going off in his body.

When he got to Cody's room, he peered inside. At first glance, he seemed fine. He was asleep. He'd kicked the sheets off, and he looked so little, his body curved, arms clutching his red blanket.

But as Jude's vision adjusted to the dark, he noticed the boy's expression. Even though his eyes were closed, emotion fluttered across his face like he was watching an action movie.

When Jude came closer, he noticed the boy's muscles flinching. He didn't know whether he should wake him or let him sleep through it. He didn't have a clue how to take care of a kid.

Then again, who better to relate to the experience of being in a strange house with people he barely knew? Jude had been a scared little boy, too. He sat on the mattress and touched Cody's back. It was so frail, the bones so delicate.

How do I make it right for him?

But there was only one answer to that question: *You make him feel safe.*

Jude stretched out beside him. He didn't want to wake him, but at the same time, he couldn't sit there and do nothing while the boy twitched and made scared little noises. So he wrapped an arm around him and held him close. "It's all right. I got you."

The boy startled and rolled onto his back. "Mister?"

"Yeah, I'm here."

"How come?" Cody blinked as if trying to wake up.

"You were having a bad dream. I wanted to make sure you're okay." Maybe he found the quiet unsettling. At the bike club, the lights were always on, and there was laughter, conversation, and music. In this house, he might hear creaking or his neighbors talking or the idling of cars.

"Is my grandpa better yet?" Cody asked.

"I don't know. But we can call him tomorrow and ask. You want to do that?"

"Yeah." The boy stared at the ceiling. "Tomorrow, I'm getting a Christmas tree. And the competition starts. I have to bring a shovel." His head shifted on the pillow to look at Jude. "Do you have one?"

"Yep." His brothers might be excited about Snowfest, but it just wasn't on his radar. But it seemed it was on Cody's, and that was all that mattered. "Do you know what we're making?"

He nodded with enthusiasm. "They were gonna make a wolf and a polar bear in a canoe, but I said I wanted a house. Big enough to walk into."

Huh. Each team worked with a twenty-five-ton block of snow. He wasn't sure how big a house they could make that would allow people to enter it. And what would they put inside? A couch and chairs, or something more elaborate like a family watching a movie together, with a big bucket of popcorn on the son's lap?

Whatever his family designed, it would be over-the-top good. The McKennas were competitive fuckers. "So that's what we're going with? A house?"

"Yeah. And I get to help with the stomping."

Everyone loved that first part of the process. The town

delivered a giant mountain of snow in the center of the square. Using wheelbarrows and buckets, each team filled a giant wooden frame and then got on top to pack it down, adding more until they reached the rim of the box.

He'd text his brothers and get in on the plan. Whatever they did, it had to be special for Cody. "Tomorrow, at the stomping, you and I can take a look at the design." Wyatt and his dad would have schematics, a list of tools, and a plan. "And you can add any last-minute touches. But for now, we need a good night's sleep. Got to be rested for the event. It takes three whole days."

Cody settled down, but his eyes were wide open.

And that brought Jude back to his original concern. "You okay in this room?"

"Yeah. I like it here."

"I'm glad. I like it here, too." Curious, Jude asked, "Where'd you sleep at the club?"

"With my grandpa. In a bag."

"A what? Oh, you mean a sleeping bag? On the floor?"

"Yeah."

"So it must be weird sleeping in a big ole bed like this."

"Yeah, it's big. I never slept in a bed like this before."

"It works for me because I like spreading out," Jude said. "But that's because I sleep like a starfish."

"What's a starfish?"

"Here. Look." Jude flipped onto his stomach, spreading out his arms and legs.

"You take up the whole bed."

"I know, right? It feels good. Try it." He shifted to the edge of the mattress to give the boy space. "Go on."

Cody flopped onto his belly and moved his arms and legs like he was making a snow angel. His shy smile did something to Jude's heart. "Look at that. You're a starfish, just like me." Jude started to get up, but fear flashed in the boy's eyes. "You okay? Want me to stay longer?"

The boy didn't answer, and his eyes cut away. Jude set a hand on Cody's head. "You got something on your mind? You can tell me anything."

"Will you stay with me till I fall asleep?"

"Yeah, absolutely."

The boy curled up like he did before, hugging his blanket to his chest. Every few seconds, he'd crack his eyelids open to see if Jude was still there.

"Buddy? There's something you should know about me."

Cody watched him warily.

"I'm always going to be honest with you. If I can't stay till you fall asleep, I'll tell you. I'll say, 'No, I can't do that.' But if I say I'll do something, you can count on it. I'll do it."

"Okay." The boy closed his eyes. He peeked at Jude two more times before his breathing slowed, his fingers relaxed, and his shoulders sagged.

This boy needed a home. A dad. He needed a routine he could count on. He *deserved* to feel safe and secure. To feel loved. Cherished. It might've been a rough start for Jude and his brothers, but they'd never doubted their dad's devotion, the certainty that they were his priority.

The impulse to hug the boy came out of nowhere, but he didn't want to wake him. That was another thing he hadn't considered. The boy's need for human touch.

It was overwhelming, all that was involved in raising a child.

He brushed a finger across the back of Cody's delicate little hand.

I've got you, little one.

Once Cody had fallen deeply asleep, Jude shifted his legs off the mattress and got up. He was startled to find Finlay in the doorway, watching. When he reached her, she hurled herself into his arms.

"You're so good with him," she said, her voice muffled by his chest. "You're so *good*."

"I have to be." He bent his knees and lifted her, carrying her back to the bedroom.

When he dropped her onto the bed, she had a concerned expression. "Are you going to stay with me tonight? Or are you going back to the guest room?"

He got it. She was waiting for him to run, to shut down, but he wasn't even feeling that impulse. He needed her. All of her. Every single piece of this woman's mind, body, heart, and soul.

He answered by peeling off her pajama bottoms, dropping his clothes on the floor, and getting under the covers with her.

He grabbed his phone off the nightstand and shot off a text.

"What was that?" she asked. "Canceling your booty call plan for tonight? Or is that a group text to your legion of women, letting them know you're off the market?"

He grinned and rolled onto his side, hiking up on an elbow. "My booty call?"

"Yeah. Don't tell me you haven't sent a text at one in the morning, looking for a hookup."

"I've never sent a booty call text. And do you want me off the market?"

"Those *are* the terms of this agreement."

"Oh, we have terms? Do you want to spell them out for me?"

"Sure." She rolled onto her side, mindlessly caressing his forearm. "Number one, you have to deliver the best orgasms of my life."

"Not a problem. Go on."

"Number two, we have to do errands together. No dividing them up to get them done faster."

"Easy. I always want to be with you."

The humor left her eyes, and sadness pinched her features.

"Hey." He shifted closer, cupping her cheek. "What just happened?"

"I don't know. I just...I would've gone a lifetime without this." She curled her hand around his wrist. "Do you feel it?"

If she meant the current that ran up his arm, across his shoulders, and down his spine, then yeah. If she meant the connection that set his pulse pounding, that made him feel as fully awake and alive as cannonballing into a glacier lake, then yes. Absolutely yes.

She gave him a pleading look. "If you hadn't shown me what I was missing, I'd have lived with that same emptiness my whole life."

The strange thing was that he understood. He'd never experienced the kind of touch that sparked on his skin.

That awakened the softer side of him. That stirred his heart. "Since I know exactly what you mean, I have to say yes to all your terms."

She smiled. "You haven't heard the others."

He made a rolling gesture with his hand. *Carry on.*

"Number three, you have to cook. Unless you want a steady diet of pumpkin bread with chocolate chips, snickerdoodles, brownies, and peshwari naan."

"Peshwari what now?"

She laughed. "It's an Indian bread with rose syrup, honey, cashews, pistachios… It's pure heaven."

"Yeah, you're gonna have to make that. But I can grill anything. Meat, fish, vegetables. How about I get the real food, and you handle the treats?"

"You're a lot more agreeable than I'd have imagined."

"There's very little I wouldn't do for you." He settled back down. "And that text went to my dad."

"At three in the morning?"

"I told him I'm not going to work nights while I'm in town." He powered down the phone and settled in next to her. "If he needs me, I can help him with admin or show up on a busy night, but other than that, I'm here for Cody." *And you.*

"Oh. Okay. That's great." Her demeanor changed, and she grew agitated. She pulled the blanket up to her chin. "I guess you won't be needing a nanny anymore, which is fine. I can pay you back in, like, monthly installments or something."

"Fee, we're not changing anything." He reached for her, pulling her into his arms. "We're in this together." If it didn't work out between them, it'd hurt like hell, but he'd squeeze the joy out of every moment they had together. "I want you as much as Cody does."

"But you won't be working. Won't this put you in a financial bind?"

Always looking out for me. "I do more than mix drinks. I flip bars, too. I have a nice savings."

"You flip them?"

"Yeah, I buy a rundown bar, give it a facelift, and then sell it. Been doing it since I got out of the Marines."

"So you own the one in Florida?"

"No, but I was thinking about it. I work in them first to see if they're worth flipping."

"And is it?"

"Might be. But only if I can buy the apartment complex next door. There's a lot of shady shit going on over there, and it's keeping people away."

"If you buy it, does that mean you'd move Cody to Florida?"

"You asked if it was worth flipping. Not whether I was going to buy it. For now, I'm staying here. I have to see where things are going with Cody."

"Okay, that's fine then. I'll be your concubine." She snuggled in closer. "This'll be fun." She ran her fingers through the hair on his chest. "Cody's so lucky to have you."

In a lot of ways, yes. But he couldn't help worrying… "What happened with Mrs. Atherton is the norm for me. What if Cody'd been there and seen the way she treated me?"

"I would've immediately shot her down. And I'd explain small-minded, grudge-holders to him."

"My champion." He kissed her cheek. "But I guarantee I'm going to get a lot more of that while I'm in town, and that means Cody will, too. He's just starting out in school. I don't want him to get branded as the bad kid." He brought her hand to his mouth and kissed her palm. "That was the whole point in keeping my distance from you."

"You keep saying that, but I'm not buying it. I think you're afraid of losing me."

"What do you mean?"

"Jude, you lost your *mom*. You might not remember much about her, but you had her for the first six years of your life, and then, she was gone. And not only that, but your dad up and moved you from the only life you knew."

"That was a long time ago," he said, even though it rang true.

"I'm not a psychologist, but I'd think such an abrupt change would deeply impact a kid."

"I had Ava." Though it sounded hollow even to him.

"And thank goodness for that, but did anyone ever help you through your loss? Did you see a therapist?"

"No. I don't remember talking about any of it."

"You were ripped out of your safe, comfortable world, and no one helped you process the loss. Why would you want a wife and kids when you learned it could all be taken away from you?"

"I had a good life." Oddly, his voice sounded faraway —like he was listening to himself through a wall. "A good family."

"Sure, but there's a six-year-old boy inside you who's still waiting for his mom to come home."

He'd crashed his bike before. An elk leaped onto Gallatin Road right in front of him. He'd veered sharply, narrowly avoiding the animal. But that same jarring, electric fear rang through him at that moment. "I never thought of it like that."

"And then, right after she died, your dad moved you, right?"

"Yeah, he needed a job with benefits right away. He applied to anything he could find, and when he got a last-minute interview in San Francisco, he packed us up and hit the road."

"How'd he wind up in Calamity, of all places?"

"He ran out of money."

"What do you mean? I'm not seeing the connection."

"He had a car full of hungry, tired kids, so he stopped at the Hole in the Wall diner to feed us but couldn't pay the bill. I guess the club president was there and saw the whole thing go down. He paid and then asked if my dad had a place to stay that night. And with four kids—one of them a newborn—he knew he wasn't going to make it to California, so he stayed. They set him up with room and board, childcare, clothes for the kids…everything. They took care of him."

"That's amazing. I never knew any of that. Do you have pictures of your mom?"

"Not a single one. From what I understand, they lived in student housing. They didn't have much of anything, to begin with, but my dad took what he could fit in the minivan and hit the road."

"Have you looked her up online?"

"There are hundreds of Mary McKennas, and I don't think she had much family."

"I guess he must've really loved her."

"My dad?" Funny, but he'd never really thought about it.

"Yeah, I mean, in all these years, he's never remarried."

"Oh, yeah. Like I said, we're just not built like that."

"There you go again. But you know what? I see you, Jude McKenna." She pointed two fingers at her eyes and then at his. "You can say it all you want, but your dad was built like that once, right? He was married and had four children. It's more likely that, after such a big loss, he isn't willing to open his heart again. I hope you don't let that happen to you."

"Maybe." He'd have to sit on what she said for a while, but it made sense. "Or maybe…" He rolled on top of her, bracing his hands on either side of her. "I haven't met the right person yet. I'm very particular, you know."

"Hmm." She scraped her fingernails down his bare back. "Impossibly high standards, huh?"

"Want to hear my criteria?" He left a trail of kisses from her cheek, down her neck to the tips of her beaded breasts. He sucked a nipple into his mouth.

"I'm going to take a wild guess here, but big boobs?"

He nodded, his tongue too busy licking. He liked the way her fingers curled into his back, and her jaw slackened. "Mm-hmm."

"A jiggly ass?"

He reached underneath her and grabbed a handful of that luscious flesh. "You get me. You really get me."

"Anything else?"

"Oh yeah. Long, silky, curly hair. It's got to spill all over me when she rides my cock."

Her hips bucked, and he took her cue to roll onto his back. She straddled him, pinning his wrists to the mattress. Her hair pooled on his chest, and she rocked her hips, letting it brush across his bare skin. "Like this?"

"Just like that." He thrust so his dick rubbed against her opening. "You better check that drawer for protection."

"Well, wait a minute. Is that number four? A willingness to have sex with you?"

"Sweetheart, it's not just about willingness. She's got to be insatiable for me."

Shifting back, she reached for him, notching him in the hot, slick cove between her legs. She rocked over his length in long, sensuous glides. "I don't know, Jude. I feel like I might just be your dream woman. Why don't we test it to be sure, see how insatiable I am?" She leaned over and opened the drawer. "Bingo." She waved the packet at him and tore it open with her teeth.

He reached for it, but she shook her head. "Not a chance, buddy. You know, it's good you weren't my first because when I used to fantasize about you, I didn't know what sex was. I pictured us kissing with closed mouths and cuddling. The first time I saw a real wiener—"

He choked out a laugh. "Never say that word again when you're sitting on my dick."

She sat back on his thighs and swept her hands up his arms, rounding his biceps, and caressing his chest. "Okay, but hear me out. A penis has always just been a penis, you know? It's just a weird-looking appendage." She pushed back on his thighs and gripped him with both hands.

He hissed in a breath when she licked him.

"But for whatever reason, yours gets me all hot and bothered. Isn't that crazy? Just looking at your cock makes me desperate to have you."

"You remember the game show and tell?" He swatted her bottom. "Let's do a little more showing." He gave her ass a shake. "Less telling."

"Patience." She sucked him into her mouth and got him soaked. "Did you know it's easier to put on a condom when you're nice and wet?" She sat up, boobs bouncing, lips wet from sucking him. "That's not something you learn in a middle school sex education class. Nope. You learn it from experience."

"You think I want to hear about the other men you've fucked right now?"

"It might excite you more if you know I have some experience under my belt."

She was being sassy, and it was cute. Batting her hand away, he fisted his swollen cock. "Do I look like I'm not excited?" He couldn't be any harder. Her eyes glazed with lust as she sucked him back into her mouth. When she licked just under the ridge, a jolt rioted through him, making his hips pitch off the mattress. "Fuck."

"See that?" Quickly, she rolled the condom down his shaft. "You're going to love having sex with me." Then she positioned herself over him. "You ready?"

"I've fantasized about fucking you since I was fourteen years old. I'm way past ready. Now, ride me."

Desire flared in her eyes, and she slowly sank down. As

she swayed her hips to accommodate his size, her eyelids fluttered closed, and she sighed in pleasure.

She made him wild. Made him want to take control, grab her ass, and move her on his hard cock, help her ride him into oblivion.

But she was all soft and sexy, and he had no choice but to settle his excited ass down and just watch. All that shiny, dark hair tumbled down her back and over her shoulders. It shook and shimmied, giving him glimpses of tight pink nipples.

When she placed her hands behind her, all that hair cascaded onto his thighs, affording him a view of her glorious breasts.

She was so beautiful, so sexy, and he couldn't believe he got to be with this woman. Overcome with emotion, he reared up and wrapped his arms around her. The kiss fired up his central nervous system and infused his blood with a volatile blend of lust and wild, deep affection.

He licked into her mouth, his hands on her back, sliding down to her ass. Gripping her cheeks, he lifted her and slammed her down on him, meeting her downstrokes with hard punches of his hips. But this position limited him, and he needed room.

With one hand cradling her head and the other on her bottom, he tipped her back onto the mattress, not once breaking the mouths apart. Luxurious strokes of their tongues and her soft moans and sighs excited him beyond reason. He wanted to drive into her until he relieved himself of this voracious hunger.

But at the same time, he never wanted it to end. He

wanted to kiss her, feel her bare tits against his chest, and hear her sexy sounds forever.

"I always knew your skin would be this soft." Gently, he sucked her earlobe. "That's number five, by the way. She has to have the softest skin." He nuzzled her neck, breathing in her feminine scent. "Six. She has to smell just like you."

"I'm doing pretty good here."

"You are." He grinned as his fingertips skimmed across her collarbone, dipping into her cleavage, and then, he pinched her nipple.

Her back arched. "Oh."

"Seven. She has to be kind. Smart. Generous."

"So all three come under the same heading?"

He chuckled. "Eight. She's great with kids."

"Eight's a lot. For me, there's only one, and that's that he gets the job done. Can you stick it in, please?"

He pressed his forehead to her chest and laughed. Yes, he laughed. While having a raging boner.

But nothing was going to rush his exploration of her lush body. He licked her nipples, pushing her breasts together and loving the erotic plumpness. "Number nine. She has to make me laugh. When we're together, I have to forget the entire world and lose myself in her. In how she makes me feel. How she frees me." A thought struck him, and he lifted his head to look into her heavy-lidded eyes. "You know what I just realized?"

She pushed the hair off his damp cheeks. "Tell me?"

"I thought freedom was riding my bike from one city to the next, but the truth is, I'm on the run." From the identity this town had given him. *No. Finlay's right.* He was on the run because the one thing he craved—a family, roots, this woman—might be taken away from him. "And I only know that because my heart—my happiness—is right here in this bed."

He raised up on his arms and pressed the tip of his cock into her opening. Watching her eyes burn with desire, he slowly pushed inside. He wanted to feel every single cell light up, experience every sensation, every shift in her expression. "Number ten. She has to make me feel alive. Happy." He slid in all the way, until his cock was coated in her desire and buried in her hot, welcoming pussy. "And number eleven. She has to be you. Only you."

"Oh, Jude." Her voice was drenched in affection.

With a hand under her ass, he tilted her hips, adjusting until he heard her moan in satisfaction. Once he found the friction she needed, he drove into her, keeping a relentless pace that had her head tipping back and her hips thrusting to meet his. Sure, he was attracted to her, but the kerosene for his arousal was affection. He just liked her so much. Liked being with her, helping her, making her laugh. He liked the man he was with her.

He drilled into her, watching her come apart. It was such a turn-on, the way she lost herself so completely.

Until she opened her eyes, and their gazes connected. Locked. And the strangest thing happened. A thunderbolt shocked his system. His breath hitched. His rhythm faltered.

He soared miles past lust and entered a whole new territory.

Never taking their eyes off each other, he fucked her. His body burned. Perspiration trickled down his back. His senses heightened terrifyingly. It was almost as if he were being split wide open. Like a laser beam of light hit the center of his solar plexus, splintering every cell in his body.

She writhed beneath him, gripped fistfuls of his hair, and bit his shoulder to muffle the cries of her release.

His climax came fast and furious, howling through him like a tornado, severing his ties to earth, and sending him blasting into a universe of blinding light and pure euphoria.

He let out a guttural cry, and she clamped her arms and legs around him. It was the closest to fusion he'd ever experienced with another human being.

His body spasmed, each orgasm more powerful than the one before it. He'd never experienced anything like it.

Finally, he collapsed to her side, and she nestled up against him.

It was perfect. *She* was perfect.

Chapter Eighteen

In that drowsy state before fully waking, Finlay lingered in the memories of Jude's hands on her.

There was nothing tentative about that man. He took what he wanted, and what he wanted was *her*. His size and strength made her feel—well, if not exactly petite, then at least just right. His hunger for her drowned all the whispers of insecurity.

He kissed like he couldn't get enough, touched like she drove him wild, and snuggled like he couldn't bear to be apart from her.

Mmm. So good. He'd clung to her all night, making her feel so…wanted. So desirable.

They were so good together. For the past few days, she'd been truly, deeply happy. She had everything she'd ever dreamed of.

Just last night, with the living room lit by a roaring fire and blinking lights, the three of them had snuggled on the couch, reading books before bed. The way she and Jude had looked at each other over the boy's head and smiled, the connection…

It was everything she'd ever dreamed of…

Unease slid under her skin. Because it wasn't real. Cody wasn't her son, and Jude—

A heady mix of desire, affection, lust, and happiness collided in her chest.

Being with him was better than any fantasy she'd ever had, but it was one thing to believe he wasn't built for domesticity, and another thing entirely to understand he'd never recovered from the loss of his mom.

She wasn't sure he *could* recover from that. And that meant he might never be able to give her the kind of relationship she needed. And now that she knew what it could be like with him, she knew she'd never accept less. Not from him, not from anyone.

He'd warned her about this. He'd said it was dangerous, that playing happy family would end badly.

But you know what? I don't have a Magic 8 Ball. I can't see the future.

I sure don't have to sabotage it, either. She'd just have to see how it played out, and if he pulled a runner or started shutting down…well, she'd know it was time to leave.

She supposed it was time to get up. Since Jude and Cody had gone to the park for the stomp, she'd slept in for the first time in ages. Her body was deliciously sore, and she stretched before stacking some pillows and sitting up.

Unplugging her phone from the charger, she checked for messages, happy to see Jude had texted pictures. The first was one of Cody leaning over a table, examining a series of sketches. She smiled at his look of concentration and loved seeing him surrounded by all those big men.

The next was the professional photo of all the teams gathered in the town square. And the third was of the six guys standing on top of the wooden mold the town provided for each team, jumping on the snow, making it so compact they couldn't dig a finger into it to make a tunnel.

Seeing Cody laugh so hard filled her with joy. She'd wanted to go with them, wanted to be part of the fun, but Jude needed to bond with the boy on his own. Not with her as the safety blanket.

It was the right thing to do, but she did feel a little left out.

A truck engine rumbled in the distance. It could be anyone, of course, but she threw off the covers, grabbed a fresh pair of panties out of her dresser, and quickly dressed.

Her heart pounded, and she nearly toppled down the stairs in her eagerness to greet him. She wanted to launch herself into his arms the moment he walked in the door, but she knew he wouldn't be alone. As she crossed the living room, she noticed boxes on the dining room table. Her body recognized them before her mind did because awareness burst under her skin. Quickly, she detoured to open one, just to be sure. And yep—Pyrex measuring cup, a whisk, and boxes of melt-and-pour mixtures.

Jude had gone into the attic and brought down her soap-making boxes. That man was terrible for her central nervous system. Smiling at his thoughtfulness, she quickly put the boxes on top of the washing machine in the mudroom. She didn't want Cody getting into the essential oils.

Truck doors slammed, and by the time she'd safely stored both boxes, boots were hitting the wood foyer.

"Miss O'Neill." Cody came racing into the kitchen. He was breathless with excitement, and, from the way he ran with his fists and arms rotating from side to side, he'd clearly adopted the McKenna swagger. "We're gonna make gingerbread cookies."

She laughed, her heart so full. "Okay, sweet boy." She pulled him in close for a hug, breathing in the scents of baby shampoo and cold air. "You had fun?"

"Yeah." He pulled away. "We're gonna go with my idea and make a gingerbread house with windows. Inside, I said there should be a family opening presents, and Uncle Wyatt said, 'What kinda family?' and I said, 'Guys like us,' and he said, 'But if we want to win, we've got to do something different,' so we're gonna do some other stuff to make it special."

"That sounds fantastic." Hope burned brightly inside her. He might always be damaged by the neglect in his formative years, but he had the spirit to overcome and embrace the gifts the McKenna family would give him. "Okay, let me check and see if we have the ingredients for gingerbread." She opened the cabinet and checked the top shelf. Flour, brown sugar, molasses. "Yep, we can do it."

"Good, 'cause Grampa says we're gonna try gingerbread cocoa, and I said I never had gingerbread before, and he said, 'Well, we're gonna make some cookies' so I can try it."

The men stopped talking, and Finlay's gaze shot to

them. Who did he mean? Carlo was in Idaho, and Jude's dad was the one who had a thing for hot chocolate.

Was he calling Gunnar Grampa? *Already?*

Oh, man. She hoped Jude would get to adopt him. A squeeze of doubt pinched the back of her neck. Because she'd been in that courtroom. She'd seen the way Judge Adams had looked at him.

He might've granted Jude temporary custody, but would he sign adoption papers? But she couldn't worry about that now. Not when she had a kitchen full of McKennas and a little boy who'd never been this talkative in his life.

"Us guys are hungry." Cody gestured to the men crowding her kitchen.

"Well, these cookies take a little bit of time to make because you have to chill the dough, but maybe I could make sandwiches?"

Gunnar pulled two cocoa packets out of the back pocket of his black jeans and set them on the counter. "Know what takes ten minutes to make?"

Cody looked up at him with reverence, waiting for the answer.

"Gingerbread pancakes." Gunnar gave her a chin nod. "Since you've got the ingredients, you mind if I take over your kitchen?"

"Not at all." In fact, she loved it.

"Pancakes, it is." Gunnar looked at the kitchen table. "Grab a chair."

Boone brought one over and lifted Cody onto it. It was interesting to see what roles the men fell into. Jude pulled a griddle from the drawer under the oven and two ceramic stacking bowls from the cabinet. Gunnar cracked eggs and whisked the ingredients, while Wyatt silently measured and neatly set the table with plates, napkins, and drinks.

A natural rhythm created over a lifetime of being a family.

She didn't have a history like that, and as an outsider, her heart gave a little twist of longing. Because she'd love to slot right in and find her own role with them.

But this is good for Cody, and that's all that matters.

Working at the kitchen table, she used the same supplies to make a batch of cookie dough. The kitchen was warm from the oven and stove and loud from the conversation and laughter. She smiled at their inside jokes—she was actually coming to understand them—and was happy to see Cody so relaxed. Securing the dough in plastic wrap, she brought it to the refrigerator.

They were all having so much fun, she figured she'd slip away, take a shower, and get ready for the day.

Until muscular arms belted around her waist, and a chin settled on her shoulder. "I missed you." He smelled of cinnamon and cloves.

She wanted to sink into his embrace. To turn into the shelter of his arms and bask in his strength and affection. But she hesitated because she knew herself. She'd go all in. She'd give him every ounce of herself.

But what if he couldn't give it back? What if he didn't have a whole heart since he'd cut off the oxygen to a big chunk of it after his mom's passing?

Oh, come on. Was there really any decision to make? If she held herself back, she'd guarantee she'd never have a life with him. No, she had no choice. She had to give him everything she had. No hiding. No pretending. And no holding back. She tipped her head back against his shoulder. "I missed you, too, but I want you to bond with him."

"I get that, but it'll happen naturally. I want you with me." His body heated up, his arms tightened, and at the same moment he lowered his lips to press a kiss on her cheek, she turned to tell him she wanted to be with him, too. But when his mouth landed over hers, it shut down all her thoughts.

This man swept her away with his sweet intimacy. His big hand held her jaw, and his tongue slipped inside, tangling with hers. When they were connected like that, all her worries and fears melted into a puddle. No one could predict the future, but she would give everything she had to get the outcome she wanted.

"Mister?" Cody called.

Their mouths jerked apart, but Jude kept his arms around her. "Yeah?"

Cody eyed them curiously. "Did you get hurt, Miss O'Neill? You made a sound like you was hurt."

"I did, yeah." She started to pull away, but Jude gripped her. Confused, she looked down to see a bulge in his jeans. Desire rocketed through her. "But Jude's making it all better." Oh boy, they were in serious trouble.

"You need a Band-Aid?" Cody asked. "I know where they are."

"I'm okay, but thank you. I appreciate that very much."

"You want some cocoa? We don't got anymore gingerbread, but I can make you a reg'lar one."

"I'd love a cup of cocoa. Thank you."

"I'll get it." Cody dashed to the stove. "We gotta make Miss O'Neill a hot chocolate. She got hurt, but Mister's making it all better."

"I'll bet he's making it better," Boone said.

"Don't start," Gunnar said. "Get the milk."

Taking one last moment with Jude, she ran her fingers through his hair. "You doing okay down there?"

"You've got your hands on me, and I can smell everything we did last night on your skin. So no, Fee. I'm not okay. I'm as hard as an anvil, and I want to drill you so hard you can't walk for the rest of the day."

She feigned a swoony sigh. "You make my heart flutter."

"You gauge how much I want you by how hard I fuck. That's plenty romantic."

"You're right."

"You want that more than words."

"I do. I love how much you want me." She pressed her hips against him.

He hissed in a breath. "I'm kicking everyone out, and we're instituting nap time around here."

She laughed. "No, you're not. Cody loves having them around. Besides, we're going to get the Christmas tree."

"Right. Okay, then, let's get those pancakes in our bellies and get a move on. But the kid's going to bed early tonight."

Before they joined the rest of the family, she said, "Did you notice that even though he loves being around your family, and they're making him pancakes and cocoa, he still wanted to get me a Band-Aid?"

"Yeah, I got that."

"Very few five-year-olds are that compassionate. You got a good one there."

"I know that. I do. Both of you are making me a better man."

She tugged on his hand, forcing him to turn back to her. "You're already a good man. We're just your reason to own it."

Chapter Nineteen

"First batch done." Gunnar set the platter on the table. "Go on and eat. There's more coming."

Chairs scraped, the brothers threw their usual barbs, and a frisson of joy tripped down her spine. She'd imagined a clean-cut husband and children who looked just like the two of them. Not rugged, tattooed bikers who were some of the most generous men she'd ever known. Not an orphaned little boy, desperate for family.

Focusing on her vision board had cut her off from a whole world of possibilities.

"What do you usually do for Christmas?" Boone asked her.

"If Willa's in town, I help out at the inn. It's really fun. Her dad dresses up as Santa, and they have carolers and cookie decorating… He even leaves a trail of powdered reindeer footprints."

"What about your family?" Gunnar asked from the stove.

She could see how weird her answer sounded to mention her friend and not her parents. "We find time to get together, but the village pays more over the holidays, and the guests are extra demanding, so they both work a lot. My mom and I exchange presents on Christmas morning. My dad…" She shrugged. How did she explain Buck O'Neill? "He's invited to a lot of parties."

The men went silent, concentrating on their pancakes, the only sound the clink of forks on plates. *Way to make things awkward.* Well, they'd asked, and she'd told the truth.

Butter sizzled on the griddle, and Cody said, "Can I make Amy a present?"

Thanks for the distraction.

"Yeah, of course," Jude said. "What'd you have in mind?"

"I don't know." Cody looked at her.

"Do you want to give her some of the gingerbread cookies?" Finlay asked. "Tomorrow's the holiday party. We can wrap them up nicely and put them in your backpack. Does that sound good?"

"That's the last day of school, right?" Jude asked.

Cody sat back in his chair, looking uneasy. "It's my last day? I don't get to go anymore?"

"No, no." She set down her fork. "It's the last day before winter break. Preschool gets a whole month off."

"I still go to school?"

"Yes. They're just taking a break for the holidays. You'll go back in January."

"Okay." The boy looked deep in thought. "If I'm not

gonna see her, I'd better make a picture, too. She'll be sad without me."

"That's a great idea. You've got that new art table in your room with all the crayons and paper." Finlay smiled at Gunnar, who quickly turned back to the griddle.

Cody dropped out of his chair and ran off.

"Wait," Gunnar called. "What about the pancakes?"

"I'm not hungry."

After the boy reached the stairs, Boone asked, "Who the hell's Amy?"

"A kid in his class," Jude said.

"Maybe Jude wouldn't have gotten suspended so much if he'd had an Amy." Boone laughed. "You remember Ms. Duncan?" he asked his brothers. "Oh, man. She was such a bitch to me, and I never knew why. Until one day, when she asked a question, and no one but me raised a hand to answer. She wouldn't call on me—acted like I was invisible —so, finally, I just called it out, and she said, 'That's enough, Jude.' Can you believe it? He hadn't been in her class in six years, and she still called me by his name."

Boone was too busy laughing to notice the way his brother's shoulders tightened.

"Remember when Decker got a D on that essay in Mr. Branson's history class?" Boone asked. "He stayed after to find out what was wrong with it, and Mr. Branson skimmed the paper, handed it back with a shit-eating grin, and said, 'Nothing, Decker. Nothing at all.'"

"Well, Mr. Branson was an asshole." Everyone shot Finlay a look. Which was fair. She didn't usually swear. But couldn't Boone see the effect this conversation was having on his brother? "You know, not everyone should be a teacher. If you can't see the kids as individuals, if you can't see what's really going on behind a vest and a bad attitude, then you shouldn't work with children."

"Okay, next batch." Gunnar interrupted the conversation with a fresh platter of steaming pancakes.

She got his message to change the conversation. "What about you guys? What do you do for the holidays?"

"Usually, we have a big dinner for Christmas Eve—" Wyatt began.

"Rack of lamb," Gunnar said on his way back to the griddle.

"And then a bunch of side dishes." Wyatt stabbed a pancake with his fork and brought it to his plate. "My client's making me pozole, so I'll bring that."

"Your client?" Finlay wondered if he meant someone he was seeing. Why would a pet owner make him soup?

"Yeah, that's why he lives in an Airstream and not a damn house," Boone said as he poured syrup. "He trades his services for weird shit like socks and—"

"Pozole." Gunnar looked at Boone like he couldn't understand how his son didn't get it. "Fair trade to me." To Wyatt, he said, "Trim the dog's nails or something and get her to double the batch."

Wyatt blew out a breath of frustration. "I don't groom pets."

"Sorry, trim the talons on the raptor," Gunnar said.

"Squeeze the cougar's anal glands," Jude said.

They all cracked up. Tension broken, Finlay went back to eating, but she wished Jude didn't keep everything inside. She knew how much he hated the way his reputation had impacted them, but *they* didn't.

"Okay, so Wyatt's bringing pozole," Gunnar said. "What else?"

"I'll bring snacks," Boone said. "Chips, pretzels."

"Yeah, because Christmas Eve is just like a tailgate party," Wyatt said. "Step it up."

"Oh, okay," Boone said. "Would you prefer a baked brie? Maybe a cranberry crostini?"

"I'm not eating cranberry crostini," Jude said.

"Bring a jar of salsa and call it done," Gunnar said.

"Sounds good to me," Boone said. "You ever try those lime chips? They slap so hard."

Okay, clearly, this was a potluck kind of thing. She had to participate, but she didn't really cook. "Can I bring dessert?"

"Sure," Gunnar said. "What're you thinking?"

"Bring whatever you want," Boone said.

"Says someone who doesn't give a crap what he puts in his cakehole." Gunnar poured the warm hot chocolate into mugs. He set two on the table and then called up the stairs, "Cocoa's ready."

"Be right there," the boy called from his room.

Gunnar made his way back to the table. "So, dessert?"

"I'd love to make a Bûche de Noël." Finlay could already see the fork tines she'd draw in the chocolate icing to look like bark, the plastic frogs and snakes she'd add for decoration.

Do they sell moss at the craft store?

"Works for me." Gunnar seemed pleased.

"He usually buys one from The Singing Baker or Coco's Chocolates," Jude said. "So that's perfect."

"Oh, good." She liked that she had something meaningful to offer. "I've always wanted to make one."

"Cool." Gunnar went back into the kitchen to pour two more mugs full of cocoa. He brought them to the table. "What's he doing up there? I'm gonna check."

"Don't rush him. He's making a present." Wyatt's chair scraped back. "I'll bring his cocoa."

"I've got a way with the ladies," Boone teased. "I'll help him with the card."

"You know how creepy that sounds, right?" Wyatt asked.

All three headed for the stairs, leaving her alone with Jude.

She got up to clear the plates, and Jude followed her to the sink. As she rinsed, he loaded the dishwasher. She couldn't help noticing his goofy smile. "What're you thinking about?"

"You stood up for me." He kissed her on the mouth.

"Well, somebody had to. You're not responsible for lousy teachers."

"Look at you, getting all worked up." He slid his fingers through her hair. "You're beautiful." His gaze was soft and warm. "You make me happy."

He overwhelmed her. His affection, his scent, his size and strength. She couldn't think, couldn't form a sentence…could barely take a breath. It almost felt like a déjà vu moment, though she'd never imagined being in a home with his dad and brothers, eating gingerbread pancakes and drinking hot cocoa.

He shut off the faucet, gripped her under her arms, and set her on the counter. Pushing her legs open with his hips, he set one hand on her cheek while the other slid into her hair. He kissed her with such devotion, such worship, that her body pulsed with need.

His urgency, his desperation burned hot enough to incinerate the barrier that kept their bodies from fusing. She needed it. The way he wanted her… It made her whole.

Gunnar barked out a laugh, and heavy boots hit the stairs.

Their mouths tore apart, but their bodies stayed pressed together. She tangled her fingers in his hair. "I can't believe I get to kiss you in my kitchen on a Sunday morning."

Cody came crashing into the room, followed by the three men. "Look what I made, Miss O'Neill. The guys said I did a good job." He handed her a drawing. "I'm going to give it to Amy in school tomorrow. Don't fold it 'cause it'll get ugly."

"I won't fold it." He'd drawn a picture of two stick figures standing in a grassy field, flowers growing on long, droopy stems. Next to them was a crude swing set. "Oh, she's going to love this." She wiped the cocoa mustache off his upper lip.

"All right, we're out of here," Gunnar said. "What's the plan? You want Christmas Eve at my place or here?"

"Yours," Jude said. "But let's have Christmas here so Cody can open his presents."

"You sure you want all of us to come over?" his dad asked her.

"Yes." She answered a little too quickly, but she knew

they understood what it would mean to Cody to have the whole family here.

"Sounds good," Gunnar said. "I'll bring the groceries and cook so you guys can just enjoy Christmas Day as a family."

With her mom and dad, she'd be apologetic. She'd worry about imposing, causing them more work. But Gunnar wasn't like that. He was genuine. All she could do was smile. "That sounds perfect."

He gave her a sharp nod. "Invite your folks."

"Oh, they won't come."

"Up to them whether they do or not." The older man shrugged. "At least, they'll know they're welcome."

"Gunnar, I want to be you when I grow up." It hadn't even occurred to her that she could emotionally detach from the people who hurt her. *They can choose to be in my life or not. It's up to them.*

After the three guys left, Jude and Finlay finished cleaning the kitchen. She put the ingredients away while he wiped the counters. "Your mom can come for breakfast. Keep up that tradition with her."

"To be honest, I think she'll be relieved to hear I have other plans. She doesn't really *want* to do anything. And I get it. She has a demanding job. It's not just the crazy hours. It's the ridiculous requests, too. A woman once called her at three in the morning because her feet were cold, and all her socks were wet from skiing. Keep in mind, all the houses and condos have washers and dryers."

"And your dad? He'd rather party?"

"Right, but he only goes to the ones where he can

make connections. People who'll hire him to caddy or give golf lessons. Or to go on outrageous snowboarding trips."

"Got it." Jude smacked the faucet and snatched a dry dish towel off the counter. He pulled her in for a hug. "You deserve so much more than they gave you."

"I think I'm just starting to see that."

As he drove to the tree farm, Finlay exchanged text messages with her parents about Christmas plans while Cody dozed in his booster seat. Between the cloud cover, the black leather interior, and the Mustang's low ceiling, the world was dark, cozy…intimate.

Contentment surged through him.

This is happiness.

Whatever he'd experienced before Finlay? That was not it. Being with her gave it a whole new definition.

Up until this moment, he'd never really fit into his skin. He couldn't explain it. He'd just never belonged anywhere. Even in his family, he'd always felt like an outsider, like the black sheep. He'd just never felt truly himself. And that was why he'd been on the run.

He wasn't chasing freedom—he was fleeing.

But with her, everything clicked into place. He was exactly where he needed to be.

When she finished, she set her phone in the cupholder. "I'm supposed to be on my honeymoon right now."

She might as well have hit him with a shovel. He'd

gotten so caught up in his own feelings that he'd lost sight of the fact she was still in the thick of a life crisis.

What had he been thinking? Of course she wasn't ready to jump from a lifelong commitment into a new relationship in a week.

You're playing house.

"Right about now, it'd be really hitting me."

"What would?" he asked.

"All the stuff we were working toward—the wedding, buying the house—is over, so it'd just be us. Alone. And, at this point, we'd realize we don't have anything to talk about. We probably wouldn't be having…" She glanced behind her to make sure Cody couldn't hear them over the roar of the engine. With the red blanket clutched to his chest, his cheeks pink from the heat in the car, he watched out the window. "Sex because we're so exhausted from all the planning, and I wouldn't care. I didn't need it from him."

"Ever?"

"Not really. I figured that was normal after being with the same person for two years. But what really hit me while I was texting my parents is that my marriage would be a continuation of the loneliness I grew up with. And it'd be so familiar, I wouldn't have even noticed." She looked down at her hands. "Until you came along and showed me what I've been missing."

Happiness flared, filling his heart and rushing into his veins. "I need you to be very specific right now."

"Oh, come on. You know—"

"No, I don't."

"I just… I think about you constantly. I want my

hands on you all the time. When something pops into my mind, you're the one I want to share it with. For thirty years, I only took up one tiny corner of my life, and you've just opened all these rooms I didn't know existed." She let out a laugh. "Don't let this go to your head."

"It's going straight to my cock. But go on."

"Mister?" Cody called.

"I take that back," he muttered. "Stop talking." He eyed the boy in the rearview mirror. "Yeah?"

"When are we getting a tree?"

"You see that sign up ahead?" Jude pointed.

Cody peered between the seats. When he saw it, he nodded.

"That's the farm. We're here."

Cody's legs kicked out in anticipation, and he balled his blanket in his lap. "I want to get a really big one."

Finlay turned to him. "Should we put white lights on it or colored ones?"

"Colored ones. I want red, green, and blue lights."

"You got it." She took in the woods around her. "Is this whole area the tree farm?"

"I don't know much about it." He'd just been a kid tromping through the snow with his family, arguing over which tree was better and taking turns with the saw. "When was the last time you were here?"

"Fifth grade, with Leia. That was my canon event." She laughed as if it were a joke. "We'd been friends for years, of course, but that trip crystallized my idea of a family. Like, she and her brother were fighting in the back seat, her parents were talking quietly up front—in a way you just knew they liked each other. *That* wasn't something I was used to. We all got cups of hot apple cider, her dad carried the saw, and we sang along to the piped-in Christmas carols on the wagon ride. The whole experience was right out of a movie."

"Well, here you are, living it yourself." Nearing the turn, he slowed.

"Except it's not real. This is a fake engagement, and I'm just the nanny." She reached for his arm. "I don't mean it like that, so you don't need to say anything. I promise I'm not feeling sorry for myself. I'm just saying I'm *not* living it. And that's okay because, thanks to my marriage blowing up, I'm learning the difference between reality and fantasy. And throwing out the map, living life on the fly? It's not so bad. In fact, it's kind of exciting."

They passed under an arched ranch sign strung with twinkling lights. The trees lining the road held giant ornaments, their limbs sagging under the weight. The parking area wasn't too crowded, which wasn't a surprise since Christmas was only a few days away. Pulling into a spot, he cut the engine and leaned across the console to kiss her on the mouth, relieved she wasn't hung up on her ex and glad she'd thrown out the vision board.

Since I'm not on it.

She unbuckled her seat belt. "But that's probably because I get to sleep naked with you, eat pancakes with hilarious and uncouth men, and make Christmas magic for a little boy who needs a home."

As soon as Cody got out of his booster seat, Jude helped him out of the car. The three of them held hands—the boy in the middle—and headed for the big white tent. When Cody saw the penned reindeer, he broke away from them and bolted. They quickly caught up with him as he watched other kids feeding the animals.

"Can I do that, too?" the boy asked.

"Yeah, of course." Jude grabbed a cup of something called magic moss. "But it says you have to clean your hands first." He lifted the boy to the dispenser and helped him rub the sanitizer all over. "There you go." He offered him the little paper cup.

Cody knelt in the snow and held out the delicate moss for a reindeer. He glanced up at them with a big grin. "He likes it."

"He does." This moment was surreal. The reversal of roles from a kid to the grownup was wild.

"It's easy, isn't it?" she asked quietly so Cody couldn't hear. "To put a child first. It comes naturally. I mean, you changed your whole life for a boy just because of a phone call."

At first, he thought she was reading his mind. But then, he remembered what she'd said in the car. "You're thinking about your parents?"

"Yeah. I'm seeing them from a whole different perspective now that I'm living with you and Cody." She looked up at him like she needed confirmation.

He didn't want to speak badly about them. She was figuring things out on her own. "They're just built differently."

"Yeah, I guess. It's just so easy, though. I can't even imagine making my kids be quiet on Christmas morning so I could sleep in. Or telling them I can't be bothered to decorate a tree or make cookies. I mean..." She set her hand on Cody's head, and he glanced up at her with pure delight. "What's more important than this?"

He wrapped an arm around her, drawing her close. "Nothing, Fee. Nothing's more important." At that moment, he wanted to make the magic for her. Give her everything she ever wanted. Shower her with attention and gifts. Anything to make her feel in her heart that she was worthy and loveable and the best person he knew.

A family joined them, holding cups of steaming hot chocolate and freshly made doughnuts. Cody jumped to his feet. "Can we get those?"

"Of course," Finlay said. "Let's go."

It wasn't too crowded in the tent, so they got in line for their snacks. She lifted Cody into her arms so he could see the choices.

"What can I get you?" the woman behind the table asked. "Cider or cocoa?"

"Is it good quality?" the boy asked.

The woman froze. Then she burst out laughing. "No, sir, it is not." She reached under the table and held up a tub of powdered mixture. "My aunt buys it in bulk, and we offer it for free, so nope. It probably doesn't even have real chocolate in it. The best I can offer is it'll warm you up."

"Sorry. He's—" Jude began.

"I'm an offshando," Cody said.

Since he'd heard the word so many damn times, Jude knew exactly what the boy was saying. "My dad calls himself an aficionado. But we need to warm up, so we'll take three cocoas."

"Got it." The woman filled three cups and handed one to Cody. "Tell me what you think."

The little boy took a sip. "It's all right. But it's not as good as my grandpa's."

The woman laughed and handed them a bag of doughnuts. "Have fun."

Next, they headed for the table that held saws and twine. The rumble of an engine had him quickly knocking back his cocoa, dumping the cup into a garbage can, and grabbing the necessary equipment. "All right, let's get on the wagon."

"We get to ride that?" Cody watched in awe as the tractor came to a stop and the families got off the wagon it was towing.

"We sure do." Finlay held her cup in her mittened hands. "It'll take us out into the fields where we can pick our tree."

As they waited their turn to board the hay-strewn wagon, Jude showed her a map stapled to a pole. "These are the different types of trees. Know which one you want?"

"I'm literally in hog heaven right now. I have my cocoa, a bag of warm doughnuts, and my two favorite guys. I'll be happy with anything you guys want."

"Douglas fir, it is." He noticed Cody had finished his cocoa. "You want to toss the cup in that garbage can?"

Cody nodded and dashed off.

Finlay moved in beside him. "Is that what your family usually gets?"

"I'm sure we've switched it up over the years, but that was the one on your vision board."

She gazed up at him with pure affection. "How do you remember that?"

"I remember everything." He brushed the hair off her shoulder, eyeing the smooth column of her neck and remembering breathing in her soft, sweet scent just hours ago. "I don't think you get how into you I was."

"I'm starting to."

It was their turn to board, so he called out to Cody. "Let's go, buddy."

Just as they started up the steps, a man shouted, "Jude McKenna? I thought they ran you out of town."

Chapter Twenty

THE SHOCK RUNNING THROUGH HIM WAS sickeningly familiar.

The replay of his past played in his mind.

Hey, you. Get back here.

Show me your backpack. Go on, open it.

We need you to come with us.

You son of a bitch.

Jude turned to find an old man stalking toward him.

"Jason." His wife caught hold of his arm. "Don't do this."

"Like hell I won't." The man shrugged out of her hold and moved closer. Addressing Finlay, the man pointed at Jude. "Do you know who he is? Because I don't think you'd have a child with him if you did."

Whatever shit he'd done in the past, Finlay O'Neill would not be paying the price. Jude blocked the man from her and the boy. "Not in front of my family."

"Well, look at that." The man seethed. "Now that you have a wife and kid, you care. Funny how that works.

Well, let me tell you something, you piece of shit. I'm not rich like some of the people in this town. I saved my entire life for that car. I had it three days before you and your loser friends crashed it. And don't tell me you were too young to know what you were doing. You were eighteen. That's old enough to know the difference between right and wrong."

"Jason, you're upsetting the boy," his wife said.

His eyes gleamed with anger, and it was clear he wasn't backing down. "That was an original '65 Mustang. My dad and I worked on it every weekend for fifteen years. And in one joyride from a bunch of punk-ass kids, it was gone. Totaled."

"That's enough." Jude would not tolerate upsetting Cody.

But before he could shut the man down, Finlay stepped in front of him. "Sir? With all due respect, that night he was on his way to me. To take me to the prom. He had no part in the situation—"

"You're going to stand up for this piece of shit?" The man reached for her arm.

Rage set his skin on fire. Before the old man could make contact, Jude stepped in front of her. "Keep your hands off my wife." His voice was so hard, so cold, the farm went dead quiet around them. But Cody was watching, and he planned on staying in town, so it was time to take a stand. "I'm sorry for what happened to your car. I'd be upset if some stupid kids destroyed a project I worked on with my dad, but I didn't steal it, and I didn't drive it, so you're not going to talk to me like this."

"You're a goddamn liar, and the judge kicking you out of town is proof of that."

"Hey." The cocoa and doughnut woman stormed up in a beanie lit up with LED Christmas lights. "Unless you want nothing but coal in your stocking," she said to the man, "it's time for you to head on out. This is a Christmas tree farm. There are children here, and Santa's very disappointed in your behavior. Now, I'm going to ask you nicely to leave the premises. You'll be awfully embarrassed if a bunch of elves have to escort you off the property."

"I can't believe you," his wife snapped, clearly mortified. "Let's go."

"He crashed my car," the man whined as his wife led him away.

After they left, the woman with the twinkling hat waved them aside, out of the line. "Hi, I'm so sorry about that. I'm Molly Bright." She gestured at the nearest sign that read *Merry Bright's Christmas Tree Farm*.

"It's not your fault." Finlay shook her hand. "But thank you for stepping in like that. I'm Finlay, and this is Jude, my fiancé, and Cody, our boy. So you own the farm?"

Adrenaline still coursed through him, and he held Cody's shoulders, pulling him close. He hated that his past ruined a fun family event, but he was glad he'd stood up for himself. It felt good.

"Technically, my aunt does," the woman said. "But I grew up here. We moved when I was a kid. I'm sure you've heard all about it. Never mind." She rolled her eyes. "Big scandal."

"With the Bright family?" Finlay asked. "I've lived

here all my life, and I've never heard anything negative about you guys. Everyone loves the Brights."

"Ah, well. That's because I'm actually Molly Winters."

"Oh, the Winters." Finlay nodded. "Yes, I remember them."

"Right, so, since my parents kept up their antics wherever we moved, I decided to cut ties and legally change my last name to my mom's maiden name. But I love my aunt and the farm, so I come for a visit whenever I can." She turned to Jude. "I've been yelled at before, so I get it. You'd think after all these years, people would forget. Or at least not associate me with their crimes, but…small towns, short memories."

"Jude says the same thing. Do you still have friends here?" Finlay asked. "Anyone you hang out with when you come to town?"

Of course, she would ask that. She knew what it was like to be excluded.

"Oh, gosh no. I'll be forever associated with what my parents did. But it's fine. I'm here to help my aunt and spend the holiday with her. It's all good."

"Well, my friends and I are going to Wild Billy's tonight if you want to join us."

He wanted to pinch her ass for lying. She had no such plans. But it was such a sweet gesture, he could only keep his mouth shut and admire the hell out of her.

"Yeah, I'd love that." She pressed her lips together and drew in a breath. "Thank you."

"Awesome." Finlay pulled out her phone. "Here. Text yourself, and then I'll let you know what time we'll be there."

Molly's teeth sank into the tips of her glove as she pulled it off to type. "I can't wait. Thank you."

Finlay slid the phone back into her pocket. "We'll talk soon. And thank you for stepping in back there." After Molly took off, Finlay slid her arm through his. "You okay?"

They'd missed one ride, so they had to wait for the next wagon. "Sure." To be honest, he wanted to get the hell out of there. Ride the Gallatin Road all the way to Yellowstone. Fuck the cold. Fuck the snow. Just leave this town in his rearview mirror.

But the little boy looking up at him with worry in his eyes was his reason to fight against the impulse. He lifted him into his arms, and Cody clutched Jude's leather jacket. "Sorry about that."

"That man was mad at you."

"Yeah." Jude exhaled, calming down for the boy's sake. "He was."

"What'd you do?"

"He actually didn't do anything wrong," Finlay said, always his protector. "His friends did it. Unfortunately, that man took it out on Jude, which wasn't very nice."

"That man was mean." There was a question in Cody's eyes, as if he wanted more of an explanation.

Well, he wouldn't lie to this kid. "He was upset, and I understand that. I may not have crashed his car, but my friends did. I shouldn't have hung out with kids who did bad things. That's my fault, and I learned my lesson."

"That's okay." Cody patted his shoulder. "You're all right."

Maybe it was the crash of adrenaline, but his heart

swelled so quickly it didn't fit in his chest. This pure-hearted boy, so filled with compassion at five years old… *I'm supposed to take care of him, not the other way around.* He cleared his throat and looked away. "Thanks."

An engine sputtered, and the next tractor pulled up and came to a stop. In the time it took to board and find their seats on the hay-strewn bench, Jude managed to calm down. He'd never seen the point in correcting people's assumptions about him, and he still didn't know if it would work. But Finlay was right that his *Fuck you and the horse you rode in on* attitude wasn't doing anything but cementing their impressions of him.

So he could stay away and continue to haul the chip on his shoulder, or he could be the man Finlay and Cody needed him to be. Because the idea of walking away from her was unthinkable, and he sure as hell wouldn't give up his boy.

Over the piped-in Christmas carols, Finlay kept up a conversation with Cody. It was clear she was trying to cheer him up as she pointed out the cute hand-painted wooden signs lining the path and the playful animated elves peering out through the trees. It was all festive and fun, and he appreciated her effort to get him back in the spirit of the occasion.

Which was interesting, considering how important this day was to her.

And maybe that was the answer right there. Being in a relationship, taking care of this boy… Jude's feelings, his needs, took a back seat to theirs. They came first, no matter what.

When the bumpy ride came to a stop, he got up.

"Ready to pick our tree?" The boy nodded, and Jude carried him off the wagon. "Let's do this."

Several people gathered around a map of the forest and the various types of trees. "Douglas fir are that way," Jude said, and they headed off, their boots crunching in the snow. Rays of sunlight streaked through thick cloud cover, and pine and woodsmoke scented the air. "You get to choose any tree you want, okay?"

"I do?" When Jude nodded, Cody wriggled free and took off into the woods.

"Stay close, buddy," Jude called as they trudged along.

"That night when your friends called you, did you know what they'd done?" Finlay asked.

"No, I didn't ask. All I knew was they needed a ride, and the police were after them." He watched Cody dart from one row to another and then back, never quite running out of sight.

"Would you make a different choice today?" she asked.

"Probably." He rubbed the back of his neck. "But back then, I felt I owed it to them."

"I get it. They were your friends when no one else would be." She reached for his hand. "Well, that's two down."

"Two what?"

"Of the ten people who remember what you did as a child."

Only Finlay could pull him out of his dark headspace. "Yeah? So I only have to go through this shit eight more times?"

"Exactly. But it'll be worth it." She tipped her chin to

the little boy who was gazing up at a tree as if it were Santa himself.

"Is that the one?" Jude called, but the boy shook his head and moved on. "What's he looking for?"

"I don't know," Finlay said. "But you have to admire his determination."

"Yeah, he's a good kid." He watched the boy gazing up at the treetops. "Doesn't seem like the old man ruined his day."

"I think that's because of the way you handled it. It was a scary encounter, but you didn't get aggressive or physical, so it showed him he was safe. That *you're* safe. You kept your cool, and you stated your truth."

"This one," Cody called, standing before a giant Nordic fir.

Somehow, they'd wound up in a whole other field. "You good with that?" he asked Finlay.

"I love it. But will it fit in my living room?"

"We'll make it fit." He dropped to his knees in the crunchy snow. "You ready to help me cut it down?" he asked Cody.

Finlay parted the branches at the base, and the two of them crawled under the tree. Jude did the initial sawing while Cody watched intently. When the cut was deep enough, he gave Cody a turn. Covering the little boy's hands with his own, they sawed the rest of the way.

"Good job." They scrambled out and stood. "Now, we push it over. On the count of three, we're all going to say, *Timber*. You ready?"

Cody nodded enthusiastically as all three of them reached for the trunk.

"One, two, three…" he said, and they all gave it a shove. "Timber."

With a crack, the tree crashed to the ground, landing with a bounce.

"Is it mine?" Cody asked. "Is this *my* Christmas tree?"

"It sure is," Finlay said.

With his gloved hands, Jude lifted it by the freshly cut base and dragged it back to the road. "Let's take it home."

As they waited for the tractor, Finlay reached into the white wax bag and pulled out a doughnut for each of them. "We need sustenance after all that work."

Together, they waited, breathing in the cold air and chewing on their apple cider snacks.

"What are we gonna put on the tree?" Cody asked.

"Grampa got us lights and decorations," Finlay said. "We could make our own decorations. Would you like that?"

He nodded, with white sugar around his mouth and on his dark blue parka. "At school, we painted these little balls and popsicle sticks. Can I put them on the tree?"

"Yeah, of course," Jude said. "We'll do that when we get home."

Once they loaded their tree onto the wagon, they settled onto the bench seat. Cody climbed onto his lap, and Finlay sat right next to him. He wrapped an arm around her.

She leaned up and whispered in his ear, "Your wife, huh?"

I did say that, didn't I?

He grinned.

He liked the sound of it a whole hell of a lot.

Chapter Twenty-One

With Christmas a few days away, it was hard to round up Finlay's usual group of friends, and Eloise couldn't get a sitter, so it wound up being just her and Ava.

But it turned out okay because Blue Fire had shown up for a surprise show, and they happened to be one of Molly's favorite bands.

"I can't believe this is happening." Her new friend ogled the lead singer of the band. "I've probably seen them ten times. Slater Vaughn is so hot."

"And extremely taken." Ava gave a chin nod to his wife, who was hanging out at the bar.

Apparently, the band was recording at Gigi Cavanaugh's studio and decided to do an impromptu gig at Wild Billy's. The place was packed, the dance floor full, and the crowd was going wild for the indie/rock music.

Word had spread quickly about the surprise concert, so Gunnar had called in all his servers. At first, she'd been happy to see Jude, but it didn't take long for women to start hitting on him. *So, that's fun.* If she didn't want to get to know Molly, she'd go home and relieve Wyatt from babysitting duty.

She didn't need to reenact her childhood.

Molly leaned across the table. "I'm confused. Are you and Jude engaged or married? Because he called you his wife."

"He *what?*" Ava practically jumped out of her chair. "His *wife?*"

"Engaged." She didn't want to lie to her new friend, but Cody's well-being was at stake. When this whole situation was resolved, she'd tell her the truth.

"Well, that's sweet, then. He already feels married to you." Molly took a sip of her drink. "Is his dad's name Billy?"

"No, it's Gunnar," Finlay said. "Why?"

"This place is called Wild Billy's. Who'd he name it after? A grandfather or something?"

Finlay laughed. "You know what? I have no idea. This place has always been a bar, but when Gunnar bought it, he renamed it Wild Billy's. I'll have to ask him about it." Her gaze wandered back to Jude. He was talking to the same woman who'd been hanging around for the past ten minutes.

Flirting came with the job of bartender—she got that —but watching it happen was a special kind of torture. She'd felt it as a kid, sure. But now that she'd actually slept with him, it was like a thousand pinpricks to her heart. And mostly, it made her consider the obvious: *We're living together, we're having sex…but what are we?*

He's into me, I know that.

But what does it mean?

They assigned different values to sex. For her, it meant commitment. But what did it mean for a man who'd never been in a relationship before?

Keep your hands off my wife.

A shudder ran through her. She'd liked that a lot. He'd been so threatening. So possessive.

When she glanced over at him again, he was gone. She sat up straighter, scanning the room, and found him walking off with the smoking-hot blonde. *Where's he going?* He followed the woman to a table on the edge of the dance floor and waited while she grabbed her purse and said goodbye to her friends. Then the two of them headed out together.

When the pretty blonde cast a look at him over her shoulder, she had a flirty, sparkling smile.

Jealousy twisted through her, hot as a poker.

She didn't think for one second he'd hook up with a woman while they were fake engaged, and while she was sitting right there in his bar. Besides, he'd made his feelings clear about her. She knew she had nothing to worry about.

Then please explain why my stomach's in a knot, and I want to cry?

Okay, this is ridiculous. She needed a minute to pull herself together. "Hey, I'll be right back, okay?"

They broke from their conversation to eye her questioningly.

She forced a smile. "Just have to go to the bathroom." She tried to act nonchalant, but her muscles had gone tight, and her movements were jerky and awkward. Dodging servers and squeezing between chairs, she made her way around the dance floor. She just—*God*—she just needed space.

It was just so familiar. All through high school, she'd had to watch girls pass him notes, meet him under the bleachers, have sex with him in their cars.

I know it's not high school. I know that.

But I'm just so emotionally invested in this man.

I want him so much.

She ducked into the bathroom and stood at the sink. Her cheeks were flushed, her pupils dilated.

It's all right.

Everything's fine.

The door opened, and two women entered, laughing. She didn't want to see anyone right then, so she slipped into a stall. In the small, enclosed space, she released a tight breath. Maybe her reaction wasn't about him sleeping with someone tonight or next week. Maybe it was because she knew, deep down, she couldn't keep him. He didn't want a home, a family, a dog, a lawn mower, and one vacation a year. It wasn't his thing.

Sure, he had Cody, but that didn't mean he had to live in suburbia and shop at membership warehouse clubs. He didn't have to host barbecues in the backyard. He was the type of man who invented his life.

While I have a playbook.

Yeah, but you're throwing it away, remember?

Am I, though? She might toss out the vision board, but she still wanted that life. She wanted to host Super Bowl parties and spend her weekends watching her kids play soccer and learn piano.

Mostly, she loved Calamity and wanted to stay here.

She had zero interest in wandering the country. She wanted roots.

Then, there you go. That's that.

You like him, but you might not be compatible.

But when the panic over losing him kicked up again, she decided to give herself a gift.

You can be with him for five more weeks.

Just enjoy this time with him. Because, realistically, she'd just walked away from her wedding. She wasn't ready for a relationship, either.

Okay, there you go.

She couldn't say she felt a whole lot better, but she needed to get back out there and spend time with her friends.

You can crash out later tonight.

Leaving the stall, she washed her hands, ran a finger under each eye to clean up the mascara smudges, and then left. When she stepped out, she slammed right into a wall of heat and muscle.

Jude grabbed her arms. "What's going on?"

"Nothing." She averted her gaze. "I just went to the bathroom."

"Bullshit." He shook his head. "You ran like the building was on fire. Now, what happened?" A man moved past them to get to the men's room, and Jude pulled her farther down the hallway.

"Nothing. Excuse me." She tried to slide around him, but he blocked her way. "I have to get back to my table."

"Cool. Soon as you talk to me, you can do that."

"Jude—" What was the point of pretending? This man could read her like no one else. "Fine. I spent the whole night watching women flirt with you, and then, you left with a beautiful blonde—"

"You mean Kelsey?"

"Well, I don't know her name."

"So what, you think I had a quickie in the parking lot?"

"No." It did sound ridiculous. "That's not the point."

"Some tourist asshole was getting aggressive with her, and she asked me to walk her to her car."

"That was nice of you. And that's, you know, I'm sure part of your job. I just…I think we shouldn't have sex anymore." *Yes, that's good. That's the point.*

Wait, no. I want sex with him.

Didn't I just give myself permission to do it for five more weeks?

No. She shook her head. "I can't do it. I'm just not cut out for it."

His eyes flared, and his features tightened. "For sex?"

"No, I like sex. I like it with you. But…"

"But women are going to ask me to walk them to their cars, and I won't be able to keep from fucking them in their back seats?" He took a step back, folding his arms across his chest. "My bare white ass pumping for everyone in the parking lot to see?" He pressed his lips together in a look of feigned concern. "My dad wants to hand the bar over to me. He's gonna be *pissed.*"

"No, it's not that. I trust you. I really do. It's more about me." She pulled him to the end of the hallway. "It's been a wild week, and my emotions are all over the place. And when I saw all those women flirting with you, it just sent me spiraling."

"Because?"

"Because I'm a forever girl, Jude." It was a relief to say it out loud. "I've only ever dated with a purpose. Right now, I'm living with the boy I had a crush on in high school, and I'm getting to know the man who's so much better in real life than my fantasies, and I know it might not go anywhere. We want different things, and—"

"You're scared."

"I'm terrified." She let out a breath.

"You done now?"

She nodded, still unsettled.

"I can't make any promises. I don't know if the judge will even consider my adoption request. *You* left a wedding a week ago, and I don't know where your head is at."

That was fair.

"But if you think, after I finally got you into my bed, that I'd even *look* at another woman, you're out of your mind. You know why I came to the village back in high school? Because you were my peace. My quiet place. There was nowhere I'd rather be than with you."

"I felt the same way."

"I rubbed myself raw fantasizing about you. And now that I know what it's like to touch you, to watch you fall apart under my tongue, no one—do you hear me, Fee? No one exists outside of you. That's the *only* thing I'm 100 percent certain about."

She believed him so thoroughly that she flung herself into his arms. He got a fistful of her hair and yanked her head back, planting a kiss on her mouth and stealing the breath from her lungs.

He kissed her mercilessly, almost as if punishing her

for doubting him. His big hands gripped her bottom and lifted her off the floor. As he carried her into a dark cove, her ankles locked around his waist. Pressing her against the wall, he devoured her while grinding his hard erection against her core.

His hunger enflamed her. She needed more. Needed to rip off his clothes and feel his hot skin against hers. She was going to die if she didn't get his mouth and hands on her. His familiar scent of clean clothes, pine, and woodsmoke ignited all her senses. The throbbing between her legs demanded relief. "Jude." She sounded desperate, breathy. "I have to…*God*."

He set her down, unzipped her jeans, and yanked them to her ankles. Spinning her around, he set her hands on the wall.

A shiver of delicious naughtiness sizzled through her. "Someone will see us."

"You want me to stop?"

"No." It was so wrong. She would never do something like this. She lowered her head to hide her smile.

He smacked her ass. "You gonna be bad for me?" His cock pushed into her opening, teasing.

A frenzy of need made it impossible to answer. All she could do was jut her ass out. She needed more. She needed him all the way inside.

"Yeah. That's my girl."

With the combination of sounds from a wrapper tearing, the wail of guitars from the music, and the thump of bass and drums, anticipation built to an unbearable crescendo. Finally, he gripped her hips and, with a punch of his hips, plunged inside. A sizzle exploded in her core and spread like a flashfire to the tips of her fingers and soles of her feet.

He pounded into her recklessly, desperately. Leaning forward, he cupped her breasts, squeezing them in his big hands. He reached between her legs to stroke her sensitive bud.

He was everywhere. His scent, his hands, his mouth, his teeth biting her shoulder. From deep within her body, the roar began, rising in intensity, churning and spinning desire into a lust so intense, she had to curl her toes and fingers to keep herself grounded.

Heat exploded, as she came in a rush so blinding, so shattering, her knees buckled. With a hand on her pelvis to hold her up, he slammed up against her, punching his hips in short, ferocious bursts.

Finally, he pulled out and turned her around, enfolding her in his arms. "Never doubt me again." He kissed her mouth. "No one will ever compare to you."

Chapter Twenty-Two

When they walked in the door, they were surprised to find Boone and Cody playing with Duplo blocks on the living room floor.

Where'd Wyatt go?

And what was the boy doing up so late?

Boone clocked their surprised expressions—it was one in the morning, after all—and stood to go. "Uncle Wyatt got a call and had to go take care of something, and Mr. Big Ears here overheard the whole thing."

Cody came rushing over. "It's a coyote, and his tongue got cut off, and there was blood everywhere, and he might be dead."

"Okay, hang on, buddy." Jude lifted him into his arms, swiping the hair out of his eyes. The dark circles worried him. "Tell me what happened."

Boone grabbed his coat. "A coyote got into a garbage can and got his tongue stuck in a can of corn. It's not cut off, and the coyote's going to be just fine. I gotta go. I'll see you both in the morning for Snowfest, right?" He touched the top of Cody's head and held his gaze. "The coyote's okay."

Jude walked his brother to the door. "Hey, man, thanks for coming."

"Any time." He paused, uncharacteristically uncomfortable. "So who all came to girls' night?"

"It was Ava and a new friend, Molly," Finlay said, putting the blocks back into the box. "Eloise couldn't get a sitter."

His gaze cut away, frustration pulling his lips tight. "See you bright and early for the festival."

"We'll be there." After the door shut, Jude headed to the couch and sat down, settling Cody on his lap. It was late, but he didn't want the boy in bed, imagining worst-case scenarios.

He got his phone out of his pocket and texted his brother.

> Jude: You got a second to talk to Cody? He's upset about the coyote.

It didn't even take a minute before his phone rang, and Wyatt's face appeared on the screen. "Hey. Can I talk to Cody?"

"Yeah, of course." Jude handed the phone to the boy.

"Is he still bleeding?" Cody asked. "Is he dead?"

"No, he's not. He's sleeping. Come on. I'll show you." Wyatt flipped the camera around and showed the rows of metal kennels at his rehab center. "See this guy? That's a rabbit."

"What happened to him?" Cody asked.

"He got into a fight with a cat, but he's okay. See him nibbling those carrots?"

Cody nodded.

"And this guy?" Wyatt moved along. "That's a cougar. He got sick."

"Is he going to die?"

"Nope. We got him all fixed up. He should be going home in a few days."

Jude had heard about that. Someone had poisoned the mountain lion. *Glad he's okay.*

"And this is the coyote." The animal was pacing in its small cage. "See that? He's fine."

"He's not bleeding."

"No, he's not. He's healthy and strong. We'll release him as soon as his tongue's healed." The camera flipped back around. "I didn't know you'd overheard my conversation, or I would've explained the situation. I'm sorry about that. Now, we've got to be at the park at seven in the morning. We should all get some sleep."

Cody nodded, rubbing his eyes. "Good night, Uncle Wyatt."

"'Night, bud."

Hearing Cody call his dad "Grampa" and his brothers "Uncle" really got to him. Maybe it was the idea of bringing this lost, lonely boy into his family. Giving him stability he'd never had.

In his mind's eye, he could see the five of them in a circle, arms around each other, the boy in the center. Protected. Safe.

Loved.

And it made him think about what Finlay said about

six-year-old Jude. Maybe, in some way, he was healing himself through Cody.

After the call disconnected, Jude got up, ready to put the boy to bed. He smiled when Finlay breezed into the living room, looking fresh and pretty, not giving away a hint she'd just been railed in the hallway of his dad's bar.

She handed Cody a tumbler. "Here's some warm milk. It'll help you get to sleep."

The boy just stared at her for a moment. "You look pretty."

"Well, thank you." She pressed a kiss to the boy's cheek. "That's a very nice thing to hear."

And right then, with Cody sandwiched between them, he got it. A magical Christmas wasn't lights and stockings hung on the mantel. *It's us.*

Together.

As a family.

What they had was special, and if she doubted him for even a second, then it was on him. He wasn't letting her know how serious he was about her. He had to crack himself wide open to banish any doubt she had about his intentions.

"Come on. Let's get you to bed." Funny how, at the start of all this, he'd warned Finlay not to get too attached. He'd told her this was dangerous. *And look at me now.* He was the one at risk for a broken heart.

When he got upstairs, he placed the tumbler on the nightstand, settled Cody in bed, and tucked him under the covers. Jude sat on the edge of the mattress. "You have a good time with your uncles tonight?" Man, he was grateful for his brothers. They'd embraced this boy like he'd always been part of the family.

"Uncle Wyatt brought Nerf guns, and we ran around the house, shooting each other. It was fun. And then, he counted how long I could hold my breath in the bathtub, and he made a fort with sheets and blankets, and then, we ate popcorn and read books."

"That sounds like a lot of fun." He'd have to thank his brother tomorrow. Both of them. They'd said they were in this with him, and now, they'd shown him. He got up. "We'd better get some sleep. We've got a big day tomorrow." Not only was shaping a block of snow into a recognizable form tough, but his family was competitive. They wanted that trophy. "Good night." He kissed Cody on his forehead and headed for the door.

"Mister?"

It was starting to bother him. How his family got titles, and all he got was Mister. "Yeah?"

"I told Uncle Wyatt I want to get Miss O'Neill something for Christmas, and he said I should make something, but I don't know what to do."

His mind went blank. He had no idea what to make. And Christmas was three days away. "I can help you. You have anything in mind?" It had been so chaotic and busy, he hadn't considered gifts.

"Uncle Wyatt got out his phone and looked stuff up. He said we could draw her pictures, but I want to do something else, so he kept looking and said I could make her a chocolate cake in a jar, and I know she likes cake, so can we do that? And I want to make Grampa hot chocolate in a jar. Can we do that, too?"

It struck him how petty it was to worry about what Cody called him. *The only thing that matters is that he trusts me and comes to me for help. Knowing he can depend on me.*

Swear to God, if they let me adopt him, I will protect this boy with my life.

"Yeah, we can do that." Of course, when he set his stupid ego aside, he could see that everyone had told Cody what to call them. Finlay was his teacher, so he'd only heard her referred to as Miss O'Neill. His brothers called themselves Uncles, and his dad referred to himself as Grandpa.

I'll have to do the same thing. Once I figure out what he should call me.

Because if I don't get to keep him, I can't have him calling me Dad.

"What're you making Miss O'Neill?" Cody asked.

His mouth opened, but no words came out. Because he hadn't given it a single thought. And that sucked. "I don't know, but I'm glad you asked."

"Why?"

She deserves the world. She deserves to be showered in love. "I want to make sure I do something special for her. Let's both give it some thought, and we'll talk about it on our way to the park. Maybe after we're done working, we can go to the store and get supplies."

"Okay. And can we make something for Uncle Boone and Uncle Wyatt?"

"Absolutely."

"I don't know how to make cocoa in a jar."

This kid's mind was racing. "I'll look it up and see, and we'll get presents made for everybody in time for Christmas. You have my word on it." He speared his fingers through the boy's hair, pushing it off his forehead. "You're a good boy, and I'm proud of you."

Even in the darkness, he could see Cody gazing up at him. He could almost see the shift from wariness to a newfound trust.

He leaned over and kissed his forehead, breathing in the scent of soap and little boy. "Good night."

Leaving the door ajar, he stepped out and looked down the hallway. The light was on in Finlay's room, and water flowed through the pipes. While she got ready for bed, he texted Ava.

Jude: You drinking tea and reading?

An introvert, she had a whole unwinding process after she came home from socializing, so he figured she'd be up.

Ava: You know it. What's up? Need something?

Jude: I do. Can I call you?

Ava: Always.

He quietly headed back down the stairs. As he looked out the window, he imagined mowing the lawn and rolling garbage bins out to the curb. He wasn't raised in a family neighborhood, and he'd never imagined that life.

But really, it wouldn't be so bad.

He brought up Ava's name and hit Connect. Unsurprisingly, she answered right away.

"What's going on?" she asked. "Everything all right with Cody?"

"Yeah. He's good." *No, talk to her. Tell her.* Make the effort. "When you said kids are resilient, I didn't get it. But now, watching him settle in, going from being shy and quiet to talking my ear off…"

"It's good, Jude. Really good."

"It is. Yes."

"But? Come on. I hear the worry."

"But what if I can't keep him? He's letting down his guard, trusting us—"

"We'll fight with everything we can to make sure you keep him, but honey, there are no guarantees. And if it doesn't go your way, he will always have this Christmas to remember what love and safety felt like. No matter where life takes him, he'll have this gift you gave him as proof there's love and good people in the world."

"You're right." He didn't realize the weight of his worries until she'd lifted them off his shoulders. "He seems happy."

"You guys make it easy."

"What do you mean?" Not a soul was outside. The moonlight illuminated the snow, making the crystals glitter.

"You brought him right into the family, and he already feels like he belongs. All of you did that, and it's just wonderful. You're doing a beautiful thing, Jude. You're a good man."

She was a teacher, so she said things like that to everyone. But for him, it sank deeply. Most of his life, he'd heard his name called with disgust. Or with a snap of anger.

So when he got praise, it spread through him like warm maple syrup. "Thanks, Ava. I'm grateful for you, you know that, right?"

She didn't answer right away, and when she did, her voice sounded thick. "Where did that come from?"

"We might've called you a nanny or a babysitter, but you were as close to a mom as we could get. I'm pretty sure you're the reason I didn't turn out like Marco."

"Oh, Jude. Thank you for saying that, but it's just not true. You want to know what I think?" She didn't wait for his answer. "Of all the kids, you were the most sensitive. All you wanted was to cuddle on the couch and read books and eat cookies." He could hear the smile in her voice. "But that wasn't going to happen in a biker club."

"It happened with you."

"And you'll make it happen with Cody."

"I'll try my damnedest." Unfortunately, though, that fate was up to a judge who thought the worst of him. "Yeah, so, anyhow, I want to get something nice for Finlay for Christmas. Any suggestions?"

"Well, I'd probably get her a cute water tumbler because she doesn't remember to drink during the day. Or maybe something for the house, like a toaster, since her ex wouldn't buy one because he thought it was 'the most unnecessary appliance in the world.' You can just put bread in the oven, right?"

"I'm hearing a 'but.'"

"But that's because of *my* relationship with her. What you choose is based on yours. What have you guys talked about? What has she mentioned? What's she looked at in a store that she liked but would never buy for herself?"

"We haven't gone shopping for anything but food and clothes for Cody."

"Oh, come on. There's a real bond between you—anyone can see it. I think you know her pretty well. Just, whatever you do, don't get her a toaster." She laughed. "That would hurt her feelings."

"She hasn't mentioned anything. What do I do?"

"Pay attention, figure out what she's into."

"She used to make soap, and I know she likes to bake." He thought about the moose slippers she used to wear, and it made him smile. He'd get her a pair of those. Maybe matching ones for Cody. The whole family. Yeah, that'd be cute.

"It doesn't have to be expensive. Just meaningful. But I will say, I think she's more of an acts-of-service kind of person."

"A what? I don't know what that means."

"You know the five love languages, right?" Ava asked.

"No."

"Basically, it's figuring out how your partner receives love. Because if you need physical touch, and she only gives you gifts, you're going to be hurt and angry all the time. You'll assume she likes to shop when, really, she's trying to do nice things for you. See what I mean?"

"I do."

"Figure out Finlay's love language and be sure to give it to her."

"What's an act of service? Do I change the oil in her

car while she's making dinner? Change the light bulb in that downstairs bathroom?"

"Yes. Do those things, for sure. But to really hit her in the feels, you'll want to do something sweeter."

"Like?"

"Jude, sweetheart." Her tone softened like it used to when she'd come into his room after he'd been suspended and wanted to talk to him. "That's for you to figure out."

"Christmas is in three days."

"Given how closely you watch her, I think you know exactly what makes her feel loved."

Two things came to mind. "My time and attention."

"See that? You know her heart."

Confidence rolled in. "I think I do." And that was when he knew exactly what he was going to do. "Hey, can you watch Cody tomorrow night?"

"Of course. I'd be happy to."

"And can you get me into the gym at the high school?"

"Legally, you know I can't do that."

"But as the closest person I have to a mom, can you?"

Ava laughed. "You play dirty."

Jude chuckled as he disconnected.

He had a plan.

And step one starts now.

Chapter Twenty-Three

AFTER CHECKING ON CODY, FINLAY PRACTICALLY floated down the hallway. She couldn't wait to see Jude. During the day, they were surrounded by people, so it was only nighttime when he was all hers.

And she craved the kind of intimacy he gave. He focused on her, making her feel like the most interesting and sexy woman alive.

As she entered her room, she caught the scent of gardenias and heard the bathtub filling.

What's going on?

She came to an almost comical stop. Because a dozen candles blazed on every dresser and nightstand. *He found my stash?* She'd kept them in a box in the laundry room, not bothering to unpack since she hadn't seen a need. Her romantic relationship had ended, and with a houseful of guests, when would she have time alone to read or take a spa night for herself?

Curious, she peeked into the bathroom and found even more candles.

And Jude, standing there in his black jeans and boots, was pouring gardenia-scented oil into the tub. *What on earth?* She stepped all the way inside to see little pink rubber duckies bobbing on the water's surface.

Rubber ducks? Could anything be more adorable? She couldn't believe it.

No one's ever done anything like this for me.

She pushed past him to get a closer look. "What're you doing?"

With a startled expression, he jerked upright. "You had a busy day." He seemed rattled. "I thought you might want to relax."

"With rubber duckies?" She fished one out to get a closer look. It had an orange beak and was surrounded by a pattern of white hearts. "This is adorable. Where did you find them?"

"At Bazoo's."

"When we bought Cody's clothes?" She remembered that first day, when she'd told him she felt like a rubber ducky floating in a bathtub.

And he bought pink ones. *For me.*

He calls me Ducky.

He nodded. "They were in a plastic box at the checkout counter. Grabbed a handful while I was paying."

"You grabbed a handful of pink rubber duckies." It wasn't a question. It was a statement. Because she was floored. "This is the sweetest thing anyone's ever done for me. Thank you."

"It's overkill, right?" He gestured to the tub. "Candles and rubber ducks? I should've picked one or the other."

"No, it's absolutely perfect." She touched his arm.

"Seriously, I love it so much." Overloaded with her own emotions, it took her a moment to process his discomfort.

He let out a breath. "Do you even like baths?"

It struck her that he'd never had a girlfriend before. He'd never done sweet gestures like this.

But he's doing it for me.

"I love them." Holding his gaze, she kicked off her slippers and pulled down her sweatpants.

Seriously, sweatpants? Could she try to be less sexy?

But you know what? With his eyes all hot like that, he practically commanded her to take off her shirt and toss it aside. As he watched, she unhooked her bra and let it drop. And there she stood, naked in front of him. If she had any doubts or insecurities about her body, the color flooding his cheeks banished them.

The muscles in his jaw flexed. His hands curled into fists. "I'll let you enjoy it." He started to go but then turned back. "Do you want your book?"

"No, thank you." She dipped a toe into the hot water.

"I should've asked. How do you like your bath?"

"With a hot biker in it." It was just the right temperature, so she sank down and let it cover her. "Aren't you going to join me?" Flowers filled her senses, and her skin felt silky and soft.

His gaze was fixed on her nipples, now slick with oil. "Fuck, yeah." Gripping the back of his shirt, he yanked it off. He kicked off his boots, jerked down his jeans, and then stood there watching, as if unsure what to do.

He was such a confident man, so it was hard to watch him flounder. She lifted her pink-painted toes and splashed the water. "Sit with me."

Getting in on the opposite side, his big body sloshed water over the edge. "I'm not going to fit." He tossed out a few rubber ducks.

"You fit just fine." She pulled on his ankles, stretching his legs as far as they could go on either side of her. Still, his knees poked out of the water like tree trunks.

He lifted her calf and began kneading the sole of her foot. "Did you have a good day?"

It felt so delicious, she tipped her head back and moaned. "Mm hmm."

"After that guy ruined our time at the Christmas farm, and you thought I was hooking up with someone at the bar, and Cody flipped out over a coyote, you can still say that?"

"Yes, because we got to cut down our own Christmas tree, my hot biker called me his *wife*, I got to have sex with that same man in a bar"—the naughtiest and most exciting thing she'd ever done—"and Cody got to be loved and cared for by three wonderful men. And then, to top it all off, my hot biker drew me a bath." She snatched up a floating duck and waved it at him.

"That's probably a better way to spin it." Cupping his hands, he doused water on his chest and arms.

As it coursed over his skin, she realized this was the first time she could see his tattoos in the light. "I remember these." She sat up to run her fingers around the tribal ink circling his left biceps and covering his right shoulder. "But you've got a lot of new ones." Her fingertips traced down his chest. "Is this a chevron?'

"Yeah. My rank." Goose bumps pebbled his skin. "Sergeant."

"And this one?" It was an upside-down triangle. At the top, it said "First." In the center, a sword drove through the number seven.

"Battalion and regiment."

Almost all his ink was black except for one block divided into four squares. "Oh, I like this. Tell me about it."

"My brothers and I have nicknames. I'm Grizz." He tapped the bear. "Wyatt's Honey Badger." He moved onto the bottom row and touched the football. "Decker's Clutch, and Boone's—"

"Hotshot?" She rubbed the flames.

"Good guess." One corner of his mouth hitched into a grin.

The rush of water when they shifted, the flickering candles, and his big body taking up so much space lit a fuse in her core. Boy, she'd had it all wrong, hadn't she? Thinking shared goals meant true love.

No, it was wanting someone so badly you'd climb out of your comfort zone to make them happy. Loving them so much you'd work hard to heal your broken bits for them.

Her gaze landed on a design that didn't fit. "Wait, what's that one?" Her brain tried to make sense of it within the context of his other tattoos. She lifted his arm to get a better look at his rib cage. "Is that a moose?" It made no sense. Every tattoo was serious, meaningful. This was a goofy moose with antlers. "That's so funny because it looks just like a pair of—"

"Slippers. The ones you had when you were eighteen and ran out of your apartment."

"You remember—" *Oh.* It took her a moment, but it all clicked into place. "*Jude.*"

She'd always known there was more to him than the inked, dark, and broody badass, but she'd only seen glimmers. Tonight, he'd given her a glimpse into his soul.

And it was beautiful.

No one had seen this side of him, and he'd chosen to share it with her. "I'm the luckiest woman in the world." She surged forward and plastered herself across his chest.

He caught her and held on tightly. With a hand cupping the back of her head, he whispered in her ear, "So the bath was a good idea?"

She turned her face into his neck and laughed. "Very good." But this position wasn't comfortable for either of them, so she kissed his cheek and returned to her side of the tub. "I had no idea you felt this way about me." But she couldn't waste time wondering how it would've changed her life if she'd known. Everything had led to this moment. "Any others I should know about?"

"Well, there's this one." He twisted around to show a realistic tattoo of a compass and a map. "It's Calamity. See? This is Wild Wolff Village."

"I love that. It's gorgeous." But she caught something else. "Wait, what's this one? A *whale*?"

"Yeah, that was Decker's stuffed animal when he was a kid."

"Why did you get that inked on your skin?"

"Just a memory. Of the night we left." He grew contemplative, lifting his hand and watching water spill out of it. "I've never told anyone about it."

"Why?"

"I don't know." He shifted, causing a ruckus with the ducks. "It always felt like something secretive, the way we left. There was an urgency."

"What do you remember?"

"I guess my memories are more feelings than pictures. I knew my mom was in labor. She was having Boone, and there was excitement around that. A lot of movement. Later, though, it changed to something scary. Terrifying. Mom was gone. She wasn't coming back."

"And no one ever sat you down and explained what happened?"

"Not really, no."

"I mean, it's like Cody, right? How can he make sense of all these changes if no one talks to him? It just lives like a fear inside him."

He held her gaze for a moment, and she could tell he was letting it sink in. "The only vivid memory I have is my dad waking me up in the middle of the night, shaking my shoulder, and whispering to go get Decker. I couldn't tell you what my dad looked like twenty-two years ago or what color my blanket was, but I do remember the urgency."

"You understood the assignment."

"Yeah, exactly." He rewarded her with a smile that said he liked how well she understood him.

"Do you remember getting Decker?"

He shrugged. "Mostly, the fear in his eyes. That's what made me go back in and grab his whale." He tapped the tattoo. "It was his favorite stuffed animal. I have a few flashes of being in a car at night, my dad driving, but nothing else until we walked into the club. And that's about it."

"Did your dad tell you why you had to leave so suddenly?"

"The only thing I know is that he was getting his MBA, and he relied on my mom and student loans to handle bills and kids. So when she died, he had no child-care, no income, and four kids."

"That's awful."

"Yeah. He said if the club president hadn't taken us in —given him food, clothing, beds…childcare—he didn't know what he'd do. He had a newborn."

"I can't even imagine. You know, sometimes I think you're stuck on the idea of birth order. That you're supposed to be the responsible one, but given what happened, it just doesn't apply here. No one experienced the trauma the way you did. Certainly not Boone, who doesn't remember a thing. I'll bet if you talk to your dad, you'll get a whole other perspective on what happened. It might help the way you see things." She laughed. "Which is great advice from someone who's all talk and no action."

He hooked his hands under her knees and pulled her closer. "You've never talked to your parents?"

She had to put her hands on his shoulders to steady herself. "Nope. I can't think of anything worse than them showing up to something because I guilted them into it. It sucks, but I just don't rank on their list of priorities."

"But if you never talk to them, you'll never know what they're thinking."

"Maybe. But nothing can change the fact that I was an accident."

"What do you mean, an accident?" He sat straighter, sloshing water out of the tub. "They told you that? That's bullshit."

She appreciated his outrage but squeezed his hand to calm him down. "My parents met the summer before college when they were working as ski lift operators. They hooked up a few times, and when my mom got pregnant, they made the decision to have me. They gave up college and tried to raise me together, but it didn't work. They're just too different. My dad's the life of the party, and my mom—well, you know what? I don't know who she'd be without the resentment and bitterness about the way her life turned out. Bottom line, I stole their futures. And they never recovered." She held up a hand. "I don't mean it like it sounds. They do love me—"

He put a finger over her lips.

She smiled. "I'm doing it again."

He nodded. "You don't have to justify or sugarcoat it. You can tell me exactly how it makes you feel."

"Well, here's the thing. It took me a long time to figure out I'm not the reason their lives didn't work out the way they wanted." She pushed the damp hair off her shoulders. "They could've gone back to school. If they couldn't afford a university, they could've started at a community college. They could've taken turns. My mom could've supported them while my dad got his degree, and then he could've returned the favor. All I know is I'm not the reason they both work at Wild Wolff Village, and I'm not the reason neither of them married again. It's just not my fault their lives suck. I might've been an accident, but there were a million different paths they could've taken."

"Bullshit. You're no accident." He rolled on top of her, knocking her back. Waves of water crashed to the floor. "You're a gift." He crushed her to his chest. "You're *my* gift." Gripping her ass, he lifted them out of the tub. "Because I get to kiss you." He pressed his mouth over hers, softly, sweetly. "Here." He left a trail of kisses along the column of her neck.

He carried her to the bed, both of them dripping wet, and tossed her onto the mattress. His body covered hers. "Here." He covered her breast with his mouth, his tongue swirling over the beaded tip. "And here."

Her back arched, and she let out a shaky, "Oh."

He kissed a path down her stomach, leaving a flurry of goose bumps in his wake.

She couldn't believe this was happening. That this incredible man saw her, wanted her…took care of her.

What she felt was so big. It was need. It was hunger. It was…

Love.

Pure and simple.

Something she'd never truly felt before, and something she could never live without now that she had it.

But would it last? That was the thing. It was their circumstances that drew them together, made everything so intense.

She didn't think she could bear it if, after their six weeks were up, his feelings faded.

And she was left alone with all these feelings.

It would break her.

Chapter Twenty-Four

STEP TWO HAD THEM ALL LINING UP AT THE BOTTOM of the stairs: Jude, Cody, his dad, his brothers, and Ava. But what he'd thought was a great idea yesterday…he wasn't so sure about now.

Basically, he was sweating underneath the tuxedo jacket.

"Thanks for helping us today, little man." Boone gave Cody a fist bump. "You did good work."

"Did you have fun?" Ava asked.

The little boy looked up. "Us guys worked real hard."

Us guys.

Cute.

"I'm sure you did," she said. "I'll stop by tomorrow and take a look."

"All's we did today is jump on the snow and start… um." Cody gazed up at Jude for help.

"Carving," Jude said at the same time Boone said, "Designing."

"Well, I can't wait to see it," Ava said. "And it sounds like hard work. Maybe I'll bring some snacks."

"Yeah, we need 'em," Cody said. "We sure get hungry out there. And it's cold."

"That's why they set up a tent with food and hot chocolate," Gunnar said. "It's for the teams. Let's not make Ava do more work."

"I don't mind," Ava said. "I want to see what you've done."

Pressing his hands together, Jude glanced up the stairs. He'd only told Finlay they were having a date night, but if she expected dinner at a nice restaurant, she'd be disappointed. He'd told her to dress up, but that could mean anything.

He probably should've given her a heads-up. Something that wouldn't spoil the surprise.

"You came up with some good ideas, Cody," his dad said. "I think we've got a winner."

"Oh, we're winning all right," Boone said. "Especially with that sleigh on the roof."

"That'll take a lot of extra time," Wyatt said.

"Yeah, well, Jude's here, so we've got an extra pair of hands," Boone said. "We'll get it done."

He'd barely slept last night. Once he'd come up with the idea, he'd had to put it in motion. That meant he'd stayed up for hours creating a playlist. And then, he'd had to make a list of supplies.

He was damn lucky his family had stepped in to help. After a morning of back-breaking work with chisels and saws and a twenty-five-ton block of snow, they hadn't hesitated to head over to the gym and set it all up while he and Cody went to the tuxedo shop and showered.

He appreciated the hell out of them.

"What's the matter with you?" Boone whacked his shoulder.

"Nothing." He said it automatically, but who was he kidding? Between the sweat and wringing hands, they knew he was a mess. "It's a stupid idea. I don't know what I was thinking."

"Oh no, honey. It's a great idea." Ava had her phone camera aimed and ready. "She'll love it."

"Look." Cody stood beside him, the box in his hand. "Here she comes."

As Fee hit the top of the stairs, she stopped to take in the scene. "What in the world's going on?" Outfitted in a black dress and high heels, her hair blown out in shiny waves, and red lipstick slashed across her mouth, she looked sexy and elegant.

Once she stepped into the living room, she bent her knees to take the box Cody held out to her. "Look at you in a tux." She ran her fingers down the little boy's jacket. "Aren't you handsome?" She opened the box. "Oh, this is so pretty." After sniffing the corsage, she broke into a warm smile. "Thank you, Cody." Then she looked at Jude. "Did I not dress right? I thought we were going out to dinner?"

"We are," Jude said. "And you're perfect." She was magnificent. He loved the Finlay who was tousled from his hands and sleepy-eyed after a good fucking, but this elegant version made him wish he'd shaved and trimmed his hair.

"Then why the tuxes?" she asked.

"Mister did something bad and ruined your date, so he wants to re…reen…" Cody glanced up at Jude once again.

"Reenact," he said.

"Yeah." Cody nodded. "He wants to renact it."

"You're not talking about the *prom*, are you?" She seemed surprised.

He nodded, unsure whether it was a look of horrified or delighted shock. But he didn't want to waste his family's efforts, so he needed to usher them along.

"And you're all part of this?" She took in the lineup, tears glazing her eyes and pink flooding her cheeks. "I don't even know what to say. You're the nicest people I've ever met. Thank you." She fell into Gunnar's arms, and he patted her back.

His dad grunted, making Jude and his brothers laugh.

She made her way down the line, crouching when she got to the little boy. "Will you help me put it on?" Cody held the elastic band open while she slid her hand through. When she stood, she wiped the moisture under her eyes. She faced Jude with a dazzling smile and pulled him in for a hug. "This is such a sweet thing to do."

The modest dress molded her hour-glass curves. He wanted to peel it off and kiss her while he filled his palms with her tits. He wanted to drop to his knees, hike up her skirt, and taste her pussy. He gave her a look that said, *Later, you're all mine.*

"Okay, picture time." Ava positioned everyone for a series of photographs, some with just the couple, others with Cody in the middle, and a selfie with the entire family together. Everyone was joking and laughing, and all he wanted was to get her alone. His hands itched to cup her ass, pull her close… He just wanted her all to himself.

"All right, that's enough." He led her to the door and pulled her long wool coat from the closet.

"Now, you kids have fun," Ava said.

Jude held it out for her, and she slid her arms in. He couldn't resist kissing her cheek and breathing in her soft, floral scent.

"Who is this guy?" Boone said. "I don't know what's happening, but I want my brother back."

"Leave it," Wyatt said.

Just as they headed out, Boone called, "Hey, Grizz."

Jude turned just in time to catch a condom to his chin. It dropped to the floor.

"What's that?" Cody called.

"Let's just say, it's going to keep you an only child." Boone laughed.

Pocketing it, Jude crouched in front of Cody and gave him a hug. "You be good for Grandpa, okay?"

"I will. We're gonna make ornaments for the tree."

"That sounds great. You have fun."

The boy inched closer, fingering Jude's bow tie. "Are you coming home?" he whispered.

"Yes, I am. But it'll be late, so I won't see you till morning."

"Do I gotta be real quiet while you sleep it off?"

Jesus. Sometimes he couldn't stand the wounds in this boy's heart. "No, Cody." He glanced up to see the concern on his brothers' faces. "If you get up and want some company, wake me up, okay? You don't have to be quiet, and I'll never have to sleep anything off."

"In the morning, will you make me pancakes like Grampa does?"

"Yes. If that's what you want, I'll make them."

"You promise?"

Holding his gaze with firmness and sincerity, Jude said, "I promise." He decided they needed a symbol of trust, so he made a fist with his thumb up. When they bumped, he showed the boy how to tap their thumbs together.

Cody let out a huff of breath, which sounded a lot like relief. "Okay." He stepped back and joined his grandpa and uncles.

As they stepped out into the cold evening, Finlay hooked her arm through his. "I sure hope you get to adopt him."

"I do, too."

"You were meant to be in his life. You and only you." She noticed the headlights at the curb, and her steps faltered. "You rented a limo?" She stopped on the walkway and turned to him. "You didn't have to do this."

He caught her hand and brought it to his mouth. "I spent a lot of time thinking about what it must've felt like for you to wait for me, to think I played you, and it made me sick. I wish I'd made a better choice that night." He turned it over and kissed her palm. "But I promise to make better ones from now on." As they headed to the sidewalk, a couple approached them.

"Oh, hello." A tall woman in a black coat smiled. "I've

been meaning to come over and introduce myself. I'm Jenna, and this is my husband, Brian."

"It's nice to meet you." Finlay held out her hand. "I'm Finlay, and this is Jude, my fiancé."

"Well, let's walk together." The middle-aged woman lifted a covered casserole dish. "I always bring homemade pasta. It's my grandma's recipe, and they love it." When she took in their outfits, her forehead crinkled. "I think you might be a little overdressed."

Finlay looked across the street. A few houses down, Mrs. Atherton's place was lit up, every window blazing with yellow light. The front door opened, and a family walked in.

Tonight's the neighborhood Christmas party.

Something Fee's dreamed of since she was a kid.

And instead of going to that, she'll be in a high school gym.

Alone with me.

Well, this sucks.

"Actually, we weren't invited." Finlay unhooked her arm from his and clasped his hand. "But we couldn't have gone anyway. It's date night."

"What do you mean, you weren't invited?" The woman was clearly confused. "Did you check your mailbox?"

"That has to be a mistake," the husband said. "Everyone's welcome. Just come with us. We'll introduce you around."

Jude's family had worked hard to decorate the gym, but his priority was Fee's happiness. He gave her hand a squeeze, making sure she knew it was okay to change things up.

But her smile was true when she said to the couple, "Thank you. I appreciate that, but Jude's made special plans for us. Have a good night."

The couple continued across the street, and Jude cupped her elbow as he led her to the limo. He opened the door and followed her in. Inside, it was dark and rich with the scent of leather. Two glasses and a bottle of chilled champagne waited in the console.

She seemed impressed. "I've never been in a limo before."

"Me neither. But it's a lot more comfortable than a party bus." He nodded to the driver in the rearview mirror, and they glided away from the curb.

She tipped her head back on the seat and sighed. "This is amazing. I've been going nonstop, unpacking, decorating, cooking, shopping…and it's such a treat to take a moment for myself. I can't remember the last time I took a bath, did my makeup—" She froze. "Oh. I can't believe I said that when, a little over a week ago, I pampered myself for my wedding." And then, she shook her head in disbelief. "Isn't that wild? How much has changed in a week? I'm living a whole new life."

Even though he'd asked a few times, he still needed to check in. "Any regrets?"

"Absolutely not. I've never been so…" She tilted her head in contemplation. "You know, I was going to say happy. But that's not what this feels like."

He couldn't resist pressing a kiss on her cheek. It held

the faint scent of her gardenia bath salts. "What's it feel like?"

"Contentment." She sighed, leaning against him. "A couple of years ago, I took a perfume-making class. Ava won it in a school auction, and she took a few of us with her. Up until that moment, I'd only ever wanted to be a teacher. But in that room, with the beakers and droppers and essential oils, this weird sensation came over me. I don't know how to explain it, but it was like it all clicked into place, and I thought, *This is me*."

"Is that how you got into essential oils?"

"Yes, exactly."

"And you gave it up because Matt didn't think it was the best use of your time?"

She tucked her head into his chest. "Okay, we've already determined I was a butthead." She smiled. "But honestly, it was more than that. It was the fact that I trusted my vision board more than my own heart."

"Not anymore. Now, you get to make new choices." He poured their champagne and raised his flute for a toast. "To fresh starts." He pressed a kiss to her mouth. "I can't believe I get to be with you."

"It's wild, isn't it? How we found our way back to each other?" She tried to climb onto his lap, but the fabric trapped her legs. She flopped back down. "If I weren't wearing this dress, I'd be riding you right now."

He hauled her onto his lap sideways. "You can ride me later, but for now, we're going back to high school. To the night that changed everything. Back then, I didn't think I was good for you, but now, I know I'm only as good as I want to be." He tipped his forehead to hers.

"But you'll still be bad, right?" She scraped her nails across his scalp. "Every now and then?"

This fucking woman. Clamping his hand on the back of her head, he slammed their mouths together. His heart thundered, and his cock went as hard as a pole. She wriggled on his lap, like she wanted him to break through the barrier of their clothing and fuck her.

Hunger consumed him, drove him. As he kissed her, he tried to reach into the top of her dress, but it was too tight. Finding the zipper, he pulled the tab down enough to give him access to her tits. He got a handful of warm, plump flesh, and she arched her back, moaning.

"Okay. We've got to stop." He zipped her back up. "I'm going to rip your dress apart if we don't." Lifting her, he plunked her down on the seat next to him and closed his eyes to try to regain control over his raging body. Clothing rustled, the seat belt latched, and he gulped in air to calm himself down. "It's supposed to be a romantic night."

"Trust me. It is." She patted his thigh. "You're nailing it."

I want to nail you. "I'm trying to make you feel special. Not maul you."

"You make me feel like the sexiest woman in the world. And you know what? It doesn't matter what we're doing. I don't need anything but time with you."

He smiled at her as the pieces fell into place. "Quality time."

"What?"

"Your love language. I'm thinking it's quality time, acts of service—"

"And words of affirmation. How did you know about that?"

"Ava. I asked her what to get you for Christmas, and she said I had to figure that out on my own. I have to learn how you receive love."

"So you looked up *love languages*?" Again, she unlatched her belt and tried to get on his lap. "Screw the dress. I'm going to rip it open at the seams."

He laughed and set her back down. "Hold that thought. We're here." The limo pulled into the school parking lot.

She was fiddling with her seat belt, so she didn't look out the window. "You know what's funny? Here we are trying to reenact high school, but this"—she wagged a finger between them—"doesn't feel like it did in high school. I'm not a girl crushing on a boy I can't have. I'm a woman getting to know a man and discovering we're so much better than I ever imagined we could be together."

As they neared the back entrance, he grew anxious. She was expecting a romantic dinner with candles and wine. Instead, he'd set up a date in a gymnasium that stunk of sweat.

This is stupid.

It wasn't too late to change things up.

"Hang on a sec. Just want to check on something." He pulled out his phone.

Jude: May-day May-day. Bailing out. What's a nice restaurant I can take her to instead?

Boone: She hates it?

Wyatt: Sweetwater Resort and Spa. It's
new and fancy.

Ava: Hold on. What did she say?

Jude: She hasn't been inside. We're just
pulling up. But she's expecting an
elegant restaurant, not a smelly gym.

Ava: Stop worrying. She'll love it.

Wyatt: Remember why you're doing this.
It's not about feeding her steak and
chocolate mousse.

His brother was right about that. Damn, that helped calm him down.

Ava: Yes! It's an apology. It's healing a
wound.

Dad: And if she hates it, pack the shit up
and take her out to dinner.

Jude: Good point. Thanks.

Feeling better, he pocketed his phone. "Ready to go?"

She leaned over to look out the window. "We're at school?"

"Yep." After sliding out, he reached back inside for her hand. Like some dude in a movie, he linked their arms and walked her to the entrance.

The door was propped open, so all he had to do was push, and they stepped through a curtain of streamers. She came to a stop when she saw what his family had done.

It was a big gym, so they'd only decorated one section with balloons and crepe paper. A folding table with a ruffled paper tablecloth held a punch bowl and various snacks. Music played softly from a tablet.

Finlay picked up a bag. "Ghost pepper chips?"

Jude laughed. "That's Boone. It's a joke in our family to see who can eat the spiciest food. So far, he's the winner."

"Are you saying your *brothers* did this?"

"The whole family. Ava got us into the gym, and my brothers and dad did the rest."

"I can't believe this." She gestured around the area. "You did all this for me."

"One decision cost me a lifetime with you." He gazed into eyes brimming with gratitude and affection. "I don't know what would've happened if I'd said no to Marco that night, but knowing what it's like with you now, I have no doubt I'd have done anything to keep you." Which meant he wouldn't have had to go through twelve years of exile and loneliness.

"I'd have done anything to stay with you, too."

He believed that. He believed in them. "When I was lying on my cot in an FOB in Afghanistan and had enough distance to get a clear picture of my past, I understood my loyalty to my friends was not more important than my integrity."

"That's pretty insightful for a jarhead."

He laughed, but he wasn't finished. "So when you asked if I'd make the same choice today, the answer is no. Because now, I get it. A real friend wouldn't ask me to betray my values, my morals, or my own happiness." He reached for her. "I'll never do that again."

As they swayed to All-4-One's "I Swear," she set a

shaky hand on his chest. "This is all so sweet, so romantic, but Jude…what're we doing?"

"What do you mean?"

She gazed up at him, those hazel eyes clouded with worry. "I'm trying not to blur the lines. I know we can't make promises beyond this six-week fake engagement, but when you do something like this for me…when you say those things… It's confusing."

A sense of urgency took hold. "I know it's too soon. You just walked away from your wedding, but I'll wait as long as you need. I've never felt this way for anybody but you, and I never will. It was you twelve years ago, and it's still you today."

"But what happens when Carlo comes home, and he's healthy, and he wants Cody back… What happens to us?"

"This isn't about Cody. It's never been about him. It's about you. It's us." He cupped her neck, forcing her to look him in the eyes. "I've wanted you since I was eleven years old."

"Eleven? I thought you said fourteen?"

"Fourteen was when I wanted to touch your boobs. But in sixth grade, it was a whole different kind of want." The memory dropped into his mind so vividly that the same emotions seized him. "Do you remember when Mr. Pettino asked if anyone wanted to volunteer to spend time with the preschoolers?"

"Oh." She stuttered out a laugh. "Yes. I jumped out of my seat, waving my hand. I was desperate for him to pick me."

"I'd always thought you were pretty, but when you raised your hand like that, you were…" *Luminous.* "I don't know how to explain it. You lit up like the Fourth of July. Back then, everyone was worried about being cool, wearing the right clothes, hanging out with the right people, but you knew exactly what you wanted, and you went for it, not giving a shit what anyone thought about you."

"Well, that was after Leia dumped me, so maybe I had nothing to lose." She was teasing, but he wouldn't let her dismiss it.

"I'll bet that's the *reason* she kicked you out of her group. Not because you didn't have money, but because you wouldn't fall in line. You've just always followed your own tune, and she couldn't stand it."

"I never thought about it like that, but it's possible. Because, yeah, her friends went along with everything she did." She sifted her fingers through his hair. "But let's get back to the part where you fell for me when you were eleven."

"Words of affirmation," he muttered, kissing first one cheek, then the other, then the tip of her nose, and finally, her sweet mouth.

"Jude McKenna." She sighed. "Talking love languages." She fanned herself.

Laughing, he caught her around the waist. "You see what a man'll do when he wants a woman?"

Her smile faded, and her eyes filled with awe. "Yeah. I really do."

Chapter Twenty-Five

As Jude crossed the living room, he took in the Christmas wonderland they'd created for Cody. Strings of lights twinkled, bright red stockings rimmed with bands of white fur hung off the mantel, and embers still glowed from their evening in front of the fireplace. It smelled of cinnamon, pine, and the sugar cookies Cody and Fee had baked.

They were all getting so close. It was good. Great, even. But he couldn't get Fee's question out of his mind: *What if Carlo took Cody back?*

The boy had become an integral part of their lives. Earlier in the day, when Jude had taken a break from carving out the interior of the snow house, he'd glanced into the white tent to find his dad and Cody having a hot cocoa together.

What would happen if he was pulled from the McKenna family?

Bringing him into the family was the right thing to

do, no question. But how many times could a person open his heart and trust when people kept leaving him?

He had to talk to Carlo. He set the water bottles down on a table and pulled his phone out of his gym shorts.

Jude: Hope rehab's going well. I know Christmas Eve is tomorrow, but I wanted to talk to you about Cody.

Before he could pick up the bottles, his phone rang. "Hey."

"Is everything all right?" Carlo cleared the roughness out of his voice.

"Yeah, all good. Sorry, I should've started with that. He's fine."

"Oh." Carlo chuckled. "Scared me."

"I didn't mean to wake you."

"You didn't. I'm a night owl. So what's up?"

"You never really spelled it out, so if I got it wrong, tell me, and we'll forget about it." He held his breath. Because there was no taking a statement like this back. "But I'd like to adopt Cody."

"Hoo-ey." Carlo let out a shaky breath. "Yes. That's exactly what I want. It'll give me a lot of peace of mind. Good kid, yeah?"

"The best. I'll wait till after the holidays, but by the first week of January, I'm going to talk to an attorney and get the process started. You think you'll be back in town by then?"

"That might be a little too soon, but I'll be available for anything you need to make it happen. Now, listen, you'll need a house and money for clothes and food.

School supplies. I'll make you the executor of the trust so you can use the money I set aside for him."

"That's Cody's money. It'll put him through college, get him a car, whatever he needs." But he knew what this man needed to hear. "I've got him, Carlo. I'll take care of him." A fist squeezed his lungs, bringing a sting of tears to his eyes. He blinked them away.

He didn't know how badly he wanted this until he got Carlo's encouragement.

"Best Christmas present ever." The older man sounded lighter than Jude had ever heard.

"Yeah." His gaze landed on the wooden puzzle Cody was working, the pile of books on the coffee table, and his superhero tumbler. "For all of us."

"All right, then. Talk later."

Snatching up the water bottles, Jude climbed the stairs. Judge Adams might not be inclined to grant him custody, but he'd figure out what he needed to do to change his mind.

When he checked on Cody, he found him fast asleep and clutching the red blanket. The rush of emotion came hard and fast, and he had to blink back tears. This boy… It was more than wanting to protect him and give him a home.

I love him.

I do.

Man, he was a mess of feelings these days. The past few weeks had shaken him up, and now, the cork had popped off. There was no holding anything back.

Tomorrow, they'd talk about what the boy should call him. He was done with Mister.

He hurried down the hallway, eager to tell Fee about the phone call. As he entered the bedroom, the yellow lamplight turned her hair to a fiery bronze. She rubbed lotion into her hands, her gaze softening when she saw him. "Is he still knocked out?"

"Yeah." *She's so pretty.* He tossed the water bottles onto the floor and stalked toward the bed.

"He couldn't stop talking about working with the 'guys' today. I heard all about carving out the interior of the house while Wyatt worked on a sled, and I guess Boone's decided to make actual reindeer. He said the only thing missing was Santa, but that you guys wouldn't have time to put that much detail in."

"There's only one more day left, so we'll just have his feet sticking out of the chimney. But yeah, he had a blast." He landed on top of her, bracing his weight with a hand at either side of her head. "You smell good."

Since she wasn't plucking her T-shirt away from her chest, he got a good view of her beaded nipples and the slight jiggle as she talked. He was about to slide his hand under the soft cotton when he noticed the logo.

University of Washington? "You went to UCLA."

"I know. So?"

He sat back on his heels. "Then whose shirt are you wearing?"

She had to look down. "Oh, it's Matt's. I sleep in it sometimes because it's so big and soft."

He got out of bed and pulled her up by her arms. "Not anymore."

"What? No, it's just a shirt. It doesn't mean anything. If you think I have an emotional attachment to—Jude!"

He yanked the fabric up and over her head. Tossing it aside, he said, "You need a big shirt, I'll get you one. But you're not wearing another man's shirt around me."

"Well, gosh, tiger, whatever will I wear?" Her eyes gleamed with excitement, and she did a little shimmy. Those luscious, plump breasts bounced. "I'll have to sleep naked."

He unbuckled his belt and whipped it out of his jeans. It landed with a clink on the floor. At the sound, her eyes went hot and sultry. "Give me that ass."

Was there anything sexier than the way she pulled down her white lace panties and kicked them off with a pink-painted toe and then crawled onto the mattress, hiking her plump, peach-shaped ass in the air? Hell, no, there wasn't.

He untied his boots, stripped off his socks, briefs, and T-shirt, and then caressed a cheek with his hand. "Come here." Gripping her hips, he hauled her up against him, sliding his cock along her soft, wet core.

My God, I want this woman.

He leaned over her body, running his hands up her sides and then cupping her tits. He knew just how she liked to be touched, so he slowly nudged into her opening while gently massaging her breasts. When she was rocking back against him and moaning, and he couldn't take it anymore, he slid deep inside his woman.

Just before straightening, he pinched her nipples and felt the rush of pleasure soak him. Yeah, he knew what she liked. Clamping his hands on her hips, he rammed into her, giving them both the friction and pace they needed.

She lowered her forehead to the mattress, her hips

rocking, meeting his thrusts, and the sound of the skin slapping mixed with the slick heat and tight clutch of her pussy turned him wild.

He lost control, fucking her so hard her fingers fisted in the blanket. Just before he reached that point of no return, he knew he had to get her there first. But just as he reached between her legs to get her off, she tipped her head back with a cry, and her hips ground hard against him.

Hearing her come undone snapped his last tether. He couldn't hold back. His release exploded out of him in hot spurts, each one so intense his body shook with tremors. He held her tight to his body, his fingers digging into her skin, until he let out a harsh exhalation.

Easing out, he smacked her ass, leaving a trail of kisses up her spine and cupping her tits. "You're perfect. Fucking perfect."

When he collapsed beside her, he pulled her close. Her hand settled on his forearm, and lamplight glinted off the diamond engagement ring.

Oh hell no. We're done with that.

He tugged it off her finger.

"Jude, we need it, remember? We have to look engaged."

"I'll get you something tomorrow."

"You're not spending a dime on a ring I'll wear for four more weeks."

We'll see about that.

Finlay had gone to high school with the Cavanaugh sisters, so it seemed the smartest choice to launch her side hustle with a friendly face. Still, she entered Harley Lu Emporium with a knot in her stomach.

She went right to the checkout counter. "Excuse me. Is Lulu here? She's an old friend of mine, and I'd like to pitch a product to her."

"No, but Harley is."

She didn't know the former pro surfer, but she was Lu's partner, so Finlay had to go for it. "Do you think I could speak with her for a moment?"

You should've made appointments. Been professional about it.

In this context, you're not a friend. You're a businesswoman.

"Sure. She's in the office. You can just knock on the door." The young woman pointed, and Finlay set off.

As she moved down the aisles of the gourmet grocery store, she noticed all the yummy treats. Fancy crackers and packets of crumpets, cookies she knew Cody would gobble up, and then, at the end of the aisle, a whole shelf of hot cocoa mixes. She smiled. Did Gunnar know about this store? He must. He was, after all, an aficionado.

When she reached the door labeled *Office*, she knocked. The unique and luscious scents from her soaps floated out of her tote bag. Yes, she was nervous, but she knew she had a great product.

"Come on in," a muffled voice called.

Finlay hitched the strap higher on her shoulder and turned the knob.

You got this.

A beautiful, very fit woman sat behind a desk. "Hi. What can I do for you?"

"I'm Finlay O'Neill. I went to high school with Lulu, and I was hoping I could show her a fun product I've developed."

"Oh, sorry. She's not here. She's off doing Christmas stuff with her family, but you can lay it on me."

"Thank you. I appreciate that." She pulled her tote off her shoulder. "I know my timing's terrible. I shouldn't be bothering you around the holidays."

"No worries. I'm single, and my family's not around, so it's no big deal."

Wait—she was alone? "Well, if you don't have plans for Christmas, you're welcome to join us." Finlay wanted to punch herself in the face. *This isn't a social call. It's business.*

"That's nice of you, but I'll be working. Someone's got to run the place."

"Well, I'm going to leave you my card anyway, so please know you're very welcome. We've got a lot of people coming, and you'll fit right in. Anyway…" She lifted the heavy tote. "I have something I think will be a good fit for your store." In addition to food, they sold high-end kitchen and bath products. "You're my first pitch, so if I'm doing it all wrong, please forgive me."

Harley broke into a warm smile. "You're fine. Show me what you've got." She came around her desk, and they both dropped into comfortable chairs.

Okay, girl. This is it.

Finlay loved teaching, and she was good at it. The hard part was that, while the children changed each year, the job didn't. There were only so many ways to make ornaments or to switch up the curriculum. Only so many age-appropriate songs to sing with her class.

And she really loved tinkering with essential oils and molding soap into fun shapes. But did she have something special, or was she just another person hawking a homemade product?

Only one way to find out…

Finlay pulled out her prettily wrapped boxes. Since it would be months before anyone stocked her items, she'd chosen a spring design with flowers and raffia ribbon. The perfumed scent swirled around them. Pride filled her. It was all just so lovely. *Wait till she sees the shapes.* "Now, I know you've got tons of fancy soaps on your shelves, but mine are different."

Harley closed her eyes and breathed in. "Smells divine."

"Right? So first, I use mango butter and avocado oil to make it luxuriously moisturizing, but then…" *This is the good part.* "I create my own scents."

"What do you mean?"

"I use what I learned in a perfume-making class to design soaps scented with essential oils." She handed over one with dinosaur-wrapping. "This is for kids, obviously. It's my newest line." *Thank you, Cody.* "There's a little plastic dinosaur embedded in it." She pulled out another one. "And this one…"

"Let me guess." Harley reached for the package wrapped in colorful blocks. "Legos."

"You got it."

"Very cute." The owner sniffed it. "It smells like cherry candy."

"Yep. And inside, there's a Lego person. And for adults, I have these." She handed over a floral package. "There's nothing inside, but it's flower-shaped and smells like gardenia and tuberose. There's no end to the unique scents I can make."

Harley closed her eyes and sniffed the package. "Delicious. I could bathe in this. I want it in my sheets and my towels." When she opened her eyes, she grinned. "I love this idea."

"Can I leave some samples for you to try? I want you to see how moisturizing they are."

"You sure can. I probably won't get back to you until January."

"Oh, of course. Believe me, I know I shouldn't be hawking my soap two days before Christmas. I just wanted to start with Lu."

"Don't worry about it. I'll drop some at her house and let her know you stopped by. But honestly, I can tell you right now, we'd be happy to stock it and see what our customers think."

Finlay got up. "Thank you so much for taking the time to talk to me. Have a great holiday." *Don't invite her. Keep it about business.* But when she got to the door, she turned around. "If you can't come for Christmas, maybe you'd like to join me and my friends for a girls' night out the first Friday in January?"

"That's really nice of you to include me."

See? She's totally noncommittal. She doesn't even know you. "My contact info is on the card attached to the bag. I hope you'll join us." She headed out the door. "Happy holidays!"

By the time she'd crossed the street and entered the park, she'd swapped embarrassment with pride. *I did it. I made my first pitch.* She couldn't wait to tell Jude.

The competition ended today, so while the judges made their rounds, the teams packed up their tools and loaded their trucks. As she headed to the McKennas' section, she marveled at the sculptures. How did they come up with these ideas?

She loved the bear with a fish in its claws. Another good one was the mermaid wearing a beanie and scarf around her neck and eating what looked to be a take-out box of french fries.

But when she got to Jude's entry, she knew without a doubt they'd win. Their attention to detail was exceptional. The gingerbread-style house had shutters, a bag of toys in the sleigh on the roof, and Santa's booted feet sticking out of the chimney. She couldn't believe the artistry. Since the guys were nowhere to be found, she slipped inside.

In it, they had a fireplace with stockings hanging off the mantel and a dining room table with three mugs and a plate of cookies. Voices approached—probably the judges—so she turned to leave when something caught her eye.

Under the table rested a pair of moose slippers. She recognized the antlers of the ones she'd owned when she was eighteen.

Just like Jude's tattoo.

She turned to go and found the man himself blocking the snow house. "You're obsessed with my slippers."

"I'm obsessed with you. Now, come on. We have to get out of here. They're judging ours next."

She stepped out of it and hugged him. "You're so sweet."

"Did you see it, Miss O'Neill?" Cody came running up to them.

"I sure did. It's amazing."

"We're gonna win," the boy said. "'Cause that's what us guys do."

"I sure hope so. But even if you don't, it was a lot of fun working together, wasn't it?"

"Yeah." He broke into a shy smile. "It was."

Gunnar, Wyatt, and Boone strode toward them, a wall of muscle, scruff, and motorcycle boots. Heads turned, and people froze as the bad boys of Calamity Falls parted the crowd.

"You guys, this is outstanding." Finlay greeted each one with a hug. "You've outdone yourselves."

"Thanks," Gunnar said in his gruff way.

"Come on." Boone rested his big hand on Cody's head. "Ready for some hot chocolate?"

"We sure earned it," Cody said.

Jude smiled, and as they headed over, she found herself in the middle of these men who'd so readily adopted her into their circle. She just loved being part of them.

That punch of adrenaline flooded her system—as it always did—when she thought of the text conversation she'd had with her mom that morning.

On the way to the tree farm, she'd invited her parents to Christmas Eve at Gunnar's and Christmas Day at her house. Initially, her mom said she'd try to make it.

It had really grated on her, so when she'd woken up that morning, she'd pushed it.

> Finlay: I get that you have to work, but I need you to know how it feels as your daughter to hear you say you'll "try to make it" for a holiday as important as Christmas. It hurts. I don't want to feel like a burden to my own mom.
>
> Mom: You're my daughter, and I love you very much. You are not a burden. I'm sorry if I ever made you feel that way. But I work with people 24/7, and I just don't have the bandwidth to dive into a whole new family after spending two years getting to know the Joneses. I know you need to be part of a big family, but I'm happy with our little one. Why don't we find a few hours to spend together, just you and me, and we can open our presents then?

She didn't know if her mom meant it as a dig, but "I know you need to be part of a big family" had wormed its way into her brain and taken root.

Because she did want that. She'd had it with Matt, and there was no question she'd thrown herself right into the McKennas.

How did she know what was real and what was driven by the lonely little girl who taped pictures onto her vision board?

Her thoughts were interrupted when she entered the tent and ran into Eloise and her baby. Her friend looked a little frantic. "What's going on?"

"I got hired to photograph Snowfest, but the sitter

canceled at the last minute, and I don't know what to do. I can't just bail, but I also can't take—"

Boone stepped between them and yanked the stroller out of Eloise's hands. "I've got her."

"I can't ask you to babysit."

"You didn't," he said pointedly.

"Don't you have to work?" Eloise asked.

"I'm off for two days. Now, go. Before you lose the job."

She held his gaze, two combatants unwilling to back down.

Finlay touched her friend's shoulder. "Just go, okay? Your baby's safe with us."

Eloise sighed. "Okay. Thank you. I'll try to get it done as quickly as I can."

"Take your time." Boone pushed the stroller to an empty table and sat down.

After her friend left, Cody tugged on Finlay's arm. "Could we get cocoa now? I'm cold."

"Yes, of course." But as they got in line, she saw Matt and his little girl at a nearby table. Chloe stood on a chair, stomping her little booted feet, as she munched a chocolate muffin. Finlay couldn't help but smile at him.

As she headed over, he stood, one hand gripping his daughter's arm.

"She's a firecracker." Finlay noticed how much the little girl looked like him.

"She is."

It was awkward for a moment. Neither knew how to greet the other. But Finlay wasn't about to hug him. "How's it going?"

"It's okay. We're living with my mom till I figure things out. She watches her while I'm at work."

She'd never seen him so uncomfortable. Undoubtedly, he had a lot to say to her, but this wasn't the right setting to get into it. "You're lucky to have her."

"I am, yeah. Eventually, I'll get my own place, get a nanny or something. I don't know. I'm not exactly thinking clearly at the moment." He blew out a breath. "It turns out the only reason my ex decided to tell me about my daughter is because she's going back to school full-time, so she needs my help. I've been thrown into this. I haven't had a chance to process anything else."

"That's awful. I'm sorry she did that to you."

"Yeah. It's been an adjustment to say the least." His gaze landed on Cody. "So it's true, then? You're engaged to that biker?"

A twinge of uncertainty hit her. It seemed cruel to let him believe a lie that would hurt him so deeply, but on the other hand, what choice did she have? "His name is Jude, and we've known each other a long time."

"That's not an answer."

"What makes you think you deserve one?" She instantly regretted snapping at him in front of the children. "I'm sorry." They lived in the same town and had to find a way to be pleasant with each other.

"Finlay, two weeks ago, we were getting *married*."

"I'm well aware."

"If you could move on that fast… It pretty much invalidates our entire relationship."

I think you managed that one all by yourself. But no matter what he'd done, she still couldn't blame him for being upset. If the situations were reversed, she'd be, too. "We had a lot of cracks in it already." But she didn't see any reason to get into it. He was the one who'd chosen to deceive her. She didn't owe him any explanation. "At least she seems to be adjusting well." She smiled at the little girl who was happily chomping away.

"I Cwo-ie."

"I know you are, cutie. And that looks yummy."

The little girl nodded in an exaggerated way. She was adorable.

"I really wish you were doing this with me," Matt said. "You'd be a great stepmom." He studied Cody. "Well, I guess that's what you are. Just to someone else's child." Tenderly, he brushed the hair off his daughter's cheek. "I messed up."

"Why, though?" she asked. "Why didn't you tell me?"

"I don't know. I guess part of me didn't want to believe it. I just wanted to marry you and get to the good part where we had kids and my buddies would come over to watch games. We had plans, and she wasn't in them." He had the decency to lower his chin and shake his head. "That didn't come out right."

"No, I know what you meant." And she was so damn grateful for the way things turned out, she really couldn't be angry with him anymore. "Do you think you and your ex will get back together? Become a family?"

"Are you kidding?" Anger and disgust twisted his features. "She *lied* to me. I'll never trust her again. Never."

Finlay waited, not saying a word. It only took a moment for him to get it.

When he did, he drew in a deep breath. "Yeah. I get

it." He looked her right in the eyes. "I'm sorry. I blew up everything, and I'll regret it for the rest of my life."

His remorse softened her. "I think we're both going to be okay."

He lowered his gaze to her ring finger, and a bolt of fear sizzled through her.

Until she remembered. Jude had taken it off. *Oh, thank God. Can you imagine if I'd still been wearing it?*

On the other hand, what would he make of a bare ring finger? If he said anything to his well-connected mom, it could surely get back to the judge. She really needed to get out of there.

"Daddy, look." Chloe raised both her chocolate-smeared hands and grinned with her muffin-covered teeth. "I'm a monster."

"Yeah, punkin'." He grabbed a napkin and made a useless attempt to wipe her mouth. "A cute one." When he turned back to Finlay, he was smiling. "I guess we both got what we wanted—just not the way we'd expected it to go."

That might be true for Matt. He had a daughter.

But for me? Right now, I'm just playing house.

Chapter Twenty-Six

On Christmas morning, everyone got to the house early, and Jude appreciated that. His brothers weren't used to small kids, but they'd jumped right in to give Cody the best possible holiday.

Ava had her own family events, so she couldn't come, but she'd stopped by the night before with her famous strata. *"This way, you can just pop it into the oven and not worry about breakfast. Just enjoy being together and opening presents."*

He pulled out his phone to text her.

Jude: An easy breakfast was a great idea. Thanks for the strata. Hope you have a great Christmas.

After sending her a picture of the family gathered around the tree and taking turns opening presents, he pocketed his phone.

"Mister, look what I got." Cody raced over, his whole body vibrating with excitement.

It was a Lego Emergency Responder set. "That's cool." He gave his firefighter brother a chin nod. "Good one."

"Come on," Boone said, waving Cody over. "Let's get started."

"Can I?" The boy looked up at Jude with anticipation.

Warmth spread through him. This was the moment it happened, and he mentally recorded it. It wasn't the baths or reading before bed. It wasn't making Cody brush his teeth or even holding his hand as they walked across the park to join their team for Snowfest.

No, the moment he felt like a dad was when his boy asked permission, exactly as he would've done with a parent.

And you know, it's a pretty good feeling. At once, it held the weight of responsibility and the joy of being the one who got to give this boy a beautiful life. "You bet." As Cody ran off, Jude pulled on his shoulder. "Make sure you thank your uncle Boone."

"I will." He ran the obstacle course around presents, boxes, and balled up wrapping paper to get to his uncle.

As the two of them settled on the rug near the huge, twinkling tree, Jude watched the scene with an unbelievably full heart. Christmas carols played on the speakers, a fire crackled and snapped in the hearth, and his family— except for Decker, who had a game—sat around his living room.

This moment erased the uncomfortable feelings of his childhood and replaced them with love. Love for his brothers, his dad, this little boy who drank up every drop of his family's attention. And her.

Finlay.

I love her. With all my heart.

She was busy opening gifts, so he didn't want to bother her, but he couldn't keep it all inside. So he sent a text instead.

> Jude: You're so beautiful. I'm watching you talk to Wyatt, and the heat from the fire's making your cheeks rosy. And all I can think is I want this forever. Us. You and me.

She clutched the gift certificate his dad gave her to a high-end soap-making supplier and got up to hug him. Her curls tumbled down her back, one lock dipping into her cleavage. When she smiled, his heart thundered, sending a rush of blood through his body.

He loved Finlay O'Neill, and he knew he wanted to spend the rest of his life with her.

If he could, he'd propose right then. But she wouldn't like that. She'd want something private and meaningful. Just between the two of them.

Also, he should probably wait till the dust was fully settled after her wedding.

Soon, though.

His dad glanced over, saw him watching, and came over to Jude. "She's the one."

"She is. Always has been." Jude grinned. "I've wanted her since I was a kid."

"Took you long enough."

"Yeah, well. I wasn't ready for her back then."

"But you are now?" There was something watchful in his dad's eyes, something probing in his tone.

Sure, he got it. His dad was worried he'd mess up. Because the only version of Jude he'd known was the fuck-up. "I am." It was time to talk to him. "Dad, I'm not that same kid. I don't get into trouble anymore."

"I know." But he sounded wary.

"I'm sorry for how hard I made things for you. I don't know why I was such a piece of shit."

Even though his dad lowered his chin, Jude couldn't miss the color rushing into his cheeks. He tugged at his scruff.

Jude rarely saw his dad upset, so he didn't know what to do. He panned the room. Cody worked intently, taking Boone's guidance. Fee gestured with her hands while Wyatt listened to her story. The fire popped and crackled, and Christmas carols played softly in the background.

But not a single thought came to mind that would convince his dad to believe him. "If I can adopt Cody, I'll raise him here. You'll see I've changed." There was no other way to prove himself.

His dad's head jerked up. "You didn't fuck up. I did."

Oh. That was not what he expected to hear.

"Not a day goes by that I don't wish I'd done things differently with you," his dad said.

"After your mom passed, I panicked. I had a newborn, three toddlers, and no income. Nothing but student loans." He looked gutted. "I was not a good father."

A fierceness took hold. "I don't know what you're talking about. You were great. You put up with all my shit. So many times, I thought you'd kick me out, but you were patient and worked hard to get me on the right path. I don't know why I couldn't find it. I don't know why I had to fuck up all the time."

"What were you supposed to do? Sit at the table and learn the multiplication tables in a bike club?" his dad snapped. "You were unsupervised and unprotected."

"I had Ava."

"When we got there, Ava was getting her master's degree. She'd help out when she could, but she had classes and student teaching gigs. After she graduated, she got a job. You and the boys were alone a lot more than you remember. You needed a father. You needed guidance, and I wasn't there."

"I don't know what you're talking about. You had to make a living. And the moment you got stable, you moved us out."

"That's right, but you were twelve when we left. Too young to understand that. All you knew was that you went from having a mom and dad to having to fend for yourself. And thank fuck you're such a good person because you protected your brothers. You did what I should've done. So if you want to know why they didn't get into trouble like you did, it was because of you. You watched out for them. You were a confused, scared kid, so yeah, you ran wild. But even when you did that, you were always a good man at heart. And I'm damn proud of you." His dad hauled him up against his chest and hugged him. It was the first time they'd shown each other affection in years, and he hadn't known how much he'd needed his dad's love until he finally allowed himself to feel it.

Jude squeezed him hard, digging his face into the crook of his neck.

His dad pulled him back. "Makes me real happy to see you with Finlay and Cody. The whole time you've been away, I've blamed myself."

"What? No. It wasn't your fault. It was because of the mess I made of my reputation here."

"You were a mama's boy." His dad's soft grin was reminiscent. "And that comfort got taken from you. But maybe now, you've got it back." His gaze slid to Finlay. "Did you open your gift from me?"

Jude had forgotten about that. It was a plain white envelope shoved into his stocking. He pulled it out of his back pocket, wrinkled and bent. "This?"

His dad nodded. "Do with it what you want. It's my way of letting you know you'll always have a home here. I hope you'll give me the chance to be the dad you should have had back then."

His heart cracked, and sorrow bled from the fissures. "Dad—"

"Open it."

All these years, they'd both gotten it wrong. So much lost time. Tearing it open, he pulled out a legal document. "What is this?"

"Go on and read it."

Jude scanned the legalese until a picture formed. "A deed? You're giving me land?"

"Over the years, I've been buying up acreage around my property. With four boys, it just made sense." He cleared his throat. "And I'm giving you some of it."

"Fifty acres. You're giving me fifty acres in Calamity Falls? Dad, I can't accept this."

"I want you here. I want you to raise Cody here."

"I don't know what to say. All this time, I thought I'd made life harder for you than it needed to be, and here you are, apologizing to me."

"Let me ask you something. If you got a call from school, telling you Cody put a snake in someone's mailbox, are you going to think he's a piece of shit? Or are you going to try to figure out why he's acting out and find ways to get him on the right track?"

A tide of relief crashed over him because he fully understood what his dad was saying. "I'll always stand up for Cody, the way you did for me. Thanks, Dad."

"I know Finlay's got her dream house, but maybe this can be a weekend cabin or something. Maybe you can build her a studio to make her soap. Either way, might be good for Cody to grow up fishing and snowboarding and running wild in the woods with his dad and uncles."

"I can't think of anything I'd rather do. Which makes no sense, considering I was planning to flip a bar in Florida and remain single and childless two weeks ago. And, Dad?"

His dad swallowed, still fighting emotion.

"Thank you. For accepting Cody and bringing Finlay into the family. All of it. It means a lot."

The front door opened, and Ava walked in, arms loaded. Wyatt headed over to relieve her of a platter.

His dad watched her intently. "What're you doin' here?"

"Dad." Wyatt's tone held a warning.

"She knows I don't mean it like that. She's part of the family, but she said she'd be with her folks."

"Holidays are hard when I don't have my girls," Ava

said with a sad smile. "Makes me happy to be with my boys."

Boone ambled over, Cody right behind him. "Well, we love you, and we're glad you're here." He reached for the shopping bags. "Let me get those."

His dad helped her out of her coat. "The girls having a good Christmas?"

"Seems like it." She sighed. "I guess it just never gets easier. They won't be home till after New Year's."

"Sucks." He said it gruffly. "You staying for dinner?"

"I ate with my family, and I'm stuffed. But I have room for Finlay's cake. She's an amazing baker."

"Let me get the Yorkshire pudding into the oven." His dad started for the kitchen.

Jude checked his phone. "Well, hang on. We're waiting for Finlay's parents."

"What time are they supposed to be here?" his dad asked.

"Her mom's working, but she said she'd try to stop by. I told her dad what time we eat, so hopefully, he'll be here."

"Well, text 'em, and see when they're coming. Don't want a dried-out prime rib." His dad and Ava headed into the kitchen.

Boone, Wyatt, and Cody returned to the Lego set, and Jude went straight for his woman, wrapping an arm around her and drawing her close. That floral scent threw him back to the two of them alone, under the covers, his hands on her warm body. "Good Christmas?"

"The best." She leaned into him, but he didn't like her troubled expression.

"What's wrong?"

"I just don't want you to wait for my parents. My mom gets paid triple time for working on Christmas, and my dad—" Her jaw snapped shut.

"Your dad?" He waited for more.

"You know what?" She looked around the room, resolve tightening her features. "I'll text him right now."

Chapter Twenty-Seven

FINLAY WENT UP TO HER ROOM. SHE NEEDED SPACE. She needed to think.

But she couldn't work this one out on her own so she called her best friend.

Willa answered on the first ring. "Merry Christmas."

"Merry Christmas." She didn't hear noises in the background, so it was true. "You really are alone today?"

"Oh, I had plans, but everything blew up, and if I don't get this case back on track, they'll fire me—even though it's not my fault. Are you having a good time with the McKennas?"

"Well, that's the thing." She paced to the window and looked down at her backyard. It was a perfectly square lot, with plenty of room for the swing set Jude would build in the spring. "I'm about to blow my life up."

"Okay. Am I pulling the pin or snatching the grenade out of your hands?"

Good question. "I've been thinking a lot about my parents, and how I tiptoe around them. I take the crumbs they offer and say thank you. And…I think I'm done doing that."

"So we're lobbing it."

"I think so, but before I do it, I need to think it through. Make a list of pros and cons."

"I think it's less about the number in each column and more about the quality, because doing it will empower you."

Just hearing her friend say it out loud gave her a punch of determination.

"And not doing it will keep you in limbo," her friend continued. "But, really, Fee, what's the worst thing that could happen?"

Her parents wouldn't disown her. She wasn't worried about that. "The worst? If I tell them, and they just keep doing what they're doing, then I'll know I don't matter."

"And that'll hurt, for sure. But—"

"It already hurts. And I'm done with the status quo."

"There you go."

"I love you, Willa."

"I love you, too. Let me know how it goes."

She pressed a hand to the cold glass, wanting to anchor herself in the moment. It felt so monumental, like there'd be a before and an after. Right then, she at least had parents. But challenging them, calling them out… Well, it could mean losing them altogether.

But what do I have? Her mom hadn't even gone to her engagement party.

Okay, I'm going to do it. She called her mom first. That would be the easiest, since she wouldn't try to play her.

She'd cut to the chase, whereas her dad would cajole and make light of the situation.

Aw, you know I love ya, kid.

No, Dad. I really don't.

But it was no surprise that neither answered their phones. It wasn't even a letdown—that was how accustomed she was to her parents not taking her calls. Sure, her mom was working, and her dad was very likely at a party telling a story. He probably had no clue his phone was ringing.

But that was the thing. Neither of her parents was thinking about her on Christmas Day. She pulled up the family chat.

> Finlay: Merry Christmas!

She had to get her thoughts together, get the right tone so it didn't sound like she was throwing a tantrum. She didn't want to sound bitter or angry. Just speak from the heart.

> Finlay: Mom, you said something to me the other day, about how I swapped one family for another. And I suppose it looks like that, but I really do care about Jude.

Ugh. You're rambling.

No, actually, she was getting to her point.

> Finlay: You said you know I need to be part of a big family, like that was a negative thing, but you know what? I want it so badly because I grew up with one that gave me the bare minimum.

Oh, maybe she *was* a little angry.

> Finlay: And now that I'm making Christmas magic for a little boy who's not even mine, and being welcomed into a family I just met, I can see how very little you both did to make me feel special. I didn't even need much. I certainly didn't ask for much.

You know what? This feels good.

> Finlay: In any event, I'm done making myself small for both of you. I'm done being convenient.

Oh yes. This is what I want to say.

> Finlay: I love you both very much, but here I am, spending yet another Christmas with a family that's not mine— no call from either of you, no real attempt to make plans. So going forward, if you want a relationship with me, the ball's in your court.

She didn't just hit Send. She punched it.

And damn, it felt good.

The laughter and conversation drew her back downstairs. The cinnamon-scented air made her stomach growl.

Even before she hit the living room, her dad texted back.

> Dad: Heard. On my way. Text me the
> address again.

Well, look at that. That was all it had taken. She smiled. *My dad's spending Christmas with me.*

After a feast of prime rib, Yorkshire pudding, and roasted carrots and potatoes, Finlay sat back in her seat, Jude's arm slung across her shoulders. She liked the way he kept his hands on her. It let her know he wanted her, was thinking about her.

They just fit, and she'd never had that with anyone before.

As always, everyone was laughing and having a great time. Especially Jude. He wasn't acting like his usual dark and broody, observant self. Like he was an outsider.

"Someone's wiped out." She smiled at Cody, who was having a hard time keeping his eyes open.

"I'll put him to bed." Jude leaned over and whispered in the boy's ear. "Hey, buddy. Need to close your eyes for a few minutes?"

The boy's head wobbled in his attempt to shake it. "I want to stay here."

"How about you stay here and close your eyes?"

"Okay."

When Jude lifted him onto his lap, the boy collapsed against his chest. In about five seconds, he was out cold, his body boneless.

It was the sweetest sight, how well they were bonding.

Her phone vibrated, so she peeked at the screen—but only because her dad still hadn't shown up yet. But no, it was just a spam text.

She had to get her parents out of her mind. *This is nothing new.*

"So what's the plan?" Wyatt asked, looking at Cody.

"Carlo's attorney's going to get started on the adoption papers, and we'll talk on January second."

"That must give him so much peace of mind," Finlay said. "To know his grandson's in good hands."

"I told him we'll find a place for him to live right near us," Jude said. "We want him to stay as involved as he wants."

"My heart is full," Ava said. "This makes me happy."

"And what about you two?" Boone wagged a finger between them.

"Don't do that," Wyatt said quietly.

"Do what?" Boone asked. "It's a legit question. They're obviously together. She's more than a nanny."

"Why don't we let them figure that out," Ava said. "It's new."

"It doesn't feel new." Jude seemed surprised he'd said it out loud, but he didn't back off. "I've wanted her more than half my life. Even when I moved away, she was still in here." He looked at Finlay. "You've owned my heart since I was eleven. It doesn't feel new at all. It's inevitable."

She almost couldn't believe he was saying these things. It was like every teenage fantasy of him she'd ever had come to life. "It does." It struck her—why she'd settled for a love like Matt's. She'd been *grateful* to find someone who wanted to do the same things she did. She'd appreciated his interest because it was so much more focused than anything her parents had given her.

But with Jude… *My God, what a gift.*

I deserve this kind of love.

"Hey, man," Boone teased. "This is the singles table. The sappy couple table's in the kitchen. Go on, get out of here."

"You taking over Wild Billy's?" Wyatt asked.

"Yeah, looks like it." Jude turned to her for confirmation, as if she had a say in it.

She could only nod. *Did* she have a say in what he did? *Is that where we are?*

"Okay, cool." Wyatt nodded. "So you're not moving."

"Things've obviously gone to hell without me here, so no, I'm not going anywhere." Jude's gaze hit Boone, then Wyatt. "Gotta keep you two assholes in line."

"Hey." Boone snatched a bread roll and tossed it at Jude.

Jude reached to catch it, but it glanced off the side of the Snowfest first-place trophy that sat in the center of the table and hit Cody's head. "Thanks for making my point."

Cody woke up and rubbed the back of his hand over his eyes. "What hit me?"

"It was a roll." Jude shot his brother a chastising look. "Uncle Boone thought he was funny, but he's not. We don't do things like that, do we? That's not acceptable—" In a flash, Jude rose out of his seat, clutching Cody, and stuffed the soft roll down Boone's black T-shirt.

Cody cracked up.

"You did not want to do that." Boone grabbed a prime rib bone off his plate and waved it threateningly.

"Okay, cave man," Jude said. "What're you going to do with that?"

Holding the bone aloft, Boone's other arm whipped low, and he snatched the last Yorkshire pudding popover out of the basket and sent it flying out.

"Credit for deflection," Wyatt said. "I didn't see that coming."

"Can we have a nice meal for once?" his dad called. "It's Christmas."

Ava clapped her hands and stood. "Game time." The guys froze. "Bring me five things that begin with the letter R. You have five minutes. Winner gets five home-cooked dinners."

All three brothers took off. Gunnar watched, shaking his head while fighting a grin.

"Hey, you don't need food," Finlay called to Jude. "*I* make you a home-cooked meal most nights."

"Yeah, exactly." Jude held Cody tightly. "We'd better win, buddy. Am I right?"

"Excuse me?" But she was laughing. He wasn't wrong.

Cody's legs were kicking as if he were riding a horse, urging Jude to hurry up. "Come on. Hurry." His grin stretched wide across his face, eyes lit up with happiness.

It was the best thing she'd ever seen. Jude and Cody were so right together.

His brothers were calling out each item they found: "Ribbon, Rope, Rice…"

Ava shouted, "You went right past the reindeer," but

Jude had a clear target. He grabbed the little basket of rocks Cody had collected as a gift to Wyatt and brought it back to the table.

"Done in two minutes." He lifted Cody's arm, and they celebrated their easy win.

His brothers came over with their arms full. Boone stared at the basket. "Why do you always do that?"

"Why don't you learn to do the same thing already?" Jude asked.

The doorbell rang, and everyone quieted down.

"Who's that?" Gunnar asked.

She checked her phone.

Dad: Here.

"It's my dad." She practically jumped out of her chair and ran for the door. When she threw it open, her heart flipped over. *He came. He's here.*

He stood there, tall, burly, his cheeks red, lips chapped from the cold. "Hey, kiddo."

"Hey, Dad. Come on in." *It worked. I can't believe he's here.* "You're just in time for dessert."

"Yeah, I don't have a lot of time. I have to get back. We've got a couple of movie stars in town, and they're talking about having me set up a pro tournament here next summer. But I wanted to talk to you." He stepped inside and cupped her elbows. "Can we go somewhere private?"

"Sure. Let me introduce you to everyone." She led him to the dining room table that was now strewn with rocks, a radio, raspberries, running shoes, ribbon, and rope.

"Dad, this is the McKenna family." She took hold of his arm. "This is my dad, Buck O'Neill."

The men stood and shook her dad's hand.

"You wouldn't believe why I'm late. A big ole bison decided to hang out right there on 191, holding up traffic. Brought his buddies out, too." He grabbed a popover from the basket and took a big bite. "Hope you don't mind if I steal my little girl away for a minute."

"Not at all," Ava said, and instead of sitting back down, everyone got busy clearing the table for dessert.

The garage would be too cold, so she led him into the mudroom. "Is everything all right?"

"I don't know. You tell me. Your mom and I talked about that text you sent. I figured I'd talk to you after the holidays, but I don't think I can wait that long. Had to come over and say my piece."

"Your piece? I thought…" So he wasn't spending Christmas with her? "I don't understand."

"Look, it's your life, and I'll never tell you what to do," her dad said. "But I'm looking from the outside in, and it sure looks like you traded your problems for someone else's."

"Dad, no." Finlay let out an exasperated breath. "It's not like that at all."

"You're living in the house you bought with Matt, only you swapped him out for some dude with a kid that's not even his."

"He's not some dude. Dad, I care about him. He's a great guy."

"Well, hang on. I'm not saying I have a problem with Jude. He seems like an okay guy. Nice family. But you've got to check yourself here, Finny. Make sure you're not getting carried away with the fantasy of a family. Because that kid is not yours. You're just the nanny, right?"

"I mean, that's how it started, yes. But it's not like that anymore. I have real feelings for Jude, and I know he feels the same way."

"Okay, but we're talking about a single guy who just got custody of a kid. And he conveniently has a school-teacher around to help him out. Hon, you just ran from your wedding. This is a time of crisis for both of you. Emotions are running high. I'm just saying, it doesn't feel real to me."

"I can't believe you're saying this to me. You think I'm not smart enough to know the difference between reality and fantasy? That I'm so lost I'd let myself be manipulated by a guy who's afraid of being a single dad? Is that really what you think of me?"

"Now, take it easy. I'm here because I love you, and your mom and I are worried. Keep in mind, I've got no skin in this game. All I want is for you to be happy, and this looks like a recipe for disaster." Her dad reached for the back door. "I have to get back to the party, but let's you and me go out to dinner tomorrow night. We'll talk more, and I promise to make more of an effort, sweet pea. Hate that you don't feel loved."

Before he could open it, Jude stepped into the mud room. "It's real for me."

Both of them swung around. *Oh God.* How much had he heard?

"My feelings for your daughter have nothing to do with raising Cody. I'm not afraid to adopt him by myself, but even if I were, I have three brothers, a dad, and the woman who raised me helping out. I don't need Finlay for that. I need her because I'm falling in love with her. Make no mistake, whether I get to adopt Cody or not, I want to be with your daughter."

Chapter Twenty-Eight

JUDE COULDN'T SLEEP.

The house was quiet. Fee was asleep and draped over him. Everything was fine.

Except it wasn't. Something was different. He knew her. Knew the faraway look in her eyes when she was troubled, the pout of her lips when she was lost in thought. She was smart, thoughtful, and plugged in, so when she'd put the milk next to the cereal in the pantry, he'd known she was distracted.

He wasn't worried about what Fee's dad said—they'd talked about it, and she'd assured him she wouldn't take advice from parents who hardly even knew her.

Well, that wasn't entirely true. Because the man's logic was indisputable. From an outsider's perspective, it *did* look like Fee had latched on to Jude's problems to avoid facing her own. She *had* jumped right in to help him with Cody.

He knew in his heart they were meant to be together, but maybe she needed time to make peace with her past relationship and clear some space for the new one.

He just didn't know.

A shaft of moonlight spilled across her naked body, highlighting her sexy thigh, and all that silky dark hair splayed across his chest. Her scent filled him, kicking up visceral memories of hearing her laughter, catching her hand in his while taking a family walk, and sitting quietly on the couch with her feet in his lap as they watched a movie.

Just a few hours ago, she'd ridden him with abandon, her hair brushing his thighs, her full tits bouncing. At the memory, desire ignited into lust, and he rolled onto his side, burying his face in her neck and just breathing her in. She stirred, making a sexy "mmm" sound.

His fingers skimmed her collarbone, landing on the plump rise of her breast. The nipple hardened, and he shifted lower so he could taste the hot little bead.

"Jude," she whispered, her fingernails scraping across his scalp.

He cupped her jaw, forcing her to look at him. "Are we okay?" He needed to know.

"Yes. Of course."

He swallowed her breathy voice with a kiss he hoped would banish any doubt she had, any ugly thought her parents put into her head. And it seemed to work.

In the darkest part of the night, the only sounds the rustle of sheets and the gasps and sighs of the woman he loved with all his heart, he knew he'd found bliss. Threading their fingers together, he raised her arms over her head, nudged her legs open, and rocked against her opening. She was wet and hot, and after a few easy thrusts, he slid deep inside.

Every cell in his body burst like champagne bubbles. He lowered his arms, so his chest brushed over hers. He wanted to feel her plush tits and hear her breathy sighs.

"I love you." He took his time with slow, sensuous glides in and out of her slick heat. His heart thundered, and blood roared in his ears. "I love you so much."

Stay with me.

Don't leave me.

She wrenched her hands free to grip his ass, drawing him tighter to her. Her back arched, and she met his hips with frantic thrusts. "Jude. I love you. I love you. I love you."

She wanted more, faster, and he gave it to her. He drove into her so hard that she had to brace her palms on the headboard. He reached under her, hiking up her ass and shifting the angle of friction, until she cried out. Fiery sparks ignited, and she gushed all over his swollen cock. "*Jude.*"

Hearing her cry out his name like that drove him past the point of return. Spasms wracked his body as one climax after another had his hips twisting, punching, and writhing, sending his spirit soaring into euphoria.

When the shudders stopped, his thrusts slowed, turned lazy, and he lingered inside her. It just felt so delicious, so good.

Finally, he settled back down beside her, pulling her close. Peace enveloped him, and he started to doze. Nothing felt as good as having a sated, warm Finlay boneless and satisfied in his arms.

He could handle her needing some time alone. He could handle her needing space. He'd understand that.

But he didn't think he'd survive her walking away.

When Finlay woke up, she had to shut her eyes against the light flooding into the bedroom.

She still wasn't used to sleeping in so late, but Jude was just so *passionate*. He wore her out in the best way. Though, really, she didn't know what she'd do when school started back up again.

The chilly air had her pulling up the blanket, which made her realize her human heating pad was not wrapped around her. Her eyelids popped open to find Jude was gone.

Wow. She must've been out cold not to even notice Cody coming in, asking for breakfast. She thought of Jude in his gray sweatpants, hanging low on his hips, shirtless at the stove, as he flipped pancakes and chatted while the little boy stood on a chair at his side, and all she wanted was to be there with them.

Well, really, she wanted to run her hands all over that beautiful ink and kiss the silly moose tattoo with the floppy antlers. *He did that for me.*

She could hardly believe it. All the years spent thinking it was an unrequited crush—when he'd been feeling it, too.

Wanting to see him, she quickly got out of bed and pulled on her pajamas. She shoved her feet into her slippers and headed down the hallway.

As expected, Cody's bed was empty, but she didn't smell melting butter or pancakes. Curious, she headed downstairs. Colored lights twinkled on the tree, and the basket of pinecones by the hearth filled the house with the scent of cinnamon.

It was all just so lovely and perfect.

On the dining room table, she found a note.

> *Fee,*
> *Took Cody snowboarding with the family. Thought you could use a day off. You've been working so hard—take a spa day! Ava will be over around ten to go with you.*
> *Miss you already,*
> *J*

Next to it was a stack of bills. He'd left her money to go to the spa.

Her heart shriveled. She didn't know why the note hurt her feelings. Maybe because he hadn't included her in the "family's" plans? No, that wasn't fair. The brothers were allowed to do things on their own. And it was good for Cody to bond with them.

It was just…what did he mean by a day off? That was something you'd say to a nanny. Not a girlfriend or a lover. The wording was just…off-putting.

In fact, the whole thing made her uneasy. *Since when do I do spa days?*

But also, this was Cody's first time on the slopes. She didn't want to miss that.

. . .

Just stop. You're overreacting.

It's fine.

In the kitchen, she found a pot of coffee keeping warm, a bowl in the sink, and dust from cereal on the counter. She filled her *I love my teacher* mug, dumped a little too much caramel macchiato creamer, which she did when she was upset—sugar was her happy pill—*sue me*—and then wandered to the mudroom and glanced out at the snow-covered backyard.

She took a sip, letting the buttery caramel and creamy sweetness comfort her. When had he made these plans? He'd never mentioned them.

And why didn't he wake me up? He could've at least asked if I wanted to go.

Cold seeped in, and she wished she'd thrown on a sweatshirt or a robe. But it woke her fully, and she got a stab of fear when she remembered they'd said "I love you" to each other.

That was a big deal.

It's huge.

But it was in the heat of the moment, so maybe it didn't count?

Or maybe it scared him, and that was why he'd taken off?

The fear spread at an alarming rate, invading her entire body. Because that would be so like him to shut down after they got really close.

Oh, stop it. You're looking for trouble. She headed back

into the kitchen, grabbed a sponge, and cleaned up the cereal dust.

Rinsed out the coffee pot.

Unloaded the dishwasher. As she stacked the plates, she realized she hated them. They were too formal and not her taste at all. As soon as they'd closed on the house, Matt's mom began sending all kinds of basic household items. Trash bins that matched the tissue boxes and soap dishes. A cute lacquered tray for the ottoman.

That was really nice of her. She'd thanked her at the time, of course. Mrs. Jones had been nothing but kind. She'd welcomed Finlay into her life and done everything she could to give them a beautiful wedding and a good start as a married couple.

And since running from the wedding, I haven't reached out to her. None of this is her fault.

I'll call her and thank her for everything.

It was just that none of this stuff was her style. Not to be ungrateful—she truly appreciated Mrs. Jones's generosity—*but where am I in this place?*

And if she were really honest, she only got the house because of her. It wasn't like they'd toured a bunch of homes and *chosen* this one. It had just become available, and they'd grabbed it. But if she'd had her choice, she'd have preferred the blue Craftsman up the street.

Back in the mudroom, she swept the dirt and grit and found a pair of Cody's socks sticking out of his sneakers, so she tossed them into the washing machine and got a load going. As she was folding the clothes, her phone buzzed with a text message.

> Ava: I'm here! Hope you're ready to get
> pampered.

She looked at the neatly folded stacks. Jude's. Cody's. Hers. It felt so completely right. Like in her gut, she knew she was exactly where she needed to be, yet…

Everything was wrong.

As she crossed the living room to let Ava in, she realized none of the furniture was hers. Not a single thing. In fact, other than her clothes and the *I love my teacher* mug, *nothing* was hers.

I know you want to be part of a big family.

Her mom was right about that. But did she want it so badly that she'd disappear into anyone's world? Like, if it hadn't been the McKennas, would she have dived right in?

She'd stepped right into Matt's life, and she'd done it again with Jude's.

You've got to check yourself here, Finny. Make sure you're not getting carried away with the fantasy of a family.

Her dad was right. She had gotten carried away with the fantasy of Jude's big, loving, generous, fun family.

He was right to be worried. She had traded her problems for Jude's.

She let Ava in. "Morning."

The smile fell right off her friend's face. "Oh. You're not ready to go?"

"I just woke up. Haven't even had a chance to finish my coffee." She started back for the kitchen. "Come on in. Want a cup?"

"Sure." Ava sounded hesitant but followed her.

Of course, the coffee maker was empty, the pot drying

in the rack. "Sorry. I wasn't thinking." She rolled her eyes. "I'm not used to sleeping so late. I'm a little out of it. Let me make a fresh one."

"No, no." Ava moved to the machine Gunnar had bought. "I'll just use this." She sorted through the basket full of pods and found one. "Are you looking forward to your spa day?"

"To be honest, I've never had one."

"Never had a massage?"

Finlay shook her head. The window over the sink looked right at the fence between her and her neighbor's yard. She didn't like that. She'd rather look at the backyard.

"Oh, you'll love it. Gunnar used to spoil me with them when I worked for him. He always gave spa gift cards as my holiday bonus."

Finlay glanced back at the dining room table to the neat pile of cash.

I did exactly what Jude warned me about. I blurred the lines.

And look at me now. Two nannies drinking coffee and getting ready to enjoy the *holiday bonus* from their employers.

"Ava, I don't…this is not…" She couldn't even finish her sentence.

Because it seemed that, finally, after two and a half weeks of avoiding it, she was about to crash out.

Chapter Twenty-Nine

CODY HAD NEVER SNOWBOARDED BEFORE, SO THEY didn't stay on the mountain long. But at least he'd learned to balance himself and had a few good runs. There'd be plenty of time to teach him.

"He's a natural," Boone said.

"Yep," Wyatt said. "Athletic, just like his uncle Decker."

Jude laughed. He knew what was coming.

"You don't have to play professional ball to be athletic," Boone said. "I haul seventy-five pounds of gear into a fire. On top of that, I carry out two-hundred-pound bodies. Trust me, I could kick his ass in stamina and endurance tests."

"Just to be sure, we'll set up a course in the backyard this spring," Wyatt said, obviously not giving a single shit about who would win.

"Damn right, we will."

After lunch on the mountain, they'd come back to his dad's place. Cody and his grandpa were in the kitchen making cocoa, while Jude sat with his brothers in the living room, itching to get home. Hopefully, she was enjoying her day. After the spa, maybe she'd spend time working with her soap. Or watching mindless TV. Whatever she needed. He just wanted to pamper her.

He loved her so damn much, it almost felt like he was making up for lost time. He didn't want to overwhelm her. And while he was glad he'd finally told her how he felt, he probably shouldn't have told her while they were fucking. Should've waited for the right time. He'd have to make a nice dinner or something. Maybe take a drive. Make it a special moment.

The box in his pocket dug into his thigh, and he pulled it out. He'd never bought jewelry for a woman before, so he wouldn't mind getting his brothers' opinion. "Hey, what do you guys think?"

Boone looked at it like it was a turd. "Where'd you get that?"

"I stopped at the jeweler's on the way home." He'd gotten the text that it was ready.

Wyatt flipped the lid open. "It's not exactly traditional, but it's very nice."

Boone glanced at it. "Wait, you're proposing?"

"Yes." He didn't know why his brother sounded so surprised. "Where'd you think this relationship was going?"

"It hasn't even been three weeks. What's the rush?"

"When you know, you know."

Boone plucked the ring out of its nest. "So, what, you just walked into the store and bought it?"

"I actually bought it a few days ago." He'd liked the

setting because the center stone represented them, and the smaller diamonds surrounding it symbolized the children they'd have. "But I made a few changes. I think she'll like the rose gold, and I got a different diamond."

"A pink one?" Boone asked.

Jude smiled. "She's a pink girl." Plus, they were rare, and he wanted her to always wear a reminder of how special she was.

"What the hell?" his dad muttered from the kitchen. A moment later, he strode into the living room with a serious expression and looked right at Jude. "My office. Now."

As he got up and followed his dad, he called out to his brothers. "Watch Cody for me?" Once inside the library-like room with floor-to-ceiling bookcases and a huge desk, he closed the door behind him. "What's up?"

"Finlay wants to sell her house." His dad handed over his phone.

Finlay: Thank you so much for your kindness and generosity, but I have decided to put my house on the market.

What the fuck? This can't be right. He continued reading.

Finlay: Given the location, I'm sure to get a buyer, so I'm going to begin the process of moving out. You've been so incredibly kind and generous, and I appreciate everything you've done, but I'm going to return all the furniture you bought. I've rented a truck and hired a few guys to load it.

"I've been gone six hours. When did all this happen?" Had she been planning it? Why the hell hadn't she discussed it with him?

> Finlay: I know this is sudden, and I don't want to inconvenience you, so I can rent a storage unit. You let me know where to deliver everything.

Jude had to read the text twice to make sure he understood. "This makes no sense." Tossing the phone to his dad, he blew out of the room and beelined to the front door. "Take care of Cody." It slammed behind him.

He fired up the truck and backed out, kicking out snow and gravel.

And then, he gunned it back to town.

The entire drive, he replayed the last twenty-four hours. Last night, they'd made love twice, and he'd said he loved her. This morning, he'd awakened to a string of text messages from his family.

> Wyatt: We're outside right now. Let's get Cody up on a board.

> Boone: Wake up, asshole! The pow is epic!

But scrolling through a timeline wouldn't bring clarity because her behavior *did* make sense. He'd been expecting this. *She can't go from a life with Matt straight into a life with me.*

All the pampering in the world couldn't help her end one relationship before starting another.

Even as he acknowledged the truth, he couldn't help

wondering if he'd gotten it wrong. *Should I have taken her with me?* Was it the spa day that set her off?

Ava loved that kind of thing. That wasn't a bad gift, was it?

Acts of service, quality time, and physical touch.

Shit. Fuck. He had gotten it wrong. He'd given her a gift instead of spending quality time with her.

All right, I can fix it.

Killing the engine, he jogged to the front door and let himself inside. Immediately, he slammed into a stack of boxes. Trash bags heavy with clothes and toys filled the foyer.

"Finlay," he hollered, racing to the kitchen. Out of the corner of his eye, he caught a flash of green. The money he'd left her sat untouched on the dining room table.

Yeah, he'd fucked up big time with that one.

As he dashed back out to the living room, he found her at the top of the stairs. He'd never seen her so wrecked. "Sweetheart." She stood there with red-rimmed eyes, hair in a pile on top of her head, and her sleeves pushed up to her elbows. He took the stairs three at a time, reaching for her the moment he got to the top.

But she reared back, holding her hands out to ward him off.

"What happened?" Again, his mind scrambled across the past day and a half. He was missing some key thing, but he couldn't seem to think straight.

"Nothing." She wouldn't look at him.

"Finlay, for God's sake, talk to me. This is your house on Bloom Lane. You can't sell it. What did I do?" he roared.

His panicked tone seemed to snap her out of her fog. "It's not about you. It's me." Dodging him, she started down the stairs. "I can't have a fresh start by living here."

Okay, good. It's not about me. I didn't fuck up. "That's fine. We can move into my dad's place." He didn't care where they lived. As long as they were together, what did it matter?

When she reached the bottom, she turned to him, crossing her arms over her chest. "I'm moving in with my mom."

"Like hell you are. That's the last place you want to be."

"It's not ideal, but my realtor thinks she's already got a buyer. It won't be forever. As soon as I get my money out, I'll find another place to live."

"And where will Cody sleep? On the floor? In a sleeping bag?" Because he was not going to focus on the part of the sentence that didn't include him.

Confusion crossed her features. But the moment awareness struck, her shoulders pushed back. "I think it's best if the two of you go to your dad's."

"Wait, you're getting rid of me, too?" The axis of his world tipped, then spun. He couldn't seem to get his bearings. *I've lost her?*

"Jude, please. This is so hard for me."

"Hard for *you*?" Urgency sharpened his mind. He had to get through to her. "Finlay, I love you. I've never…I'm not *ever* going to love anyone else. You're it for me. So don't tell me it's hard for *you* to dump *me*. If you do this, if you walk away, I will never be the same. Do you understand that?"

Tears spilled down her cheeks, and her shoulders curved in. "Please stop. Please."

"It was easy to want you when I was a kid because it was from a distance. But now? Now, I know you. I know how you like your coffee and what temperature you like when you shower. I know the song you hum when you're baking. I know your heart and mind...I know your soul. And that makes me the luckiest man in the fucking world. Don't do this. Do not break up with me."

"I know it's awful, but I have to, Jude. I don't know what I'm doing."

"I'll tell you what you don't do. You don't throw us away. You come to me, and we'll handle it together. Sell the house, I don't care. We can live in a camper on the side of the road, and I won't care. Whatever it is, we'll get through it together."

"I can't do that. If I stay with you, I'll never know if I'm hiding in your problems instead of handling my own. I'll never know if you love me because of our situation. You always ran from me when things got intense with us, but now, you have no choice but to stay. For Cody's sake. Do you see that I need time to sort it all out?"

Of course he did. He'd been saying it all along. "Yes." Which meant he had to let her go. But he stood there, frozen, terrified that if he broke the connection, he'd never see her again. He'd lose her for good. "Okay. I'll go. I'll give you..." His mind blanked out, so he resorted to action. He grabbed some of the garbage bags and tossed them into the back of his truck. He loaded the boxes. His heart raced, and perspiration dripped down his back.

When he finished, he turned to her. "What do I tell Cody?"

She stood on the porch watching him with the same anguish he felt—as if *he* was leaving *her*. "You paid for me, right? I'm still your nanny."

The money. Reality flipped like a coin, tails turning to heads. "Oh shit. *Fuck*, no. That's not what I meant. I was trying to pamper you. I wanted you to feel special. Loved."

"Let's not get into it right now. I'm not thinking clearly."

"Okay, okay. We don't have to talk about anything. But it's not over, right? We're only taking time apart?"

"Yes. That's right. I just need…time. If we're truly meant to be—"

"We are truly meant for each other, and I'll prove it by giving you this space." He got into the truck.

She stepped off the porch. "You'll get your money back."

"I don't want it."

"And I'll put the furniture in storage until your dad tells me where to put it."

Fuck that. "It'll go in the next house we buy together."

Chapter Thirty

JUDE WAS DEVASTATED. THERE WAS NO OTHER WORD for it.

Fear shadowed him, a constant presence. But he fought like hell because he couldn't give in to it. Not when he had a little boy in his care.

They'd been living with his dad for two days now, and they'd kept busy, ice-skating in Wild Wolff Village and grabbing milk-shakes at the Hole in the Wall diner. Today, he'd built a bonfire for the two of them in the backyard, and they were making s'mores.

Even bundled up in parkas and wool hats and the blankets Jude had thrown over them, it was still freezing.

With a sticky hand, Cody tapped his leg. "Mister?"

"Yeah?"

"What happens when you go?"

"Go where?" When he prodded the fire with a long stick, sparks flew into the frigid air. Because of all the changes—moving and not living with Finlay anymore—

he'd decided to work from home till after the New Year. "I'm not sure what you mean."

"You know, like Grandpa's gone and Miss O'Neill's gone. When you're gone, who do I have?"

It hit so hard, it knocked the air out of his lungs. He was stunned. He couldn't answer. A dozen thoughts came to mind—all of them empty words of reassurance. But he'd worked hard to earn this boy's trust, and he couldn't promise a future with any of them. He didn't know *his* future with Finlay or whether he'd get to adopt Cody.

But damn, the idea that his little boy lived with such frightening thoughts tore him up inside. Heart aching, he hauled the boy onto his lap. "Your grandpa's getting better every day, and I know he can't wait to get back to you. And Miss O'Neill's not gone. You see her and talk to her every day." And while he couldn't make promises, there was one thing he knew to be true. "And me? I don't want to be anywhere else but with you."

The boy sat perfectly still, and Jude wished he knew what he was thinking. It didn't seem like he'd soothed Cody's worries. He tipped the boy's chin so he could look into his eyes and feel the sincerity of his words. "I love you, Cody. I don't know what the future holds, but I can promise you, I will do everything in my power to keep us together forever."

The boy held his gaze, studying, weighing, deciding. Finally, he gave a barely noticeable nod.

"And I'd sure appreciate it if you didn't call me Mister anymore."

"What should I call you?"

"It's up to you. You can call me Jude…"

The little boy cocked his head. "Can I call you Dad? Like I did that guy who's you 'cept in another place?"

Whoever got to raise this beautiful, sensitive, smart boy would be the luckiest guy in the world. *It better be me.* "Yeah, Cody. You can call me Dad. I'd like that a lot." He hugged him and kissed his temple.

"Is it time to go to Amy's yet?"

Jude burst out laughing. *Guess he's okay.* "No, not yet." When he'd brought him onto his lap, the blankets had slipped off, so he snatched them from the ground and settled them over them again. "Is it too cold? Do you want to go in?"

"No. I just don't want to be late."

"I won't get you there late. We'll leave in half an hour." As hard as he tried, he couldn't stop thinking about Finlay. He held on to hope by his fingernails. He would not succumb to doubt. He wouldn't allow himself to entertain the idea that she'd decide to move on without him.

She wouldn't. A love like theirs? Not a chance.

Still, every second that ticked by without a call from her threatened his sanity. Taking care of Cody tethered him, but it was hard because everything in this town reminded him of her. Of them.

Us.

There will always be an us. There's no world where Jude and Finlay aren't living in it as one.

Boots crunched on fresh snow, and a bag came flying, landing in his lap. Wyatt dropped into the Adirondack chair next to him.

Jude held up the beef jerky. "Thanks."

"You've been out here a long time. Don't want you two starving to death."

"I'm heading into town to pick up some groceries," his dad said, lagging a few steps behind. "Want me to drop Cody off for his playdate?"

"It's early, isn't it?" Jude asked, but Cody was already scrambling off his lap.

"Yeah, Grampa. Good idea. Let's go."

The moment his dad clasped Cody's sticky hand, he grimaced and shot Jude a look that said, *Thanks for the warning.*

Jude laughed. "Be sure to wash up before you go."

"I will," Cody called.

His brother shuddered. "My nuts're gonna freeze off out here."

"Didn't invite you."

"Can we at least be sad inside?" Wyatt leaned closer to the fire.

"Again, didn't invite you."

"Fine. But if I get frostbite—"

Jude whipped off the blanket and tossed it at his brother to shut him up.

They sat in silence for a few moments. Wind whistled through the branches, and the fire popped and crackled. "She's coming back," Wyatt said.

"I know that. I just don't know what to do in the meantime. Do I text her?" He wrote her messages all the time but stopped himself from hitting Send. "She's at her mom's, and I know she hates it there. Can I send her cookies? Chocolate-covered strawberries?"

A bag hit the back of his head and dropped to the

ground. "No, dumbass. Leave her alone." Boone plunked his ass into the chair on Jude's other side. "Damn, it's cold." He opened the bottle of whiskey.

Jude pulled three red plastic cups out of the bag and held them out one at a time so his brother could pour into them. Once filled, they tapped them together and knocked them back.

Instantly, his blood warmed, and his skin prickled. Which matched his internal situation. Because as much as he didn't want company at the moment, he appreciated his brothers' support.

"What went wrong?" Boone asked.

"I left her money. For a spa day." He paused before adding the kicker. "With Ava."

Both his brothers gave him a side-eye. "Our former nanny?" Wyatt asked.

"I know. You think I don't know? I was in a hurry to leave, and I wanted to do something nice for her. Instead, I made her feel like a babysitter." He tipped his head back. "I fucked up."

"I don't think she broke up with you over that." Boone poured more whiskey. "Finlay's not like that. She'd have just called you out on it."

True. But it was the final push. "Acts of service, quality time, and words of affirmation. Those work. But receiving gifts? I don't think that's one of hers."

"What're you talking about?" Boone set his cup in the snow and reached for the beef jerky.

"Love languages."

"How about you just speak the *English* language?" Boone tore the bag open. "I don't know what you're saying right now."

"I love her. And I can't lose her."

"You're not going to." Wyatt sounded awfully sure about that. "This doesn't have to do with money or gifts. She needs time, that's all. But she's not going anywhere. You guys are great together."

"She sold her house. I don't think you get how big a deal that is. She's always wanted to live on Bloom Lane."

"That's the house she bought with her ex," Boone said. "Why would she want to live there with you and Cody?"

Jude held his brother's gaze, the whiskey making his nerves jangly. "I get that, but she was crying. She was upset. And I couldn't help her. She didn't want me to."

"I think…" Wyatt stared at the fire. "She's got to get through this on her own, and you've got to trust she'll come back to you."

I hope he's right.

"Can we go inside now?" Boone said. "I can't feel my nuts." He grabbed the shovel and dumped snow over the flames.

As Jude got up, he snatched the paper bag off the ground and stuffed the graham crackers, chocolate, and marshmallows inside.

"Can you ever feel your nut sac?" Wyatt asked as they headed into the house.

"Why would you even ask that?" Boone said. "Obviously, no one's ever licked your balls."

"I'm talking about in general," Wyatt said. "Just in daily life. You don't feel them any more than you feel your toes or fingers."

"Dude, I feel my balls." Boone opened the door, and

they all filed into the house. "When my jeans ride up, or I run too fast. You never had a dog ram his face into your junk?"

The heat inside the house made his skin burn. Jude sat on the bench in the mudroom and untied his boots, kicking them off. "When she's sad, she likes sweets. I want to send her some of that Harley and Lu's fancy ice cream she likes."

"Or you can give her the space she asked for." Boone hung his jacket on a hook.

"It's a tough call." Wyatt led the way into the kitchen. "You don't want silence to come across like you don't care."

Oh shit. He couldn't let her think that. Not for a second. "Then I'm going to do it. I'll send her—"

The doorbell rang.

Finlay? Yes. He knew it. In his socks, Jude took off, nearly sliding and falling on his ass, but he righted himself in the need to get to her. He threw the door open, shocked to see the sheriff.

It was the apology in the woman's eyes that gave his stomach a hard twist. She held out an envelope. "Hate to be the bearer of bad news, but there's been a motion filed about Cody. You'll need to appear before Judge Adams to sort it out."

"What is this?" Jude took the envelope and tore it open. *Notice to Appear.*

"It's a hearing to determine guardianship," the sheriff said. "Because of a material representation to the court."

"What the fuck?" Boone muttered under his breath.

"Will he take Cody from us?" Wyatt asked.

"It's possible." She studied the three of them as if deciding how much to say. "Look, it's a small town. People talk, and the judge's wife has lots of friends. Someone told her you and Finlay aren't really engaged. Whoever it was contacted Family Services."

"Shit." *Who would do something like that?* "He can't revoke custody. Cody's happy here. We take good care of him. We're his home."

"Tell that to the judge tomorrow morning at nine," the sheriff said.

"Is there anything I can do?" Jude asked.

"Show him the man you've become, not the kid you used to be. And it wouldn't hurt to get Finlay there."

Finlay didn't have space in her childhood bedroom to play with essential oils, but she could still tinker with the formula for her soap. She wanted something super luxurious.

As she set out her new molds on the bathroom counter, her phone rang. *Willa.* "Hey."

"Happy New Year!" Her friend had to shout over the party noises in the background.

"Yep. You, too." Though she was barely hanging on, she tried to rally for her friend.

"Oh, Fee. You're breaking my heart. Hang on." A moment later, the noises dulled. "Okay, I'm in the bathroom. How are you?"

Guess she hadn't done a very good job. "I'm freaking out." Tucking the phone on her shoulder, she washed and dried her hands and headed back to her bed. "He might lose Cody over my stupid, impulsive lie."

She had daily outings and phone calls with the boy, so yesterday, when the phone rang, she was surprised to see Jude's face on the screen. After telling her about the Motion to Appear, he begged her not to blame herself. Yeah, like that was going to happen.

It's totally my fault.

But he'd asked her to show up in court, and that was the very least she could do.

"You have to stop kicking yourself. If you hadn't lied, Jude probably wouldn't have gotten custody."

"That's true. So how do I fix it? How can I help?"

"You tell the truth. The reason you did it, your feelings for both of them, the kind of father-figure Jude is... I mean, that's all you can do."

"You make it sound so simple, but this judge already hates him."

"The judge wants what's best for the boy, I promise you that."

"I just... Why can't I think straight? What's wrong with me?"

"I don't know why you're so hard on yourself. You've been through a lot of upheaval. All you need is some time."

"Yeah, but look what I do with my time." She stuttered out a laugh. "I moved out of my house the day after I got an offer." In fact, she'd told the realtor to keep scrolling down her wait list until she found someone who could move in right away. Within an hour, they'd found someone willing to pay cash, buy it as-is, and close quickly. Until the money hit her bank account, she'd be living in her old bedroom. "I walked away from the only man I've ever loved, and I hurt a little boy in the process."

"I don't think it's unreasonable for you to have an identity crisis. There was the you before Jude, and the you after. I think it's fair to give your mind a few days to catch up with your heart."

"But when it finally does, do you think he'll still want me?"

"Girl. Seriously?" Willa asked. "What did he send you today?"

She got up to look at the delivery cards she'd tacked to her old corkboard.

> *Miss you,*
> *J*

That was for the week of prepared meals that the gourmet store had delivered.

> *Stopped by for more cocoa and saw this.*
> *Take a bite of each one and tell me your favorite.*
> *J*

That one came with a giant box of chocolates from Coco's. Good girl that she was, she'd done as she was told and taken a bite of each one. It would've been so much more fun to do it with Jude, all snuggled up in bed, wearing pajamas, lamplight casting a yellow glow on her white duvet.

But she hadn't let him know her favorite.

She should've, though. She should've given him something.

But as much as she missed him, as much as she believed he loved her, there was just a tiny thorn lodged in her deep tissue, a reminder that he might only want her because of the situation.

"Today, I got a spa basket. It has foot scrub, nail polish, a face mask, a candle, bath salts, and some pink rubber duckies."

"Pink…what? That came in the basket? That's so cute. My dad should offer that to his guests. Where did it come from?"

"He put it together himself."

I got it wrong last time, so I'm trying again.
This one's from my heart, not my wallet.
]

"Really? That was sweet. So when are you going to put him out of his misery?"

That was the thing. How did she dislodge the doubt? Would it ever go away?

She didn't want to be Ava in thirty years, loving a man she couldn't have. And wouldn't it be worse if Jude actually married her and only realized ten years down the line that he'd needed a nanny/mom for Cody and didn't love her the way a husband should love his wife?

Not that it felt that way when they were together, but still. Her mind was fuzzy and overloaded. "Wills, my judgment was so wrong. Like, *so* wrong. How can I trust myself after almost marrying Matt?"

"Well, you thought planning out your life would keep you safe, and it didn't. What choice do you have but to go with your gut this time?"

A knock on the door had her lowering the phone. "Yes?"

"Your dad's here," her mom called through the closed door.

My dad? Why? "I have to go. My dad stopped by on his way to a New Year's Eve party. Have a great time tonight, and we'll talk tomorrow."

"Love you."

"Love you harder." She disconnected and headed out of her room. Only when she saw her parents all dressed up did she realize she was wearing the same pajamas she'd slept in. "Hey."

"You got another package." Her mom handed her a thick manila envelope.

"Oh, thanks. Wait, does anyone deliver on a holiday?"

"I brought it." Her dad lifted a big box toward her.

But she didn't take it. "You saw him?"

"His family's having a little shindig, so I stopped by for a bit." Her dad set the box on the table. "Open it."

"How is he? How's Cody?"

"Ah, well. He's kind of a mess, if I'm honest. But Cody's great. Living his best life."

"Do you think he'll lose custody?" She couldn't say she regretted the lie—not if it enabled Cody to have the McKennas for the holidays. But she didn't want the boy to suffer for her mistake.

"It's hard to say," her mom said. "But we'll all show up at the courthouse. We'll do what we can to support him."

She opened the thick envelope and pulled out architectural designs. *What are these?*

Her parents went into the kitchen to grab the champagne. While they were busy pouring, Finlay opened the card.

Now that you're free of the past, let's invent a future together.
    Happy New Year,
    J

Happiness detonated in her chest, and her spirits soared. She wanted that so badly.

And maybe that was the answer right there. She didn't have to stay away from the man she loved. They just had to build a life of their own invention.

"Happy New Year!" Her parents came back wearing party hats and blowing noisemakers, and her mom handed her a plastic flute of champagne.

"Thank you." It was only then that she noticed the decorations. The floor was littered with silver, purple, and gold balloons, and a sparkly banner stretched across the living room wall. "I must really be a mess if you're throwing me a party."

"No, it's not that," her mom said. "We wanted to talk to you. What you said the other day, about making yourself small for us?"

"That hit hard." Her dad jammed his hands into the pockets of his khakis.

"Well, I'm sorry, but it's true." She wouldn't back

down even if it hurt their feelings. "I tried to take up as little space as possible so you wouldn't mind having me around."

"Oh, Finlay. No. We loved spending time with you. Who wouldn't? You're so full of life and have such great ideas." Her mom set her flute down. "I swear, that's not at all how it was. Honey, I admired you. You had a vision, a direction. I never had that. Look at me. I've been in the same job for over twenty years."

"You've got to understand," her dad said. "You were always driven, and you were on a good path. We agreed, as long as you weren't getting into trouble, that we'd let you do your own thing. Why would we get in your way?"

"Because I wanted your support. I wanted to feel like we were a family. Like I mattered. I mean, I know I was a mistake, but you could've at least—"

"Whoa, whoa, whoa." Her dad made a T-sign with his hands. "Time-out. You were unexpected, that's true. You were a big surprise, but we've never—not once—thought of you as a mistake."

"I thought you resented me for taking away the future you'd planned on." She said it mostly to her mom.

"Well, that's the thing, Finny. I didn't have any idea what I wanted to do. And if I wasn't the fun mom you wanted, it's because I was tired. I work with extremely demanding people, and I have to be on for them all day and night. Honestly, I thought I could be myself around you. I thought we were comfortable together."

"But now that we know how you feel, we're going to make some changes." Her dad brought her in for a hug. "We love you, sweetheart."

"Very much." Her mom joined them, wrapping her arms around both their backs.

"You guys." Tears blurred her vision, and the kink in her heart she'd always lived with eased. "You don't have to change your life for me." She pulled away. "You can show up in other ways."

"Well, tonight, we're going to love you up," her dad said. "And if you'll look in the damn box Jude gave you, you'll see we're all set for a fun night in."

She pulled open the flaps to find a canister of hot chocolate, chips, pretzels, and five different varieties of cookies. "This is so sweet of him." An urgent need to connect with him rushed up hard and fast, and she reached for her phone.

Finlay: I love tonight's gift. Thank you.

She wanted to tell him about the conversation with her parents but didn't think it would be fair. Either she was with him or she wasn't. Still, she couldn't resist saying one more thing.

Finlay: I miss you.

Okay, two more things.

Finlay: I miss us.

"Ready to ply?" Her dad held up a game of Scrabble. "Yeah, let's do it."

Chapter Thirty-One

The court reporter adjusted the height and angle of her stenotype machine, and the security officer read something on his phone.

Jude hoped he never had to stand in that courtroom again.

Behind him, the noise level grew higher, and he turned around, surprised to see every seat filled with familiar faces. "What's going on?" he mouthed to his dad.

"Support," his dad mouthed back with a shrug.

"You got this." Ava gave him a thumbs-up.

Finlay wasn't there yet, and that had his anxiety spiking. He needed her. Not just so the judge could see they were still in each other's lives, but for his own peace of mind. She quieted him. With her, he knew he could get through anything.

His attorney tapped his wrist, making him swing back around to find the judge entering.

"All rise," the bailiff said. "The Ninth Judicial District

Court, Teton County, Wyoming, is now in session, the Honorable Judge Adams presiding."

Fabric swished, and a table leg shrieked on the wood floor as everyone got to their feet. The judge sat down, put on his reading glasses, and glanced at his notes. "Please be seated." He looked right at Jude. "We're here today at the request of Family Services in the matter of the guardianship of Cody Rossi, specifically regarding allegations concerning the fitness of the current guardian, Jude McKenna."

In the quiet courtroom, he heard a whispered, "Excuse me, excuse me, excuse me." He turned to find Finlay taking a seat in the row behind him. Relief whipped through him.

"Mr. McKenna, we're only halfway through your temporary guardianship."

The judge's disgusted tone snapped his attention back to the bench. "Yes, sir."

"And here we are, discussing fraud and misrepresentation. I'm not sure you understand how seriously the court takes deception in custody matters."

"I do, sir. Absolutely."

The judge nodded. "When you last appeared before me, I had reservations. Your history in this town gave me pause. The only reason I granted that petition was because Ms. O'Neill assured this court you were engaged and that the child would be in her care, as well."

"She has been. We've been living at her home."

"Family Services informs me the home has recently been sold."

They didn't need to live on Bloom Lane to be guardians. "That's correct."

"They also tell me you're not engaged to Ms. O'Neill. Is that true?"

"We are not currently engaged."

"If that's the case, it suggests you're the same person who thought rules didn't apply to him twelve years ago. Mr. McKenna, you have committed fraud against this court, and I relied upon false information to make this ruling. It is within my power to revoke temporary guardianship, but as Mr. Rossi is currently unable to leave Idaho, that would mean his grandson would be placed in the care of a foster family. How do you feel about that?"

"I hate it. I think it's the worst possible outcome for him. His mom abandoned him at birth, his dad died, and his grandfather's in no position to raise a little boy."

"Which is why we're having a hearing instead of removing the child. I'm willing to hear your side, but I ask you, how can I entrust the care of him to you when you lied to the court?"

"If I were the kid you remember, I wouldn't want you to grant me custody. But I'm not that kid. I'm a man, a Marine, a son, a brother, and a caregiver to an orphaned boy. I didn't lie under oath. I went along with it because you clearly weren't going to grant me temporary custody, and you ended the hearing before asking for confirmation. But I love that boy, and I treat him like my son because that's what he is to me. You won't find anyone better to raise him than me."

"Twelve years ago, you didn't steal a car, but you were the getaway driver. Three weeks ago, you didn't lie, but you went along with a deception. How are you going to be a strong role model and parent for this child if you can't help yourself from being an accomplice in your friends' criminal activity?"

That was enough. He'd been polite. He'd been deferential. But Judge Adams had just crossed a line. "You're talking about two different situations. At eighteen, I made a bad choice out of misplaced loyalty. My time in the military and away from home taught me that lesson. Three weeks ago, the only woman I've ever loved stood up in court and said we're engaged. Frankly, I was floored. Dumbfounded. And thrilled. And in the three weeks since she made that statement, we've fallen deeply in love. She's the sun, and I'm her moon. She's the air I breathe. She's the best person I know, and the only woman I want to spend the rest of my life with. I didn't lie to you then, and I'm not lying now when I tell you I would marry her right this minute in this courtroom, with my friends and family as witnesses." He whipped around to look at her, worried he'd freaked her out, but her features were soft, and tears glistened in her eyes.

She rose. "Judge Adams, may I speak?"

The judge nodded.

"I lied about being engaged, but I didn't lie when I said I've loved this man half my life." She shifted her focus to Jude. "I've been a butthead. I thought there was something wrong with my judgment because I was willing to marry a man like Matt, but I was so wrong. I have great judgment. World-class judgment. I could be a Supreme Court judge for how good my judgment is. Because I choose you, Jude McKenna, to spend the rest of my life with. I love you, and I probably should've said that in private, but I'm not stuffing myself into little boxes anymore. I'm living my life out loud." Lifting both arms, she shouted, "I love you!" Her ebullient laughter filled the courtroom. "I love you, Jude McKenna."

"Woo-hoo," Ava shouted.

"Live your truth," someone else called.

"That's my girl," her dad said in his booming voice.

"Here we go again." Judge Adams slammed the gavel. "That's enough. This hearing is over."

Just as Jude reached for Finlay across the partition, the judge called out, "Mr. McKenna, when you're ready to make this guardianship permanent through adoption proceedings, my clerk can provide you with the necessary paperwork. Based on what I've seen today, I don't anticipate any objections from this court."

"You sound really happy, Fee."

"I am. I've never been happier." Most of her time with Matt was spent planning a wedding. That meant searching for a gown, tasting cakes, visiting venues, and choosing invitations—all that stuff. It was busy and lots of fun. But this new life with Jude—even though in some ways it was more chaotic with adoption and figuring out where to live —had brought her a level of peace she'd never once had. Because it was real. It was authentic.

And she had true love.

"So he filed the adoption papers?" Willa asked.

"Yep. On our way out of the courtroom. And since he

already has temporary custody and the consent of Cody's guardian, they told us they can streamline the process."

"Thank God. Get this behind you and get that boy settled in as a McKenna."

"Yes, exactly. And we're house hunting. As much as we love living at Gunnar's, we want to get our own place, be our own little family unit."

"I love it. Do you have any showings lined up?'

"I've been to a few, but there's always something weird or wrong with the layout, you know? Actually, I've been looking at those floor plans Jude gave me on New Year's Eve. I think we're going to build."

"That'll take a long time. What about the home visits from Family Services? Are you worried they won't see stability?"

"No, we've got that at Gunnar's. They just need to see he's in a safe place with a loving family." *And with three uncles, three grandpas—if you include Carlo, Gunnar, and her dad—two grandmas—with Ava and her mom—and two parents who really love each other, Cody's rich with love.*

"Hey, I have good news. I handed those soap samples out to the lawyers in my firm, and the response was fantastic. Throw up a website, and we'll be selling them like hotcakes."

"That's awesome. Thank you, but I'm not quite ready for that." Before launching an online store, she wanted to get some local traction. She'd test the market in Calamity first, see what worked and what didn't. "I appreciate your support, though. So how're things going with Blaze? Did you have a great time with him in the Bahamas?"

Willa laughed. "His name's Camden."

"Oh, right. Sorry." She was only teasing. She knew the guy's name. It was just that he looked like the cover model for a Harlequin Romance novel.

"I got a 'Hey, girlie' message on Splashagram from his long-distance girlfriend in Indiana, so I kicked him to the curb."

"What a jerk." Boots on the stairs had her looking up just as Jude came into the walk-out basement that Gunnar had turned into her "studio." She liked that. No, she wasn't an artist, but his family made her work seem important.

"Hey. Do you have a second?" Jude seemed nervous.

"Yeah, of course," she whispered. "Hey, Wills, I have to go. Talk later?"

"Yep. Be good."

"Always." She disconnected.

He picked up a bar of soap shaped like a pinecone and sniffed it. "That's nice. I'd use it."

"Oh, yay. I'm happy to hear that. Would you mind trying it out for a few days? I've changed the formula and want to make sure it's moisturizing but not greasy." She reached for the boxes that had just come in. "Look. I bought these from a company in Iceland."

"What are they?" He examined the adorable molds. "Puffins?"

She nodded.

"Cute." He seemed preoccupied.

"What's up? You okay?" She ran her hand up his arm, all the way to his big, round biceps. A thought struck her, and her pulse quickened with dread. "You haven't heard anything from Family Services, have you?"

"No, nothing. We're good. Listen, I don't want to interrupt your time making soap, but could you take a drive with me? We can pick Cody up from his playdate with Amy on the way back."

"Sure." That was the thing about him. He respected the things she valued. He didn't tell her to hold off on building a business, to focus on her job and Cody. She really loved that about him. He supported her wholeheartedly. "I'd love to."

"Great. Wear your boots."

"Where are you taking me? Should I change?" In her sweats and moose slippers, she wasn't fit for a public outing.

"Not at all. It'll just be us."

She grabbed her boots on the way out to the garage, got into the car, and put them on as he backed out.

A fresh snow had fallen the night before, so the highway looked like a Christmas postcard. The Teton Range rose tall and jagged on one side, and the bison preserve spread out for miles on the other.

But her focus was on the man driving the car. He'd forgotten to wear a jacket, so his muscles were on clear display in that black T-shirt and jeans. Now that she'd gotten to trace his ink with her tongue and hands, they held so much more meaning to her. She would never get tired of looking at him.

Jude McKenna was the sexiest man alive.

His hands flexed on the wheel.

"Why're you so nervous?" she asked.

"I'm not."

"Oh, I get it. I'm the side piece, right? And you're

taking me to meet your other family? Is this the moment I find out about your double life?"

"Yes, Finlay. It's exhausting trying to please two women, so I'm hoping to merge the two. Are you open to being a sister wife? Wait. Don't answer until you meet her. If you don't hit it off, I don't know what I'll do."

"Oh, that's cute. Real funny. Don't be misled by the wholesome schoolteacher vibe I've got going. There's a whole other side of me you don't want to unleash."

"Oh, I'm pretty sure I do want to unleash it." He smiled. "But no, you're too insatiable for me to have another woman." He slowed to make a turn down a driveway that had been recently plowed.

"Where are we?" She leaned forward to get a better view.

"I never told you what my dad gave us for Christmas."

What does that mean? "I got the gift certificate."

"Yeah, but there's something else." After parking, he got out and met her in front of the truck. He reached for her hand, and they walked into a clearing. "This is ours."

Snow weighed heavily on lodgepole pine branches, and wind whispered through the forest. "I'm a little confused."

"Over the years, he's been buying up land as it hits the market. I think he's got an idea to create some big compound for all of us."

The jagged mountains created a dramatic backdrop against the winter wonderland. "It's just so…majestic." There was no other word to describe the beauty of nature in this magical place. "I feel like I'm going to see Bambi walk out of the woods. Maybe birds holding a string of twinkling lights."

"Yeah, it's great, but if you want to live closer to town, that's fine. There's a great fly-fishing river going through it, so we can always just have a cabin out here."

"Jude?" It was freezing, but…was that sweat beading on his forehead? Why did this make him so nervous? "I love it."

"But to live?"

"Yes, to live. Are you kidding me? I can't think of a better place to raise our family. What about you? Are you thinking about something else?"

He let out a breath she hadn't known he was holding. "Honestly, I could live in a yurt as long as I've got you."

"Might make more sense. I wouldn't have to worry about cooking."

He laughed. "But we couldn't fuck. Not with Cody in there with us."

"Jude, I would love to build a house here with you. I wanted to live closer to town so I could have barbecues and block parties. Community. But between our families and friends, we already have that. I'm so blessed. I want you, I want Cody, and I want the three of us to invent our lives together."

"I want that, too."

"But it scares you?" Maybe it was the idea of all those kids he knew she wanted.

"Nothing scares me about a future with you." He turned to her, eyes burning with passion. "I love you, Fee. I love everything about you. In a thousand lifetimes, I would only ever choose you." And then, the love of her life, the man she'd loved since she was a teenager, got down on one knee in the snow. "Finlay O'Neill, will you marry me? Will you build a house and a life with me and fill it with babies and love?"

Joy burst from her heart like solar flares. "Yes, yes, yes. A million times yes." She hurled herself against him, and the feel of his strong arms holding her, claiming her, protecting her, was the greatest gift in this world.

"Life with me won't look anything like your vision board."

"Those were pictures of someone else's home and husband and children. I want to create a life and family with *you*. I want it to be us, our vision. I want us to build something together."

He kissed her deeply, coaxing her tongue into play. He pulled away. "Do I really get to be with you for the rest of my life?"

"I know, right? After all the loneliness, the wrong people… We finally found what we were looking for in each other. I'm the luckiest woman in the world."

"Oh." He dug into his pocket. "Shit. I forgot." He pulled a rich blue velvet case out of his pocket and flicked it open. The pink oval diamond surrounded by smaller clear ones was absolutely stunning.

"It's gorgeous." Her hand shook as he slipped it onto her finger. "I've never seen anything so beautiful."

Cupping her jaw, he rubbed her cheek with his thumb as he gazed into her eyes. "I have. And now, I get to look at you every day for the rest of my life."

Epilogue

HIS DAD RAN WILD BILLY'S SO WELL THAT IT HADN'T taken Jude long to get the hang of it. That said, it was a hell of a lot of work. And some days were rough.

Like today. It always sucked to fire someone. But he'd watched the video feed, and the new bartender could be seen making occasional runs out to his car to drop liquor bottles in his trunk. It had to be done.

After checking that item off his to-do list, he turned his attention to the promotional campaign. He'd invited the winners of the Teton County rodeo to visit at the end of the season, so he'd had flyers and posters made and taken an ad out in the *Calamity Gazette*. *Should be a good crowd for that.*

The office door opened, and Wyatt walked in. "Hey." Jude found the file on his computer and opened it. "What're you doing here?"

"Had to come into town for some supplies."

Why did his brother sound weird? "You're practically a

hermit, and you have supplies delivered, so what're you talking about?"

"I come into town when I need…things."

"Yeah? Like what?" Other than visiting his family, his brother rarely left his clinic or his Airstream. "I don't see any shopping bags."

"They're in the car. The point is, I'm in town. Want to grab a sandwich or something?"

In twenty-eight years, his brother had never even eaten a sandwich. Wyatt didn't like putting food between "dry bread," and mayonnaise made him gag. But something was up, and if his brother needed him, he'd drop everything. "Yeah, sure. Let's get lunch." He closed his file and logged out of his computer. "I know this place that slathers on extra mayonnaise. It's really creamy and thick. It's not like snot at all."

His brother turned green. "Stop, okay? That's disgusting." They headed out the back door into the alley. "It doesn't have to be a sandwich. That's just another way to say, 'Let's get lunch.'"

"You could've said tacos. 'Let's grab tacos.' Or a burger. People say that, too. But you said 'sandwich,' specifically, so I think you've got a hankering for some thick slices of bread. So dry, they'll suck the saliva right out of your mouth. Oh, you know what? We could put congealed cheese between them. That would be good." He got into his brother's car and waited till Wyatt got behind the wheel before he leaned over the seat to look for the *supplies*. "I don't see any shopping bags."

"They're in the trunk. Can you just put your damn belt on?"

"Sure. What's the rush?"

"I'm hungry."

"For a sandwich? Maybe you can get ciabatta bread." That was his brother's least favorite kind of bread because he said it was like eating foam peanuts. "With an extra glop of mayo."

His brother's lips pressed tightly together, and he looked sick. When he turned onto Main Street, he pulled up in front of Coco's Chocolates. "Hang on. I have to pick something up."

"Oh. More 'supplies'?" But Jude got out of the car and followed his brother inside. Since Cody and his grandpa had bonded over cocoa, Jude had become a regular here, so he waved to the woman behind the counter.

"Let me go grab your cake," she said to Wyatt.

"What do you need a cake for?" Jude asked after she left.

"For a party."

"You're going to a party?" he asked.

His brother kept his gaze on the display of chocolates. "Mm-hmm."

"You going to do karaoke? Beer pong? Fuck a random in the bathroom?" All the things Wyatt said he hated about parties.

The door opened, and Boone walked in. "Hey, man. What's up?"

"What're you doing here?" Jude suspected this wasn't a coincidence.

"Saw Wyatt's car out front. Figured something big was going on if he came into town."

"Oh, fuck off," Wyatt said. "Both of you.

"We're on our way to get *sandwiches*," Jude said. "But first, he has to pick up a cake to bring to a *party*."

"No shit? I want a sandwich. With mayonnaise and some roasted red peppers. Those suckers go down like eels." Boone elbowed his brother. "Can I come to the party?"

"Yeah, sure," Wyatt said in a dull tone.

"Is it like a cook-out, where we stand around a grill and shoot the shit?" Boone laughed because that was another thing their brother hated about parties.

After they got the cake, they stepped outside. "I walked here, so you mind giving me a ride?" Boone asked.

Wyatt didn't bother answering, so the youngest brother got into the back seat, and they put the cake box on his lap. "Hey, can you do me a favor? Can you stop at the tux shop?"

Jude twisted around in his seat. "What for?"

"Got a thing to go to."

"What thing?" Jude asked. "You've never worn a tux in your life."

"Sure, I have."

"Okay, fine. Since prom, you've never worn one."

Boone wore a shit-eating grin. "Well, I am now."

Wyatt turned into the parking lot of a strip mall and kept the engine running. Setting the cake on the seat beside him, Boone hopped out. "Be right back."

The moment the door shut, Jude turned to his brother. "Okay, what's going on? You're not going to a party, and he doesn't need a tux."

But before he could answer, the back door opened, and Decker slid in. "Hey, man. What's up?"

"Okay, what're we doing here? Playing clown car? Who's next?" When neither answered, Jude pulled out his phone to see if he'd missed a text message. "Am I forgetting something? A birthday? Anniversary?"

What would require a tux in July?

"Whose anniversary?" Decker opened the cake box and peered inside. "Why so small?"

"That's just the top layer," Wyatt said. "The kids were running around, knocked into the table, and it fell off."

"What kids?" Jude asked.

"Cody and Amy."

Cody knocked a cake over? "Where did this happen? He's at camp today."

But Boone was jogging back to the car, arms loaded with black tuxedoes. "Got 'em. Let's go."

Jude turned to Decker. "And what stop do you need to make?"

"Thanks for asking." Decker flashed his superstar smile. "Can you hang a left at the light? I just need to run into the flower shop real quick."

"All right, that's enough," Jude shouted. "Just tell me what's going on?"

"That cake looks good," Decker said. "The whole car smells like chocolate."

"Stop," Boone snapped.

"Come on," Decker said. "Just a swipe. The frosting's the best part."

It took another hour to finally get to their destination, which happened to be their dad's house. Cars and trucks were parked everywhere. "Is anyone going to tell me why

Dad's throwing a party? And why am I the only one in the dark?"

As they got out of the car, Boone shoved a tux at him. "Get dressed and meet us out back."

Jude slipped into the bathroom off the kitchen and quickly changed clothes. Only when he caught up with his brothers again on the terrace did he finally get the answer to his questions. A hundred white folding chairs faced a flower-strewn arbor. "Who's getting married?" His first thought, when he saw how pretty Ava looked with a white flower in her hair, was to seek out his dad.

Sure, he'd wondered about it over the years. There was some kind of weird energy between the two of them, but neither had ever once shown an interest in dating or getting married.

He found his dad shaking out a tablecloth, the white fabric floating in the air before settling over a long folding table. "It's not Dad and Ava, is it?"

"Getting *married*?" Boone burst out laughing. "Do you pay attention to anything? Ava's dating some cop."

"She is? I didn't know that." Then who? He searched the crowd for a wedding gown.

The late afternoon sun streaked through giant clouds, casting dramatic shadows across the lawn. A white van was parked near the row of tables, and caterers were hauling out food. Guests gathered near the make shift bar and talked in clusters around the pool, which was covered with a dance floor.

Why would a wedding be a surprise for Jude? Were his brothers just fucking with him?

But the entire world blurred as one woman came into

crystal-clear focus. Finlay O'Neill wore a pale pink dress with a tight top and full, frothy skirt. A crown of white flowers laced with pink satin ribbon was perched on her head. She stood under an arch of peonies in every shade of pink—from bright fuchsia to cherry blossom to blush.

Her smile burned through his confusion, and everything clicked into place. "It's me. I'm getting married today."

"Yeah, man." Boone pulled him into a hug. "Happy for you."

"Congratulations." Wyatt took his turn. "Real happy for you."

And then, Decker. "You got a good one."

All three of his brothers got a hold of him, and in the clutch, Boone said, "Proud of you, brother."

Jude couldn't take his gaze off his bride.

My bride.

I'm getting married.

For the first two months after they'd gotten engaged, he'd asked about setting a date just about every day. After enough rejection, he'd accepted that it just wasn't on her radar. She was focused on helping Cody adjust, teaching her students, building her soap business, and designing their future home. So he'd backed off and asked her to tell him when she was ready.

She's ready now.

As he soaked up the beauty of his family and this life he'd stumbled into, all because the woman of his dreams had run out of a church and climbed onto the back of his bike, he heard a little voice shout, "Dad!"

His son came running over and slammed into him. "Were you surprised? Did I keep a good secret?"

Jude picked him up. "You kept a great secret. I don't know how you did it."

"I wanted to tell you so many times, but Mom kept reminding me how fun it'd be to see your face."

"Did you see it?" Jude asked, smiling.

"Dude, everyone saw it," Decker said. "The moment you laid eyes on your bride, you got this creepy look."

"It wasn't creepy," Wyatt said. "Don't say that."

"Oh, yeah? What would you call this?" Decker made an exaggerated expression of a lovestruck fool, and Cody laughed his head off.

"You did, Dad. You looked just like that."

"Man, I am *never* getting married," Decker said.

"Hey, a football keeps you warm at night." Jude tipped his chin toward his bride. "I get her." That lush body, her caring nature, and sense of humor…Finlay had it all. She was everything to him. His best friend, his lover, and his partner in life. "Let's go see Mom." Setting Cody on his feet, he headed down the petal-strewn aisle.

"Isn't she pretty, Dad? She looks like a princess."

"She's the most beautiful woman in the world. We're so lucky to be with her." Every time he saw her across a crowded room or spotted her in a grocery store, he still got that same hit of attraction. He would never stop wanting her.

As they reached her, she beamed a smile at him. "Jude McKenna, will you marry me?"

"Nothing I want more." He leaned in to kiss her, but she put a hand on his chest.

"No, sir. We haven't gotten to that part yet." Still, her gaze dropped to his mouth, and her tongue made a slow slide along her bottom lip. But she snapped out of it. "I hope you don't mind the surprise."

"Not at all." That was one of the best things about being with her. She kept things fun.

"Good. Because it's go-time." She waved at Ava, who set a flower arrangement on the table before heading over.

Halfway down the aisle, she clapped her hands to get everyone moving over to the arbor. "Let's get these two married." When she reached the altar, she smoothed Cody's hair. "You know what you've got to do."

He nodded. "I'm on it."

"How long have you been planning this?" Jude watched his boy take off. "And how did you keep it a secret when everyone we know was in on it?"

"Well, it's a funny story. Remember when Willa was in town for that meeting with the Petticoat Rulers?"

"Sure."

"Well, Knox Holliday happened to be there, too. And we got to talking, and I told her our story. She said to let her know when we're ready to get married because she'd love to make me a dress. And it just struck me that I *was* ready. More than ready. And then, we all started talking about what kind of wedding I wanted, and her sister-in-law, Stella, was there, so she threw out ideas, and from there…it all just sort of happened. Honestly, I didn't plan a single thing. Everyone took a role and ran with it."

"A role? What do you mean?"

She gestured to the yard. "Gunnar said he'd handle the food, so he talked to Delilah Lua, the executive chef at

Wally's, and then Coco Cavanaugh said she'd make the cake. Knox designed the dress, Wild Heart Florals offered up bouquets… I mean, everyone just pitched in."

"Why?" It didn't make sense to him. He barely knew most of these people.

"Well, I mean, I've taught most of their kids, and your dad helped grow their businesses." She touched his arm. "Mostly, I think people see you around town with Cody and think you're awesome."

"That makes no sense. I'm like any other dad."

She smiled, shaking her head. "Remember the photo of you and Cody during the Bamboozled Duck Race? You're looking all dark and dangerous in your black jeans and boots with your beard and long hair, and there you are with a six-year-old boy on your lap, licking ice cream cones at the lake and watching the duck boats float down the river."

He did remember that. What was so special about getting a cone with your boy?

"Well, that photo has more likes and comments than anything else on Calamity's Splashagram page. But also, I think everyone's just really happy for us."

"I don't know what to say." He'd felt like an outcast his entire life in Calamity, so to have everyone showing up like this…

"It helps that you haven't made that scary face in a while, so you've given them a chance to get to know you."

He tugged on his beard. "I guess I should've shaved."

"Nope." She shook her head. "I love you exactly the way you are. Your beard is sexy. Your bike's sexy. Your ass is sexy. Everything about you gets me hot and bothered. I love our life, and I want to stand in front of everyone we know and celebrate us becoming a family."

"I don't know what to say other than thank you. Thank you for loving me and giving me a true home." Overwhelmed, all he could do was say, "I love you."

"And you make me feel it every single day. Not just with your words, but also with the way you make my coffee every morning. And when I forgot my lunch on that field trip to Yellowstone? You left an important meeting to ride out there and bring it to me. You make me feel special and important and…" Her features softened, and she smiled. "Totally, perfectly loved."

He knew another way to let her know how loved she was, so he yanked her up to his chest and kissed the living daylights out of her.

As always, she melted against him, throwing her arms around his neck and filling his senses with her touch, her taste, and those sexy little moans.

"Oh, honest to God, you two." Ava pushed them apart and stepped between them. "Give me ten minutes, and then you can make out all you want."

They pulled apart, but he liked her lips all shiny and wet. Liked the well-loved look in her eyes. "Let's get a move on, then."

"Uh, no," Boone called from the front row. "They can wait till they're home."

"There are children present," Decker said.

"All right. Hush now." Ava stood under the arch and faced the guests who'd taken their seats. "Our bride has decided to skip the formality of walking down the aisle to focus on the heart of the matter, the joining of two people to form the greatest bond this world offers, which is the formation of a family."

Finlay looked at her father. "Sorry, Dad. You can have a dance, though."

"Hey, I have a front-row seat. All good on my end." Buck grinned. "Happy for you, sweetheart."

"It took a community to pull this wedding together, so thank you to everyone who helped," Ava began. "We're here to celebrate the bride and groom's love, but before I start the ceremony, I'd like to begin with a little story." Ava gave him a warm smile. "Jude was six years old when I met him. He was wide-eyed and watchful, barely said more than two words, but he wasn't hard to read at all. Because Jude might've been scared in that new environment, but he shoved his own feelings aside to take care of his brothers. And let me tell you, his brothers were four, two, and three months old when they showed up on the doorstep of a biker club."

When Finlay reached for his hand, it anchored him. He didn't know where Ava was going, but he sure as hell didn't want to visit a childhood of reckless mistakes.

"I knew he was special from the moment I met him," Ava said. "He was smart, clever, and deeply sensitive. He's got the biggest heart of anyone I know, and there's no one else on this earth I'd want to see him with than our dear, sweet, generous, kind Finlay."

"Oh." His bride let out a shaky breath. "Thank you."

"Finlay treats every child in her classroom as if they

were her own. She makes them feel like their every thought matters. And she's an includer. If she sees someone sitting alone, she'll invite them to sit at her table. She's got the biggest heart of anyone I've ever known, and there's no one I'd want to see her with more than Jude."

He glanced at his bride to find her beaming that warm, affectionate smile at him. "Sounds like we're a perfect match."

"And now, we'll begin," Ava said. "Today, two separate lives will become one. Jude, do you take Finlay to be your lawfully wedded wife, to love her, honor her, protect her, and keep her happy for the rest of your lives?"

"Oh, hell yeah," he blurted out. When their guests laughed, his neck heated, and he said, "Sorry, I wasn't expecting any of this." He cleared his throat. "Uh, yes. Yes, I do."

Ava nodded. "Finlay, do you take Jude to be your lawfully wedded husband, to love him, honor him, protect him, and keep him happy for the rest of your lives?"

"I do." The two simple words were drenched in emotion.

And he loved it.

"And now for the rings." Ava looked at the row of seats behind Jude.

"Well, wait a second," he said. "What about the vows?"

"I didn't give you a chance to think about them," Finlay said. "So I figured we'd skip that part. Besides, we live our promises every day anyway."

"No, I want to say them." It meant a lot to him.

"But you're not prepared."

"I've been preparing since the day I asked you to marry me a year and a half ago."

Finlay grinned with a look that said, *Go for it.*

He reached for her hands, forming a bridge between them. Leaves shushed, and her long, wavy hair fluttered in the breeze. With her pink lips and rosy cheeks, he was lost in her beauty.

But he'd asked to exchange vows, and he was damn well going to deliver. "Fee, I wasn't man enough to ask you out on a date back in high school. I told myself it was because I didn't want to ruin your reputation, but the truth was, you intimidated me. You knew exactly who you were and what you wanted, and nothing would stop you from getting it. I admired the hell out of you back then—"

"That's two swear words, Dad," Cody grumbled from the first row.

"Okay. After the ceremony, you can tell me the two chores of yours I'll have to do as punishment."

His brothers and dad laughed.

"Now, where was I?" he asked.

"Telling me how perfect I am." Finlay's eyes shone with joy. It was the most beautiful sight he'd ever seen. This woman glowed from within.

"I admired you back then and am completely in awe of the woman you've become. You're the best mom to our boy, the best partner a man could ask for, and I can't believe I wasted so many years thinking I didn't deserve you. Instead, I wish I'd made myself good enough for you."

She leaned in and cupped his cheek. "You've always been the man I wanted. Always."

He held her hand against his face. "You're the bright, shining star I orbit around, and I will do everything I can to make all your dreams come true."

"Don't you know?" Her hand slipped away and clasped his again between them. "*You're* my dream. You've always been the one. No one in this world makes me feel more special. Throughout my life, I've tried to make myself smaller, to fit into a nice little box where I wouldn't be too much of anything. And you let me be all that I am. With you, I'm exactly enough. Don't you see? There's nothing better in this world than being with someone who loves me for who I am and encourages me to be my whole self. Jude McKenna, you're the love of my life, and I will cherish you every single moment of our lives together."

"Well." Ava blinked back tears. "We need to move on to the rings before I'm a sobbing mess."

Jude's dad nudged Cody, who got up and delivered a velvet pillow with two rings embedded in the folds. Jude smiled when he saw the band he'd bought for her a year and a half ago. "You found it, huh?" He'd hidden it in the back of her closet, in an old pair of moose slippers.

"Don't tell me you just learned something new about me," Finlay said.

"She's a snoop," Willa called. "Can't keep anything from her."

As everyone laughed, he plucked it out of its nest.

"As you place this ring on her finger, please repeat after me," Ava said. "With this ring, I pledge an eternity of love, faithfulness, and honor."

Jude slid the band onto her left finger. "With this ring, I pledge an eternity of love, faithfulness, and honor."

When it was Finlay's turn, her hands shook. "With this ring, I pledge an eternity of love, faithfulness, and honor."

He wanted to scoop her into his arms and run back to the house. He wanted to love her all night long. "What about a honeymoon?" He pulled her up close, whispering into her ear. "I want you all to myself."

Finlay sighed. "I want that, too, but that's something we'll plan together." She grinned. "But we do get to spend the night at the Sweetwater Inn and Resort." She glanced at the owner and gave her a smile of gratitude.

"We've also got a place in Iceland, if you want," the owner's husband and retired movie star, Trevor Montgomery, called out.

"We can hash out the details later," Ava said. "Let them get to that kiss. By the power vested in me by the State of Wyoming, I now pronounce you husband and wife."

Jude hooked an arm around Fee's back and hauled her up against him. Tilting his head, he kissed her with love, awe, and utter gratitude that he got to be with this woman for the rest of his life.

But something changed, love sparked into lust, the kiss turned hot, and he was helpless against the desire burning in his blood. When Fee hitched a leg up his thigh, he remembered Cody and his brothers and his dad and half the town were watching, so he tipped her back, her long hair dusting the ground.

While kissing him, she lifted her bouquet into the air and tossed it.

They were laughing now, giddy, so he barely heard Willa say, "Oh, hell no. Here, you take it."

"Not me," Eloise said. "Here."

"Oh no," Molly said. "Thank you, but—"

"Guys, it's flowers," someone said. "Not a hot potato."

Everyone laughed.

"Thank you for marrying me," he whispered against the sexy mouth that drove him wild.

"Oh, please. I've been trying to put a ring on it since I was fifteen years old."

"And look at us now," he said. "Living our happily ever after." He straightened, waving their son over, and the three of them made a Cody sandwich. "I love you both more than anything. You're my whole world."

The boy sighed and rested his head on Jude's shoulder. "I love you, Dad."

The beautiful moment was interrupted when a woman called out, "Excuse me? I'm looking for Decker McKenna?" She looked left, then right. "I'm sorry to interrupt, but this is really important."

Everyone quieted down because the stranger was holding a little girl's hand.

Thank you for reading Can't Get Over You! Want more of Finlay, Jude, and Cody? Grab this beautiful scene that's sure to warm your heart right here!

And if you want more of the McKenna Brothers,

Decker's story is up next in *Until I Found You.* You're going to love watching this pie-making quarterback fall in love with a strong, feisty woman…and the little girl he didn't know he had. #footballromance #singledad #surprisebaby #steamy #foundfamily

For more of Calamity Falls, where the people are wild at heart and the romance is off the hook, check out the whole series:

The Calamity Falls series

The Bowie Brothers
KEEP ON LOVING YOU
WE BELONG TOGETHER
THE VERY THOUGHT OF YOU
JUST THE WAY YOU ARE

The Cavanaugh Sisters
IT WAS ALWAYS YOU
CAN'T HELP FALLING IN LOVE
COME AWAY WITH ME
WHOLE LOTTA LOVE
YOU'RE STILL THE ONE

The Renegades (Hockey)
THE DEEPER I FALL
LOVE ME LIKE YOU DO
TRULY, MADLY, DEEPLY
NEVER IN MY WILDEST DREAMS

The McKenna Brothers (The bad boys of Calamity Falls)
CAN'T GET OVER YOU
UNTIL I FOUND YOU

Mistletoe and Silver Foxes
ALL I WANT FOR CHRISTMAS IS YOU
WHEN YOU WERE MINE

The Wild Wolff Village Serials
KISS ME SLOWLY
ANYWHERE WITH YOU
BABY I'M YOURS

Have you read the Rock Star Romance series? Come meet the sexy rockers of Blue Fire:

YOU REALLY GOT ME
I WANT YOU TO WANT ME
TAKE ME HOME TONIGHT
MORE THAN A FEELING

Get ready for *Until I Found You*, the next book in the McKenna Brothers series, coming June 2026! You're going to love watching this pie-making quarterback fall in love with a strong, feisty woman…and the little girl he didn't know he had. #footballromance #singledad #surprisebaby #steamy #foundfamily

Come hang out with me on Facebook, TikTok, <u>Instagram, Goodreads, and Pinterest</u> or in my private reader group!

Read the first chapter of UNTIL I FOUND YOU, coming June 2026!

"Ten minutes," Willa Holland called to her dad.

"Got it. I'll get a pot of coffee going."

This inn had been in her family for generations, so she was both touched and relieved by the outpouring of support from the townspeople helping her bring it back to its former glory.

They'd cleared out the entire place—the beds, dressers, cutlery, cleaning supplies, everything—so, why did she hear water running through the pipes? She had to go check it out. "Be right back."

As she dashed across the saloon and up the grand staircase, the ghosts of piano players and costumed servers singing bawdy songs danced around her and, for a moment, her heart ached. How had it all slipped away?

Because you left Dad to run everything all on his own.

No, no, no. Don't go there. That was the whole point of taking a leave of absence from work.

We're bringing it back.

Only this time, they'd have a manager, a bookkeeper… a full staff to help him run things. He'd never be alone again.

At the top of the stairs, light from an open door spilled into the hallway, and a woman in a flirty white dress and hot pink cowboy boots walked out of Room 201. She headed in the opposite direction, toward the back of the inn.

"Excuse me?" Willa called.

The woman kept going.

"*Hey.* Hang on. What're you doing here?" They'd found housing for the guests who'd booked a year in advance and hadn't taken new reservations in months. There shouldn't be anyone under this roof.

Finally, the woman stopped and turned around and waved. "Hi. It's just me. Ariel. I work here."

Willa hurried to catch up. They'd been shut down for a week. *No one works here.* As she passed the open door, she took a quick glance into the room. Perfume lingered in the air, and early morning sunlight slanted in through the windows. As expected, it was empty—

Except for the jeans and biker boots tossed carelessly aside and the naked man lying on a nest of blankets.

What the hell?

He was face down, one arm cocked, elbow jutting out…and that ass.

It was the shape of a peach, the cheeks hard and round. *That's hot.*

She tore her gaze away. "Wait. You're not leaving him behind, are you?"

"I'm late for work. I have to."

"Now, wait a minute." None of this made sense. "We're shut down for renovations. How'd you get in?"

"I work in housekeeping. My aunt gave me the master key."

"Who's your aunt?"

"Marjorie."

"I'm not buying it." *Not for a second.* "She's worked here for thirty years. She'd never do that."

"She said I'd still have my job in three months when you reopen, so I just kept it." The young woman plucked an old-fashioned brass key out of her handbag. "Do you want it back?"

"Yes, I want it back." The audacity of this girl. She snatched it out of her hand and shoved it in her pocket. "What made you think it was okay to crash in one of the rooms?"

"I mean, there's nothing here. It's not like I could steal anything." She continued down the hallway.

"Hang on. There's a man in that room."

"I know. I met him last night at Wild Billy's." The fringe on her boots swung as she walked. "He didn't want to go to my apartment because he said my roommates might recognize him. Well, also, he couldn't walk very far —he's got a bum knee—" She cocked her head. "Or maybe it's his ankle? I don't know. But he could hardly walk, so I brought him here." She reached the stairs. "Bye now."

Oh, hell, no. "You have to take him with you."

"Oh, he's not going anywhere. He's had a bunch of shots and a painkiller."

"Well, you can't just leave him here. Who is he?"

"I don't know." She got about halfway down the stairs before stopping to turn around. "I think he's like an athlete? I'm not sure, but everyone was buying him drinks and wanting him to sign stuff. Sorry, I've really got to go. If I'm late again, I'll lose my job."

"I've got an entire crew showing up in ten minutes to start working."

"Definitely don't let them see him. He wouldn't like that." She reached the door and pushed it open. "Bye."

"Not cool," Willa shouted. *Well, now what?* She sure didn't have "removal of an unconscious naked man" on her to-do list.

Whatever. It was on it now. She turned and headed back to the room to assess the situation. Her heart fell when she stepped inside and took in the emptiness. Part of the inn's appeal was its history. Each suite was named after the outlaws who'd once slept there. So it was sad to see it without the red velvet curtains and gold tasseled ties, the dressing table, four-poster bed, and vintage dresser.

Literally the only thing in the room was the naked man, his clothes, and a few blankets.

Is he even alive? She crouched at his side to check. The good news: The rise and fall of his back meant he was breathing. The bad news: This man was out cold.

Okay, simple solution. She'd find his phone and call someone on his contact list. Except when she rooted through his jeans' pockets, she didn't find one. He didn't even have a wallet. *You've got to be kidding me. Who goes to a bar without money or an ID?*

So, now what? The man was built of solid muscle. Pair that with him being buck naked, and she had a problem.

She couldn't touch him, let alone move him on her own. She pulled out her phone to text her dad, but right then, trucks rumbled outside, and doors slammed.

In a mountain town, summer was a contractor's busy season, so they'd created a timeline that would get everyone in and out as quickly as possible. Besides, everyone was working for free, so she wouldn't take that for granted. Not for a second.

No, she had to handle this herself.

> **Willa:** Got a little problem to take care of. Can you get the workers started?

> **Dad:** Sure. Everything okay? Need my help?

> **Willa:** I got this. Be down soon.

She slid her phone back into her pocket. "Okay, buddy. It's time to get up." Objectively speaking, his body was a work of art. He had broad shoulders that tapered to a trim waist, powerful thighs, big, clean feet, and neatly trimmed dark blond hair.

I could bounce quarters off that ass.

All right. Enough with the ass. She didn't see how she could lift him on her own, but the woman said he'd signed autographs at the bar, so he must be some kind of minor celebrity. And in the hospitality industry, discretion kept you in business. The Wild Rose Inn and Saloon was already struggling. She didn't need a lawsuit from this guy. Or for word to get out that she'd treated some hotshot poorly.

Which meant she was on her own.

"Hello?" She leaned closer to his ear. "You're naked, so I don't want to touch you, but I really need you to get up right now." Maybe she *should* get her dad up there. This guy was big. Powerful.

Voices filled the saloon, and soon, they'd be coming up the stairs and cutting holes in the walls.

"Okay, buddy. I hate to do this, but you leave me no other choice." She went into the bathroom—now stripped of everything but a sink, toilet, and medicine cabinet—filled both hands with cold water, and shut off the faucet with her elbow. Then, she came back and tossed it onto his head.

"Wha—?" He jolted, his face a mask of pain. His head tipped back, and his knee bent. "Fuck."

"Are you okay?" She dropped to her knees. "Oh, my God, I'm so sorry. I forgot you're injured." *What have I done? That was so mean.* But the laughter from downstairs meant she had to get moving. "The thing is, people are on their way up, and if you don't want pictures of you hitting social media, we have to get out of here."

With his eyes squeezed shut, he seemed to hold his breath, frozen in the same position for several moments. Finally, his body relaxed, but he didn't open his eyes. "Where's the rabbit?"

"The *what*? Don't tell me you guys brought an animal in here." *Can you imagine?* How would she even find it? "You have to let me know if you did. We're renovating this entire place. It could get hurt."

"She put the rabbit in the pudding cup." His eyes rolled back in his head, and then he was out.

"No, no, no. Wake up. Come on now." She nudged

his shoulder. "Let's get you dressed, okay?" *So, there isn't a rabbit, right? He's just loopy from the painkillers?*

"Coach is gonna be *pissed*." He slurred his words.

"Sounds like you've got a lot on your plate, what with the rabbit, the pudding cup, and the coach, but we'll tackle each thing one at a time, okay? First, let's get your pants on."

"What about the fiffle?"

"The fiffle's fine, I promise." She reached under his arm and pulled, but it was like trying to lift a tree that had fallen in the forest. Frustration flared into agitation. She couldn't lift him, couldn't risk his or the inn's reputation to get help…what was she supposed to do? When boots trampled on the stairs, she pinched his beautifully rounded biceps.

"Ow." He jerked his arm away. "Why'd you do that?"

"Because in five minutes, an entire team of construction workers is going to walk into this room and see you naked on the floor. I don't follow sports, so I have no idea who you are, but this is a small town, and news spreads fast. Now, I'm sorry, but you either get up, or you're on your own."

"What about the pudding cup?" He sounded annoyed more than anything.

"I'll get one on the way to your house or hotel or wherever you're staying. Now, *get up*." She tugged on his arm, and thankfully, he rose. But only to a sitting position. "That's fine. We can start with the shirt." She plucked it off some kind of stand—*Oh. It's a walking boot. So, not a knee injury.* "Lift up your arms, Peach Butt."

"What am I going to tell Coach?" He swayed, ready to

topple over, but she shoved her knee behind his back to prop him up.

Lifting first one arm, then the other, she wrestled the T-shirt over his head.

"I don't feel good," he said. "Show me your boobs."

She burst out laughing. "You're a good-looking guy, but you've got no game. You need to work on that." She reached for the jeans. "Please get your pants on by yourself, okay?" She shook his shoulder. "Hey. Stay awake. I'm not touching your junk, so you really need to do this on your own."

But he'd gone lifeless again.

"Fine. I'll get them on your legs, but you'll have to take it from there." After lining them up, she got the right foot in but wasn't sure what to do about the left, since that seemed to be the injured ankle. She did it gingerly, gently, and managed to get the pants all the way to his knees.

Now what?

Well, whatever you do, don't look at his junk.

Don't do it.

Do not look—

Oh, crap. She looked.

And found he was half-hard.

"Like what you see?" He wore a dopey smile, but his eyes were still half-closed.

"Well, it's big, I'll give you that. But if you don't know how to use it—and with pickup lines like that, I'm positive you don't—then it's just a regular ole dick." She sat back on her heels, trying to figure out how to get his pants on. "Okay. Here's what we're going to do." She eased him back onto the floor and gently stretched out his legs, trying very hard not to look at his private part, but that was impossible because it was growing. "You need to put that thing away."

"She likes it in a pudding cup."

She raised both her hands. "Hey, no judgment. Whatever happens between consenting adults is none of my business. All I'm asking is that you get it out of my sight."

"She's cute, but she's not mine. She's not. Oh, fucking fiffle." His head lolled backwards.

What was he trying to say? *Fiffle…falafel? Maybe people?*

Forget it. Focus. "I need you to lift your butt, and if you don't, I'm going to pinch it."

He obliged, lifting his ass, but in doing so, he cried out in pain. "It's fine, Coach. It's nothing. I'm fixing it."

Sounded like his coach didn't know about his injury. "You really do have a lot going on. I wish I could help you, but unless you need an attorney, there's not much I can do. Now, come on. We're almost done." His arms wouldn't cooperate, so she straddled him. "Lift. One more time."

"Grab the fiffle."

"You better not be talking about your dick."

"No, no. The fiffle. Where is she? She's so little. Have you seen her? They say she's mine, but she can't be. She's not."

"Are you talking about a rabbit? Or a child?" She slid her hands under his naked butt and urged him to lift. Thankfully, he did, and she got the jeans all the way up. But now, she had a problem. Because she couldn't button anything until he tucked himself away. "Sir, I'm willing to help you, but I'm not touching your junk."

"My junk." He snickered.

"Come on." She took a few steps back, grabbed his wrists, and tugged. When he got up, he swayed, and she had to wrap her arms around him to keep him from landing on the floor. "Now, put it in your pants. Do it now."

He seemed to understand because he got the job done, and she was able to button him up.

"Stay." She pointed a finger at him before grabbing the boot. "Here you go. Now, step into it."

With her guidance, he got his left foot inside. "Did we get the results back? Is she mine?"

Did he mean *paternity* test? She couldn't even imagine what he was going through. "Oh, man, buddy. You're breaking my heart." She got it all Velcroed up. "Okay, let's go."

She glanced around to make sure he hadn't left anything behind and led him down the hallway.

"Why's the room spinning?" he asked.

"Apparently—and I'm not pointing fingers here—but someone mixed painkillers with alcohol. That's a no-no. Even for masters of the universe like you."

At the bottom of the staircase, she pushed out the door that led to the parking lot. In the bright sunlight of a Calamity Falls morning, she filled her lungs with the cool, crisp, clean mountain air. It was so unlike what she was used to in New York City, and she loved it.

After getting him into his seat and carefully lifting his

boot into the footwell, she reached across to buckle him in.

He sniffed her hair. "You smell good."

"Thank you."

"Are we going to see her?"

"Sure." She got him secured and then rounded the Jeep to her side. "Just tell me where she is, and I'll take you."

"This is bad. This is so bad."

"Yeah, it doesn't sound good, and I'm sorry for that. I really am, but I blew up my entire career to get this inn back on track, and I have to oversee this project. If you can't tell me where you're going, I'll have to drop you at the police station."

"You know who scares me? That girl. She scares me. She says I'm her *father*. Can you believe it? *Me*?"

"I'm sure it's hard to wrap your head around something like that, but my dad always says 'Fear comes from uncertainty.' And it's only when you face your fears that you conquer them. So, that's what you're going to do. You're going to face her, deal with the test, and then kick some serious ass. Right?"

"Kick ass," he mumbled.

"Now, what's your address?"

He had his head tipped back and his eyes closed. "Is she there?"

"I don't know where she is, but I'm going to guess she's in very good hands."

"She's not. She's got no hands. No one's got her."

"Well, let's go to your house and see what we can do."

His head snapped up. "Really? You'll take me?" His plaintive tone really messed with her.

She'd do whatever she could to help him. "Yeah, I'll take you wherever you need to go." She reached for his hand and gave it a squeeze. "No matter what's wrong, it's all going to work out. You have to believe that." She leaned forward, ready to put the address into her GPS. "Where're we going?"

"1140 Bella Canyon Road."

That didn't sound familiar, but then, she hadn't lived in Calamity for over a decade, and there'd been lots of new construction over the years. She punched it in, but the only place that came up was a thousand miles away. "Los Angeles?"

"My rabbit likes my fiffle."

"I'll bet all the girls like it, but I'm not driving to LA, so…where to?"

When he shifted in his seat, his boot cracked against the console, and he cried out in pain.

"Well, that settles it. There's only one place I can take you and your fiffle."

It took her twenty minutes to get to the rehab center. She only knew about it because the men who ran it were snowboard and ski champions. Famous athletes from around the world trained and recovered from injuries there. She couldn't think of a safer place for him to be.

Her companion had fallen back asleep, so when she pulled to a stop in front of the facility, she roused him. "Hey, buddy. It's time to wake up."

His eyelids fluttered before opening and, for the first

time, he seemed to actually see her. He broke into a grin. "Hello, gorgeous."

"Don't even start. You're not my type." She grabbed her phone out of the cupholder, found the facility in her web browser, and hit Call.

"Bowie Antigravity Training Center. How can I direct your call?"

"Okay, hear me out because this is kind of a weird request, but I've got an athlete in my car. I don't know who he is, only that he's injured. I don't know where to take him other than here. Can I leave him with you guys?"

"I, uh…" The woman laughed. "I don't know what to say. I've never had a request like that. Hang on a minute, okay?"

"Sure." She glanced at her companion to find him slumped against the window again. "Nuh-uh." She shook his shoulder. "You've got to stay awake for this. They're not going to take you if you're unconscious. Come on now."

He blinked and shook his head like a wet dog. "Is she here?"

"No, it's just me. But help is on the way." *Hopefully.*

His features softened. "You're sure pretty."

"Yeah, I get that a lot." Not really, but what could she say to that? He was looking at her through painkiller goggles.

"Ma'am?" The receptionist came back on the line.

"Yep. I'm here."

"Fin Bowie's on his way out to see you."

Though he was a few years ahead of her, he was kind of a legend in high school. And, since his name was on the marquee, she breathed a sigh of relief. "Perfect, thank you." She cut the engine and unbuckled. "Good news, Mr. Fiffle. You've reached your destination." She got out of the car and waited as a very tall, fit, gorgeous man came down the walkway.

He reached out a hand. "Fin Bowie."

"Hi, I'm Willa Holland. My family owns the Wild Rose Inn and Saloon."

"Love that place. What can I do for you?"

"Well, I've got this guy who's a little down on his luck." She gestured to the Jeep.

"An athlete, you said?"

"I don't personally know him or his situation, but yes, that's what I was told. He's got a mix of pain pills and shots in him, so he's out of it. He doesn't have a phone or a wallet, so I figured I could either take him to the police station or here."

"I'm not sure what I can do for him. If he's injured, he's probably working with someone already."

The car door opened, and the booted foot hit the ground. She felt so bad for this guy, and she wanted to get him the help he so obviously needed, but at the same time, she didn't want to embarrass him. "Do you have scholarships for athletes who don't have the resources to come here?" she whispered.

"Sure, we do, but I can't help him if he doesn't have any ID."

She was out of time, and she couldn't in good conscience abandon this guy. "What if I pay for the first few days? Please? He really needs help. If you give him room and board, if he can see a doctor who'll take X-rays, or, you know, evaluate him, then we can at least get him in good enough condition to start figuring things out."

But Fin was watching Mr. Fiffle unfold his big body out of the car and straighten to his full height. A spark of humor lit the owner's eyes.

"Look, this isn't funny. I know he's a mess, but he's worried about his coach finding out. If I give you my credit card, can you just take care of him for a few days, get him on his feet? Please?"

Mr. Fiffle clonked his way up to them. He shielded his eyes with a hand. "What's going on? Where am I?"

"Willa, are you pranking me?" Fin asked.

"Of course not. Why would you even think that?"

"Because this is Decker McKenna. He's a Super Bowl champion who led the league in touchdowns last year." Fin broke out in a grin. "Pretty sure he doesn't need a scholarship."

About the Author

Award-winning author Erika Kelly writes sexy and emotional small town romance. Married to the love of her life and raising four children, she lives in the southwest, drinks a lot of tea, and is always waiting for her cats to get off her keyboard.

https://www.erikakellybooks.com/

www.ingramcontent.com/pod-product-compliance
Lightning Source LLC
Chambersburg PA
CBHW031434200726
48289CB00001BA/75